THUNDER OVER THE
SUPERSTITIONS

THUNDER OVER THE SUPERSTITIONS

ROGUE LAWMAN: A GIDEON HAWK WESTERN

PETER BRANDVOLD

FIVE STAR
A part of Gale, Cengage Learning

Including a bonus story featuring the Rio Concho Kid: Blood and Lust in Old Mexico

GALE
CENGAGE Learning·

Farmington Hills, Mich • San Francisco • New York • Waterville, Maine
Meriden, Conn • Mason, Ohio • Chicago

GALE
CENGAGE Learning®

LIBRARY OF CONGRESS CATALOGING-IN-PUBLICATION DATA

Brandvold, Peter.
    Thunder over the superstitions : rogue lawman : a Gideon Hawk western / Peter Brandvold. — First edition.
      pages ; cm
    "Including a bonus story featuring the Rio Concho Kid: Blood and Lust in Old Mexico."
    ISBN 978-1-4328-3010-6 (hardcover) — ISBN 1-4328-3010-4 (hardcover) — ISBN 978-1-4328-3007-6 (ebook) — ISBN 1-4328-3007-4 (ebook)
    I. Title.
    PS3552.R3236T46 2015
    813'.54—dc23   2015012955

First Edition. First Printing: October 2015
Find us on Facebook– https://www.facebook.com/FiveStarCengage
Visit our website– http://www.gale.cengage.com/fivestar/
Contact Five Star™ Publishing at FiveStar@cengage.com

For who else but James and Livia Reasoner

CONTENTS

CHAPTER 1
THE LAUGHING LADY

The rogue lawman, Gideon Hawk, smelled blood on the howling wind.

Beneath the wind, he heard the pattering of an off-key piano. The music, if you could call it that, emanated from somewhere ahead in the dusty, wind-battered desert settlement on the outskirts of which he halted his grulla.

A weathered sign along the road announced SPOTTED HORSE, ARIZ. TERR.

Hawk slid his big, silver-plated Russian Model Smith & Wesson .44 from its holster positioned for the cross draw on his left hip. He flipped the latch on the top-break revolver with his gloved thumb, breaking it open. He filled the cylinder's one empty chamber with a bullet from his shell belt, then snapped the gun closed.

He returned the pistol to its holster and filled the empty chamber in his horn-gripped Colt, which occupied the holster on his right hip, strapped around his waist by a second shell belt. He returned that gun, too, to its holster but did not snap the keeper thong home across the hammer. He let the straps dangle freely, both pistols ready to be drawn.

Hawk had followed a killer here. A killer carrying one of Hawk's own bullets in his hide. It was the killer's blood that Hawk smelled on the wind. The piano's pattering did not sound like a funeral dirge, but it might as well have been, because Hawk intended for the music, if you could call it that, to be the last notes his quarry ever heard.

He loosened his Henry repeater in the scabbard strapped to his saddle, the walnut stock with brass butt plate jutting up above his right stirrup fender. Then he nudged the horse ahead down the broad street. Shabby, false-fronted buildings loomed to both sides, obscured by windblown dirt and tumbleweeds.

Shingles hanging beneath porch eaves squawked on rusty chains. The dirt and sand of the desert ticked against the buildings and porch floors and caused a rocking chair to jounce back and forth jerkily, as though an angry ghost were seated in it.

As Hawk rode, the piano's feckless patter grew gradually louder though the moaning wind often obscured it.

A door opened on Hawk's left. A lean, gray-bearded man bound to a wheelchair heaved himself over the doorjamb of the Spotted Horse town marshal's office. A five-pointed star was pinned to his wool shirt, half hidden by his left suspender. He was not only lean but scrawny, his legs appearing withered in his faded denims. He wore a weathered, funnel-brimmed Stetson down low over his eyes. As he came out onto the jailhouse's narrow stoop, his blue-eyed gaze found the tall rider straddling the grulla in the street before him.

The old man stopped instantly. He glanced up the street, toward where a lone horse stood at a hitch rack fronting a saloon, and then glanced once more at the tall stranger in the black frock coat, string tie, and low-crowned, flat-brimmed black hat wielding a Henry rifle and wearing two pistols on his hips.

The town marshal jerked his chair back into the jailhouse and slammed the door.

Hawk looked at the horse standing at the hitch rack a block beyond him, the wind blowing the calico's black tail up under its belly. That's where the piano's din seemed to be originating. He touched spurs to the grulla's flanks and, looking around cautiously, wary of an ambush, continued up the street.

A couple of minutes later, he put his horse up to the right of the calico tied to the hitch rack of the Laughing Lady Saloon, and dismounted. While the two horses touched noses, getting to know each other, Hawk tied the grulla's reins to the hitch rack and then shucked his Henry from its scabbard.

He cast his glance once more toward the opposite side of the street, making sure no bushwhackers were drawing beads on him. He noted nothing more portentous than several windows in which "Closed" signs dangled in the mid-afternoon of a business day.

Hawk looked at the saloon before him, a shabby adobe-brick affair with a brush-roofed gallery. It was indeed from inside this place that someone was trying to play the piano. They'd switched songs now. This one Hawk couldn't recognize. He doubted if anyone could, except possibly the girl who was humming along with it.

Hawk climbed the three steps to the gallery, his spurs trilling. He pushed through the batwings, and stepped to the right quickly so as not to backlight himself. Loudly, he racked a shell into the Henry's breech as he looked around, his eyes accustomed to quick adjustments from light to dark.

The piano stopped caterwauling. The girl sitting in front of it, on the far side of the bar running along the wall's right side, turned to him. She was clad in a black corset and bustier, with sheer black stockings attached to frilly red garter belts.

She was a pretty, round-faced Mexican with flashing eyes and black feather earrings partly concealed by her long, straight black hair. Her hair was dark enough to make her at least half Indian. Part Apache or Pima, judging by the symmetry of her face, the boldness of her eyes. She had a long, knotted, pink scar running down from the middle of her cheek and ending just beneath her jawline. Its contrast accentuated her beauty.

11

When the piano's last raucous notes had finished reverberating, Hawk could hear only the wind's keening and muffled voices coming from the ceiling.

The girl was the only one in the long, dingy saloon outfitted with a dozen or so tables and rickety chairs. She rose from the piano bench and, keeping her oblique, dark gaze on Hawk, strolled behind the bar, her high-heeled black shoes tapping on the floor puncheons. The feather earrings danced along her neck.

She stopped about halfway down the bar. She leaned forward on her elbows, giving Hawk a good look at her cleavage, and absently traced the scar with her finger. "Drink?"

Hawk glanced around once more, at the wooden staircase rising at the rear of the room, just beyond the piano. There was a colorfully woven rug at the foot of it, an unlit bracket lamp hanging on the wall over the rug. Above the lamp was the snarling head of a mountain lion.

Hawk glanced at the low ceiling through which the voices continued to filter—one high and shrill, the other low and even.

"That him up there?"

"Him," the girl said, frowning curiously and thoughtfully tapping her right index finger against her lower lip. "Hmmmm. By 'him' do you mean the owner of the calico?"

She may have looked half Indian, but she did not speak in the flat tones of most Natives annunciating English. This girl's English was easy and lilting though touched with a very slight Spanish accent. Raised on the border among several races, most likely.

Hawk stared at her without expression on his severe-featured, mustached face that betrayed his own mixed bloodline. His father had been a Ute, his mother a Scandinavian immigrant. It was the jade of her eyes that made his own such a contrast to his otherwise aboriginal appearance with beak-like nose and jutting, dimpled chin. Unlike most Indians, however, Hawk's sideburns were thick, and his brushy mustache drooped toward his mouth corners. He kept his dark-brown hair closely cropped.

The girl's mocking half smile faded, and she blinked once slowly as she said, "Doc's with him. Diggin' that bullet out of him. Yours, I take it?"

A shrill cry came hurling down the stairs: "*Ow!* Oh, Christ—that hurt like hell, you old devil!"

The low voice said something Hawk couldn't make out.

The shrill voice said, "Bullshit, you take it easy with that thing or I'll . . ."

The shrill voice trailed off as the other, lower voice said something in calming, reassuring tones.

The girl said, "You'd swear he never took a bullet before."

Hawk moved into the room, loosened the string tie around his neck, and set his rifle down on the table nearest the batwings. "Doesn't sound like I'll be goin' anywhere till that bullet's out of him. I'll take that drink if the offer's still good."

"Offer's good if your money's good."

Hawk kicked out a chair, dug a coin out of his pants pocket, and flipped it off his thumb. It flashed in the window light as it arced toward the girl, who snatched it out of the air with one practiced hand.

She looked at the coin and arched a brow. "For that, you can have a drink, and"—her cheeks dimpled as she offered a lusty smile—"pretty much anything else that ain't nailed down."

"Just the drink will do me for now."

"Whiskey?"

Hawk nodded and doffed his hat as he sagged into his chair. He set the hat down on the table, over his rifle, and raked a hand through his close-shorn hair. He continued to hear the voices in the second story, with an occasional curse and boot stomp, but the hysterics were apparently over.

13

The girl filled two shot glasses and set them on a wooden tray. She folded a newspaper and set that on the tray, as well, glancing at Hawk and smiling. "Like something to read?"

Hawk shook his head. "Just the drink. Be pullin' out soon."

"Well, just in case," she said, and moved out from around the bar. As she approached his table, he saw that the corset and bustier were damned near sheer enough to reveal every inch of her nice, full-busted body.

She kept her eyes on him as she set the whiskey in front of him. She set the change from his half eagle down beside the shot glass. She kept the other shot glass on the tray with the folded newspaper as she sat down in a chair across from him.

"Business got slow after he arrived," she said. "It was like the wind blew him in. All the *hombres* who took shelter in here *from* the wind blew on out like the trash being scattered around town." She shook her head once and sipped her whiskey. "Who is he?"

"Clyde Leroy Miller," Hawk said. "Otherwise known as Pima."

"Pretty bad fella, this Pima Miller?"

"About as bad as they come."

She chuckled incredulously. "How bad? Just for conversation's sake and all, since you don't seem to care to take me upstairs and let me earn the rest of that half eagle, which I'm rather good at, if I may say so myself."

Hawk threw back half of his own whiskey, set the glass back down on the table, turned it between his thumb and index finger. Pima Miller and the sawbones were still talking, so he didn't mind sitting here chinning with the whore. He had a mind to take her upstairs.

His loins were heavy, for he hadn't been with a woman in weeks. But he couldn't chance losing his edge.

Not this afternoon, with his quarry near.

Hawk said, "He and his gang robbed the bank in Kingman. Shot the president, vice president, locked the customers inside, and burned the place to the ground. They shot the Kingman marshal on their way out of town, dropped two posse members the next day."

"You're the posse now?"

"Close enough."

"Lawman?"

"That's right."

"Where's your badge?"

Hawk slid the lapel of his black frock coat to one side, revealing his sun-and-moon deputy US marshal's badge. The whore leaned forward slightly in her chair, frowned as she studied the three ounces of tin-plated copper.

"I hate to tell you this," she said with a dubious look. "But you're wearin' it upside down."

"Yep."

Her look was skeptical. "May I ask why?"

"It's an upside-down world . . . full of upside-down laws."

"And you're an upside-down lawman . . . ?"

"Houndin' upside-down owlhoots." Hawk grinned as he threw back the last of his shot.

She studied him, nodding slowly, tentatively. Of course, she'd spied the glint of madness in his keen, jade eyes. Most did eventually. Some sooner than others.

Hawk was well aware it was there, for he'd seen it while shaving in a looking glass and hadn't been one bit surprised or bothered. It had come with the black territory he'd begun riding in the forever-dark days in the wake of his son's murder and his wife's self-hanging. Linda had hanged herself from the tree in their backyard right after Jubal's funeral.

The whore glanced at the stairs to her right. "Where's the rest of his bunch?"

"Feedin' mountain lions and coyotes along the trail between here and Kingman, Miss . . ."

"Vivienne."

"Wildcats gotta eat, too, Miss Vivienne."

"And you're . . . ?"

Hawk dipped his chin, narrowed his jade eyes. "The upside-down lawman who's about to drill a bullet through your pretty head, Miss Vivienne."

Chapter 2
Sawbones Wanted

Hawk stared at the whore sitting across the table from him.

Vivienne stared back at him, her eyes intense. Hawk glanced down at the tray sitting just right of her half-empty shot glass. She had her hand beneath the folded newspaper atop the tray.

"Shoot me?" she said, wrinkling the skin above the bridge of her nose. "Why on earth would you do such a nasty thing, Mister Upside-down Lawman?"

"Slide your hand very slowly out from beneath that newspaper."

"What?"

Hawk waited. Her eyes flickered slightly. Color rose in her pretty cheeks, the scar turning paler, as she slid her hand slowly out from under the newspaper. She slid the hand over the lip of the tray and over the edge of the table to her lap.

Hawk reached across the table and flipped the newspaper off of the tray. A small, black, double-barreled pocket pistol with ivory grips glared up at him—a very small but very deadly coiled snake.

The girl grabbed her right forearm with her other hand and sort of scrunched her shoulders together, pooching her lips out and averting her gaze from Hawk's.

Hawk picked up the gun. He flicked the loading gate open and spun the cylinder, letting all five cartridges plunk to the table, where they rolled. Then he tossed the gun over the batwings, which the wind was jostling, and into the street.

"How much did he pay you?"

Vivienne shrugged, smiled bashfully, and again traced the scar with her finger. "A half eagle."

Hawk gave an ironic chuff. Then he turned toward the stairs, and frowned.

No more sounds were coming from the second story.

Apprehension was a cold finger pressed to the small of the rogue lawman's back. He stared at the ceiling, ears pricked. No sound except the wind's moaning and the ratcheting clicks of the batwings.

"What room's he in?" Hawk asked Vivienne.

"Three."

Hawk picked up the Henry, glanced at the girl staring up at him gravely. "One peep out of you . . . ," he said softly, menacingly.

Vivienne turned her mouth corners down.

Hawk strode quickly to the stairs. He climbed the steps two at a time, stopped at the landing and, holding the rifle up high across his chest, looked up toward the second floor.

Nothing.

He climbed the second landing and stopped at the top. To his right and on the left side of the dim hall carpeted with a soiled red runner, a door stood partway open. He moved slowly, one step at a time, wincing at each creak of the floor beneath the runner, to the half-open door.

He kicked the door wide and stood crouched over the Henry, which he extended straight out from his right hip, sliding it quickly from right to left and back again. The room smelled like sweat, blood, and whiskey. The lone, brass-framed bed, which nearly filled the small room, was rumpled, sheets bloodstained.

A gray-headed man in a black suit sat in a chair near the bed's right-front corner, beside an open window. The man's head was tipped to his chest, as though he were sleeping though he wore spectacles and a stethoscope.

He looked as though someone had splashed him with a full bucket of red paint.

Hawk moved to him in two quick, long strides and pushed his head up and back with his rifle barrel, revealing the wide, deep gash stretching from one ear to the other. The cut was so deep that Hawk could see the man's spine through pale sinews and liver-colored muck. A bloody scalpel lay on the floor near his blood-splattered shoes.

Hawk let the dead pill roller's head drop back down to his chest and crouched to look out the window beside him.

A hay wagon was just then making its way along the main street, two beefy mules in the traces. A gray-bearded old man in overalls was shaking the reins over the mules' backs.

Wind tore at the hay in the wagon box. There was a deep depression in the hay pile. As the wagon passed from Hawk's right to his left, Hawk saw a murky, black-hatted figure in a light-blue shirt, suspenders, and black neckerchief running down a cross street, bits of hay clinging to his boots.

Hawk grimaced as he raised the Henry to his shoulder, aimed quickly, and fired. The rifle leaped and roared, setting Hawk's ears to ringing in the close confines of the hotel room. The bullet blew up dust about six inches behind the heel of Pima Miller's scissoring right boot.

The killer glanced over his shoulder as Hawk ejected the spent cartridge casing. Hawk aimed again, squeezed the Henry's trigger, and watched his second bullet plume dust about a foot in front of where the last one had, another four inches shy of its mark.

And then Hawk could have sworn that Pima Miller cast him a taunting grin over his left shoulder as the outlaw continued running in a shambling, wounded sort of way, and disappeared around the rear corner of an old adobe church.

Hawk raked out a curse as he swung around and ran out of the room. He dropped down the stairs threes steps at a time, raising a ruckus that sounded like thunderclaps. Vivienne stood by the piano she'd been playing earlier, wringing her hands together in front of her see-through corset and regarding Hawk warily.

"I do apologize," Hawk grunted as he ran past the girl on his way toward the front of the Laughing Lady.

"What for?" the girl called after him.

"The town's out a sawbones!"

Hawk tipped his head low against the howling wind and ran up the street to the west. He ran one block and then turned into the cross street and sprinted for the back of the church.

He took his time scouring the area behind the church for Pima Miller, wary of an ambush. But then he crossed a rocky arroyo and found a little adobe shack and a stable and stock pen sitting in a clearing among wind-jostled mesquites and palo verdes. A corral of cottonwood poles flanked the shack, with a half dozen or so horses milling under a brush arbor.

Goats bleated in the stock pen. Dust rose and swirled, peppered with hay as well as the shit from goats, chickens, and horses.

Hawk stopped at the edge of the wash, facing the farmyard. The shack was no larger than the goat pen. It was cracked and discolored and several of the ironwood branches forming its roof lifted in the wind.

As Hawk surveyed the shack, a man stepped out of its front door, ducking his head and then donning his hat. He carried a rifle in his right hand. His long, cream-colored duster blew in the wind.

Another man stepped out behind him, also ducking through the low door and donning his hat. Two more men followed the second one, and a minute later, Hawk was facing five men armed with rifles. Four stood over six feet tall. The second man from the left was a full head shorter and dressed all in black leather except for a billowy red neckerchief whipping around in the gale.

Black mustaches drooped down over his mouth corners. He was the only one of the five not holding a rifle but held his hands over the two .45s on his hips.

None of these men was Pima Miller. Hawk guessed that Miller was holed up inside the shack from which the raucous strains of a baby's cries were whipped and torn by the wind.

Hawk recognized a couple of the hard-eyed, bearded faces from the wanted dodgers residing in his saddlebags. Two of these men he knew for sure had prices on their heads. They probably all did. But that didn't matter to Hawk. He'd take the bounty money; he'd be foolish not to. He and his horse had to eat, same as everyone else.

But mostly these men needed killing and Gideon Hawk believed he'd been placed on this earth to do just that—kill men who needed killing. It was as if some judicious spook whispered in his ear which ones needed killing and which ones did not.

Rare it was that Hawk's trail led to a man who did not need a bullet in his head, however. Some needed two, just to be sure. And none needed proper burials. If such men had been placed here for a reason at all, it could be only to feed the carrion eaters.

The man standing to the right of the short, black-clad *hombre* stared incredulously at the rogue lawman, and said, "Gideon *Hawk* . . . ?"

Hawk said, "You had to know our paths would cross sooner or later, Frye."

Leonard Frye—wanted for sundry offenses including bank robbery and murder. He'd also raped a young schoolteacher near the creek by which she'd taken her class for a picnic.

"Why's that?" Frye asked.

" 'Cause when a man needs killing as badly as you do, and for as long as you have, it's what I'd call *inevitable.*"

The short man glanced at Leonard Frye and said something out of the corner of his mouth. Hawk couldn't hear the words but he did hear Frye's response: "Shut up."

The last man to the right of the group scrunched up his face and said, "What—you think you're God or somethin'?"

"Yeah," Hawk said. "Somethin' like that."

Inside the shack, the baby continued to cry. Hawk kept one eye on the open door and the shuttered windows, wary of Pima Miller flinging a shot at him.

Leonard Frye opened and closed his hands around the Winchester he held across his chest. He shaped a cockeyed grin, narrowing one eye. "Five against one, Hawk!"

As Hawk snapped his rifle to his shoulder, he said, "Nope—just four, Leonard!"

He drilled a round, black hole in the middle of Leonard Frye's forehead. Frye didn't make a sound as Hawk's bullet snapped his head back sharply and sent him staggering, hang-jawed, dead on his feet, dropping his rifle. The others jerked to immediate life, but Hawk dropped the short man before the little man could snap off a single round with his fancy .45s.

And then, as the others opened up on him, Hawk pivoted to his right and dove behind a dilapidated handcart moldering at the base of a barrel cactus. Slugs splatted into the side of the handcart and plowed up dirt and sand around Hawk. One bullet tore through the rotten handcart to sear a short line across his right cheek.

Hawk rolled away from the handcart to the other side of the barrel cactus. The three remaining shooters stood crouched and firing their rifles from their hips.

They'd lost track of Hawk for three vital seconds. The rogue lawman took advantage by shooting out from the right side of the barrel cactus. His aim was muddy from this position, however, and he managed to clip one man only in the knee. By the time he'd emptied the Henry, he'd wounded only one more. Tossing the empty rifle aside, he pulled both pistols.

Lead hammered the ground in front of him.

The smell of cordite was pepper on the breeze.

Hawk pulled his head back behind the cactus as two bullets plunked into it, spraying pulp and thorns. Hawk triggered his Russian around the cactus's left side. The bullet clanked off a rifle and plowed into the jaw of one of the shooters, who screamed and dropped his weapon as he buried his face in his hands.

The two others were backing up, eyes bright with anxiety, apparently looking for cover behind them.

Hawk aimed his Colt carefully around the right side of the cactus, and drilled one of the retreaters in the belly. As that man folded like a jackknife, bellowing curses, Hawk drilled the other one in the left shoulder. As the man screamed and jerked back, Hawk's Colt leaped and roared again. The bullet slammed into the man's neck, just right of his Adam's apple.

The shooter dropped his rifle and twisted around and fell. He rolled over onto his back, rose to a half-sitting position, and tried bringing his rifle up once more.

Hawk gained a knee, aimed the Colt carefully. The wounded shooter stared at him, terror in his wide-open eyes. He opened his mouth to scream. The rogue lawman's next shot shattered the man's front teeth and shredded his tongue before blowing out the back of his head.

Spying movement near the cabin, Hawk jerked his head toward the door to see Pima Miller grinning at him over the Remington he was aiming straight out in his right hand. Miller's gloved left hand was clamped over the bloodstain just above his left hip.

Hawk pulled his head back behind the cactus, and Miller's slug went hurling through the air where Hawk's face had been a quarter second before.

Hawk fired both his pistols toward the cabin.

Miller gritted his teeth as he jerked back inside, and then he was gone, nothing but dark doorway where he'd been.

And then Hawk was running toward the open door with both pistols cocked and raised.

Inside, the baby was screaming louder.

CHAPTER 3
MOTHER AND CHILD

Hawk bolted through the open door, threw himself to the right, and pressed his back against the wall. He knocked a shelf loose of its moorings, and the shelf and several clay containers and airtight tins crashed to the floor.

Ignoring the din, the rogue lawman shifted both his aimed pistols around, looking for a target in the shack's rough-hewn, sparsely furnished, dingy interior. The shack was long and deep.

At the rear were two windows. The right window's shutter was open. In the yard beyond it, Miller was gaining his feet, looking back through the window at Hawk. He was smiling but his unshaven cheeks appeared drawn and haggard. His long, cinnamon mustaches beneath the beak-like nose and close-set eyes were buffeting in the wind.

The wounded killer raised his Remington, and Hawk ducked as the pistol stabbed flames toward him, popping flatly. The slug slammed into the wall over Hawk's crouching body.

Hawk rose, raising his pistols to his shoulder. He held fire. Pima Miller was no longer in the window.

Hawk bolted forward. He ran between a cluttered wooden eating table and the wall on the right, past what he thought was a person slumped on a sofa and a crate hanging from the ceiling by ropes. This crate was where the baby's cries seemed to be originating.

None of these messages that Hawk's senses were sending to his brain seemed very significant at the moment. His gaze was riveted on the window beyond which he'd seen Pima Miller.

As Hawk reached the window, he stopped and aimed his Russian out the opening. A small adobe barn and corral lay about sixty yards away, amid low shrubs, cacti, and blowing grit. The horses were standing beneath the brush arbor, their tails blowing in the wind.

Another horse—this one saddled—was tied to the corral gate. A burlap feed sack hung from its ears. Another horse was galloping off through shrubs flanking the corral's right side. As the horse and rider—Pima Miller in his blue shirt and black hat—swung to the right, following a shallow wash, Hawk aimed quickly at the obscured figure, and fired.

Miller and the horse were twisting and turning too violently down the wash for accurate shooting. Hawk's slugs plumed dust, spanged off rocks, and snapped mesquite branches.

Hearing himself curse loudly, Hawk continued firing, with both pistols now leaping in his hands, until the hammers clicked benignly against the firing pins.

He loosed another bellowing curse as he stared off toward where Pima Miller had been only a few seconds before and where there was only blowing grit and jostling branches. The horse tied to the corral gate shook its feed sack free of its ears, shook its head again, and whinnied.

Behind Hawk, the baby was crying loudly, shrilly.

He remembered the slumped figure.

He walked back along the table cluttered with all manner of weapon—pistols, rifles, and knives—as well as ammunition of several calibers. There were plates with food on them, a board with a half a loaf of crumbly brown bread, a pot of beans, a saucer bearing goat cheese.

But Hawk's attention wasn't on the cluttered table but on the figure slumped across the red velvet fainting couch which, with its scrolled arms and legs, looked as out of place here as would a zebra in the corral out back.

The girl was hanging half off of the couch's left side, her head on the floor, arms dangling. She wore a cheap, green dress of embroidered cotton. Her feet were bare, brown legs dirty. Hawk dropped to a knee beside the girl hanging off the arm of the couch, and cleared his throat tentatively.

"Miss . . . ?"

When he received no response, he took her arms and pulled her to a sitting position atop the couch. He immediately saw why she hadn't responded. There was a ragged-edged hole in her forehead, sort of centered between the bridge of her nose and her left eye.

Her large, brown eyes were open and staring at Hawk's chest. Long, straight, raven hair hung down past her shoulders and along her slender, brown arms. An Apache girl, judging by her skin color and the broad flatness and rounded cheekbones of her pretty face.

She wore a doubled necklace of .45-caliber cartridges strung with braided horsehair around her neck. The cartridges winked dully in the dull light from the window at the end of the room— the window through which Hawk had let Pima Miller flee.

The baby continued to cry loudly, stridently. So loudly at times that Hawk's eardrums rattled and ached. Feeling as though someone had stuck a stiletto in his guts, the rogue law-man stepped over to the crate hanging by ropes from two rusty hooks in the ceiling.

The peach crate was padded with a folded, striped blanket— part of a horse blanket. The little brown child inside the crate lay crying up at Hawk, its tiny, round, brown face crumpled in misery. The child—a boy, Hawk thought—squeezed his eyes shut with every bellowing scream. There was a momentary pause in the screams as the child filled its tiny lungs, and then the screams resumed.

The boy's tiny hands, each little larger than the tip of Hawk's own fingers, flailed in the air between the boy and Hawk.

Flailed for the comfort of its mother . . .

"Nan-tee."

The voice sounding just off of Hawk's right shoulder caused him to jerk with a start. He turned to see Vivienne standing beside him, staring at the dead woman sitting on the fainting couch. The saloon girl held a blanket around her bare shoulders.

"Nan-tee," Vivienne said. "Miller's woman."

"That his, too?" Hawk nodded toward the child in the peach crate.

Vivienne nodded. She reached into the peach crate, wrapped her hands around the child clad in an oilskin diaper, and lifted him out of the box. She pressed the boy's tear-streaked cheek to her own scarred cheek and then held him fast against her breast, rocking him gently.

Hawk tore his beleaguered gaze from the child to the boy's dead mother.

"Miller?" Vivienne said.

"Out the window," Hawk said tonelessly.

The child had stopped crying. The silence now on the lee side of the gunfire and the infant's wails was funereal. Outside, the wind howled and moaned like a hungry, stalking animal.

"He left her here," Hawk said. "Left the boy here."

"That is understandable," Vivienne said, continuing to rock the child gently. "He is a bastard. A *pendejo*. I never knew what she saw in him—Nan-tee. She was always fond of the outlaws, though. The rest of the town was scared of her . . . because of *them*." She looked around at the small shack cluttered with food, guns, tack, and ammunition. "Scared of this place."

"This where they holed up—Miller's bunch?"

"For two, three weeks at a time," Vivienne said, and then

cooed to the child who had taken comfort in the saloon girl's touch.

"They would ride in, and business would dry up in Spotted Horse, just as it has done for the past week, since they last rode in." Vivienne stared at him for a time, frown lines cut across her light-brown forehead, above her curious brown eyes.

"Who are you?" she whispered.

"The man who killed the child's mother," Hawk said again in the same hollow, toneless voice as before, as he continued to stare at the child nuzzling Vivienne's breast, trying to get to the nipple behind the see-through corset. Some invisible specter was turning that stiletto in his guts, probing around inside him as though fishing for his heart.

Wretched damned world . . .

"I know a woman who will care for him," Vivienne said as thunder rumbled in the distance, beneath the wind. "He will be better off without her and Miller."

"No child is better off without his ma," Hawk said.

Vivienne turned and walked out of the shack, gently rocking the child against her chest.

Hawk stared down at Nan-tee. As the dead woman, her hair blowing in the wind funneling through the shack, stared blindly across the room, he had a vision of his own wife's face as Linda had dangled from that big cottonwood in their backyard in the little, Midwestern town of Crossroads, in the miserable hours after they'd buried their son who too had been hanged.

Only Jubal had been hanged by Three-Fingers Ned Meade as payback against Hawk. Before he'd gone rogue because of Meade and the crooked county prosecutor who had turned Meade free on a technicality he'd found in the law, Hawk had brought Meade's perverted younger brother to justice.

Linda had hanged herself out of grief.

Nan-tee's face was now Linda's face, framed in tousled,

yellow-blonde hair, staring at him as though pleading with him to forgive her for not being strong enough to live in this world without their boy.

Hawk drew a deep, raspy breath. He raised his hands to his face, raked them down his cheeks, rubbing away the tears.

Then he turned away from the dead woman, and followed Vivienne and the child back across the wash.

As Hawk approached the Laughing Lady, he stopped in the middle of the street, which was empty except for blowing dust and tumbleweeds. Vivienne walked out of the saloon, the child in her arms wrapped in a green army blanket. The whore had changed into baggy denims and a wool shirt, a green bandanna wrapped over her head.

She moved down the porch steps and untied Pima Miller's horse from the hitch rack. She sidled the horse to the porch steps, climbed to the top step, and stepped into the saddle.

She swung the calico toward Hawk, cradling the child in one arm against her chest. She canted her head toward the Laughing Lady. "Help yourself. I won't be long."

She pointed the horse west and rammed the heels of her moccasin-clad feet against the horse's ribs. The calico lunged forward and galloped out of the windblown town, the girl's long, black hair blowing out behind her.

Hawk looked at his grulla for a full minute before he actually saw the horse. Practical matters returned to him, washing up behind the patina of the dead Nan-tee in his head, and he led the horse off to the Spotted Horse Livery & Feed Barn, which he'd noticed when he'd first ridden into town.

He paid the young Mexican who ran the place to stable and care for his horse. He paid him an extra eagle to drag away the outlaws lying in the yard outside of Nan-tee's adobe. He instructed the liveryman to leave them in a draw far enough downwind of town that their scent wouldn't foul the air in Spotted Horse.

He paid him an extra eagle to bury Nan-tee in the yard behind her cabin.

Whatever the Apache woman had been, she'd been the baby's mother, as well, and to Hawk's mind that set her nominally above the carrion feeders.

Then he went back to the Laughing Lady and drained half a bottle of whiskey, sitting out on the porch, watching large, sooty storm clouds roll in from the west. Near nightfall, when the rain had started, the wind howling in earnest and the thunder clapping brutally, causing the saloon's timbers to creek, Vivienne rode back into town.

The baby was no longer with her.

She stabled the horse, returned to the saloon, and carried a fresh bottle and two glasses out onto the porch. She sat down beside Hawk, wrapped in her blanket, both legs curled beneath her, and they drank together and stared out into the rain-lashed, stormy night.

Neither said a word even after they'd gone upstairs together.

CHAPTER 4
RIDER ON THE STORM

Sitting atop a low hill beneath a wind-lashed palo verde, the coyote watched the figure slowly take shape out of the early darkness and hammering rain.

At first, the coyote thought the rider might be a sick deer or a gimpy burro that had strayed away from some miner's diggings. He might be able to take down such a beast and chew out the liver and bladder to carry back to his burrow and dine in relative comfort, out of the thundering storm.

The coyote, wet and bedraggled, its tail curled forward around its left back leg, pricked its ears and worked its nose, all senses alert as it stared at the moving figure.

As the silhouette beyond the slanting, white javelins of the rain mounted a low hill about fifty yards from the coyote's hill, the coyote saw that what he had been watching and hoping would be a meal was, to its dismay, a horse and a human rider. The coyote smelled the horse now, though the beast of human burden was downwind from the coyote, and it smelled the copper smell of blood.

The man's blood.

The coyote had smelled such blood before, as well as the blood of young wild horses that he and his pack had taken down when the coyote itself was young. The man was injured, but he was mounted safely atop the horse that continued plodding toward the coyote.

As the horse and low-hunkered rider continued plodding

toward the coyote, the coyote gave a disgruntled mewl deep in its throat, turned, ducked under a low-hanging branch of the palo verde, and loped off down the backside of the hill.

It faded into the storm, hoping to maybe find a drowned fawn in one of the flooded arroyos.

Pima Miller, dozing in the saddle, had felt the horse stop. Now he looked over the dun's head to see what had halted it.

An arroyo stretched across the desert path about twenty yards ahead. Through the thin line of storm-beaten willows and mesquites, Miller saw the butterscotch water sliding between the banks that appeared to have a twenty-, maybe thirty-yard gap between them.

Occasional leafy branches went bobbing past, twisting and turning with the current.

In the stormy sky, lightning flashed. Thunder peeled like a malevolent god slapping his hands together and laughing.

Miller looked down at his left side. Just above his hip, blood mixed with the rain. It was oozing out of the hole in his shirt. The wound, two days old, felt like a rat was trying to chew its way out of him.

He'd had no idea who'd been dogging him until Frye had identified him back at Nan-tee's place.

Gideon Hawk, otherwise known as the rogue lawman.

Persistent damned son of a bitch!

Miller lifted his head, and water sluiced off the brim to tumble down his back and onto his saddle, soaking him further though he probably couldn't get much wetter than he already was. He'd left Spotted Horse two hours ago, and the rain had started soon after. A summer monsoon. It could rain all night.

Miller needed shelter.

The sawbones in Spotted Horse had dug the bullet out of his

hide, but he hadn't sewn the wound closed. Miller hadn't time for that. The son of a bitch who'd been dogging him for the past four days, killing Wayne and Pierson and T. J. and then Dick Overcast, was warming his heels.

Now the outlaw needed a ranch cabin or a goat herder's shack. Even a cave would do. Anywhere he could hole up out of the weather and catch a couple hours of shut-eye.

Miller straightened his back, clamping his left hand to the wound in his side, and rammed his spurs into the dun's flanks.

"Come on, you ewe-necked hammerhead!" the outlaw bellowed savagely into the wind. The horse leaped ahead at the man's sudden, angry onslaught. "Let's get across that arroyo!"

The horse trotted through the trees and stopped at the edge of the water, furiously shaking its head.

"He-yahhh!" Miller bellowed.

He hadn't needed to. A sudden thunder burst, sounding like that dark god pounding an empty, giant steel barrel with an ax handle, nudged the frightened beast on into the stream. Almost instantly, the horse was in up to its neck, the cold, dirty water closing up over Miller's legs. As it reached his crotch, he sucked a breath through gritted teeth and shuddered.

He felt the horse working furiously beneath him, grunting and whickering, trying to keep moving, to keep its head above the water.

"Come on, goddamnit!" the outlaw shouted, half the sentence drowned by another thunderclap, which came about two seconds off the heels of a lightning flash so close that Miller thought he could smell brimstone above the fresh, muddy scent of the sodden desert.

The horse was sliding downstream faster than it was moving forward. Fury burned through the pain-racked outlaw. He whipped his rein ends against the mount's right hip. That caused the horse to lurch beneath him.

Miller was about to lash the beast again but stopped when three crossed witches' fingers of lightning flashed just ahead and left. The pink, blue-limned strike was so near, it lit up the roiling stream for one full second—long enough for Miller to see that the arroyo was at least twice as wide as he'd first thought it was.

"Holy shit!" he yelled, fear ensconcing him in its large, chill hand.

This wasn't no average wash. A wash out here that wide had to be Jackass Gulch—a killer when it came to gully washers like the one Miller now found himself in the midst of.

"Come on, you cayuse!" the outlaw bellowed, whipping the horse's left hip without mercy, grinding his spurs against the mount's flanks.

The horse lunged forward once, twice, three times. Then Miller heard it give what sounded like a giant yawn. Only he knew it was a groan that meant the horse was done for.

"Shit!" Miller cried as the horse, too weak to swim any longer against such a raging current, began sliding nearly straight down the center of the stream.

The horse sort of fluttered in the water. It dropped a good foot, and then suddenly Miller found himself floating on top of the saddle, his boots slipping free of the stirrups and his legs sliding out from beneath him.

He fought for the saddle horn, but suddenly the horse dropped farther beneath him. It turned onto its side, and Miller flailed with all his limbs, trying desperately to stay above the current. Then, like a helping hand, something solid and black swept toward him. He'd barely glimpsed it, whatever it was, riding low in the water before him, and he gave a soggy grunt as he threw both arms up.

They caught the tree, hooked around the trunk that was about as large around as his own torso. It stopped him abruptly.

Wet bark ground into his nose and forehead. A broken point of the tree stabbed his side about six inches beneath his armpit. He smiled at the pain because it only meant that he had something solid to hold onto, something he could ride down the arroyo until he could find his way to one of the banks.

As he clung to the tree, however, he realized he wasn't moving. He glanced to his left. Another lightning flash revealed the muddy bank out from which the tree extended. Apparently, the wind had torn it out of the ground by its roots.

He'd been thrown a buoy!

Grinding his teeth against the pain in his left side, Miller walked his hands along the side of the fallen cottonwood, slowly making his way, handhold by handhold, to the bank. As he did, the rain continued to pour down on him. The skies rumbled and clapped demonically. Lightning flashed so brightly that at times he was blinded. The darkness between flashes was surreal.

His boots scraped against the bank beneath the water. Continuing to crawl along the side of the tree, Miller made his way up the bank. When his legs were nearly out of the water, he climbed the rest of the four feet through the mud and sodden gravel to the top and lay there for a time, cheek to the earth, catching his breath and sending a silent prayer to whatever dark god had saved his worthless hide.

He chuckled.

The chuckle died on his lips, however, when he remembered the cold-eyed bastard who'd been dogging him. He looked behind and out beyond the tree extending into the wash, which was narrower here than it had been upstream, and probed the rainy night for signs that Gideon Hawk had followed him.

Nothing moved but the wind and the rain and the water sliding behind him, occasionally whipped to a creamy froth.

Most men wouldn't follow in weather like this. But Miller had heard Hawk's reputation. Most men on the frontier, especially *outlaw* men, were well aware of the green-eyed half-breed who wore the deputy US marshal's badge upside down on his vest.

The crazy-loco son of a bitch who went around killing outlaws like they were rats scurrying around a trash dump. The man was worse than the lowest of bounty hunters.

Hawk didn't hunt men for the bounty on their heads. He hunted them to kill them for his own demonic satisfaction.

It was said that the loco son of a bitch, in his own messed-up mind, was still killing the man who'd hanged his boy. Over and over again, with each outlaw Hawk murdered, he was killing "Three-Fingers" Ned Meade.

Over and over and over again . . .

Miller shuddered from an extra chill, just thinking about the rogue lawman out there somewhere in the murky darkness, hunting him with the sure-footed, cold-blooded, razor-edged senses of a stalking puma.

Miller filled his lungs and yelled across the wash behind him, "I ain't Three-Fingers Ned, you son of a bitch! He's *dead*! You done *killed* him, for chrissakes!"

Miller sucked a damp breath, chuckled again. He himself was getting crazier than a tree full of owls. Hawk wasn't out here. He was probably still holed up in Spotted Horse, waiting for the storm to break.

"Damn fool," Miller admonished himself, groaning against his sundry miseries as he heaved himself to his feet.

He looked around and then slogged off through the willows and cottonwoods, the storm-tossed trees and shrubs dancing around him like drunken witches. He didn't know how long he'd walked, practically dragging his boot toes, before he came to a trail.

He studied the trail beneath his boots carefully for a time. It was a graded trace scored with deep wheel furrows. Many of them. Of course, the furrows were filled with water now, and the rain was splashing into them like bullets fired from heaven, but they were furrows, just the same.

Miller's heart quickened hopefully. He'd come to the Butterfield stage road. At last, he had a trail to follow. Trails lead somewhere. This trail would lead to a settlement, eventually.

He'd taken only twenty or thirty steps before he stopped again. He'd spied something off the trail's left side.

Lights.

The silhouettes of buildings shifted amid the lights. Then Miller heard what sounded like the clattering of a windmill's blades.

He saw the sign slanting in the mud along the trail, beside a tall saguaro: SUPERSTITION RELAY STATION.

Miller swerved from the trail and entered what he now saw was a broad yard. The windmill lay just ahead and right, clattering raucously beneath the storm's din. Just beyond lay a long, low cabin, its lamp-lit windows beckoning.

Miller grinned. He brushed his hand across the holster thonged on his right thigh. His Remington was still snugged down in the sodden leather. The cartridges were likely so damp they wouldn't fire, but the people in the cabin wouldn't know that.

"Halloo the cabin!" Miller laughed, his words swallowed by the thunder. "Wet and weary traveler out here!"

CHAPTER 5
THE GIRL AT SUPERSTITION STATION

Miller was glad there was no dog in the station yard.

If there had been, he'd no doubt be aware of it by now, as he quietly mounted the steps of the front stoop that sat on stone pylons. The dog would likely be nipping at his heels and raising one hell of a ruckus, ruining the outlaw's chance at surprising those within.

Miller didn't hate dogs, but dogs were almost never an outlaw's friend.

His Remington in his right hand, Miller moved to the window to the right of the front door. There was a thin red curtain that Miller could see through. Staring through the sashed pane, he grinned. And then he moved back to the door.

He opened the screen door, held it open with his right boot, and then tripped the metal latch of the inside door with his left hand.

When the latch clicked, he cocked the Remy, drew the door open, and stepped inside quickly, pulling the door closed behind him.

The girl sitting at the long, wooden table to Miller's left jerked her head toward him, and gasped. She'd been wrapping wet rawhide around a pick handle, but now she raised both hands from the table as she started to rise from the bench.

A long-haired old man had his back to Miller. He must have been hard of hearing. He apparently hadn't heard the door open or the trill of Miller's spurs as the outlaw had stepped over the doorjamb. Only when the girl, crouched over the table and staring wide-eyed at the intruder, said, "Uh . . . um . . . old man—I think we got *com-pany!*" did the oldster turn his head to look over his left shoulder.

He dropped the coffee mug he'd just refilled from a black pot. As the mug hit the braided rug beneath the old man's boots with a dull thunk, the oldster reached for a double-barreled shotgun leaning against a ceiling post.

"No, no, no," Pima Miller said, wagging his head and trying not to shiver against the cold that had penetrated his bones. "Now, why would you want to go and shoot a weary traveler on such a cold, wet night?"

The old man forestalled his movement toward the shotgun, and turned full around to face Miller. He had a big, craggy, warty face, with a blue-gray Vandyke beard that accented the ruddiness of his sun-seared cheeks. His pale-blue eyes flashed angrily as he said, "Maybe on account o' that weary traveler comin' in here unannounced and holdin' a pistol on me!"

His voice was hoarse, raspy with age and tobacco smoke. He had a coal-black wart, large as a coat button, beneath his right eye.

A hissing sounded.

At first, Miller thought the girl had made it. But then he saw on the other end of the table, beyond a pile of miscellaneous leather and burlap pack gear, a large cat. It was standing on the table, its back humped, and it was glaring at Miller and hissing raucously.

It was no ordinary cat. This one was twice the size of your average larger-than-average kitty, and its ears were tufted. It head was large and round, eyes glowing like copper pennies.

"Christ!" Miller said, swinging the Remy toward the beast. "You got a damn *bobcat* in here?"

The girl said, "Don't shoot, ya damn fool. He's friendly!"

"Don't look friendly to me!"

The girl looked at the cat. "Claws, pipe down!"

"Yeah. Pipe down, Claws!" Miller said through gritted teeth—or he would have gritted them if they hadn't been clattering so violently—"or I'll drill a forty-four round through your mangy hide!"

"Claws!" the girl yelled, hooking her thumb over her left shoulder.

The cat leaped down from the table with a solid thump and dashed up a narrow wooden staircase beyond a fieldstone fireplace in which flames danced. The stairs led to a loft. The cat dashed into the loft and plopped down to stare through the cottonwood-pole rail above the kitchen.

The cat's copper eyes glowed menacingly beneath the silhouettes of its tufted ears.

"Who in the hell has a bobcat for a pet?" Miller said in disgust, waving his cocked pistol around, wondering what other surprises lay in store for him here. "Anymore o' them things?"

"No, he's the only one," the girl said.

"Any dogs?"

"No, the old man don't like dogs."

"Any other *people* here?"

"Nope," the old man said, holding his disdainful gaze on the interloper from the other side of the table.

"Any hostlers out in the barn?"

"I'm the only hostler here," the old man said. "The line's too cheap to hire more."

"When's the next stage due?"

"Not till tomorrow," the girl said. "Likely won't get through till the next day, with this weather an' all." She gave a saucy, mocking smile as her hazel eyes raked Miller's soggy frame up and down. "But I guess you know all about that, don't you?"

"Jodi, quit talkin' to this man!" the old man ordered.

"You're the one best shut up!" Miller stomped around the table. His icy glare caused the old man—he had to be pushing seventy—to move his Adam's apple up and down in his stringy neck and take one step back toward the range.

Miller set his pistol on the end of the table and picked up the double-barreled shotgun—a cheap, Belgium-made affair stamped Cambridge Arms Co. A twelve-gauge, it was a side-by-side hammer gun. Miller breeched it. Both barrels were filled with live shells.

He snapped it closed, shoved his Remington back down in its holster, and aimed the shotgun at the old man's pendulous belly. "Now, how 'bout I blow a hole through you, old man?"

"Ah, shit!" the old man complained, raising his hands to his shoulders. "You got no cause to do that. Take what you want and go!"

Miller looked at the girl, who was still standing in front of the table. She stood only an inch or so over five feet, but she was about as comely as they came. Not much over seventeen, if that, and her pretty, heart-shaped, hazel-eyed face was framed by thick, tawny curls. She was dressed in a coarse work shirt and overalls, but the body beneath those crude duds was well filled out in all the best places.

She blushed under the outlaw's scrutiny.

"Except her!" the old man snarled. "You can't have her!"

"She yours?"

"Yes, she's mine. She's my *granddaughter.* She belongs to me, and if you touch one hair on her head . . ." The old man seemed to realize the ridiculousness of his threat. He swallowed again and looked at the twelve-gauge in Miller's hands.

Miller laughed. Then he shuddered as the cold continued to rack him, and turned to the old man. "Whiskey!"

"I ain't got no whiskey!" The old man lowered his voice, and his right eye flashed shrewdly. "I got bacanora. That'll take the

42

chill out of your bones . . . if you're man enough."

"Oh, don't give me that shit, you old fool. Break out the ba-canora, for chrissakes." Miller looked at the girl. "Was he born a fool or did he get this way in his old age?"

"He's been a fool for as long as I've known him." The girl glanced at the old man jeeringly.

The old man glanced back at her, swelling his nostrils, as he reached toward a high shelf above the dry sink right of the range. "I told you not to talk to him. You mind me!"

"You shut up, old man. Just pour me a tall one and sit down at that table and keep your hands up where I can keep an eye on 'em. You try anything, I'll blast you, and this girl won't be your concern no more."

Miller cut his eyes to her again. Again, her cheeks flushed, though she otherwise betrayed no expression.

"Oh, I know you will," the old man said, pouring out the grapefruit-colored agave-derived alcohol into a tin cup and slid-ing it across the table to Miller. "I know who you are. I recognized you as soon as you came in here."

"You did? Who am I?"

"Pima Miller."

Miller sipped the bacanora. It punched the back of his throat like a fist wrapped in barbed-wire then pulverized his vocal chords as it raked down into his belly to burn holes through his stomach lining. He choked out, "No, shit—I *am*?"

"Sure, you are." The old man splashed bacanora into another cup. "And I'll thank you not to use that saloon talk in front of my granddaughter."

"Well, old man, I reckon you have me at a disadvantage." Miller laughed as he opened and closed his hands around the shotgun aimed at the old man's belly. "Albeit a small one." He cut his eyes to the girl again. "And I'll bet she's heard worse talk than that."

The girl just stared at him. There was no more fear in her eyes. Her eyes were bold, frank, and her mouth was turned slightly up at the corners.

The old man was about to say something else, but Miller wagged the shotgun at him and said, "Sit down there, and shut up, old man. Drink your busthead. And keep them paws up where I can see 'em." He looked at the girl. "You—Jodi. Can you sew?"

"Of course I can sew," she said. "What do you need sewn?"

"Me."

Miller walked around the table and into the small parlor area fronting the fire. There was a large, braided rug in there, as well as a rocking chair. He sagged into the rocker, and, holding the shotgun slack across his knees, kicked out of his boots. "Fetch a needle and catgut, and if you're shy, you better avert your eyes. Because I'm gonna get buck naked so I can dry out in front of this nice fire here. Damn, it's a nice one, too. Lordy, that heat feels good!"

"You can't get naked in here!" the old man roared.

"And bring me a blanket," Miller said as the girl climbed the stairs to the loft. "Make that two!"

"She ain't your slave," the old man scolded from the table, where he was sitting now and slowly packing his pipe. "And I done told you to keep your clothes on, you owlhoot!"

"Ah, shit—I know who you are." Miller was standing and unbuttoning his shirt. "Sure enough—this is the Superstition Station, so you gotta be Old Man Zimmerman. Sure enough, I heard of you." He glanced at the loft where the girl was moving around and the cat was still staring down at Miller. "Heard of your granddaughter, too."

"So you have," the old man said, glaring over his pipe at the outlaw, who shucked out of his shirt and tossed it down in front of the fire.

Miller glanced at the pick on the table. The girl appeared to have been greasing a pair of old saddlebags, as well, and also working on a pack frame.

"You two go off in the desert, I hear," Miller said, thoughtful. "Up into the Superstitions."

"So what?"

"You lookin' for that old mine?" Miller grinned. "That old mine that that old Dutchman from Phoenix supposedly found?" His grin broadened. "The lost Peralta diggin's?"

"Like I said," the old man snarled, scratching a match to life atop the table and touching it to the bowl of his porcelain-bowled meerschaum. "So what if we do? Look around. You'll see we ain't found nothin'. Nothin' but coyotes, Apaches, and rattlesnakes."

"No, but I'll bet you two know them mountains like the backs of your hands by now." Miller shoved his denims down to his knees and sat back down in the rocking chair. He looked at the girl moving down the stairs with a wicker sewing kit hooked over one arm. "Sure enough—I bet you two know every nook and cranny of that country."

"Jodi, look away, fer chrissakes!" the old man bellowed, choking on pipe smoke. "Can't you see this crazy owlhoot's half *nek-kid*?!" His anger appeared to dwindle quickly as another thought dawned on him.

He turned to Miller. "Say, who in the hell's doggin' you, anyways?"

45

CHAPTER 6
THE MEANEST SON OF A BITCH
IN THE TERRITORY

The next dawn, Miller opened his eyes in the Zimmerman cabin's loft, and saw a wildcat staring at him devilishly, ready to pounce.

"Holy shit!" the outlaw screamed, and reached toward where he usually positioned his pistol when he bedded down either outside or indoors.

But the gun wasn't there. Instead, he grabbed a handful of Miss Jodi Zimmerman's hair, causing the girl to groan and lift her head from her pillow.

"What the hell?" the girl complained, glancing over her bare right shoulder at him.

Miller rose to a half-sitting position, drawing the sheet up protectively against his chest while he flailed his right hand for his pistol and stared at the beast that didn't seem so ready to pounce, after all. Jodi's bobcat, Claws, lounged atop the mirrored dresser off the foot of the brass bed that took up most of the space in the cluttered loft.

The cat stared at the outlaw with a vague, almost bored interest, slowly blinking its copper eyes. It curled its tail and flicked it and then gave a mewl as it climbed to its feet, humping its back as it stretched.

It dropped over the side of the dresser to land on the floor and give another, louder mewl.

Miller remembered that he'd laid Old Man Zimmerman's shotgun on the floor beside the bed, and he turned over too

46

quickly, reaching for it. The stitches the girl had sewn his wound closed with barked and showed their own nasty fangs, chewing into him, and he forestalled the effort and clutched his side with a yelp.

"Turn your horns in," the girl said in a sleep-raspy voice. "It's just Claws." She glanced toward the cottonwood rail running along the edge of the loft, and yelled, "Old man, let Claws out!"

Miller lay back against his pillow, clutching his side. The girl had sewed it up tight as a drum. It didn't appear to have bled at all last night. And generally the wound felt better. He probably owed that to all the Mexican busthead he'd drunk the night before, though the dull pain in his head was no doubt the cost.

Miller smacked his lips together—his mouth tasted like a tarantula had crawled inside and died under his tongue—and said, "The old man ain't gonna be movin' around too much this mornin'."

He chuckled dryly.

The girl sat up and swept her tangled hair out of her face. She gave a grunt as she remembered that Miller had ordered her to tie old Zimmerman to his rocking chair before she and Miller had sauntered up to the loft together. She gave her own dry chuckle and said, "I was wonderin' why it was so quiet down there."

She threw the sheet off her naked body and dropped her long legs to the floor. Miller reached for her but she batted his hand away. "I gotta let Claws out, get a fire goin'." She gave him a sultry glare over her shoulder. "Less'n you don't want breakfast."

Miller raked his cheek brusquely against her right arm. "You behave yourself down there. Keep that old devil tied to his chair and remember I got his shotgun."

"You're a tough one, ain't ya?"

The girl spread her hand across his unshaven face, and

pushed his head back against his pillow. Then she rose and dropped a cotton nightshirt over her head. It hung down to just below her knees. She swept her hair back behind her head, yawned, and descended the loft stairs to the main room.

"Throw some grub into a cavy sack while you're at it!" Miller yelled. "We're gonna need food on the trail!"

"What trail?" she said from the main room, padding toward the door.

"The trail to Superstition," Miller said, suddenly realizing, by the buttery light angling through the loft's single, sashed window, that it was way past dawn and he had to get up and get moving before Hawk showed. Miller had no doubt he would.

The rogue lawman was known for not leaving a trail until his efforts had paid off in the form of dead men. Miller would have to fight eventually, but first he'd lead Hawk into unfamiliar territory. Into *rugged* territory. And then, when he had the high ground and the upper hand, Pima Miller would rid the frontier once and for all of the loco, upside-down lawman.

And he'd also pull down the hefty bounty he'd heard had piled up on the rogue lawman's head.

Miller rose and stumbled naked over to the dresser and threw back half a jug of stale water. He followed it up with what was left in the bacanora jug, and then picked up the shotgun, hooked his pistol belt over his shoulder, and stumbled downstairs, his knees stiff as half-set mortar from his cold swim in the arroyo. The old man sat in the rocking chair on the other side of the hearth.

He was awake, his red-rimmed, red-veined eyes open, wrists tied behind his back, ankles lashed together. He'd been gagged with a polka-dotted blue neckerchief. He sat rock-still, glowering up at Miller from beneath his shaggy brows.

Miller chuckled at him as the outlaw gathered his clothes from where he'd hung them from chair backs in front of the now-cold fire. Miller dressed and then, as the girl prepared breakfast in sullen silence, he cleaned his pistol, found a couple of boxes of .44 shells and an old-model Winchester rifle, and cleaned and loaded that, too.

Neither Miller nor the girl said anything. Of course the old man did not because Miller kept him gagged. The old man sat facing the hearth but kept his eyes rolled toward Miller in stony, hateful silence.

When Miller and Jodi had eaten, Miller told her to prepare food for the trail.

"We can't go on no trail with you," Jodi snapped, clearing the table. "We got a stage due today, tomorrow at the latest."

"You just shut up and do as I say or I'll gut-shoot both of you and leave you howlin'!" Miller glanced at the old man. "Besides, who said he was goin'? He'd just slow us down."

He looked at Jodi again. "I've heard you and him been livin' out here, running the station and combin' them mountains yonder for that Peralta gold since you was six years old. Now, I could tell from last night that that was a few years ago."

He laughed through his teeth as he turned to the old man, who started tossing his head and grunting furiously. Miller threw back the last of his coffee, rose from the table, walked over to Zimmerman, and jerked the gag down to his whiskered chin.

"What the hell you want, old man?"

"I gotta take a piss, you sonofabitch!"

Miller cursed and went back to the table. He found a folding knife among the girl's clutter, opened the knife, and held the blade up close against Zimmerman's leathery neck.

"How 'bout if I just slit your throat and put everyone whose ever had to have anything to do with you out of their misery?"

"Go ahead!" the old man barked raspily, lifting his chin to expose his lumpy throat. "I'd just as soon not live no more after what I heard up in the loft last night!"

Jodi laughed at that.

So did Miller.

He untied the old man and kicked him outside to drain his bladder off the stoop. And then he forced old Zimmerman to go on out to the barn and saddle a couple of riding horses, and to outfit them with grub sacks and canteens. He wanted a rifle sheath on one of the mounts, as well.

"They better be the best mounts in your remuda, old man," Miller barked, standing on the stoop and waving his pistol at the old man's back as Zimmerman trudged, bandy-legged and cursing profusely, off to the barn and corral in which several horses milled.

Miller walked out into the soggy, steaming yard and stared nearly straight south, toward the rusty crags forming what looked like a giant Gothic cathedral but which comprised, in fact, Superstition Mountain. It seemed to rest suspended above the misty horizon, the mountain's sheer, three-thousand-foot cliffs, pinnacles, and vertical canyons towering over the saguaro-studded desert.

Miller picked out the slender, finger-shaped peak known as Weaver's Needle. It was near that formation that the old Dutchman's mine was said to reside—formerly the mine of one Don Miguel Peralta.

But Miller cared nothing for the Dutchman's gold. He doubted it even existed. It wasn't called Superstition Mountain for nothing. All the outlaw wanted was to lure Gideon Hawk up there into that devil's maze of clefts, canyons, and washes, and shoot the holy hell out of him.

Miller looked all around the station yard, pocked with many mud puddles amid the snaking fingers of steam rising now as the morning heated up, and then he went back inside to hurry the girl. Twenty minutes later, the old man led the two horses back to the cabin, and Miller and Jodi filled their saddlebags and cavy sacks with trail supplies, including the bacon sandwiches she'd made.

Miller tied the old man up in his rocking chair. There was no reason to gag him. He could yell all he wanted. There likely wouldn't be anyone to hear him for several hours.

"He's gonna catch you, whoever he is doggin' your trail."

"Who is he?" Miller challenged the old man.

"I don't know, but whoever he is, to have Pima Miller pissin' down his leg, he must be good!" Old Man Zimmerman cackled at that, eyes sparking devilishly.

Miller unsheathed his Remy and clicked the hammer back.

"He's a mouthy old bastard," Jodi said. "But if you kill him, you're ridin' alone. Good luck gettin' into those mountains without knowin' the way. Geronimo will find you and cook you slow!"

Miller drew his index finger taut against the Remy's trigger. He could kill the old man and force the girl to show him the way, but she'd likely run him into a box canyon. She was savvy. Easier to let the old man live, he supposed.

Miller turned to her. She was holding a cavy sack over her shoulder.

"Get mounted up!" he yelled, glaring at the old man.

He depressed the Remington's hammer, left the cabin, and drew the door closed behind him.

But he couldn't stand letting the old man live. When they were two hundred yards south of the station, Miller stopped and dragged the girl off her horse. She fought him, cursing, but he finally got her hog-tied. Then he tied her horse's reins to a spindly cottonwood.

"You poison-mean son of a bitch!" she barked at him, lying belly down on the ground, legs and arms drawn up behind her back. Her pretty face was flushed with fury.

"That's right!" Miller raked out, laughing. "I'm the meanest son of a bitch in the territory!"

He galloped back toward the station yard. The trussed-up girl watched him. From her vantage, Miller was a small, brown silhouette by the time he reached the station. She stared through the fog snakes as he dismounted and leapt onto the porch.

He was out of sight for few seconds before the girl heard the dull crack of the outlaw's pistol.

Jodi stared toward the station yard. She blinked slowly. Her mouth corners rose.

CHAPTER 7
DUST AND BONE

Hawk was up at dawn, lashing two four-foot-long oak branches together with rawhide he'd found in the barn behind Nan-tee's now-vacant shack. He'd soaked the rawhide in a water trough, and now he knelt atop the two branches, where they formed a cross, and tightly wound the wet rawhide around the joint.

He tied the hide and used the back of a shovel blade to hammer the cross into the ground, at the head of Nan-tee's grave, on the far side of a shallow wash flanking the barn. He lowered the shovel, caught his breath, and looked at the mound of rocks.

Odd how he no longer felt anything but a slight, lingering guilt. He was well aware he'd orphaned the little boy, but it had been a mistake he'd declared to himself as honest. The woman's killing had been inadvertent, and he'd done as much as he could to repay Nan-tee for having killed her and orphaning her boy.

Having her buried and marking her grave was as much as he could do. Vivienne had taken the boy to an Apache woman who lived with her father and two children in a hogan-type lodge in the desert west of Spotted Horse.

Hawk said no words over the dead woman. He knew a few, but they refused to be remembered. He'd said them before, and ever since his family had been taken from him, they'd sounded laughably hollow.

He'd tried it again just a few months ago, when he and his blonde sometimes-partner Saradee Jones had visited the two graves outside the town of Crossroads in southern Dakota Territory. Hawk had been wounded in an especially violent shootout, and his nearness to his own death had fueled the urge to be near his dead family again. But to Hawk the two graves in that stark cemetery had merely been two depressions in the ground capped with wood fashioned into crosses—home to nothing more substantial than a few shovelfuls of dust and bits of bone.

Those two holes in the ground did not house his family. His family—the love and the laughter and the times he and Jubal had fished a nearby creek together—were gone. They'd been taken from Hawk and this world by Three-Fingers Ned Meade.

All they were, all they would have been . . . gone.

It was a bone that Hawk could not get out of his craw. Killing Pima Miller wouldn't do it, either. He had no illusions.

But Miller needed killing if for no other reason than a young mother had taken a bullet meant for him. But of course there were many more reasons. Miller was a killer. He'd even killed the sawbones who'd dug Hawk's bullet out of his hide. By hunting him down and killing him, Hawk would feel better.

He would feel, for an hour, maybe an hour and a half—no more than that—*better.*

And then, when the feeling passed, he'd clean and reload his weapons and look for the next man who needed killing.

Or the next woman. Women were not immune to evildoing.

Saradee Jones, for instance. There was likely no worse woman anywhere. And she needed killing. But so far, Hawk hadn't been able to drop the hammer on her. He'd only been able to feast himself on her splendid body while she taunted him for doing so.

One day, however, he would kill her. Maybe the next time he saw her, in fact.

Footsteps sounded behind Hawk. One hand went to the grips of the silver-plated Russian as he turned. He removed his hand from the gun. Vivienne walked toward him. As she made her way across the wash, she carried a burlap sack in one hand, a steaming stone mug in the other.

She wore her black hair pulled back in an enticingly sloppy French braid. A cream-colored, Mexican-style dress with red embroidering hugged her fine body, buffeting around her brown legs. The dress left her shoulders bare.

The long, pale scar running down the side of her face stood out in the weak morning light.

The grulla, saddled and ready for the trail, Hawk's Henry rifle snugged down in the saddle boot, whickered and turned to the girl, as well, switching its tail.

"Easy, fella," Hawk said, patting the horse's neck. "She's a friend."

"A friend, eh?" Vivienne smiled ironically as she climbed the shallow bank, likely remembering the passion of their previous night's coupling. She held out the coffee and the tied neck of the bag to Hawk. "Food for the trail. Parched corn for your horse. I thought you might like a cup of coffee before you go."

Hawk stared at her, vaguely puzzled.

"I had a feeling I'd find you here," she said.

"Why?"

"Just a feeling."

Hawk took the cup and the grub sack, and sipped the coffee. It was hot and black.

Vivienne folded her arms on her breasts as she looked down at Nan-tee's grave. Then she glanced at him. "Where's your wife?"

"How do you know there was a wife?"

"You look like a killer. Kill like a killer. But last night . . ." Vivienne shrugged a shoulder. "I don't know. You were nice.

Gentle. Figure there must be a woman behind that."

"There was."

"And a child?"

Hawk stared over the mug as he sipped the coffee.

"I found a carving—a wooden horse, a black stallion—on the floor in my room. It must have fallen out of your coat pocket. 'Jubal' is written on the bottom." Vivienne paused. "I wrapped it up and put it in the grub sack."

"Obliged. It's my boy's. *Was* my boy's."

"I'm sorry, Gideon. Whatever happened, I'm sorry. I hope you find peace sometime, somewhere . . . despite it all."

"Ain't likely. But I appreciate your sayin' the words, Vivienne. Just the same."

She reached out and slid a finger across the moon-and-star badge pinned upside down to his vest.

"Farewell, Upside-down Lawman. Watch your back. Pima Miller is a sneaky devil. Some say Nan-tee gave him secret Apache powers that make him extra strong, extra hard to kill."

Hawk finished the coffee and handed the cup back to Vivienne. "We'll see."

Hawk tied the grub sack to his saddle horn then stepped into the leather. He did not look back at the woman from the Laughing Lady Saloon as he put the horse into a trot through the chaparral, heading south, the same direction in which Pima Miller had headed.

As Hawk had expected, the storm had washed away most of Miller's sign. But Hawk's own Ute war chief father had taught him how to track long ago, and he'd put those skills to good use, gaining experience during the years he'd worked as a bona fide federal lawman.

He'd honed said skills to a razor's edge after he'd begun tracking men for his own satisfaction, with a hard heart and the unflappable determination of a religious fanatic. There was probably presently no better tracker on the frontier than Gideon Hawk, excepting possibly one or two Apache trackers now working for the US Army under the supervision of General Crook, or some of the Pima and Maricopa Indians whom John Walker had trained to fight Geronimo's Chiricahuas.

To complement those skills, Hawk was as patient as he was determined, and patience was key when tracking on the lee side of a desert gully washer.

Hawk had last seen Miller heading south, toward the Superstition Mountains that were now in the early morning a gray-green lump on the southern horizon. As Hawk rode through the chaparral, weaving around saguaros, barrel cactus, mesquites, and palo verdes, he saw the remnants of the previous day's rain—the desert caliche and soft clays whipped into small swirls and still-damp, miniature deltas that had eroded any markings left by the killer.

But, still, Hawk found parts of prints on the lee sides of trees and occasional boulders, where the rain had had less direct access to them. He also found several relatively fresh horse apples and even a bit of cloth clinging to a cholla branch—a few threads of blue chambray that had been torn from the same color shirt as the one Miller had been wearing when Hawk had last seen the killer.

By noon, Hawk had progressed only a mile from Spotted Horse, but as Miller's trail was leading almost directly south, he was relatively certain it would continue in that direction, toward the Superstitions whose steep, gray crags continued changing both shape and color along the southern horizon as the sun kited across the sky.

As Hawk rode and continued picking up small signs of his quarry's passing, he put himself in the mind of Miller. The killer had ridden through here during a downpour. He'd also been wounded. Those two things had likely made him a desperate man. One who had likely not been sure that Hawk hadn't been following him.

Doubtless, the man would't have cared much about which direction he was riding. He'd likely given his horse its head and just hung on, hoping to find some place in which he could cower from the lightning, thunder, and hammering rain.

Since he'd been heading south, he'd probably continued heading south.

Hawk continued his slow ride, scanning the ground as well as the flora around him, throughout most of the afternoon, wanting to make sure he was still on Miller's trail. He didn't care if it took him a week to ride five miles. As long as he was still on Miller's trail, he'd eventually catch up to the man and kill him.

He hoped Miller wouldn't die from his bullet wound before the rogue lawman could run him down. He wanted the satisfaction of being the last person the killer saw before he was sent to hell on the burning, gunpowder wings of a .44 slug.

Hawk thought the man who'd left his dead woman—killed with a bullet meant for him—and his small child behind while he'd fled into the night, thinking only of himself, deserved nothing less.

He reached a broad, deep arroyo in the early afternoon, when the distant mountains were relieved by dense shadow, the northwestern rock faces tinged yellow and salmon. Hawk stared down at the cut before him. The water, which was the color of creamed coffee, had receded halfway down the steep banks. Last night, however, it had to have been a veritable millrace.

Hawk looked around, wondering if Miller had made it across or had headed either east or west along the bank. He considered following the arroyo in both directions, but if he remembered right, the Butterfield Company had a stage route running nearby. Miller might have known about the trail and at least tried to head for it. Hawk would check the trail out first, and the first relay station he came to.

Someone might have spotted the wounded killer.

Hawk's grulla mustang crossed the arroyo easily, though it had some trouble climbing the steep opposite bank that was slick with still-wet clay. The horse's hooves slipped, and as it fought for traction, the mustang's lungs wheezed like a blacksmith's bellows.

At the top of the bank, Hawk stopped the horse, resting him, and looked around.

To his right, a saguaro leaned out over the wash. The night before, the lip of the wash had eroded enough to uproot the cactus. Now, among the bone-colored roots that had been partially torn out of the ground, something glistened in the afternoon sunshine.

Something Miller had left behind? Possibly a canteen?

Hawk swung down from the saddle, dropped to a knee beside the saguaro, reached through the roots, and took hold of the object.

He saw right away that whatever it was couldn't have belonged to Miller, for it was too deeply entangled in the saguaro's roots. However, curiosity urged him to disentangle the roots until he was holding before him a badly dented and rusted Spanish-style helmet from which the rain had washed away some of the mud. Despite the weathering, Hawk recognized the headgear by its flat, narrow brim and the high crest, like a rooster's comb, running from front to back.

Only one cheek guard clung to it. The other was likely entangled deeper in the root ball, or maybe it had long ago been blown or washed away in rains similar to that which had ravaged this desert the night before.

Hawk ran his hands along the helmet's flaking metal brim. Finding these ancient artifacts always gave him a chill. They reminded him how small and insignificant he was. Even how small and insignificant his *misery* was—merely one clipped scream among the barrage of screams and long, keening wails that comprised all of human life on earth from the first mortal forward.

He peered through the bristling chaparral toward the castle-like Superstitions rising in the south. He'd heard that a rich Mexican whose family had owned a sprawling rancho had come north on a gold-scouting expedition about forty years ago. Don Miguel Peralta had been chasing a legend that the Apaches had told Coronado about a vein of almost pure gold in the high, rugged range two hundred miles north of what is now the US–Mexico border.

Discovering that the vein was more than mere legend—that the nearly pure gold did, in fact, exist—Peralta recruited several hundred peons to work his "Sombrero Mine" deep inside the Superstitions, and over the next three years he shipped home by pack train millions of pesos' worth of nearly pure gold concentrate.

Hawk looked down at the helmet in his hands.

Could he be holding the headgear of one of Coronado's men who, exploring this country three hundred years ago, first became privy to the Apache story of almost-pure gold? The gold that Don Peralta mined later, before the Civil War, and ended up selling his life to the Apaches for?

Dust and bone . . .

Hawk heard a scream. Loud and shrill, it came from inside his own head. It was the scream of his wife when Linda learned that their boy, Jubal, had been taken off the school playground and hanged by Three-Fingers Ned Meade.

Hawk tossed the helmet aside, swung up onto the grulla's back, and continued south toward the stage road and, he hoped, more sign that he was on the trail of Pima Miller.

The wind wasn't blowing, but the rogue lawman could smell blood on the breeze . . .

CHAPTER 8
THE STAGE FROM FLAGSTAFF

The old man sat back in his rocking chair, both open eyes rolled up and slightly off-center as though he were staring at the bullet hole in his forehead.

Blood trickled from the hole past the corner of his left eye and along his nose to pool in the mustache of his blue-white Vandyke beard. His arms had been tied behind him to the spools at the back of the chair, and his ankles were bound. His lower jaw sagged, upper lips stretched back from his crooked, yellow teeth in the same snarl he'd likely given his killer.

Extending the cocked Russian in his right hand, Hawk looked around the shack. He didn't have to inspect it to know that no one else was there. A deathly silence filled the place, and dirty dishes were mounded in the dry sink to the right of the range on which were several greasy pots and pans. Flour had been spilled on the table, near a mess of freshly oiled tack and the hide-wrapped handle of a pickax. The flour told Hawk that someone had hastily packed for the trail, and that that person had likely gone with Miller.

That Miller had shot the trussed-up, defenseless old man, there was no doubt in Hawk's mind. A woman had lived here with the old man, for the kitchen, however messy, bespoke a woman's touch. The slight fragrance of lilac water mixed with the smell of man sweat and tobacco in the cabin's hot, pent-up air still humid from the previous night's storm.

Hawk turned and walked out through the cabin's open door.

He held the Russian down along his leg as he moved off the porch and walked around the yard, closely inspecting the ground. He stopped near the windmill and stared south.

Then he holstered the hog leg, stepped up onto the grulla's back, and trotted on out of the yard, following an oft-used wagon trail that appeared to meander over the low benches in the direction of the Superstitions standing tall now on the horizon, orange and pink in the light of the falling sun.

Fifteen minutes later, content that he had Miller's trail—two shod horses heading south toward the mountains—Hawk returned to the yard and unsaddled his mount in the barn. He took great care with the grulla, watering and graining the mount and then slowly, thoroughly wiping him down with an old feed sack and then currying him and cleaning out his hooves. The horse had picked up a few pebbles and cactus thorns, and they had to be tended to prevent trouble as he trailed Miller.

Hawk was well aware that without his horse, the hunt would be over. And once he left the stage station and headed up into the Superstitions, his horse would be even more essential. If the mustang went down, Hawk's own life would be over.

And Pima Miller would ride free with his hostage.

If the girl or woman was, indeed, a hostage. Hawk had seen no signs of a struggle, so he couldn't be sure. He'd heard that Miller held a devilish attraction for women, and any girl living alone out here with the now-deceased old man would probably be susceptible to the killer's charms.

Miller might be using her as a guide rather than a hostage. The cabin was filled with mining implements, as was the barn and tack room, which meant that the old man and possibly the girl were at least part-time prospectors, and likely knew the mountains well.

By the time Hawk had finished tending his own horse and feeding and watering the stage horses and three burros and headed back to the cabin, the sun had slid down behind the far western ridges that were silhouetted black against it. He saw no reason to continue after Miller that day.

Tomorrow would be soon enough. It would likely rain tonight, as already more monsoon clouds were building in the southwest, but Miller would no doubt continue to follow the well-worn trail leading south of the station yard.

Obviously, he was intending on either hiding in the mountains until his trail grew cold, or on leading his hunter into the high crags, isolating him and bushwhacking him from the ample cover of that wild country. Or maybe he intended to work through them to the south. Hawk knew that the outlaw's home territory was the desert around Tucson. He'd acquired his nickname, Pima, from having been married to a Pima girl for a time, when he'd been hauling freight to Arizona cavalry outposts in the years following the war.

That had been before he'd turned to sundry, more nefarious, means of making his living . . .

Back in the shack, Hawk built a fire in the range and untied the old man from the rocking chair. Using picks and shovels from the cabin, Hawk buried the old man behind the shack, first wrapping his body in a tattered quilt. He had to rush the job because of the storm's approach, with drumming thunder and a chill, rising breeze, but he was content that he'd ensconced the old man's body safely from the predators.

He brewed coffee on the cabin's range and sipped it outside on the porch, watching the rain come down, feeling refreshed by the chill, damp breeze. Later, he ate one of the two remaining burritos that Vivienne had made, with a pickled chili pepper she'd also packed. For dessert he sipped tequila from the small stone bottle she'd wrapped in heavy burlap, fingering the wooden stallion his boy had carved only a few days before he'd died . . .

The storm didn't last half as long as the one the night before, and Hawk was glad. It would make following Miller easier. The thunder rumbled for nearly an hour after the brunt of the storm, lightning flashing in the northeast.

The air was fresh and cool, perfumed by the desert.

Hawk slept in one of the beds in the curtained-off area of the cabin reserved for overnight passengers. He slept well, knowing that he was on a warm trail, confident that he would kill another killer soon.

That morning, just after dawn, he drank coffee and ate his last burrito and pickled chili pepper outside on the porch again. He'd saddled the grulla and tied the horse to the hitch rack fronting the cabin. As Hawk finished the burrito and washed the last bite down with another swallow of coffee, the grulla gave its tail a hard switch and turned its head to peer toward the trail curving out of the desert.

Its ears twitched as it stood, tensely staring toward the north.

Slowly, Hawk leaned forward and set his plate and cup on the porch rail. Then he reached behind him for the Henry he'd leaned against the shack. He pumped a live round in the chamber, off-cocked the hammer, and rested the rifle across his thighs.

Presently, a man's yell, muffled by distance, pierced the morning quiet and stillness. The faint din of galloping hooves followed, gradually growing louder. Many sets of hooves. As the man's yells continued, punctuated with what sounded like the pops of a small-caliber pistol but which Hawk recognized as a blacksnake being snapped over a team's back, Hawk eased his grip on the rifle.

The yells were those of a jehu haranguing his team.

A stage was approaching from the north.

65

Hawk sat back in the chair and waited, hearing the commotion growing louder until the stage came into view along the trail, the six horses lunging forward against their collars, the jehu sitting on the right side of the driver's box, whistling now more than yelling.

The shotgun messenger sat to the driver's left, cradling the sawed-off, double-bore coach gun in his arms. As the stage drew near, the jehu—a stocky man in a high-crowned, salt-encrusted cream hat and wearing a red neckerchief with white polka dots up high across his mouth and nose—eased back on the ribbons he was deftly plying in his gloved hands. Above his hands, thick leather gauntlets ringed his forearms.

The team and its trailing coach thundered into the yard. It came around the far side of the windmill and stock tank, and the jehu leaned back in the seat, pressing his boots against the dashboard, as he hauled back on the reins. The shotgun messenger was cautiously eyeing Hawk still sitting on the stage station's front stoop. The shotgun rider lowered his neckerchief, and Hawk saw that a wad of chaw was bulging his left cheek.

When the driver had the team stopped, he ripped his own neckerchief down from his nose and yelled, *"Zimmerman!"* He cast his incredulous gaze from Hawk to the closed station house door and then back toward the barn and pole corral. *"Jodi! Zimmerman!* Stage from Flagstaff!"

Hawk said, "They're not here."

He glanced through the door of the coach sitting about thirty feet straight in front of him. He thought there were four or five passengers jostling around inside the Concorde, preparing to de-stage. A woman was coughing and waving a hand in front of her face as though to clear the dust roiling around inside the cramped confines.

Hawk's gaze caught on the flash of something shiny.

A badge, perhaps?

"Where are they?" the shotgun messenger asked Hawk, looking over the driver who was just then setting the brake and spitting dust from his lips.

Hawk stared through the window of the stage door. Sure enough, one of the passengers wore a badge. From Hawk's position, it looked like the moon-and-star badge of a federal.

"Did you hear me, mister?" the bellicose shotgun messenger said, scowling at Hawk. "Where's Jodi and the old man?"

Hawk said, "The old man's dead. Buried behind the station house. Jodi—does that happen to be a male or a female?"

The driver was glowering at Hawk, apparently not certain he'd heard correctly. "Female! What's this about Zimmerman?"

"Dead," Hawk said.

The driver and the shotgun messenger glanced at each other skeptically. Then they both started to climb down off their perch.

At the same time, the stage's near door opened, and a tall man in a three-piece suit so dusty that it appeared gray stepped down into the yard. A badge was pinned to his wool vest. He cast Hawk a dark, critical stare and then he turned to help down from the stage a middle-aged woman in a green traveling frock and small straw hat trimmed with fake berries and flowers.

The next man out, also middle-aged and wearing a shabby suit and wool shirt with attached collar, appeared to be the woman's husband. His corduroy trousers were patched at the knees. The man and the woman stepped to one side, looking around with the typically harried, disoriented expressions of stage travelers—especially those who'd likely been held up on account of the weather. The man beat his bowler hat against his leg, causing more dust to billow.

As the lawman continued to regard Hawk skeptically, his eyes flicking between the Henry resting across Hawk's knees, and Hawk's face, two more men climbed heavily, wearily down from the stage behind him. These two were dressed similarly to the first man, and they also wore deputy US marshal's badges. Ever so slightly and slowly, Hawk used his left middle finger and the heel of that hand to slide his coat across his own upside-down badge, concealing it.

He didn't know if the others had noticed. He hoped not. He was not in the business of killing lawmen. Unless they got in his way.

Then they were as fair game as men like Pima Miller.

The stocky driver strode up the porch steps, batting his own hat against his thigh, and said, "You pullin' some kinda funny, mister?"

"About what?"

"About Zimmerman bein' dead?"

"Nope," Hawk said. "I never joke about death. I found him in there yesterday, tied to his rocking chair. Someone had drilled a bullet through his forehead. He was getting cold and starting to swell, so I buried him."

The driver tripped the latch, opened the door, and stepped inside, yelling, *"Zimmerman?"* He waited. "Miss Jodi?"

"I told you," Hawk said, gaining his feet. "He's around back."

The driver stepped back out of the station house. He and the shotgun messenger shared a look, and then the driver hurried back down the porch steps and walked swiftly around the corner of the cabin, heading for the rear. The shotgun messenger gave Hawk an owly look as he rested his shotgun on his shoulder, spat a dark stream of chaw onto a prickly pear, and followed the older man toward the back of the cabin.

The lawmen all looked at each other, and then two followed the jehu and the shotgun messenger around the cabin, while the third lawman and the two civilian passengers stood regarding Hawk skeptically in the morning's dwindling shadows.

Hawk stepped down off the porch. Heading for his horse, he

glanced at the middle-aged man and woman, and said, "There's coffee inside."

The man and the woman both glanced expectantly at the deputy US marshal. The federal canted his head toward the station house. He waited until the couple was inside, and then he said, "Hold on, friend."

He stepped toward Hawk, his fingers in the pockets of his butternut wool vest from which a gold-washed watch chain dangled.

He was tall and lean, fair of skin and sunburned at the nubs of his cheeks. His long, slender nose was peeling. Hawk guessed he was in his early thirties. Curly blond hair hung down beneath the flat brim of his coffee-colored Stetson, which boasted a band of rattlesnake skin.

His mouth was long and thin beneath a dragoon-style mustache. His relatively smooth cheeks showed a day-old trace of beard stubble to which dust clung. He carried himself with an air of self-importance as he sauntered toward Hawk, and stopped just off the grulla's right hip.

Hawk was standing on the horse's left side, resting his rifle across the seat of his saddle and then reaching down to tie the latigo strap beneath the horse's belly.

"If what you say is true, friend," the lawman said with a taut smile, "then you're gonna need to hang around and answer a few questions."

"I'm not your friend," Hawk said, pulling the end of the latigo through the saddle's D ring. "And I don't like it when folks get too friendly."

"You said Old Man Zimmerman was dead, friend. And I, bein' a federal lawman an' all, would like to know who killed him."

"Pima Miller killed him. But, again"—Hawk smiled at him over his saddle—"I'm not your *friend.*"

The lawman frowned. "Miller's who we're after. Chief marshal sent us down from Prescott. Miller and his gang robbed the bank in Kingman and are said to be meeting up with the rest of their gang somewhere south of Phoenix."

"No shit?"

"How do you know Miller killed Zimmerman?"

"I just know."

"Hold on, friend!"

The federal walked around the rear of the grulla. Hawk had turned out his left stirrup and was preparing to toe it and mount, when the federal lawman grabbed Hawk's arm. As Hawk turned to face him, the lawman's eyes dropped. Hawk followed the man's glance to Hawk's upside-down badge, which his coat had opened to reveal.

The lawman slowly lifted his chin. When his eyes finally met Hawk's, his brows were beetled with incredulity. "What the . . . ?"

Hawk heard the voices of the other lawmen as they strode back toward the yard from the cabin's rear.

"Let it go, friend," Hawk said, his lips quirking a frigid smile beneath his brushy mustache. "Just let it go."

The lawman's disbelieving gaze flicked from the badge again to Hawk's emerald-hard eyes. "You're . . ."

"They don't have to know," Hawk said mildly. "If they do know, it ain't gonna go well. You know that. You'll just be three dead men with no yesterday, no tomorrow."

Hawk held the lawman's gaze. The man's lower jaw sagged. His eyes were dark with fear, frustration.

"Step away. Be our secret. You boys just keep ridin' on down to Phoenix in the stagecoach there, and you see about Miller and his gang down there . . . and you just think about how you might have died today but didn't because you were smart enough to keep your mouth shut."

"There's a grave back there, sure enough," said one of the other two lawmen as they both rounded the cabin's far front corner. He stopped and nodded toward Hawk. "Have you checked him out, Alvin?"

Alvin stared uncertainly at Hawk. And then he took one step back, saying haltingly, "Yeah, I checked him out. He seen Miller in the area." He took another step straight back away from Hawk, the grulla between Hawk and the other two lawmen now approaching, the jehu and shotgun messenger behind them.

"He thinks Miller and his bunch is headed for Phoenix . . . just like we thought," Alvin said.

"What about Miss Jodi?" This from the jehu, who'd stopped with the other men near the porch steps.

"I figure they must have taken her," Hawk said, sliding his coat closed and stepping into the leather. He rested his Henry across his saddlebow and backed the grulla away from the hitch rack.

He smiled at Alvin, nodded to the other lawmen and the jehu and shotgun rider, and then swung the grulla around the cabin and put it into a jog across the yard, heading south toward the trail he'd scouted the evening before. For a time, he could hear the lawmen talking behind him. He hoped Alvin kept his mouth shut.

Hawk didn't want to kill lawmen, though he knew from experience that many were no better than the men they were paid to hunt. Some were worse.

Still, he didn't want to kill the lawmen from Prescott.

But if they trailed him, tried to impede him, he would blow them all to hell.

CHAPTER 9
DEADLY COMPANION

Miller reined his brindle bay to a halt under a lip of rock that rose out of the canyon floor like a shark's fin, and glanced behind him. He could see no movement down toward the broad neck of the canyon they'd been riding through for the past hour, so he glanced at the girl riding off his left stirrup.

"Get down and start a fire. We'll rest the horses and have lunch here."

"I'm gonna have to gather wood for that fire," Jodi said, climbing off the back of her Morgan mare. "Sure you trust I won't skin off on ya?"

She cast him a devilish grin over her shoulder.

"You stay away from that horse while you're gatherin' that wood, and you stay where I can see you. You try to run off, I'll—"

"Yeah, I know," Jodi said, tying the Morgan to an ironwood shrub in the shade of the shark's fin. "You'll run me down and tan my bare ass and then you'll hobble me and I'll ride belly down over my mare's back for the rest of our wonderful time together."

She snickered as she kicked a chunk of ironwood free of the ground, and then stooped to pick it up.

"Think it's funny, do you?" Miller snarled. "You'll see how funny it is if you try to run out on me."

He reined the bay around and rode back down the old Indian trail they'd been following into the mountains. The trail climbed a low bench overlooking the canyon mouth. Several yards from the top of the bench, Miller stopped the bay, fished old Zimmerman's spyglass out of his saddlebags, and then got down and crawled to the lip of the bench.

He telescoped the glass and stared off across the desert toward the stage station that was lost in the heat haze of the northwestern horizon. All that he could see were low, rocky bluffs, hogbacks, swales and mesas sprinkled liberally with palo verdes, saguaros, mesquites, and clay-colored rock.

Miller carefully scrutinized the desert flanking him. From time to time he glanced over his shoulder at the girl, who appeared to be dutifully gathering wood and building a fire. As the outlaw studied a low mesa rising in the northeast, movement caught his eye closer in and on his right. His heart hiccupping, he jerked the spyglass in that direction, followed a gray-brown blur of movement until the object stopped atop a flat rock.

Miller stared through the glass, adjusting the focus.

His heartbeat slowed. The outlaw shaped a wry smile. What he was looking at was none other than the girl's bobcat, Claws, who just now leaped down off the rock to lie in a wedge of shade leaning out from it.

The bobcat stared toward Miller, flicking its bobbed tail.

Miller chuckled. Then he reduced the spyglass, slipped it back into its deerskin poke, rose, and tramped down the slope to his horse. He looked back toward their noon camp. The girl had a small fire going, thin tendrils of gray smoke rising from orange flames. She was on one knee, pouring water from a canteen into a small, black coffeepot.

She glanced over her shoulder at Miller. He was too far away to see her face clearly, but he'd gotten to know her well enough to know she was smirking. Something inside him wanted to wipe that smirk off her face, to bring her to heel like a dog. He didn't care for women thinking they were better than him.

But he needed her to get him through the mountains after he bushwhacked Hawk, so he had to keep his temper on a short leash. Besides, he couldn't beat her up too badly. He needed her in good health to quell his natural male desires.

"You don't care one bit that I killed the old man, do you?" Miller asked her when he'd ridden over to the fire. He'd dismounted and was loosening the bay's latigo strap, so the horse could rest easy.

She was sitting on a rock near the fire, leaning forward, elbows on her knees, gloved hands together. She was giving him that look again. That look like she knew more than he did about something, or that she was better than he was.

Or maybe she found him funny to look at. He knew he wasn't the best-looking gent, but he had a way with women, and he'd had none too few, neither. And that kid he'd left at Nan-tee's wasn't the only son he'd sired, neither.

When she didn't say anything but merely continued to give him that faintly jeering look through those bold, hazel eyes of hers, he said, "What in the hell you lookin' at, goddamnit? What you thinkin' about?"

She hiked a shoulder and glanced away. "I'm just thinkin'."

"Why don't you answer my question?"

"What question?"

"Old Zimmerman. Your grand*paw*!"

"Oh, him," she said, shrugging again and then lifting her boot toes and staring down at them. "Well, he's dead now and I never really cared for him. The old bastard was in my way, if you want the truth. So, you killed him. You shouldn't have, but you did. I didn't have no part in it, and there wasn't nothin' I could do to stop you, so I reckon I got a good story for old Saint Pete when I see him. About *that*, anyways."

Miller stared at her, incredulous. Then he chuckled and dug

his horse's feed sack out of a saddlebag pouch. "You're a piece of work, girl. Yes, ma'am, you purely are!"

When he'd hung a feed bag of oats over the bay's ears, he started to sit down on a rock near the girl. He stopped when the stitches in his wound pulled, feeling that rat gnawing on him again. Then he eased himself down on the rock, pressing a hand over the wound and wincing.

"Don't let the coffee boil over," the girl said, rising and heading off into the brush on the far side of the horses.

"Where the hell you goin'?"

She disappeared among some boulders. He could hear her thrashing around, grunting softly. When the coffeepot started to boil, Miller used a swatch of burlap to remove it from the flames.

He dumped a handful of ground Arbuckle's into the water, let it return to a boil and then removed it from the flames again, setting the hissing pot on a rock to the right of the fire. Miller jerked his head up when the girl strode back into their little camp. She had a pocket knife in her right hand and a mess of what looked like cactus pulp in the other.

"Hey, where'd you get that knife?" Miller asked, scowling at the open blade in her hand.

"Slipped it into my boot before we left the station. Figured it might come in handy. Don't get your shorts in a twist. Open your shirt and I'll smear this prickly-pear pulp on those stitches. It'll take some of the pain away and keep it from festering."

Miller knew the remedy, as he'd been married to a Pima girl and lived among her family for a year. Those people could make a meal out of a single cholla branch. Keeping his eyes on the barlow knife in Jodi's hand, Miller jerked his shirttails out of his jeans, and pulled the shirt up to expose the wound she'd stitched closed. The wound appeared relatively clean, but some yellow fluid was leaking out through the seam in his puckered skin, between the stitches that looked like clipped cat whiskers.

As Jodi used her finger to smear the pulp into the wound, Miller sucked a sharp breath through his teeth.

"Easy!"

"Stop your caterwauling."

When she'd coated the wound with the cactus pulp, Jody brushed the excess on her trouser leg.

"I'll take that," Miller said, and reached for the knife.

She pulled it away and, grinning, sort of did a two-step around the fire before bending over and sliding the barlow back into the well of her right boot. "I haven't stuck you so far, have I?"

"You little bitch."

"Chicken shit!"

Jodi laughed and then sauntered back over to the coffeepot.

She added cold water to settle the grounds then poured them each a cup while Miller scowled at her, knowing he'd be sleeping even lighter at night than he usually did. He'd be wondering if she was going to slip the blade of that knife between his ribs. Deciding he'd deal with the knife later, he accepted a cup of steaming coffee from her, sat on a rock, and stared along their back trail.

Jodi warmed some beans and rabbit meat in a small skillet, and while they ate their burritos around the fire, she said, "Who's behind you, killer?"

Miller had been chewing and staring off toward the mouth of the canyon again. He looked at her, swallowed, sipped his coffee, and grunted, "What?"

Sitting on a rock on the far side of the fire, the girl took a big bite of her burrito and said around the unladylike mouthful, "You're nervous as a doe with a newborn fawn. What wolf you got nippin' at your hocks, killer?"

"Stop callin' me killer or I'll backhand you."

She laughed and shook a lock of her gold-blonde hair out of

her eye. "Who's doggin' your trail?"

He didn't like her mocking tone. He was starting to think he should have killed her when he'd killed the old man. Trouble was, he didn't know the Superstitions. He needed a guide.

"What's it to you?"

"Well, if he's doggin' your trail, he's doggin' mine, right?"

"Fella called Hawk." Miller turned his head to stare back down the canyon. "The *rogue lawman*, they call him."

"No kiddin'?" Jodi pitched her voice with pleasant surprise, which also riled Miller. "I've heard of him." She chewed another bite of her burrito and then chuckled again as she said, "What'd you do to get him on your trail?"

"None of your business."

"Where we headin'—you figure that might be my business?"

Miller turned to her. He chewed and sipped his coffee for a time and then he ran his sleeve across his mouth and drooping mustaches and said, "I want you to take me to high ground. Maybe a canyon like this one, but higher up in the mountains. Some place good to set a bushwhack."

"You're gonna kill him? This *rogue lawman*?"

"Yeah, I'm gonna kill him."

"From bushwhack?"

Miller's ears warmed with anger. He glared at her, chewing, and then he swallowed and pointed at her with what remained of his burrito. "You get that tone out of your voice. I don't like it."

"You can threaten me all you want, Pima," the girl said saucily. "But if you don't treat me right, I'm liable to lead you into a box canyon, let that rogue lawman fella ride right up on ya. Geronimo hides out from the army up around Weaver's Needle, but I know how to work around him—when I *want* to. Hell, I could lead you into a nest of diamondbacks. Plenty of those out here, and I know where more than a few of 'em are. A prospector named Dunleavy dug into one o' them nests, started screamin' somethin' awful. About six baby rattlers little bigger than this finger was clingin' to his arms. One dug its fangs into his *cheek*!"

She laughed and shook her head. "He was dead in an hour, but let me tell you—that was one hell of a long, loud hour, if you get my drift!"

"You done?"

"What's that?"

"Yappin'. You done?"

Jodi brushed her hand across her mouth, shook her hair back from her head. "Oh, be a sport. I'm just funnin' with ya. I'll help you out . . . as long as you tell me what's next after this."

"What do you mean—what's next?"

"What're you gonna do after you kill this *rogue lawman*?"

"I'm gonna have you lead me out of the mountains to the south. Then, you're clear. You can go back to the station, and I'll head for Mexico."

Jodi swallowed the last of her burrito and curled her upper lip at Miller. "And then you'll work back north and retrieve the money you took out of the Kingman bank."

Miller chuckled dryly. "We didn't get more than a few hundred dollars out of that bank. We hid the money along the trail. Too little to risk goin' back for. Don't worry." Miller grinned, happy to think she thought he might have the upper hand on her for a change. "I ain't holdin' out on ya. I'm broke. All I got is the shirt on my back and my gun, and that's about all."

Jodi considered that for a time. She sipped her coffee. "I might have an idea."

Miller had turned to stare back down the canyon again. Now he looked back at Jodi, whose eyes were wide and grave and missing their customary mockery. "What idea?"

"Just an idea. I'll tell you more after you back shoot this *rogue lawman* fella."

"I didn't say I was gonna back shoot him!"

"Back shoot, bushwhack. Same difference."

Miller's dark eyes glinted angrily. "You know—I was just startin' to think I might could like you."

"Easy, killer." Jodi tossed her cup down, rose from her rock, and walked around the fire. She stopped before Miller and thrust her shoulders back. Her pointed breasts jutted behind her shirt. "You be nice to me, I'll be nice to you."

Giving a smoky smile, she knelt down between his spread knees and reached for the buckle of his cartridge belt.

Chapter 10
"Drag That Soggy Boot Back North and Live to Piss Another Day, Friend!"

Deputy US Marshal Whit Chaney eased his chestnut around a bend in the wall of the canyon he and his two partners had been following throughout the day, and jerked back on the horse's reins. He frowned as he stared ahead, not liking what he was seeing.

Not liking what he was seeing at all.

The ground rose sharply about seventy yards ahead. A broad jumble of black volcanic rock studded with desert flora appeared to block the trail. From his vantage, he could see no way through it.

Had the man they'd been tracking led them into a box canyon?

He turned to his partners.

The tall, blond-headed Alvin Teagarden rode a buckskin on a parallel course about fifty yards to Chaney's left, on the other side of a dry arroyo that ran down through the canyon's center. Ralph "Hooch" Mortimer rode his dapple-gray nearest Chaney, along a game trail following the arroyo's near side. Both men had seen Chaney stop, because they too had halted their horses and were looking at him warily, apparently wondering what had spooked him.

Chaney lifted his chin toward the steep hill of jumbled rock and tangled cacti ahead of him. And then he looked down at the trail in front of his horse. About twenty yards back, he'd lost sight of the shod hoofprints he'd been following. He saw no sign of them here, either.

Those two troubling facts—the steep wall of boulders ahead of him and the sudden disappearance of the rogue lawman's sign—made Chaney's heart skip. As were most lawmen throughout the frontier, Chaney was well aware of Gideon Hawk's reputation. The man hunted bad men mercilessly. But he showed the same lack of mercy to any lawman who stood between Hawk and his prey.

And he was very, very shrewd.

Shrewd and merciless.

Bad combination.

Chaney looked toward his two compatriots once more, and raised a waylaying hand. Then he stepped down from the chestnut's back, tied the reins to a low shrub, and, slowly and quietly levering a live cartridge into his carbine's action, began walking forward.

He moved one careful step at a time, looking all around him, up and down the gradual, rocky ridges sloping toward the canyon on both sides. He followed the trail around a cabin-sized block of cracked volcanic rock, and stopped.

Ahead of him stood a saddled horse. A grulla. It was tied to a willow at the edge of the arroyo. The horse turned to look at Chaney. It twitched its ears and switched its tail and whickered softly. It stomped one of its rear hooves. That hoof and the other three hooves were wrapped in deer hide.

Chaney's heart leaped into his throat.

Movement above and to his right.

He whipped his head in that direction to see a tall, mustached man in a dark frock coat and black hat standing beside a boulder about thirty yards up the slope, on the northeast side of the canyon. The tall man shook his head gravely, jade eyes flashing in the afternoon sunlight, and pressed his cheek to the rear stock of the Henry rifle he was aiming into the canyon.

Flames lashed out of the Henry's octagonal barrel.

When Chaney heard the rifle's coughing report that whipped around the canyon like a thunderclap, he was already on the ground. He felt like someone had slammed a sledgehammer against his upper-left chest.

The rogue lawman lowered the rifle slightly and ejected the spent cartridge, which careened over his right shoulder to clatter off a rock behind him. He pumped a fresh round into the chamber and stared through his own powder smoke wafting in the air before him at the man lying supine in the canyon, grinding his spurs into the gravelly ground as he arched his back, death spasming through him.

He'd lost his hat. The high-crowned Stetson with a Texas crease lay several feet away to his left. He lifted his bald head and round face toward Hawk, his deputy US marshal's badge flashing in the sunlight from where it was pinned to his black bullhide vest over a white, blue-pinstriped shirt. He gritted his teeth beneath his gray-brown mustache.

Hawk cursed.

The man had jerked just as Hawk had fired, fouling the rogue lawman's aim. He'd meant to kill the man outright. He felt he owed him that much—for working a damned hard job for low pay, if for no other reason.

Hawk aimed again. His second shot blew the top of the man's head off and lay him flat down on the ground, boots shaking with the last of his death spasms.

Beyond him, on the other side of the large, black boulder, men shouted. A horse whinnied.

Hooves clacked on rock.

Hawk racked a fresh round into his Henry's breech. A second later, the clattering died. A horse whickered down the canyon a few yards. Hawk crouched low, holding his Henry up high across his chest, waiting.

Silence.

A hot, dry breeze blew against his back. It lifted dust along the canyon floor beneath him, and swirled it. When the mini-cyclone died, a hatted head and the end of a rifle barrel slid out from the left side of the large, black boulder.

Hawk slapped the Henry's butt plate to his shoulder, aimed quickly, and fired.

The hatted head jerked back violently. The man's entire body was revealed to Hawk as he staggered away from the boulder, to its left side, throwing his arms out and dropping his rifle. He stumbled over a rock behind him, and fell hard. Arms and legs akimbo, he jerked as his life left him.

Hawk pursed his lips with satisfaction. That man had likely not even heard the shot that had blown his lamp out.

Pumping a fresh round, Hawk dropped to a knee beside his covering rock, looking around, waiting. The third lawman was out here somewhere. He'd glassed all three on his back trail. If the lawman was smart, knowing that his two partners were dead, he'd mount up and ride off.

But if he'd been smart, he wouldn't have headed after Hawk in the first place.

Hawk held his position for ten minutes, growing impatient. He didn't want to have to kill any more lawmen. He wanted to be after Pima Miller. But he could do nothing until he'd scoured the third lawman off his trail.

Something moved along the slope on the canyon's west side. Hawk drew back behind his boulder as a slug slammed into the opposite side of it, spanging wickedly. At the same time, the belching report reached Hawk's ears. It screeched around the canyon for several seconds.

Then the man fired again. And again.

After the last echo had died, Hawk doffed his hat and edged

a look around his boulder. His keen eyes picked out the silhouetted hat and rifle barrel halfway up the canyon's west slope. Smoke was wafting in the air around the silhouette.

Hawk snaked his Henry around the side of his covering boulder and snapped off two quick shots, driving the shooter back behind a rock. Then Hawk donned his hat, bolted out from behind the boulder, and dashed around boulders and cacti, heading toward the opposite side of the canyon.

He wove through his cover like a stalking cat. The third lawman, Alvin Something-or-other, flung lead at him from the canyon's west slope. The shots screeched off rocks and plunked into saguaros and barrel cactus, raking several stems from a clump of Mormon tea. As Hawk jogged steadily along the canyon's north slope, which was the wall creating a box canyon, drawing nearer his quarry, Alvin grew more and more desperate.

His shots came faster and faster. They also came wilder and wilder.

Then there was a lull during which the man was probably reloading.

Hawk turned along the crease forming the canyon's northwest corner and began angling back downcanyon but also climbing the western slope at a slant, toward where he'd last seen Alvin's gun smoke waft. He heard the rifle crash again but could not see it from his current vantage. As he rounded a boulder and a one-armed saguaro, he saw the muzzle flash and the smoke puff.

The slug curled the air off Hawk's left shoulder.

Hawk dropped to one knee and raised his Henry. He fired just as the third lawman snapped his eyes wide in fear and pulled his head back behind a nub of rock protruding from a bed of black shale about forty yards farther up the slope.

Hawk's slug hammered the side of the rock nub, keeping the

third lawman back behind his cover. Hawk lowered the Henry, and, levering another round into the sixteen-shooter's chamber, ran up the slope, zigzagging between saguaros and boulders and piles of porous volcanic rock blown out of the earth's bowels eons ago.

The shooter fired two more rounds at him. Both flew wide. Hawk kept scrambling up the slope toward the shooter's cover. He wended his way through rocks and prickly pear, ran up past Alvin's boulder and threw himself to the ground, aiming his Henry at the backside of the rock from where Alvin Something-or-other had been shooting.

Alvin wasn't there.

Hawk saw him scrambling up the slope toward the ridge crest. He had his rifle in one hand. His boots were slipping on shale, and he was pushing off the ground with his other hand.

Hawk heaved himself to his feet, sent two quick rounds after the third lawman, and then ran up the slope behind him. Alvin glanced over his right shoulder at Hawk. His eyes widened. He was grunting and cursing under his breath, breathing hard.

He threw himself behind a rock little larger than a gravestone. Hawk saw the end of the man's rifle barrel snake around the side of the rock.

Hawk dropped to his belly and raised the Henry. A ratcheting hiss rose from ten feet in front of him, on the upslope. The diamondback was tightly coiled, button tail raised. It was sliding its flat head toward Hawk, forked tongue extended, its little, colorless eyes like tarnished pellets.

Just as the serpent appeared about to strike, Hawk blew its head off. Its headless body struck, anyway. The bloody, ragged end where its head had been fell into the dirt and gravel about a foot in front of Hawk, writhing.

The rogue lawman pumped a fresh cartridge and took aim again at the shooter's rock.

"Hold on!" the man screamed.

He'd come out from behind the rock, moving backward up the slope. He tossed his rifle away and continued stumbling backward.

"Don't shoot me!" Alvin screamed.

He'd lost his hat and his curly blond hair was caked with dust and bits of foliage. Sweat ran down his narrow cheeks. Hawk lowered the Henry, aiming it out from his hip, and strode up the slope. By the time Hawk reached the third lawman, Alvin had reached the flat, gravelly top of the ridge, a barrel cactus rising on his right.

Buzzards were circling high but quartering over the canyon in which the two dead lawmen lay.

Alvin stopped, thrust his hands up, palms out.

"Please don't shoot me. Ah, Jesus!"

Hawk stopped six feet in front of the young lawman. "You damn fool."

"Please . . . don't!" Alvin turned his head away as though he couldn't bear to look at the man who was about to kill him.

"Why'd you do it, you damn fool? Why did you get your two partners killed?"

"Ah, shit," Alvin said, licking his dry, dusty lips. "There's a reward. A big one. Governors of four territories got together, set a bounty. Twenty thousand dollars to any lawman who can prove they killed you!"

Hawk had heard about the reward, though he hadn't been sure it wasn't a mere rumor. There were lots of rumors—lies—regarding his exploits. A few years ago several territorial governors had put out a death warrant on him.

Now, this.

Hawk chuckled without mirth. "Twenty thousand dollars ain't worth a pinch of rock salt if you ain't alive to spend it."

"I know that," Alvin said. "I know that now."

"You got your partners killed."

"I know that!"

There was a dribbling sound. Hawk looked down to see that the inside of Alvin's left pants leg was wet. Liquid has splashed atop his boot, slithered down the side of the sole to roll up in the dirt.

"Drop that pistol belt," Hawk ordered.

Alvin unbuckled and dropped his pistol and shell belt inside of five seconds.

"Forget about your horse. You start walkin' north and don't stop or take even one look back, hear?"

Alvin stared at Hawk, lips trembling. "Hell, I'll die out here without my horse, my gun!"

"You'll make it back to the Superstition station. You'll be hurtin', but you'll make it. Unless you want me to shoot you right here, which, when I think about it, is all you deserve."

"No! No . . . I'll make it, all right."

"If I ever see you again, Alvin, I ain't gonna be near as generous."

"No."

"Move!" Hawk bellowed, stepping around behind the frightened lawman.

Alvin glanced back at him and then, keeping his hands raised to his shoulders, began running down the slope at an angle, heading for the canyon bottom.

Behind him, Hawk shouted, "Drag that soggy boot back north and live to piss another day, *friend*!"

CHAPTER 11
THE OUTLAW'S DILEMMA

As her Morgan lurched up an incline through greasewood and barrel cactus, Jodi glanced over her shoulder, and smiled.

Miller scowled. "What the hell you grinnin' at? You simple?"

The girl did not reply but turned her horse into a crease between two large chunks of sandstone rising from the top of the hill they were on. Miller gave a wry chuff and followed her through the crease. On the other side, the girl slid lithely down from her Morgan's back and stood looking around, her gloved fists on her hips.

"What the hell you doin'?" Miller raked out at her. "It's too early to stop."

"Not if we're where we're goin'."

"Huh?"

"This is the place I said you get could set up your bushwhack, kill that rogue lawman fella." She grinned at him again.

Miller looked around. More mushrooms of sandstone rose before him. Mesquites and cedars grew up out of cracks in the rock. Sandstone boulders stood among the growth. Miller swung down from the back of his brindle bay, tied the horse to a cedar, and then climbed up the shelving mushrooms of sandstone rock.

At the crest, he could see out over a deep, narrow valley. Really, it was more of a gorge. There were a couple of lower ridges between Miller's position and the larger canyon on the far side of which jutted an even steeper ridge than the one he was on. From here, the main canyon looked like a mere crease between ridges. He could see it where it doglegged off to his right and away.

"Best get away from the ridge, silly," Jodi said, slapping his upper arm with the back of her hand.

"Why?"

She pointed at the doglegging canyon to Miller's right. "Because if he's still on our trail, he's down there somewhere. Might see us."

Miller pointed. "That's where we came from?"

Jodi nodded. "We rode right up here—or nearly so, anyway—about an hour ago. Then circled back. The canyon trail passes about sixty yards below where we're standing." She nodded toward the canyon side of the ridge. "He'll follow our trail and you can dry gulch him from here."

Miller stared down the far side of the ridge, saw the trail angling from his right to his left beyond some rocks, catclaw, and cedar shrubs. "Shit, we rode past here. Crazy damn country."

The girl chuckled, self-satisfied.

"So he'll ride right past here—*down there*." Miller laughed and ran a gloved hand across his chin. "Yeah, that'll work."

Getting a handle on the layout, he stepped back a little, until a large thumb of sandstone and granite partly shielded him from view from the broader canyon below. "Shit—this is some crazy country. Talk about a devil's playground!"

"A fella could get lost without a good guide, couldn't he?" Jodi's tone was customarily jibing.

Miller snorted at her. But she was right. He didn't like it, but he needed her. There was such a maze of canyons in this neck of the Superstitions that a man could walk thirty yards, blink, turn around and be forever lost.

Miller retrieved his spyglass from his saddlebags, doffed his hat, and stood just off the corner of the large boulder capping the ridge. He trained the glass to the northwest, the direction from which the girl had led him, the direction from which his stalker would be coming, as well.

Miller stared for about fifteen minutes through the glass until he finally caught sight of a slow-moving shadow coming along the main canyon. A man was what the shadow appeared—a gray-brown man-shadow moving at a steady pace along Miller's back trail. The outlaw knew it was Hawk. Of course, it could be a prospector or some lone Indian, but Miller knew it was Hawk. He'd spied the same shadow on his trail early the day before, and he'd noticed it several times since.

Always moving at the same, maddeningly slow, plodding, steady speed. In no hurry whatever. Apparently, he was so sure of eventually running down his quarry that he felt no *need* to hurry.

Studying that slow-moving but purposeful shadow now moving toward him at a seeming snail's pace, Miller felt the short hairs along the back of his neck rise. His heart quickened. He remembered the man he'd seen in the yard of Nan-tee's shack, so coolly and sure-handedly dispatching Miller's second gang.

Some of the best shooters in the territory. Maybe in all of the Southwest. He'd blown them all to hell and he would have blown Miller to hell, too, if Miller hadn't had the advantage of being in the cabin, where the shadows had concealed him.

One of Hawk's bullets had drilled Miller's woman. Too bad. But better her than him. Since that afternoon, the outlaw had only considered the child he'd left behind in passing and certainly with no degree of sentimentality. He hadn't even paused to consider who would care for the boy, whom Nan-tee had called Ti-Kwah, which in her language meant sunrise.

Or was it sun*set*?

He lowered the spyglass, donned his hat, and stepped back

behind the boulder.

The girl was sitting on a rock, her back to a cedar growing up through a jagged crack running through the sandstone. She'd removed her hat and was wiping moisture from the sweatband with a spruce-green handkerchief.

"This is a special place for me," she told Miller, smiling fondly as she looked around. The large dimpled areas in the sandstone held water from last night's monsoon rain.

"How so?"

She hiked a shoulder. Her smile grew broader. "I became a woman here. On a blanket right down there."

As usual concerning this girl, Miller was incredulous. "What's that?"

"I told you—I became a *woman* here." Jodi dropped to her knees and drank from one of the rainwater-filled dimples.

"You became a woman here," Miller said, skeptically.

Jodi lifted her head, sat back on her heels, donned her hat, and looked around. "One of Geronimo's warriors found me here. Took me by surprise. Didn't seem to know whether to kill me or take me, so he *took* me. And then I killed him. Stuck one of his own arrows through his neck."

Miller just stared at her. She'd said it as though she'd just recounted a mildly successful fishing trip.

She turned her head toward him, smiled, and blinked slowly. Her eyes were dull with threat.

"Why, you're crazy," Miller said, sliding his right hand to the holster thonged on his right thigh. It brushed only leather. He looked down at it, lower jaw hanging. When he looked at the girl, she reached around behind her. When she brought her right hand forward, she was holding his Remington.

"Lookin' for this?" she asked, closing her upper teeth over her lower lip.

"How in the *hell* . . . ?"

91

As she held the gun, she raised and lowered the hammer a little with her thumb, making a faint clicking sound. "You oughta know by now, Mister Outlaw, that I ain't no little girl you should trifle with."

"How did you get my gun?" Miller demanded, facing her, spreading his boots a little more than shoulder width apart.

"Wouldn't you like to know?"

"I'll take that back."

"Why? So you can shoot me with it?"

Miller raised his voice. He didn't want to admit it, but his mouth was dry with fear. "I said I'll take that back, you little . . . !"

He let his voice trail off. She was staring at him, one eye sort of slanted in toward her nose. It was more than just a faintly devilish look. That look coupled with his pistol resting in the palm of her right hand rocked him back on his heels.

"Oh, here!" she said, tossing it up to him.

He stumbled back, catching the gun against his chest. His face was warm with embarrassment. Anger and rage made his knees feel as though they were filled with warm mud.

"Did you believe all that?"

Miller lowered the gun. "All what?"

"My story about the brave I killed?"

"Should I?"

Kneeling there on the stone-capped crest of the ridge, she smiled at him again while staring up at him from beneath her blonde brows and the low-canted brim of her hat. "If I was you, I would. And I'd also keep in mind, I got a knife in my boot. And I got this here."

She reached around behind her again. When she showed him her right hand, it was again filled with a pistol. A .41-caliber pocket pistol with ivory grips.

"Stole this off a gambler passin' through the station," Jodi said, hefting the wicked-looking little popper in her hand. "Figured it might come in handy someday."

She tossed it from hand to hand before tucking it back behind her, and rising. "Well, I reckon we'd best tend the horses and set up camp," she said with a sigh, turning away and skipping down the rocks. The little pistol was tucked behind her wide, brown belt, at the small of her slender back. "Probably gonna rain again like it usually does."

Watching her, Miller canted his head to one side and raked the fingers of his left hand down through the ginger whiskers on his cheek.

Later, after a brief rain, Miller took Old Man Zimmerman's Winchester and had a look around his and Jodi's camp.

They were on the side of a larger mountain from the top of which, staring southwest, Miller could see the formation known as Weaver's Needle. Most folks in the territory had heard about the "Dutchman," some fellow named Walzer, who'd discovered an old Mexican gold mine somewhere near Weaver's Needle, which some folks called "Sombrero" because it was also shaped like the steepled crown of the Mexican hat.

Like many who'd spent more than a week in Arizona Territory and had heard about the vein that was so rich you could literally use a hammer to break the nearly pure ore out of the walls and fill enough of a poke in just a few minutes to put yourself on easy street for the rest of your life, Miller had had a hankering to look for the mine himself.

But there were other stories, too.

Stories about many men who'd tried looking for the same mine, but the country was such a maze of cactus and rattlesnake-infested ravines and canyons that they'd become forever lost, died of thirst or starvation, been tortured and killed by Apaches, or had stumbled out of the Superstitions avoiding such fates by a hair's breadth and had vowed never to return, warning others not to try it.

Miller had heeded such warnings. Not necessarily because he feared anything the Superstitions could throw at him, but because he was basically a lazy man and preferred to make his living by a much easier means.

By stealing it from others.

Still, that brown finger of crenellated rock jutting above the cactus-studded hogbacks held an eerie fascination even for a lazy man like Pima Miller. Imagine walking into an ancient gold mine, the walls around you sparkling with gold so rich and pure it hardly needed smelting!

Miller brushed a fist across his chin, shook his head, and made his way back down the craggy peak he was on. As he did so, he stopped near a sandstone shelf, and stared down, frowning. A hoofprint marked the sandstone gravel and red caliche to the right of his right boot.

A hoofprint. Looking around, he saw several more. Two riders had passed along this mountainside, following what appeared a game trail or maybe an ancient Indian trail. The Superstitions, having been claimed for centuries by the Chiricahua Apaches, were woven with such traces. And the mount of neither rider had been shod.

Unshod horses meant Indian.

Around here, *Apache* Indian.

Chiricahua.

Miller could tell that the Chiricahuas had passed here maybe an hour before the brief rain of an hour earlier.

Cold fingers of apprehension raking his spine—Miller had heard plenty of stories of Apache torture—he dropped to a knee and studied the terrain around him. Spying no movement outside of a jackrabbit and a cactus wren perched atop a nearby saguaro, he continued on down the mountain.

He kept a .44 round seated in his carbine's chamber, his thumb on the off-cocked hammer.

By the time he saw the brindle bay and the Morgan tied to ironwood shrubs below his and the girl's camp, where they could drink from natural tanks filled with fresh rainwater, the sky had again turned the color of oily rags. Thunder rumbled like a giant's upset stomach.

Cold raindrops began splattering against the back of Miller's neck, making him wince against the chill in sharp contrast to the earlier, searing heat.

He walked up the grade beyond the horses and into the rocks where he and the girl had set up camp on a level, cactus-free strip of ground at the base of the ridge crest from where he intended to rid his trail of Hawk. The clearing was surrounded by tall boulders and cedars, which offered some protection from the rain. Jodi had erected a burlap lean-to angling out from one of the shrubs. She lay under it now, resting her head against her saddle, hat tipped down over her eyes. Her arms were folded atop her chest, boots crossed at the ankles.

Jodi appeared to be asleep, gold-blonde hair falling messily across the saddle.

Watching her, Miller's loins tingled. At the same time, apprehension continued to play a needling rhythm tapped out with cold fingers against his backbone. The girl was damned dangerous. He'd have to kill her sooner or later.

Now might be a good time, before she could get the drop on him. True, he needed her to lead him out of the mountains, but something told him she wouldn't let him get that far. Not far enough to feel independent of her.

Because she knew he'd kill her then.

He wasn't sure what her game was, but she was up to something. Could be he was just being nervy, but he didn't think so. Possibly, she knew about the twelve hundred-dollar bounty on his head, though it might have gone up since King-man. And all the torture—even Apache torture—wouldn't drag the secret out of the girl before she was ready to fess up. Miller had a keen, stone-cold feeling at the base of his breastbone that if he waited to find out what her game was, and how high the stakes were, he would be too late to save himself.

He held his carbine across his belly. He squeezed the gun in his hands. As cold as it had suddenly turned, with the rain lashing him from behind, his hands were sweating inside his gloves.

A bass voice whispered in his ear. "Kill her, fool. The rogue lawman is as good as dead. Tomorrow, after you kill him, you'll have two spare horses, plenty of guns, ammo, and grub. You know where Weaver's Needle is. Once you get there, swing west and you'll be to Phoenix in no time. Rest up there with a whore or two, a couple bottles of whiskey, a game of cards, and head on down to the border."

Miller's heart hiccupped, increased its pace. His breath grew shallow. Sweat ran down the palms of his hands, inside his gloves. He squeezed the rifle again, pressing the sweat into his gloves. He slowly thumbed the hammer back. The thunder and the rain covered the clicking sounds.

"Kill her now . . . before she kills you . . ."

Miller moved heavily forward, stopped just outside the lean-to, and stared down at the girl. His heart beat more persistently. He prodded her with his boot toe.

She used a gloved index finger to poke the brim of her hat up off her forehead. She turned to him, wrinkling the skin above the bridge of her nose. She continued to stare at him like that for a good half a minute. And then, so slowly so as to be almost imperceptible, her mouth corners rose.

Miller eased the Winchester's hammer back down.

His hands shaking, he leaned the rifle against the cedar's twisted trunk, doffed his hat, and crawled under the tarpaulin.

He woke the next morning to the smell of wood smoke. He rolled over and saw small flames licking up from several catclaw sticks. Jodi had a blanket thrown over her shoulders. It was all she was wearing. It didn't cover much of her.

She was just then filling a canteen from one of the natural rock tanks near the fire.

Miller cursed, grabbed a cedar log, and rubbed out the flames with a single swipe.

"You *crazy?*" the outlaw rasped, eyes nearly bulging from their sockets. "You tryin' to draw him in here, or *what?*"

CHAPTER 12
TURNABOUT

In the following dawn's misty shadows, Hawk followed the trail up a steep incline and into scattered cedars speckling this slope high above the main canyon. He swept his gaze from left to right and back again, and then, by instinct, he drew back on the grulla's reins.

He'd been extra cautious while following Pima Miller, because it had become obvious just after he'd killed the two federal lawmen and sent the third one hoofing it back north with a wet boot, that the girl was much more than a hostage.

She was, as Hawk had suspected, a guide.

She was also Miller's lover. He could tell that from the sign left at their bivouacs.

Hawk had learned much by studying her and Miller's tracks. He knew which horse was carrying which member of his two-party quarry from having seen two separate sets of boot prints near the separate horse prints, informing him which rider had mounted and dismounted which horse.

He knew that Miller's horse had a faint flaw in its right-rear hoof, and that the outlaw's horse was ever-so-slightly pigeon-toed. Not enough that the trait could likely be noticed by simply watching the horse walk or trot, but the indentions its shod feet left in the ground told the tale.

The girl's horse was almost always in the lead, while Miller rode behind her. She was guiding him into the mountains. That was the reason for Hawk's added caution.

He had little doubt that Miller would try to ambush him and that he'd instructed the girl to lead him to an opportune place from which to bring about the ambush. Thus, Hawk, who had set up his own ambushes and been the target of others' ambushes enough times to know what kind of terrain to look for, rode a little more slowly and with his eyes and ears especially skinned for trouble.

He sensed trouble now.

The secondary ridge on his left sloped gradually up toward a large, rectangular boulder set atop a broad sandstone dike screened in cedars and several different kinds of cactus, including a saguaro with one arm pointing down. The ridge was about seventy yards from the trail Hawk was following—the same trail that Miller and Jodi Zimmerman had followed sometime during the previous afternoon, before the rain.

A perfect distance and reasonable incline for accurate shooting by a seasoned shooter.

What also had alarms bells tolling in the rogue lawman's ears was the fact that Miller and the girl had ridden through here especially slowly, as though they'd known exactly where they were heading and were confident that, despite the storm clouds that had been building, they would arrive at their destination soon.

Hawk pulled back on the grulla's bridle reins. The horse gave a soft whicker, sensing its rider's caution, and backed up. Out of sight from the ridge, Hawk turned the grulla, rode a hundred yards back down the trail, and then turned the horse up the steep southern slope, climbing the ridge.

The grulla was sure-footed, mountain bred, and it had little trouble negotiating the incline's uncertain terrain stippled with the dangerous cholla, or "jumping" cactus, and several nasty-looking clumps of catclaw. When Hawk had gained the secondary ridge about seventy yards from where he assumed Miller was lying in ambush, he continued up the next ridge, and stopped the grulla several yards down the other side, among boulders whose pocks and pits offered the tired mount fresh rainwater.

He slipped the grulla's bit, loosened its latigo, and shucked his rifle from the saddle scabbard. He sat down on a rock to exchange his stockmen's boots for a pair of soft moccasins for easier, stealthier walking, and then headed back up and over the ridge.

Hawk moved slowly, stopping every four steps to drop to a knee to look all around him and to listen. Then he continued moving down the slope at a slant, in the direction of where he was assuming his quarry had holed up to set up an ambush.

He'd gained the lower ridge as the sun poked its head above the eastern horizon, spreading a saffron light across the stark, brown ridgetop behind him. Now he moved slower. Much slower, setting each moccasin down so slowly that neither foot made a sound.

The sun was full up, and Hawk could feel the heat building, when he finally brought up the backsides of a couple of horses tied to the base of the dike he'd spied from its other side. There was a gap in the rocks near the horses. He figured that would lead directly to Miller's and the girl's position.

But, because of the horses, it was no good.

He moved to his left, and it took him nearly a whole hour more to find access to the dike from the side opposite the horses. Slowly, he moved through several black boulders capping the dike, weaving among cedars and cacti. Suddenly, he stopped and dropped to a knee behind one of these boulders.

His heart thudded.

He smelled smoke on the breeze. Wood smoke.

For an instant, the smell confused him. Was Miller stupid enough to build a coffee fire when he knew that Hawk was moving toward him?

Hawk's hesitation distracted him. He was just about to turn and retreat when a shadow angled down on the rock slab near his right shoulder and knee. The click of a gun hammer sounded as loud as a war drum in his left ear.

The cold, round barrel was rammed up taut against the back of his head, just behind that ear.

"Don't so much as twitch, Hawk," said the menacingly reasonable voice of Pima Miller. "Just lower that Henry's hammer and set it down slow. One quick move and I'll drill a forty-four round through your brain. Don't want to, 'cause this close I'm liable to get covered in your oozin's. But I will." He heard the man's smile in what came next. "You know I will."

Hawk's heart thudded heavily. A keen frustration coupled with humiliation was a hard rock in his belly.

He'd been outsmarted. They'd figured—maybe *planned*—on him finding their camp. They'd built the fire to confuse him. It had worked. He'd let his quarry get behind him. An unforgivable mistake. One he would deservedly pay for.

Breaking through the stiff mortar of his sharp reluctance, he lowered the Henry's hammer and set the gun down on the rock slab before him.

"Now, both pistols. Set 'em down there next to the rifle. *Slow.*"

Hawk rolled his eyes to the right. Miller had backed up a few feet, holding his cocked pistol about four feet away from Hawk's head. Too far to lunge at him with any hope of being successful.

Hawk drew a deep breath. He slid the Russian and the Colt from their holsters. The snick of steel against leather was a sickening sound.

"Easy, now," Miller said behind him, shifting his weight from one boot to the other. The nervousness in the man's voice only

101

slightly tempered Hawk's chagrin at having given them the drop.

Hawk set the pistols down by the rifle.

"Get them hands up, *stand* up, and turn around slow."

Hawk raised his hands to his shoulders and turned around. Miller was about three inches shorter than the rogue lawman. The outlaw backed up a step, swabbed his lips with his tongue, twitched a smile. "Feelin' foolish?" He chuckled, continuing to shift his weight around on his hips and opening and closing his hand around the neck of his Remington's butt. "I bet you are. I bet you're feelin' right foolish!"

Footsteps sounded behind Miller. And then the girl appeared, making her way down a pile of hard, black lava flanking Miller on his left. Tawny hair tumbled to her shoulders as she let the rise's momentum carry her down the lava pile.

As she stopped at the bottom, flushed and a little breathless, she smiled, showing white teeth between pink lips. She drew her shoulders back, pushing her breasts out.

She said, "Holy shit—you got him."

She'd said it quietly, awe in her tone.

"Yep," Miller said. "I got him."

"So, that's him—the rogue lawman." The girl was walking toward Hawk, sort of swinging her hips and thrusting her breasts.

She stopped beside Miller. Her hazel eyes sparkled as she gazed up at the dark, grim-faced man before her. "Big, tall drink of water, ain't he?" she said, raking her eyes up and down his frame and across his broad shoulders, hooking her thumbs in her back trouser pockets.

Miller lunged forward. Aiming the pistol in his right hand at Hawk's face, he buried his left fist in Hawk's gut.

The sudden move had caught the rogue lawman off guard. Miller was a strong son of a bitch—Hawk would give him that.

The savage blow rammed Hawk's solar plexus back against his spine, compressing his lungs and forcing his wind out in a single, coughing chuff. Hawk's knees buckled. He hit the stone-hard ground, leaning forward, arms crossed on his belly, gasping.

Miller stepped back quickly, slanting his cocked pistol down at Hawk's head. "There—that sorta shortens him up a little, don't it?"

Rage swept through Hawk as he tried to suck air back into his lungs. His upper lip quivered as he curled it above his mouth and glared up at the grinning, narrow-eyed, ginger-bearded killer standing over him.

"Ha-ha!" Miller laughed, taking another nervous step back, as though away from a leg-trapped bear. "He didn't like that."

The girl seemed to be enjoying herself. She smiled down at Hawk, her eyes bright and shifting between the two men. She resembled a bloodthirsty spectator at a bare-knuckle bout. But then, suddenly, her smile became a frown as she turned to Miller. "Well, ain't you gonna kill him?"

"Not unless he tries somethin'. This man has a bounty on his head—the most I ever saw."

"Huh?"

"Sure enough," Miller said. "Uncle Sam has put a twenty-thousand-dollar bounty on his head. All I gotta do is turn him into the nearest federal marshal to make my claim."

"Forget it," the girl said, shaking her head. "Forget it, Pima. We can do better than that."

Miller looked at her, narrowing his eyes impatiently. "You just get back to the fire and put a pot of coffee on. Me, I'm thirsty an' hungry. I done just captured the rogue lawman his ownself!"

"Forget it, Pima. You'd best shoot this son of a bitch, or you'll regret it."

Miller gave her a mocking grin. "Now, now—no need to be

scared, little angel girl. I can tame this wildcat. Come on, Hawk. Get to your feet, turn around and keep goin' the way you was goin' before you was so rudely interrupted."

Miller chuckled again at that, but Hawk could still hear the nervous, almost giddy edge in the killer's voice.

Hawk had regained his wind though his lungs still felt pinched. He looked up at the gun Miller kept aimed at his head. Then he looked past the Remington's cocked hammer at Miller's face. The man was sweating and grinning, and Hawk wanted nothing more than to hammer the killer's face with his fists.

In good time.

Slowly, he gained his feet, wincing at the spike-like pain in his belly, the pinched feeling in his lungs. He donned his hat, letting the rawhide chin thong dangle to his chest, and then turned, stepped over his weapons, and began moving through the rocks in the direction of the fire. The fire's smoke thickened as he approached.

He stared down from the escarpment at a burlap-roofed lean-to in a small hollow among rocks. The fire lay on the other side of it. It had been built with cedar mixed with cottonwood branches to which green leaves still clung, making smoke.

"Gotta hand it to her," Miller said a ways behind him, keeping his distance. "That was the girl's idea."

"Jodi's idea," the girl said. "I got a name, Pima. Feel free to use it."

Miller chuckled at that, as well. "Fooled you—didn't it, Hawk? For a second there you thought I was dumb enough to build a fire, knowin' you was on my trail. You thought you was just gonna waltz right in and surprise us."

"Yep, you fooled me," Hawk admitted. For a second it had been true. At least, they'd baffled him long enough to move up on him. He deserved the jeering. But he hoped he'd get another chance at Miller. Doubtful, but hope kept a man alive when it was all he had.

The hope of a kill. Two kills, now, since the girl had thrown in with Miller.

Fueling that hope was the fact that Hawk had a pearl-gripped, over-and-under derringer in an inside pocket of his frock coat. As well as a short-but-deadly, antler-gripped dagger in his right boot.

Miller pressed the Remy's barrel against the small of Hawk's back. Instantly, without having to consider the move, he swung around, pinwheeling his left arm. But Miller had been anticipating the ploy, and the killer managed to pull his hand and pistol back and out of Hawk's reach, so that Hawk's fingers only brushed the end of the Remy's barrel.

Hawk froze. Miller laughed his insufferable laugh.

Flanking him, the girl shook her head slowly, darkly. "Pima, you'd best quit funnin' and kill this man before he kills you. Before he kills us both."

That riled the killer once more. Scowling at her, he said, "I thought I told you to make coffee?"

"Kill him, Pima!"

"I'm the ramrod of this little two-man gang, sweet darlin'!" Miller railed, disciplined enough to keep his eyes on Hawk. "So kindly shut your pretty mouth. It's a might better at different things than yappin', if'n you get my drift. You get over there to the fire and make me a *goddamn pot of coffee!*"

He was looking at the girl now. But Hawk did not move on him. Miller was cagey. Hawk had to bide his time. Hoping, of course, that the girl didn't get her way and he still *had* some time.

Glancing darkly at Hawk, her jaws hard, Jodi Zimmerman swung wide of both men and made her way down to the fire.

"Now, you head on down there, too, Mister Rogue Lawman,

sir," Miller ordered. "But first . . ." He grinned broadly, narrowing his little, narrow eyes. "I'd like you to remove that little popper you got residin' inside your coat."

Hawk stared at the man grinning back at him.

Slowly, he removed the derringer from his coat pocket, and tossed it to Miller. Miller pocketed the derringer, jerked his chin toward the lean-to. Hawk turned around and made his way into the diamondback's den of Miller's camp.

Well, he still had the dagger.

At least, for now.

CHAPTER 13
IN THE DIAMONDBACK'S DEN

Keeping his Remington aimed at Hawk, Miller reached into a cavy sack and pulled out a coiled rope. He tossed the rope onto the ground beside the girl, who'd just filled a coffeepot from a canteen.

"Tie him," Miller ordered.

She glared up at him. "You wanted me to make coffee!"

"Tie him first. Tie his wrists together, behind his back. Then tie his ankles. You, Mister Rogue Lawman—you sit down in front of that rock over there."

Hawk looked at the rock. It was on the far side of the little hollow from the lean-to and the fire.

Jodi looked at Miller. "You wouldn't have to worry about him if you'd shoot him."

Miller closed his eyes for a second. When he'd slowly opened them, his face was red. He drew a deep breath as though to calm himself. "If you backtalk me one more time . . ."

"Oh, all right!" the girl said, angrily tossing the coffeepot against a nearby boulder and grabbing the rope.

She walked over to where Hawk had sat down against the rock. Miller holstered his pistol, picked up a carbine, cocked it, and aimed it out from his right thigh at Hawk's head, to one side of the girl.

"One wrong move, Mister Rogue Lawman, I'll drill ya another eye."

Hawk just stared up at him.

"Lean forward and get those arms behind your back," the girl ordered from six feet away.

Hawk stared up at her, his green eyes without expression, and then he slowly complied. He gave the girl a faintly challenging look, quirking his mouth corners.

She glanced uncertainly at Miller. "You gonna shoot him if he jumps me?"

"I'll shoot him."

"You hear that, mister?" the girl said, fear coloring her cheeks and beetling her sun-bleached eyebrows. "He'll shoot you if you try anything."

Hawk said nothing. He just stared up at her with subtle menace.

The girl snorted, her jaws hard, and then she slid her eyes toward Miller once more before leaning forward, as though she were approaching the cage of a wild, freshly captured beast. Which, to her, Hawk guessed he was.

She dropped to a knee beside him and, flicking her gaze between his hands and his eyes, she wrapped the ropes around his wrists. As she stared at him, the expression in her eyes changed from apprehension to a faintly pensive cunning. He held her gaze for a time, and he got the sense that Miller had taken on a real load when he'd taken the girl away from the Superstition Station.

"What the hell you smilin' at?" Miller said.

"He ain't smiling," Jodi said, grunting as she tied a knot in the rope binding Hawk's wrists. "He's smirkin'. He knows that every second that goes by that you don't kill him, he still has a chance of killin' both of us." She stared into Hawk's gaze. "Ain't that right, mister?"

Hawk didn't say anything. The rope was cutting into his wrists.

The girl smiled, signaling a definite change in her mood. She cut the rope with a barlow knife and used the other half to bind Hawk's ankles, keeping her gaze for the most part on his, as though probing him with her shrewd, cunning mind. She glanced at Miller and then back at Hawk, her forehead creased pensively.

And then she stood and stepped away from Hawk's bound feet.

"Now, then," Miller said. "You ain't so tough, now, are ya, Mister Rogue Lawman, sir?"

The outlaw grinned as he stepped toward Hawk. The killer lifted the barrel of his carbine, swung up its brass butt, and smashed it savagely against Hawk's left cheek.

Hawk grunted as the blow slammed his head sideways against the rock.

A high-pitched screech rose in his ears and flares exploded behind his squeezed-shut eyelids as he felt the angry welt swell on his cheek. Another welt, like a smoking brand, was rising on the back of his head. He felt the wetness of blood just beneath his right eye. It dribbled down his cheek toward his jawline.

Miller laughed.

Then he lunged toward Hawk again, ramming the carbine's butt against the left side of Hawk's mouth. Again, the back of Hawk's head hammered the rock behind him. His mouth burned. He tasted the copper of blood from the cut on the inside of his upper lip. His left eyetooth throbbed.

He felt blood dribble down from the outside left corner of his mouth.

Rage boiled within him. He tried to draw back on it. Rage was a waste of energy as long as he was trussed up like a hog for the slaughter.

Still, he gritted his teeth, ignoring the barking of his left eyetooth, which felt loose, and glared up at Miller grinning down at him. Miller thrust the butt of his carbine toward Hawk

109

once more, and the rogue lawman braced himself for another blow, squeezing his eyes closed.

"Now, ain't you tough!" the girl said sarcastically. "Beating up a tied man!"

Miller stopped the rifle about four inches from Hawk's face. He looked at the girl, pursing his lips and flaring his nostrils.

"First you wanna dry gulch him," she said. "Now you wanna beat him senseless when he can't fight back." She pulled her folding knife out of her jeans pocket, and opened it. "Let me untie him. Then you two can go at it, even odds."

She held Miller's gaze with a mocking one of her own.

And then she hardened her voice as she said, "Either that or kill him. But if you keep beatin' on a defenseless man, Pima, I'm gonna think you can't handle no other kind."

Miller whipped his head back toward Hawk. His close-set eyes seemed set even closer together. They were wide with pent-up fury. He aimed the carbine's barrel at Hawk's head, and clicked the hammer back.

Hawk stared at the rifle's small, round, black maw.

As black as death.

Here it comes, he thought.

He was mildly surprised that he felt no trepidation whatever. In fact, a strange calm washed over him. He felt his mouth corners spread an almost affable smile as he continued to gaze up at the man he thought was sure to kill him.

But in Hawk's mind, he was not seeing Pima Miller. He was seeing Linda and Jubal. They were standing on a green hill in the far distance, so he couldn't see them clearly, just their silhouettes, mainly, and the fact that Linda was wearing a frilly dress that was nearly the same rich yellow as her hair.

They were smiling, beckoning. A warm wind was blowing the skirt of Linda's yellow dress and her and Jubal's hair.

They were beckoning to him. His family was beckoning him

home. Vaguely, as he stared toward them, wanting to get up from the ground and run to them, he felt a tear ooze out the corner of his right eye and roll slowly down along his nose toward his mustache.

The bullet did not come.

The mirage faded, and Hawk found himself staring up at Pima Miller, incredulous. "What're you waiting for?"

The rifle sagged in Miller's arms. As the killer stared down at Hawk, his expression was faintly surprised, befuddled.

The girl owned much the same countenance. Her lips were slightly parted, hair hanging down along both sides of her face. Her breasts rose and fell behind her shirt as she breathed.

"Nah," Miller said. "Ain't much fun in killin' a man who ain't afraid to die." He depressed the carbine's hammer and lowered the barrel. "All in good time," he said. "All in good time."

He turned to Jodi. "Where's that coffee?"

The girl held her openly fascinated gaze on Hawk. Then she turned to Miller as though she'd forgotten he was there. She smiled and started walking toward the fire. Casting her amused smile at Hawk, she said, "Comin' right up!"

Hawk was disappointed.

He'd thought he was going home.

The day passed slowly. For Hawk, sitting back against the boulder with his smashed face, it also passed miserably though the pain dulled after an hour or so.

What caused the bulk of the misery was knowing he'd been fooled. And having to watch Miller and Jodi stroll about the camp without being able to kill them.

The two had decided to stay put for the day, resting themselves as well as their horses. Miller's bullet wound still bothered the killer, which was plain from the stiff way he moved and by the long nap he took under the lean-to, while an afternoon thundershower soaked Hawk to the bone.

The girl joined the killer and when they woke up, they didn't seem to mind that Hawk was sitting only a few feet away. They coupled like back-alley curs, grunting and cursing and laughing throatily. Jodi seemed to like that Hawk could watch if he wanted to, and since he didn't have much choice, he saw her glance toward him now and then, while her hair jostled across her bare shoulders and jouncing breasts.

When they were done and dressed, the rain had stopped. The girl smiled once more at Hawk as she threw her hair back behind her shoulders and began looking for dry wood with which to build a fire.

Earlier, Miller had sent the girl off to retrieve Hawk's horse, and they'd picketed the grulla with their own. Hawk couldn't see the horses from his position, but he recognized his own mount's sporadic, nervous whickers. The grulla was no doubt able to smell Hawk, maybe even smell the dried blood on his rider's face, but he could not see him.

That fact and the strangers' presence made the horse owly.

It didn't do much for Hawk's mood, either.

As Miller and the girl sat around the fire that night, eating a jackrabbit the girl had snared and roasted, she said over her steaming coffee cup, canting her head toward Hawk, "How do you intend to turn him in for that reward money when you yourself got a bounty on your head?"

Miller forked meat and beans into his mouth and stared at her dully while he chewed. Then he picked something from between his teeth with his fingers, rubbed it on his trouser leg, and said with menacing nonchalance, "How do you know I got a bounty on my head?"

"I don't know," the girl said, hiking a shoulder. "Don't you?"

"You *know* I do."

"I *figured* you did," she said, hardening her voice with strained patience.

"That mean somethin' to you?"

Jodi studied him. She held her plate on one thigh, her coffee cup on the other thigh.

"Yeah," she said after several seconds, adding slowly, carefully enunciating every word as though for a moron to understand: "It means how in the hell do you think you're going to turn in that big drink of water over there for that twenty thousand dollars you say he's got on his head, when you yourself are wanted? I'd spell it out for you if I thought you could read!"

It was Miller's turn to study her with menacing blandness. After a while he said, quietly defensive, "I can read."

"*What?*"

"I can read, goddamnit!"

Jodi glanced over at Hawk, sitting about ten feet away. Hawk watched them, biding his time, waiting, since that was about all he could do, anyway. He sensed something happening between them. Something that might work in his favor, but he wasn't sure what that might be.

Meanwhile, he was quietly straining his wrists behind his back, trying to work the girl's knot in the ropes free. It didn't look good. She'd tied a damned tight double knot, and so far, after several hours of spontaneous work on it, he hadn't made much, if any progress, but only caused his nails to bleed.

"What're you lookin' at him for?" Miller asked the girl.

"I was wonderin' if he was makin' any more sense out of you than I am."

"Don't look at him. He ain't there. You just keep your moon-calf eyes off him. He's my worry—not yours."

"Oh, that's right—it was the bounty on your head we was talking about. And how is it you figured to turn him in, when—"

"That's what you're here for."

Again, Jodi stared across the fire at Miller as though she were having trouble understanding him.

"You don't have a bounty on your head, do you?" Miller asked her.

"None that I know of."

"So . . ."

"So I'm gonna turn that man over to the first US marshal we run into."

"Just his head." Miller grinned and looked at Hawk. "Once when we get close to Tucson, were there's an old drunken deputy US marshal posted, we'll shoot the son of a bitch, throw his head into a gunnysack, and *you'll* turn it over to old Hiram Mitchell and fill out the paperwork to put in for the reward. And when it comes, we'll split it."

"Fifty-fifty?"

"Sure," Miller said, hiking a shoulder. "I'm a fair man."

Jodi glanced over at Hawk once more. The firelight sparkled in her hazel eyes, blazed in certain strands of her hair flowing down over her shoulders.

She set her plate aside and used a scrap of burlap to remove the smoking coffeepot from the fire. She refilled both Miller's cup as well as her own and then returned the pot to the rock near the fire's glowing coals and short, dancing flames.

She sat back down, picked up her cup, and blew on it, the steam bathing her pretty face. "How do I know I can trust you?" she asked Miller.

"How do I know I can trust *you?*" Miller returned, leaning back against his saddle and crossing his legs at the ankles. "How do I know you ain't figurin' on turnin' me in for the reward on *my* head?"

"How much reward you got on your head?"

"Enough."

"How much?"

"Enough, I said."

The girl didn't let him off that easy. "How much?" she asked, gritting her own teeth and leaning toward him, hardening her jaws. She gave it as well as she got it, Hawk mused, still straining at the ropes binding his wrists.

Miller stared at her, blinked, glanced away, sheepish, and then returned his gaze to her. "Twelve hundred."

"Hah!" Jodi laughed, slapping her thigh. She hooked a thumb toward Hawk. "He's got twenty thousand on his head and you got twelve hundred on yours, and you think I'd take *yours* over *his*?"

Miller sat up, glaring at her and gritting his teeth again. "Just 'cause he has twenty thousand on his head and I only got twelve hundred don't mean a damn thing. It just means he's been at it longer, that's all! And, shit, he's a lawman! He makes them other lawmen look like fools!"

"Oh, take the hump out of your neck, Pima. I don't need your bounty, and I don't need his bounty, neither. And you don't need his bounty, neither. Too risky . . . when I got somethin' else in mind."

"Oh, this again."

"Yep, this again." The girl picked up her plate and Miller's, went over to some loose gravel between the fire and Hawk, and scraped a handful of the gravel and dirt over one of the plates, cleaning it.

She looked at Miller. "You know that old Apache gold mine everyone's been blabberin' about for years?"

"The one the Dutchman says he found?"

"That's the one."

"What about it?"

"I know where it is," Jodi said.

Miller gave a caustic chuff. "Oh, sure you do."

"I do." Jodi was cleaning the second plate. She flashed a

quick glance at Hawk and then looked over her shoulder at Miller again. "And I been waitin' for the right man to come along to help me clean it out."

CHAPTER 14
TAWNY HEAD, BLACK HEART

The night passed even more slowly for Hawk than the day had.

Miller hadn't given him anything to eat, and his hunger, coupled with the fact that he was battered, wet from the rain, and tied, made him feel as though he were balancing a smithy's anvil on his shoulders.

Miller and the girl had kicked out their fire and retired to their lean-to. They'd rutted again as before and then Miller got up to wander around with his rifle. Hawk had spied Apache sign the day before, and he had a feeling that the killer had, as well.

Miller walked around, looking tense. He smoked for a while along the top of the ridge above the lean-to, cupping the coal in the palm of his hand as he stared out over the canyon. Then, apparently satisfied they were alone, he came down off the ridge and sauntered over to Hawk.

"Only reason I'm keepin' you alive is 'cause I don't have to haul your smelly carcass through the desert to Tucson. If it was winter, you'd be dead."

Hawk didn't say anything. He kept his eyes straight ahead, not giving the man anything.

That seemed to rile Miller. He swept his right boot back, then hurled it forward, ramming the toe into Hawk's right thigh. The pain seared through the rogue lawman's leg, but he kept quiet and held still, staring straight ahead.

"That hurt," Miller said, chuckling. "I know it did."

He kicked out of his boots and crawled back under the lean-to.

Hawk dozed now and then but sometime around three thirty or four he awakened. He'd heard something, but he wasn't sure what. The horses were milling around faintly, edgily. He recognized the grulla's deep, almost soundless whicker.

Hawk looked around. The night was still, silent. Save for the starlight, it was a black as the inside of a glove. Something or someone was on the prowl near the camp. He could tell as much by the faint tingling at the base of his spine as from anything else.

The horses continued to sidle around, snorting, for another half hour. And then they settled down. And the tingling at the base of Hawk's back faded, as well.

At first light, Miller crawled out from under the lean-to. He muttered something to the girl then grabbed Hawk's Henry, stumbled past Hawk, and checked the horses. He didn't return soon, so Hawk figured he'd gone out on the scout again.

The killer must have sensed something the night before, as well.

The girl gathered more wood, built a small fire, and made coffee. When the coffee was done, she brought a cup over to Hawk, and dropped to a knee beside him.

"Want some coffee?"

"No, thanks," Hawk said.

Jodi looked genuinely surprised. "Really? You don't want no *coffee*?"

"Nope."

She stared at him, brows knit together. "You sure?" She blew the steam toward him. "Don't that smell good?"

Hawk didn't say anything.

"Jesus, you're a tough son of a bitch, ain't ya?"

Still, Hawk said nothing. She stared at him, sleep in her eyes, lines from her saddle still creasing her cheek. Fine lines from her slumber stretched out from the corners of her hazel eyes. She hadn't brushed her hair but merely tucked the tangled mess behind her ears.

She'd left the first three buttons of her shirt undone, showing a bit of white chemise and the first dip of cleavage.

"I s'pose you're thinkin' I might've poisoned it," she said.

"Just don't care for any of your coffee."

"Reckon I don't blame you. Since I was tryin' to get him to kill you an' all." The girl paused, feigned a sheepish look, pooching her lips out and casting her eyes low. "Sorry about that."

Hawk gave a droll chuckle.

She raised her eyes coyly. "Hope we didn't keep you awake last night . . . with all our carryin' on."

"I slept fine."

"Really?"

"Yep."

She studied him sidelong. "Pshaw! You heard. And I bet you were wantin' some, weren't you?" She pressed her hand against his shoulder, gave him a shove. "Come on! I know I'm purty. I ain't high-hatted or nothin', but I been told I'm easy on the eyes enough times I'm startin' to believe it." She looked off. "Seem to satisfy him well enough."

She rolled her eyes to Hawk. "You wanna kill him, don't you?"

Hawk looked at her.

"Why don't you, then?"

He continued to stare at her skeptically.

"You and me could be partners, you know. I'm gonna need a tough man to help me mine the gold out of that old hole. Geronimo and his Apaches keep a close eye on things up here. The Superstitions are the home of their Thunder God, and he's a colicky cuss. He don't like intruders. That's what us white folks are—even *half-breed* white folks."

Teasingly, she placed a finger on Hawk's long wedge of a nose, and shoved his face to one side, smiling and then folding her upper teeth over her bottom lip.

A brazen one, this girl. A coquette. A tawny-headed, black-hearted coquette.

Hawk wouldn't trust her as far as he could throw her uphill against a prairie cyclone.

"What're you sayin'?" Hawk said, feigning interest.

"I'm sayin' that if you was to throw in with me, I'd make it worth your while."

She slid her shoulders back slightly, pushing her breasts out, and slid her face down close to Hawk's. He could hear the faint crackling of her lips as she broadened her coquettish smile. "You'd be a rich man and you'd have a pretty, young girl to warm your fancy bed at night. To do things to you I bet you've never even dreamed of."

"Oh?"

"Sure. And all you have to do is promise me you'd like that . . . and you'd like to be richer than your wildest dreams . . . and promise to kill Pima . . . and you're in."

"You really think that old mine is more than legend?"

"I know." She gazed at him gravely now, her bold gaze certain. "I've seen it. The old man didn't. I kept it from him because I couldn't trust him to not get drunk and gas about it to others. He'd act like it was all his, like he found it himself. I saw it early in the spring, when I got lost out here, and I've drawn a map. It's in my saddlebags."

"What about the Apaches?"

"They're a problem. We'll have to be careful. It might come to fightin'. If it does, I'd rather have you doin' the fightin' than a man like Pima."

Jodi looked away as though to make certain they were alone,

and then she shook her hair back from her face and leaned even closer to Hawk, until he could smell her distinctly feminine fragrance mixed with the smoky, horsy smell of her clothes, and feel her breath against his cheek.

"Just between you and me," Jodi said, "Pima's weak. He's got a weak mind and a weak soul. You know. You heard him talkin'. And what's more, I can't trust him. He don't have no integrity. I can tell by lookin' at you, though, that you got integrity. You wouldn't double-cross a girl who only wanted you to kill the man you already wanted to kill yourself and make you rich and give herself to you for an added reward."

She brushed her nose against Hawk's jaw, and smiled.

"Would you?" she asked.

Hawk gazed at her, lifted his mouth corners slightly. He glanced down her shirt because he knew she wanted him to, and then he broadened his smile and narrowed his eyes lustily. "No, I wouldn't."

"We got a deal, then?"

"Deal."

The girl stared at him skeptically, considering. And then she reached into her pants pocket. Hawk had just finished using the rock behind him to grind through the rope around his wrists, and now he swung both arms forward, showing her his hands.

"No need for the knife. But I will take a gu—"

Miller's voice cut him off. *"Hey—what the hell's goin' on over there?"*

Hawk turned to see Miller running toward him on the left, climbing the rise and holding Hawk's rifle across his hips.

"Hey!" Miller shouted as he started up the rocks toward the camp.

The girl looked from Hawk's freed hands to Miller and screamed, "Pima, help!" She dropped the coffee cup and scrambled back away from the prisoner.

The rogue lawman lunged for her, intending to grab her around her neck and take the pistol she usually carried wedged against the small of her back. But Hawk's ankles were still tied, restricting his movements, and his fingers only brushed the girl's chest before he fell forward on his belly.

Miller's boots thudded. His spurs rattled. Hawk could hear the man's raspy breaths as he ran up the rocks. Hawk turned his head in time to see the killer standing over him, boots spread, glaring down and raising the Henry, barrel up.

"I was just tryin' to give him a cup of coffee!" Jodi screamed, feigning horror.

"Why, you son of a bitch!" Miller raked out just before he rammed the brass butt plate of the rifle against Hawk's right cheek.

One more smack with the Henry laid the rogue lawman out cold.

He didn't know how much later he woke. All he knew was that for a seemingly endless time his slumber had been racked with a searing pain in his head. It had felt—still felt—like someone had sunk a hatchet through his skull. His belly and hips ached and burned. Making the pain in his head worse, all his blood had seemed to pool in his brain, feeding the tender nerves.

His heart was two giant bells tolling wickedly in his ears.

As he opened his eyes, he saw the ground passing in a brown blur beneath him. The rich, warm tang of horse and leather filled his nostrils. He looked around. He'd been thrown belly down over his own saddle, across the grulla's back. That was the grinding he felt against his midsection. His wrists were tied even tighter than before.

His ankles were also tied and hung down the grulla's opposite side.

As he rode, gritting his teeth against the clanging in his head,

Hawk heard the girl and Miller talking, one of them leading the grulla. The girl was acting as though Hawk had jumped her. She was insisting Miller kill him and "get him out of their hair for good."

They wouldn't need the reward money. Not with all the gold waiting for them in that old Mexican mine.

Miller obviously, wisely, didn't trust her much more than Hawk did. The killer wanted to keep Hawk alive until he was certain the mine was real and not just one of Jodi's stories or a figment of her "tawny-headed imagination."

Hawk had to grin through his pain at that.

And then he saw his opportunity to get shed of these two.

They were traversing a razorback ridge. Just beyond him, a deep canyon dropped nearly straight down. What the hell? He couldn't be in any more pain than he was already in.

And he doubted he'd ever get another chance to free himself, another chance at hunting Miller down and killing him.

What was the worst that could happen?

That he'd join his waiting family?

Hawk laughed soundlessly.

With a low groan, Hawk funneled every ounce of his remaining strength into his arms and legs. He pitched and bobbed until he'd worked his knees up onto the grulla's back.

"Be seein' you, old pard," he muttered to the horse as, using his knees and elbows, he hurled himself into a somersault off the horse's back and into the canyon.

As he tumbled down the steep, shale-carpeted slope, he realized he'd been wrong. There was a whole other world of pain just waiting for him at the bottom of that canyon, grinning its snaggle-toothed grin.

CHAPTER 15
TORMENT CANYON

"How you feelin', sugar?"

It was the voice of Saradee Jones—intimate and lilting, faintly raspy and familiar to Hawk's ears. The outlaw girl's voice spoke to him from far away, as though from the top of the very deep well at the bottom of which he lay.

Of course, it wasn't really Saradee speaking to him. He was only dreaming the voice as he'd dreamt the voices of Linda and Jubal, whispering into his ears, urging him to let go. To release this world of aching torment and endless grief, and to walk with them over the green fields of their new home.

Where they would live together in serenity throughout eternity.

"Feelin' better? Why, I do believe you're still kickin', after all."

Saradee's voice. Or his mind's fabrication of her voice. She wouldn't be in this canyon. They'd parted ways back in his hometown of Crossroads. She'd sensed, rightly, that he'd wanted to visit the graves of Linda and Jubal alone. He hadn't seen her after that visit, had no idea where she'd gone. That wasn't unusual. Their partings had always been spontaneous and without formality, just like their infrequent liaisons.

They were not partners. At least, in Hawk's mind they were not. A few months ago, she'd saved his life in a town called Trinity Ridge, when he'd been hanged upside down from a burning gallows by the Tierney Gang, and he supposed he was beholden to her for that.

But for no other reason. She was an outlaw and a killer. Someday soon, he would kill her.

Someone touched his shoulder, jostled him slightly. Her voice again. It was starting to annoy him because it was drawing him up out of the deep well of sleep again, and away from his misery. He wanted to remain deep inside the well. He felt that rising from it would only return him to an unbearable world of pain— one that he could feel hammering at him as though on the other side of a stout, log door.

The pain was like a pack of hungry wolves yapping and howling outside that door.

"Hey, Hawk," Saradee said. Close now. Very close. Her lips seemed to be just off his left ear. "Haw-awwk," she said in her lilting singsong.

He opened his eyes, squinted against the pain that was like a railroad spike hammered through both ears. What his eyes finally focused on was something shiny. Shiny silver. A cross dangling from a rawhide thong down a girl's neck, resting atop a deep well of dark cleavage exposed by the first few buttons of a well-filled hickory shirt.

The girl's neck and chest were lightly tanned. At the first downward slope of the cleavage, on the far side of the little valley from Hawk's face, was a single, jagged-edged, whiskey-colored freckle.

"Hey," the girl said. "Quit starin' at my tits. How 'bout some water?" She jostled a hide-wrapped canteen; Hawk could hear the water sloshing around.

And then he realized how thirsty he was and that he'd been dreaming of snowmelt—of diving into a snowmelt stream and letting the water flow into his mouth, down his throat, and into his belly.

Hawk lifted his head, which he then realized was being held

up by the girl's right shoulder. She lifted the canteen across her well-filled blouse and the silver crucifix nestling at the top of her cleavage, shoving the flask toward his mouth. But Hawk found himself raising his right arm and wrapping that hand around the canteen, taking it from her.

He tipped up the canteen, pressed the metal ring of the opening to his lips, and drank thirstily.

"Easy, fella," Saradee said as water dribbled down the corners of Hawk's mouth. "It's been three days. You drink too much too soon, you'll founder."

Hawk couldn't help himself. The water tasted too good. He pulled the canteen away from his mouth, filled his now-thirsty lungs with air, and then let the water wash down his throat once more, filling his belly. Instantly, it buoyed him, made him feel better. He was like a plant that had gone too long without water.

On the other hand, for some reason, that hammering at his door now seeped through an opening, rapping that railroad spike from both ends. He hardened his jaws, gritted his teeth, pulled away from the girl, and leaned his head back against a wall.

"Hell!"

"Yeah, well, I told ya," Saradee said, taking the canteen from him. "You oughta listen to Saradee. She's here to help . . . just like always."

"Where in the hell am I?" Hawk said, dragging a ragged breath into his lungs.

He felt a strange pressure around his head and reached up to feel a bandanna tightly wrapped around his forehead and tied in back. His fingers touched crusted blood at the front and back.

Only then did he remember his tumble down the steep slope into the canyon—the raking, hammering pain in every joint, sharp rocks and cactus thorns biting into him.

"Found this old shack," Saradee said, looking around. "I think the canyon's called Torment. Leastways, it says that on an old map I took out of the stage station. I reckon that would be fitting under the circumstances, wouldn't it?"

Hawk looked around. Stone walls, mostly ruined, rose around him. There was a brush roof over his head, but most of the roof of the small casa—probably an ancient Mexican rancher's or herder's hovel—had tumbled into the barren rooms. The floor was hard-packed desert caliche.

Outside, the sun shone brightly off barren rock. A hot breeze slid a catclaw's branches back and forth in a far window. The branches scraped softly against the old stone.

A saddle and other tack lay on the floor around him. There was a fire ring mounded with gray ashes and a charred cedar branch. A coffeepot sat to one side, as did several other eating utensils, pots and pans.

Saradee's gear.

Her words had been slow to penetrate his brain. Now, as they did, he turned to her sitting close beside him. "Stage station?"

"Superstition. Shadowed you there." She huddled close to him, wrapped her hands around his left bicep. "Just can't seem to get shed of me, can you?"

He stared at her, gave a wry chuff. He wasn't surprised that she'd followed him. He wasn't sure what she wanted from him. She seemed amused by him, somehow. Amused by his venomous quest for vengeance. It seemed to attract her, keep her dogging his heels, as though she were mesmerized by his single-mindedness.

She was no more capable of love than he was, so he knew she didn't love him. He had to admit feeling something for her, though.

More than *something*.

A insatiable hunger for her body, which, young, ripe, and

supple, was impossible for any man to ignore. And once he'd fallen prey to this blonde-haired, blue-eyed succubus's bewitching wiles, the man found himself thinking about her almost constantly.

At least, when he wasn't thinking about killing.

"You followed me into the mountains."

Saradee sighed and let her hands flop against her thighs clad in skintight, light-blue denim under leather chaps. "Search me why I came. You'd think I'd have outgrown you by now, gone back to bank- and train-robbin', cold-blooded murder and my sundry other wicked ways. But when I saw you pull through Albacurk, I just couldn't help but dog you, see what kind of bailiwick you ended up in next."

She squirmed against him, kissed his cheek. Her sun-bleached blonde hair hung straight and long past her slender shoulders. It fell down both sides of her doll-like face bejeweled with the long, deep-blue eyes of an outlaw sorceress. They were crazy, taunting, eminently alluring eyes—even crazier and more taunting than Jodi Zimmerman's eyes.

She was similar to the other young outlaw woman whose path Hawk had recently crossed. But even Miss Zimmerman could learn a whole book of unspeakable lessons from the outlaw queen known as Saradee Jones, whom some said *acted* like a witch because she indeed *was* a witch.

An outlaw witch.

Pity the poor fool who let her sink her bittersweet claws into him, as Gideon Hawk had made the mistake of doing himself. Every time he laid eyes on Saradee, he rued the day he hadn't killed her before she could lure him into her bed.

Now, since she'd somehow saved his hide again—or, at least gotten a roof over his head and doctored his wounds—he knew he should be glad that he hadn't drilled a bullet through her beautiful head. But he just couldn't manage it.

Hawk found himself staring at her in disbelief at both her beauty, the pureness of which belied her malevolence, and the fact of her presence.

"That was you I sensed around Miller's camp last night, wasn't it?" Hawk said.

"I was workin' around you, tryin' to figure a way to get you out of there. Wasn't in much of a hurry, I reckon. I was kinda wondering if that randy little bitch, Miss Jodi, was going to lure you into the trap she was settin'."

Hawk chuckled as he grabbed the canteen out of her hands. "You must've been close." He threw back another deep drink.

Saradee snatched the canteen back from him. "You wanna founder?"

She returned the cap to the canteen's mouth and said, "I was scoutin' from across the canyon when you pulled that fool move, throwin' yourself off your horse. You fell a ways but you might've fallen farther. Got hung up on a ledge of sorts. Miller was going to shoot you but the girl—she's a smart one, ain't she?—she knocked his rifle away. Must've reminded him of the Apache danger. I reckon they figured you were a goner, anyway, so they moved on. I had a devil of a time gettin' you off that ledge and hauled into the canyon. Rigged a travois, dragged you around lookin' for shelter, found this place."

Saradee appraised their surroundings.

"It ain't much, but it's been home now for the past three days. I reckon it's grown on me. Don't recollect stayin' in one place this long in a month of Sundays."

"Three days, huh?"

"Three days. I bet you gotta pee like a plow horse!"

It was then that Hawk realized he was naked beneath a coarse army blanket. He lifted the blanket. Aside from a large bandage cut from a blanket wrapped taut around his ribs, and another couple of bandages wrapped around cuts on his legs, he was as naked as the day he'd been born.

Saradee had even taken off his socks.

She laughed. "Don't worry, sugar—I've seen it before." She winked at him.

Hawk cursed. Not because he was naked, but from the general wretchedness of his situation. Little modesty remained in him. He flung the blanket aside, heaved himself slowly, heavily to his feet, setting his jaws against the hammering in his head, and stumbled barefoot and naked out of the shack. A few feet beyond the front door, he evacuated his bladder on a prickly pear.

Saradee's big palomino stood hobbled nearby, in a patch of shade between a couple of mesquites growing among the rocks. The horse lowered its head, whickered softly at the naked man watering the prickly pear. Hawk looked around, saw that they were in a slight bowl surrounded by low, barren hills.

Almost straight to the west rose the finger-like formation of what was most likely the peak called Weaver's Needle. Some old prospectors called it by its Spanish name, El Sombrero.

The sun was blinding. That, coupled with the shrill, pulsating music of the cicadas, caused the ground to rise and fall around Hawk. He suddenly felt sick to his stomach. He grabbed the doorframe to steady himself but, twisting around, he dropped to his knees anyway.

Saradee was there beside him, draping one of his arms around her neck, wrapping her own arm around his waist.

"Easy does it, sugar!" Saradee said, grunting against the big man's considerable weight.

Hawk got his feet under him but his knees felt like wheel dope. He leaned against the girl but his knees were grazing the ground by the time she got him back to the crude pallet she'd made for him over leafy willow branches and burlap. Hawk lay down in the makeshift bed. He tried fighting against the nausea and the infernal swimming in his head, the pounding in his temples, but it was no use.

Outside, thunder rumbled. He glanced toward the doorway, saw the white-hot light dim slightly. Another summer storm was moving in.

More thunder rumbled like distant war drums. Hawk took that as a sign to give into his own weakness and the pressure of Saradee's hands pushing him down, and flopped back against the pallet.

He was asleep before his head had hit the saddlebag pouch that the outlaw girl had filled with sand for his pillow.

When he opened his eyes, it was dark. A small fire burned nearby. It shone in Linda's yellow-blonde hair as, straddling him naked, she rose and fell slowly, gently grinding against him. He looked down to see his wife's hands with her gold wedding band pressed against his chest. As she lifted her hips, she leaned forward, pushing comfortingly against him. As she dropped back down to his pelvis, the pressure on his chest lightened.

Hawk smiled. He was home. His smile broadened. His pain was gone. There was only Linda making love to him, her long hair obscuring her face as it cascaded down her shoulders to caress his chest, soft as corn silk, when she leaned forward.

"Oh, Gid," she whispered. "Oh . . . Gideon . . ."

Behind her now in the firelight he could see the basinet in which their baby, little Jubal, slumbered among the quilts she'd sewn for him during her pregnancy.

Hawk lifted his hands to his wife's breasts, gently massaging the full, high, cherry-tipped orbs before caressing her cheeks with his thumbs. He slid her hair back from her face with the backs of his hands.

Hawk froze, staring up at the girl straddling him.

It was not Linda's soft, light-blue eyes smiling down at him now but the glassy, nearly opaque, folly-ridden gaze of Saradee Jones.

The beautiful outlaw shook her head slowly, stretching her rich lips back from her white teeth in gentle mockery. "Not her, Gideon. Linda's dead. She's back in one of those two graves you visited back in Crossroads—remember?"

Saradee lowered her hips to his and then bowed her head and tightened her face as she ground against him, groaning hoarsely. "Just me now. Just . . . ohhh, god . . . *me!*"

Hawk tried in his mind to resist her. He could not.

His blood rose undeniably. He grunted and cupped her breasts almost savagely and drove himself up deep inside her. He pressed the back of his head fast against the blankets, cursing and squeezing her breasts as he spent himself.

Saradee sighed and collapsed against his chest.

Outside, the palomino whinnied.

Then came the thuds of many galloping horses.

Saradee gasped. As she flung her naked, sweat-slick body off of Hawk, he reached for his Henry.

CHAPTER 16
IN THUNDER GOD'S ABODE

Hawk had automatically gone for his rifle, which he'd assumed was lying where he usually kept it, to the right of his bedroll. He'd forgotten that he'd taken his leave of Miller and Jodi Zimmerman without any weapons save for the dagger he kept in his boot.

He'd remembered too late that his rifle was still with Miller. The quick, twisting move had grieved his battered ribs. As he gave an agonized grunt and pressed his right hand to his side, he heard the thunder of several horses outside the ruined hovel.

Naked, Saradee turned to Hawk.

"Here!" she hissed, and tossed him one of her silver-chased, pearl-gripped Colts.

Hawk caught the weapon against his chest. Saradee quickly threw her shirt over her shoulders and ran to the outline of a window to Hawk's left. The fire had burned down to a soft, umber glow, leaving the hovel in thick, inky shadows lightly limned in red.

Hawk spun the Colt's cylinder and, rising heavily but vaguely realizing he wasn't in as much pain as before, he moved to a window on the opposite side of the cabin from Saradee. He hunkered on one knee to the left of the empty casing and gazed out into the dark canyon.

Hooves thumped. Horses whickered softly, occasionally blowing. There was also the rasping of men. For a moment, Hawk could see nothing out there, only hear the horses and the men

133

who seemed to be circling the hovel. But then as his eyes adjusted to the night's moonless darkness, Hawk saw the quick-moving shadows maybe thirty, forty yards out from the shack.

Occasionally, starlight reflected off a face or an eye or some metallic object that the riders carried. Briefly, between two shrubs, Hawk glimpsed a patch of red. Likely a calico bandanna—the kind favored by Apaches. He could tell from the muffled hoof thuds that the horses galloping around the hovel were unshod, another sign that Apaches—likely, Chiricahuas—had come calling.

Hawk felt the chill of apprehension seep into his battered body. Out of the frying pan and into the fire. And he had neither his own pistols nor his Henry repeater. Just Saradee's Colt, which left her with maybe only one more Colt and her Winchester.

How many Indians were out there?

Hunkered down beside the window and staring out into the night, he tried to count the shadows swirling around him. They seemed to be moving at a fairly good clip on their sure-footed, desert- and mountain-bred mustangs—too fast for Hawk to get a handle on their number.

He waited, his thumb caressing the cocked hammer of Saradee's Colt. He hadn't realized how hard he'd been clamping his jaws together until they started to hurt. His palm grew slick against the Colt's pearl grips.

Movement behind Hawk. He turned to see Saradee leap the fire and run toward him. Light from the umber coals bathed her bare legs, glistened in her blonde hair and her eyes. She hunkered down on the opposite side of the window from Hawk. He could sense her anxiety as the riders continued circling.

"Injuns!" she hissed.

"Hold your fire."

"I'll hold mine if they hold theirs!"

Hawk continued staring out the window. The riders continued circling, jangling Hawk's nerves just as he knew they were doing to Saradee's. He had the urge to dress but he didn't want to turn his back on them. Besides, it wasn't cold and he might as well die naked as clothed.

Give the carrion eaters an easier time of it.

Just when Hawk thought he couldn't endure the tension any longer, the hoof thuds began to dwindle. Fewer and fewer shadows passed outside the window. Then one more passed, and that was all. The hoof thuds dwindled into the night.

Silence.

"What the hell?" Saradee said.

"Might be a trap."

Hawk rose and stiffly gathered his clothes. Even more stiffly, he wrestled his way into his longhandles, whipcord trousers, socks, and boots. He pulled his suspenders up over his long-handle top. Again, he looked for his rifle. It was so much a part of him, he felt as though one of his arms had been hacked off at the shoulder.

He tossed Saradee's Colt her to her, and picked up her Winchester carbine. She preferred pistols. He preferred a long gun. He racked a shell into the Winchester's chamber and then, thumb on the hammer, walked slowly out into the night.

In front of the door, he stopped and looked around. He did not hear Saradee move out of the shack behind him. She was as stealthy as a night-hunting puma. He only felt the slight displacement of air as she stepped up beside him. She smelled like cinnamon and the musk of love.

Hawk canted his head to his left. The girl drifted off that way. Hawk moved to his right. He didn't know the terrain like she did, so he had to move especially slowly and carefully so he wouldn't trip and give himself away or walk into an ambush.

When he figured he'd moved about fifty yards out from the

canyon, he stared off in the direction in which he was sure the Indians had headed. West. Nothing but silence out there in the stygian darkness, save for the distant yammer of a lone coyote.

Saradee's voice cleaved the silence. "Hawk."

He turned and walked back toward the shack. He stopped when he saw the cream figure of the big palomino fidgeting around the mesquite it had been tied to. Saradee stood several yards behind the horse. Some slender object slanted down before her.

Hawk moved toward her and saw the feathers trimming the wooden shaft protruding from the ground behind the palomino. An Apache war lance.

"What the hell's that mean?" the girl said, her voice pitched low with gravity.

"It means get out or they'll escort us out . . . by way of hell."

Hawk turned and walked back to the shack.

"You know, I think I'll kill you for lyin' to me, girl!"

Pima Miller glared at Jodi Zimmerman, who, sitting on her Morgan mare in one of the many shallow canyons that formed a maze in the heart of the Superstitions, turned her head this way and that. Her brows hooded her troubled eyes, and her lips were stretched, balling her cheeks in a frustrated scowl.

"I don't understand it," she said, glancing down at the penciled scrap of paper in her gloved hands. "I was careful to write down the directions and draw clear pictures of the terrain. I knew I'd have trouble finding it if I didn't, and—"

"And now, even with your map, you're still havin' trouble findin' it. And we've been out here for three days now. Three long days in this heat followin' your so-called map and your so-called *story* of the richest gold mine in all of North America."

"Oh, hush—I'm tryin' to figure."

"Tryin' to figure, huh? I'm tryin' to figure what in the hell ever got into me to listen to your wild story in the first place. Now, not only do I not have a pair of saddlebags bulgin' with nearly pure gold ore, but I don't have that rogue lawman's head in a gunnysack!" Miller wagged his head from side to side, groaning. "Did I say that head of his is worth twenty thousand dollars? Did I *say* that?"

"I believe you might've mentioned it among all your other caterwauling," Jodi said, holding the map in front of her but looking back over her left shoulder at the large, red pinnacle of El Sombrero.

The formation did indeed resemble a sombrero from this vantage—the steeple crown of the hat rising from a stark, red, boulder-strewn, cone-like mountain and presiding over the entire Superstition Range and the Salt River Valley, with the airy blue backdrop of Boulder Canyon to the southwest.

The vastness and starkness of the land here always took Jodi's breath away. It made her feel at once lonely and anxious but, also, knowing the ancient mine that the land contained, like a jewel clamped in the palm of a giant fist, it made her giddy and eager. It made her heart tap-tap-tap-tap, like an Apache war drum, in her throat, in her ears.

But, now, if she couldn't find it, knowing that she'd been so infernally close, maybe within only two hundred yards after waiting for the old man to die or for her to work up the gumption to leave him behind and ride out here alone and chip off what she could from the precious jewel and then head for far, far better climes—the disappointment would be a bottomless well.

She'd never stop falling into it.

If she couldn't find the old Peralta mine, she'd put her pistol in her mouth and blow her brains out.

How could anyone go on living, knowing the riches they'd left behind? She'd seen it! After the Dutchman from Apache

Springs had left with his two burros, she'd backtracked him, found the mine and explored it, seen the color in the walls.

It had been like the scales of a giant diamondback fashioned from raw, glittering gold!

Jodi was sweating. It was running down her cheeks, between her breasts and down her shoulders under her shirt. Her breath was short and shallow. The cicadas were screeching a raucous, throbbing rhythm that matched the throbbing of the girl's own heart.

Desperately, she looked around. There were several lesser canyons, most brush- and rock-choked, angling away from this main one they were in and which was maybe fifty yards across at its widest. The old man had said these ravines were old lava rivers from the time the Superstitions had been created by exploding volcanoes.

She glanced back over the rumpled, barren land to the southwest and El Sombrero, and then "Tsucked" her horse on ahead, looking around for some of the landmarks she'd carefully penciled on her sheet of lined notepaper.

"You best find that gold, girl."

Behind her, Miller stepped down from his saddle and removed his canteen from the horn. He was leading Hawk's grulla. They figured they'd use the rogue lawman's mount and his saddlebags for squirreling out an extra parcel of the Dutchman's gold from the mine.

"You best find it . . ." Miller let his voice taper off maliciously as he walked over to the shaded base of the arroyo's western bank, and sagged down with a grunt. "Me—I'm gonna rest here, have me some water. I think your stitches done opened up on me."

Jodi looked behind her again. She could see a little splotch of fresh blood on the outlaw's shirt.

She lifted her gaze to the red sandstone ridges rising all

around her. She'd spied Apache sign the day before, and she thought she'd sensed the red men following them, staying just out of sight. It was said that Geronimo saw himself as a keeper of the Superstitions, so to speak. The Chiricahuas had long called the mountains their physical as well as spiritual home. It was also the home of their Thunder God.

Geronimo, as did Cochise before him, wanted to keep the mountains free of the white-eyes. The Apaches haunting these mountains didn't kill as automatically and wantonly as they once had, fearing retribution from the cavalry, but gold hunters were still known to disappear in these mountains, never to be heard from again.

Somehow, the old Dutchman, as well as Jodi and the old man, had managed to steer clear of the dangerous Chiricahuas. Her time was likely running out, she thought as she continued to rake her gaze around the rocky ridges for sign of the little, dark, savage men with their coal-black hair held back by calico headbands.

The Morgan moved steadily north along the ravine. The sun shifted across the sky, angling westward. Shadows slithered along the wash and along the crags. As one particular shadow edged along the top of a boulder rising along the ravine's eastern bank, it revealed something.

Jodi looked at the map in her hands, its corners ruffling in the dry breeze.

Her heart hiccupped as she slid her gaze from the rock drawn on the map to the actual boulder rising on the eastern bank. When she saw the ancient drawing painted on the boulder's upper right corner in ochre—a stick man on foot facing down some large, round, bear-like creature with a long lance—she had to purse her lips to hold back a scream.

A smile exploding across her face, she looked back at Miller who sat against the bank, his canteen beside him, one knee raised, running a wet handkerchief back and forth across his hatless head.

"I found it!" she hissed. "Bring the horses! I found it!"

The outlaw looked at her, his mouth open, his ginger-bearded, narrow-eyed face turned sunset red by the sun. "Huh?"

Jodi beckoned broadly. "Hurry, you damn fool—I found it!"

CHAPTER 17
THE STRANGER

Hawk pressed his back against the escarpment and set his boots a little farther than shoulder-width apart. He was in the shade here in this rocky corridor, but the air was still as hot as the hobbs of hell. As he heard footsteps approaching from the boulder's other side, he told himself it was about to get hotter.

He held Saradee's carbine barrel up in front of him. The Winchester was cocked, and his right index finger was curled against the trigger, ready.

The soft, crunching falls of moccasin-clad feet stopped. A sweat bead dribbled down from Hawk's right sideburn to his jawline. He frowned, squeezing the Winchester in his hands.

Why had the brave stopped?

Then he glimpsed movement in the corner of his right eye. He turned to see a dark head wrapped in red calico and a pair of black eyes staring at him from over the top of a boulder on the other side of the ravine down which the first brave had been coming. The first brave had apparently been warned to hold his ground by the one atop the boulder who just now slid his cheek against the neck of the Winchester he was aiming at the rogue lawman.

Hawk threw himself forward against another boulder as the Apache's Winchester coughed shrilly, smoke and red flames leaping from the barrel. The slug slammed into the rock against which Hawk had pressed his back a moment before.

Shards and rock dust flew.

Hawk raised his own carbine and fired at the Indian atop the rock, who was suddenly no longer there, and then he stepped out from the gap between boulders he'd been hunkered in. The Apache whose footsteps Hawk had been hearing was just around the corner. Hawk's sudden appearance caused the brave to snap his eyes wide and trigger the carbine he was aiming straight out from his left hip.

Hawk triggered his own rifle a quarter second later. The staccato blasts echoed shrilly together. The Chiricahua's bullet hammered the boulder flanking Hawk, maybe two inches off the rogue lawman's right hip, while Hawk's slug took the brave in the gut.

The brave leaped dramatically back, as though from a coiled snake, his carbine dangling in his left hand, barrel aimed at the ground. His molasses-colored eyes flashed at Hawk as he tried to reset his feet, but then Hawk shot him again, in the forehead.

The second bullet lifted the young, stocky brave with tattoos on the insides of his cherry-brown arms, straight up and back and threw him onto the ground that Hawk's slug had painted with the red and white contents of the young warrior's skull.

Instantly, Hawk wheeled toward the boulder atop which he'd seen the other brave. The rogue lawman's second spent cartridge wheeled over his right shoulder to clatter onto the ground behind him as he pumped a live round into the chamber.

He stared at the boulder, skidding his gaze from side to side and to the top. And then, not seeing his target, he ran across the narrow ravine and along the boulder's left side. He continued running straight out behind it, stopping suddenly and wheeling to his right, expecting to see the brave hunkered down behind the privy-sized chunk of black lava.

"Hawk!" It was Saradee's voice behind him.

Hawk wheeled as a pistol popped. Ten yards behind Hawk, the second brave lowered the Spencer repeater he'd been aiming at Hawk. The Chiricahua stumbled forward on the toes of his moccasins, the fire in his eyes dying fast. He dropped the Spencer as he twisted around to see Saradee aiming one of her silver-chased Colts, gray smoke curling from the barrel.

Movement behind Saradee.

"Down!" Hawk shouted.

The girl dropped like a fifty-pound sack of cracked corn as Hawk snapped his carbine to his shoulder. Hawk fired and watched the brave who'd been coming up behind the blonde, nocking an arrow to an ash bow, fire the fletched arrow into the ground at his feet and then twist around and stagger back in the opposite direction before dropping to his knees.

He gave a guttural cry as he tried to heave himself to his feet, but then he stumbled forward and fell belly down on the ground, quivering as the life left him. Saradee, also lying belly down, lifted her wide-eyed face toward Hawk, glanced behind at the brave who'd almost perforated her pretty hide with a razor-edged strap-iron arrow point.

She turned back toward Hawk and grinned.

Hawk walked back the way he'd just come, looking around carefully. He gazed up and down the ravine before crossing it and crouching down beside the first brave he'd shot. The brave was carrying a Winchester repeater outfitted with a leather lanyard trimmed with filled cartridge loops. Kicking the dead warrior over, Hawk also found that he carried a Schofield .44 behind a red cotton sash.

Hawk slung the brave's Winchester over his own right shoulder, and pulled the Schofield out of the sash. He tripped the latch and broke open the top-break pistol. All six chambers showed brass. Hawk snapped the revolver closed and snugged it into one of his two empty holsters—the one he wore in the cross-draw position on his left hip.

Saradee moved up behind him. He saw her shadow slide

along the red, rocky ground. She was looking around cautiously. Softly, she said, "Any more?"

"Hell if I know." Hawk held out the carbine he'd borrowed. "Here."

Saradee looked at her rifle and then at the one hanging from Hawk's shoulder as well as the Schofield in his holster. Her cheeks dimpled and she shook her blonde hair back from her face. "You're racking up."

"Now, I just need a horse."

They'd left the ancient shack Hawk had been healing in two days ago. They'd had to ride double on Saradee's palomino as Hawk continued his hunt for Pima Miller. The palomino was strong, but the heat and extra weight were taking its toll, slowing them down.

Hawk needed a horse. Even if it wasn't his own grulla. Any horse would do. Even a half-broken Chiricahua mustang that likely didn't care for the smell of white men.

Or anything else about white men . . .

Hawk and Saradee had spied the Indians milling along a ridge about an hour ago, around three in the hot afternoon. Sensing an ambush, Hawk had decided to bring the ambush to the Chiricahuas. True, he and Saradee were the interlopers here. The Apaches were only protecting what they believed to be theirs, a mountain of religious significance—their Thunder God's abode. But Hawk doubted they'd mind if he didn't sell his life cheaply.

A true Chiricahua would not flinch at a mortal challenge.

The next challenge for Hawk was to secure one of the warriors' horses.

He made sure his new carbine was fully loaded and then he looked around. He sensed that the Indians had come from the north, so he stepped out into the ravine and stared in that direction.

Spying no more imminent threats, he glanced at Saradee. "Fetch your horse."

"Whatever you say, lover."

"Stop callin' me that," Hawk said, angrily squeezing his new carbine's neck as he looked around at the weird pinnacles and glyphs of rock rising in all directions.

"Don't give me orders . . . *lover.*" Saradee looked around warily. "Are you sure Miller is worth all this? Maybe you should find another killer to kill. One who hasn't embedded himself so deep in *Apacheria.*"

The sun was hammering down on Hawk, who had lost his hat sometime before Miller and the Zimmerman girl had thrown him over his horse. Now he went back to the Apache, removed the strip of calico banding the young warrior's head, and wrapped it around his own.

As he tied the cloth in back, he said, "You can leave whenever you want. You never had to ride out here in the first place."

Hawk meant it. He didn't like having her around. Or was it that he liked having her around *too much*?

She smiled at him, reached up to adjust the calico bandanna on his forehead. She'd dimpled her pretty, suntanned cheeks again. A few strands of her hair, sun-bleached nearly white, blew against his cheek. He felt the raw pull of her deep in his loins.

Her infernal pull.

"Leave and miss out on all this fun?" Saradee shook her head. "Not a chance, lover. I'll fetch my horse."

She turned and strode away. Hawk couldn't help watching her go, admiring the sway of her full, firm hips and round ass strained against her light-blue denims. Her chaps slapped against her long, slender legs as she walked, silver spurs ringing lightly.

Her hair slid back and forth along her slender back, blowing out from her face in the hot, dry breeze.

Hawk turned away from her and continued walking along the ravine. He saw the light indentations that the Apaches' moccasins had made in the caliche. He followed them into an offshooting canyon and then into an open, sandy area. He stopped in a wedge of shade, and snapped up the Winchester.

Three horses milled in the chaparral to Hawk's left. Paint Indian ponies with simple hemp hackamores and colorful Apache blankets for saddles. He was glad to see the horses but what had him riveted was the white man staked back-down to a slight rise ahead and on Hawk's right.

Hawk looked around the man, making sure he wasn't walking into a trap. When he deemed himself alone, with only the staked man for company, Hawk moved forward. He stopped at the base of the slope to which the man had been staked.

The man was groaning and turning his head from side to side, squeezing his eyes shut against the sun. He stopped moving and his eyelids flickered as he tried to see through them.

"Someone there?" To Hawk, his Old World accent sounded German. His dark-brown beard, lightly threaded with gray, hung to the middle of his chest clad in a sweat-matted, salt-stained buckskin shirt. A hide tobacco pouch hung down his chest, half-concealed by his beard.

Hawk looked around carefully and then moved up the slope to stare down at the gent. The man squinted up at Hawk. He must have seen only Hawk's dark hair and the red bandanna, for he spat out, "Miserable savages! Kill me and get it over with!" Then he grunted out several angry words in the Chiricahua tongue.

Hawk said, "Easy. I'm not gonna kill you."

When he was relatively sure no more Indians were near, Hawk let his carbine hang down his back by the lanyard. He pulled his dagger from his right boot and cut the man's wrists free of the ironwood stakes they'd been lashed to with strips of muslin that had no doubt been looted from some white settler's ranch house or wagon.

When Hawk had freed both the man's wrists, he reached down to cut loose his ankles. "How many were there?" he asked, still looking around. The only sign of the Indians were the three contentedly grazing mustangs.

The man had sat up. He was eyeing Hawk suspiciously. He had dark-brown eyes set deep in dark sockets, and a lean, weathered face. "Five jumped me," he said in a deep voice, rubbing each wrist in turn. "Somehow the devils snuck up on me. Strange. I've done good, skinnin' clear of 'em."

He seemed deeply baffled by the attack, as though he were fairly confident in his ability to avoid the Apaches.

Hawk said, "That means there's two more around here somewhere."

The man shook his head as his second ankle came free of the stake. He wore high-topped, lace-up boots, his buckskin trousers stuffed into them. Both trouser knees were patched, the patches nearly worn through to his longhandles.

"They come runnin' through here a few minutes ago," the man, who Hawk assumed was a prospector, said, glancing off toward a relatively flat stretch of rocky, brush-speckled desert to the north. "Apaches don't like a fight unless it's a sure thing."

Hawk stared to the north. He used a hand to shade his eyes. He thought he could make out two figures bobbing in the hazy, brassy distance, heading toward a distant, copper-colored, shelving ridge.

Hawk looked at the prospector. The man was studying Hawk closely, his brown eyes still skeptical. Hawk extended his hand and tried a reassuring smile.

"Hawk," he said.

The prospector had an addled air. Hawk wasn't sure if it was

147

from the attack or if he was just naturally edgy, suspicious of strangers. Something told him it was the latter.

The man slowly closed his own hand around Hawk's. He was not wearing a glove, but it felt like he was. His palm was so thoroughly calloused that if felt like a glove liberally crusted with dried mud.

He did not give his name, merely nodded slightly, one eye twitching, and then looked away. He gained his feet heavily. He was tall and broad-shouldered, potbellied, bandy-legged. He brushed dust from his trousers, picked up a canvas hat lying nearby, set it on his head, and began tramping off to the north.

"Fetch my burros," he muttered just loudly enough for Hawk to hear. He hacked up phlegm, spat to one side, and kept walking.

Hawk stared after him. Saradee put her palomino up beside the rogue lawman and stared off toward the north, lifting a gloved hand to her hat brim, shading her eyes.

"Who's that?"

"Hell if I know," Hawk said.

CHAPTER 18
GOLD!

"I can't believe this," Miller heard himself mutter. "I can't . . . I can't believe this. I must be feverish . . . . *dreamin'*!"

On his knees, he used a hammer to chip at the scale-like lumps of gold in the mine's low ceiling. He closed his eyes and lowered his head as the gold and bits of quartz and dirt rained down on him. One chunk bounced off his hat. It smarted as it raked his forehead, but he didn't mind. In fact, he barely felt it.

Miller coughed against the dust wafting in the close, shadowy confines and looked down at the gold nugget about half the size of his fist glistening up at him in the wedge of daylight angling down from a ceiling crack farther down the hole.

The crack was just beyond where Jodi was working, filling her second set of saddlebags. She chuckled as she set down her hammer and buckled the pouch she'd just filled.

"Told ya, didn't I?" she jeered. "And you thought I was lyin'."

"I did," Miller admitted, chipping away at another nugget protruding from the ceiling above his head. "I did at that." He stopped hammering at the gold and grinned at the girl, winking. He felt so light that he thought it fully possible he might float like a feather on the wind.

Float over the earth, grinning.

"May I apologize, Miss Jodi?" the killer said. "May I do that? *Sincerely?*"

"No need to apologize," Jodi said, gaining her feet and trying to heft the saddlebags onto her shoulder. No doing. The bag was way too heavy. She'd have to drag it along the ground. "Just fill them pouches and meet me outside. We'd best head on out of here before the Dutchman pays his mine another visit."

"Pshaw!" Miller said. "Chances of him makin' another visit when we're here are slim to none."

"Just the same . . ." Jodi grunted as, crouching—the ceiling was too low for her to stand up straight—she started dragging her filled saddlebags up the slant of this secondary mine shaft. "We only have these three saddlebags . . . and three horses. No point in tarryin'."

"What a shame," Miller said. "What a damn shame we don't have one more horse. Or two horses. Two big mules. Think of that!"

"We already got enough gold here to see us through two or three lifetimes, killer. Keep your mind on that. I been all through this, dreamin' at night about drivin' a whole herd of mules up here, drive 'em out loaded with gold. But, then, shit—the Apaches would probably find me, run me down."

Jodi was grunting, breathless, as she dragged the bags up the secondary shaft to the main one, her silhouetted figure growing smaller and smaller against the light of the shaft's front entrance. "No point in gettin' greedy. We just gotta take what we can carry and get out before the Apaches or the Dutchman finds us here!"

"I ain't afraid of no Dutchman," Miller said, knocking another nugget free from the ceiling. "Ain't afraid of no Apaches, neither!"

The gold and quartz thumped onto the mineshaft floor. The floor, walls, and ceiling still showed the chips and gouges from Miguel Peralta's many peon miners who'd toiled in the mine about forty years ago. They'd exploited the main vein into the mountain, and then they must have started on the secondary shaft, near the main shaft's mouth, just before they'd heard the war drums and hightailed it.

Miller and Jodi didn't have torches so they'd penetrated the mine no farther than the light. There was plenty of gold right here for the taking, and not even hard taking at that!

So, the legend was real!

Peralta had really been here, mining the gold that Coronado had heard about. It had been Apaches who'd killed Peralta and his men when they'd fled down the mountains toward Mexico with a string of gold-laden burros.

As the burros had bolted from the gunfire and flying arrows, the gold had been scattered to the four winds.

"Plenty more where that came from," Miller said, chuckling as he worked.

"What's that?" Jodi called, crouching at the entrance about fifty yards up the shaft.

"Nothin'!" Miller said. "Just talkin' to myself! We rich men tend to that, don't ya know!"

He laughed hard at that, giddy.

Giddy.

Liable to sail off on the next low cloud . . .

"Meet ya outside!" Jodi yelled. "Don't linger. Just fill them bags and pull your picket pin!"

"Yeah, yeah," Miller said, stuffing several small chunks into a pouch of the saddlebags open near his knees on the shaft floor. "Now she's gettin' all bossy. Ain't that just the way, though?"

He chuckled some more. Jodi's bossiness didn't bother Pima Miller. Nothing bothered Miller and he doubted that anything ever would bother him again.

He chuckled at that, too, and tried to stuff another couple of small nuggets into the saddlebag pouch. He pushed and tucked and tried to break the nuggets into smaller pieces.

They just wouldn't fit.

He looked down at the nuggets in his right, gloved hand. What a shame. What a damned shame. Leaving good gold behind.

He tossed the gold chunks into the darkness farther down the shaft, heard them thump and clink as they struck the floor and rolled. That made him laugh, too. Tossing gold around as though they were mere rocks. Like he was a kid skipping stones on a quiet lake.

Hah!

Miller buckled the flap on the bulging pouch, gained his feet, and began dragging the bags on up the shaft. He groaned against the hitch in his side, where the rogue lawman had shot him. The stitches were pulling free. Miller had been feeling blood welling from the wound for the past several days.

As soon as he made it down to Tucson, he'd have to have a real sawbones stitch him up again. Now that he was rich, he couldn't take any chances on not living a good, long, full life! One hell of a rich life indeed!

Hell, he was richer than Horace Tabor! He was richer than Jay Gould and all them railroad barons back east!

Hah!

Miller dragged his saddlebags up the shaft. He had to crawl to make it easier on his side, since he couldn't stand up all the way.

By the time he'd gained the entrance, where the light momentarily blinded him and the heat blasted against him like the breath of an angry dragon, he gained his feet, slung the bags over his shoulder and made his way over to where Jodi was tightening her Morgan's saddle cinches.

One pair of bulging saddlebags hung behind her cantle. The other was on the rogue lawman's grulla.

Miller headed for Hawk's horse. It was eyeing him skeptically. The girl had fed each of the horses a pile of peeled barrel cactus, as up here at the entrance to the mine nothing grew but rocks and prickly pear.

Miller grinned at her. Even with the hundred pounds of gold on his back, he felt as light as a cottonwood leaf. "Girl, I might just let you please me extra fine tonight!"

Jodi looked at him askance. "I'd rather fuck Cochise, dead as that old Injun is."

Miller eased the saddlebags across Hawk's empty saddle and turned to her, sure he'd misunderstood or that she was just back to teasing him again. "Huh?"

"You heard me."

Jodi had tightened her cinches and now she turned toward the outlaw, leaned against the side of the black, and crossed her arms on her breasts. She looked Miller up and down, and curled a nostril. "First the old man tellin' me what to do and when to do it, and don't do that, girl, do this . . . and oh, no, you done it all wrong, girl! Makin' light of me and runnin' me ragged. Treatin' me like he treated his boots, only worse. At least I didn't have to fuck the son of a bitch. But you—you think you can have it just any old time you want it. You think you deserve it because I led you to this here mine—the Dutchman's mine— and now you're just feelin' like the cock o' the walk!"

The girl spat to one side, looked at Miller again, and wrinkled her other nostril.

Miller studied her, squinting against the bright sunlight up here at the top of a small, shelving mesa straight north of El Sombrero. "Hey, now . . . I was just funnin' you, girl. I was just feelin' good, and, you know . . . funnin'. No need to get a bur in your bonnet."

"I ain't wearin' a bonnet, you jackass."

"Hey, now, you listen here!" Miller said, feeling anger burn up through all the goodness and lightness he'd been feeling.

The girl reached behind her, filled her right hand with her pocket pistol. Miller had been moving toward her but now he stopped. His anger burned hotter, brighter.

"I was gonna wait till we got to Mexico, Pima," Jodi said, aiming the pistol at his belly. "I was gonna wait till we had the gold stashed somewhere secret, where we could fish it out whenever we needed more of it. It'd have been a whole lot easier to have help gettin' the gold across the border. But you won't make it. That wound done opened up on you. Opened up bad."

Miller glanced down at his side. She'd been right. He felt as though a sharp-toothed animal were gnawing away at the bullet hole. Blood stained his shirt. The stain was at least as large around as his open hand.

"You're losin' blood fast," Jodi said. "You'll just keep losin' it faster an' faster. And your slow dyin' would just slow me down. So I'm gonna end it right here, Pima."

The girl raised the pistol and clicked the hammer back. She smiled with one half of her mouth. "I'm gonna end our delightful partnership right here."

There was the *boing!* of a bowstring being released.

A soft whistling growing louder.

The thump of the arrow tearing into flesh and bone.

"Ughh!" the girl cried, lurching forward and triggering her pistol into the ground near her boots.

Dropping the gun, she twisted around and hooked an arm behind her back, which was suddenly bristling with a red-and-blue-fletched Chiricahua arrow sticking straight out from between her shoulder blades.

The afternoon before, after Hawk's and Saradee's own encounter with the Apaches, the rogue lawman managed to run down one of the Chiricahua's horses—a cream with cinnamon

speckles across its rump and down its hips—and he and Saradee headed on down a twisting, turning arroyo to make camp
a mile away from where the Chiricahuas lay moldering in the
desert heat.

Hawk hadn't seen the old prospector since the man had
wandered off in search of his burros. He figured the man had
gone his own way, but when the purple evening shadows were
stretching long and Hawk was perched on a rock at the lip of
the arroyo, on the scout for more attackers, his Apache carbine
resting across his thighs, he saw the lone figure moving toward
him along the wash.

Two pack-laden burros flanked the bearded desert rat.

Saradee sat atop another rock on the wash's far side. Between
her and Hawk, a low fire built from the near-smokeless branches
of the catclaw shrub snapped and crackled, a pot of coffee
gurgling as it warmed. She, too, watched as the man walked
slowly toward them, his crunching foot thuds and the clomps of
the burros rising gradually in the quiet desert gloaming.

"Company for dinner tonight," Saradee said in her wistful
tone. "Hope the maid polished the silver."

As the stranger approached, he paused, blinking owlishly as
he gazed at Hawk and Saradee. He glanced down at the fire
and then swung the burrows, which he led by a stout rope,
toward the horseshoe in the wash in which Hawk and Saradee
had tethered their horses, which were now eating mesquite
beans.

A large, bloody jackrabbit hung down one side of one of the
burros, the rope around the rabbit's neck tied to the pack frame.

The old man said softly, dully, "Meat for the fire."

He didn't say so, but Hawk knew it was an offering in return
for Hawk and Saradee's intrusion on the Chiricahua's festivi-
ties, which doubtless had been about to include their seeing

how loudly and for how long they could get the prospector to scream.

"That's funny," Hawk said, eyeing the bloody rabbit. "I didn't hear a shot."

As the desert rat began removing the pack frame from the back of his stockiest burro, Hawk saw the Apache war lance hanging from the frame, amid the bulging canvas panniers. The strap iron tip of the lance was still speckled with what appeared to be fresh blood.

Hawk gave a quiet chuff in recognition of the oldster's desert survival skills. Moving around out here as silently as possible was likely the reason he was still moving around at all.

When the prospector had finished unrigging and then carefully, thoroughly tending his burros, who snorted up the parched corn he'd mounded before them, he picked up an old Springfield rifle from among his gear. He walked shyly over to the fire, thumbing his hat back off his forehead and staring up at Saradee. The girl grinned at the old German, and climbed down off the boulder she'd been sitting on, one knee raised. She walked around the fire and stuck out her hand.

"I'm Saradee. Welcome to our fire!"

The old man looked at her hand. Apparently, he'd never shaken a female hand before. Haltingly, he lifted his own and gently squeezed Saradee's hand before running fingers through his grizzled beard and saying shyly, "You're right purty."

He'd said it so quietly that Hawk had barely heard him. The rogue lawman barely heard the oldster's low, sheepish chuckles as, steeling quick, frequent, admiring glances at the well-turned-out blonde before him, he dropped to his knees, slipped a knife from his belt sheath, and began deftly dressing the jack on a rock.

When the rabbit had finished roasting, they all ate hungrily around the fire that they kept low, so the glow couldn't be seen for more than a few yards beyond it. The prospector didn't have much to say. Like most desert rats not accustomed to being around others, he was odd. He glanced around at Hawk and Saradee with a vague, speculative suspicion, as though he were wondering what they were doing out here.

He also cast Saradee several lusty looks, his glance dropping to the girl's swollen hickory shirt. Saradee pretended not to notice but only grinned over her plate or her raised coffee cup at him.

"I had one like you," the prospector said as he broke a rabbit bone and then loudly sucked out the marrow.

"You mean you had a woman," Saradee said with a dubious arch of her brows.

"Yep. I had one." The prospector rolled his dark eyes toward the darkness beyond the fire. "They killed her." He sighed, tossed his bones into the fire. "Killed her bloody, the devils."

That was the extent of his conversation for the evening except for one more sentence, spoken when they'd cleaned up their eating utensils and Hawk was about to situate himself for taking the first night watch.

The old prospector had just reclined against the bed he'd made of several blankets and a burlap feed pouch. "No need to keep scout."

And then he tipped his hat brim down over his eyes.

Hawk glanced at Saradee, who shrugged a shoulder and then spread her own bedroll. Confident that the old-timer's senses were even keener than Hawk's own, and likely finely attuned to the smell of stalking Chiricahuas, Hawk rolled out an Indian blanket and drifted into a deep, dreamless sleep.

He awoke before dawn. It was the old-timer who'd awakened him. The man was outfitting his burros on the far side of the wash. When he had them rigged up, he simply walked away, leading the burros. His and the burros' footsteps dwindled gradually against the backdrop of a single, howling coyote.

Saradee was sitting up, leaning back on her elbows.

"What do you think about him?" she asked.

"I think I'm gonna follow him," Hawk said.

"How come?"

"Got a feelin' . . ."

Hawk flung his blanket aside, rose, and grabbed his rifle.

CHAPTER 19
IN THE DINOSAUR'S MOUTH

"I'll be damned," Hawk said the next day.

"What is it?"

On one knee atop a ragged-edged, red stone ridge, Hawk trained Saradee's spyglass through a notch overlooking a broad, red stone canyon with more red crags, like gothic church steeples, looming on the other side of it. Hawk and his blonde companion were at the heart of the Superstitions, among the towering peaks, plummeting canyons, and narrow, meandering washes littered with volcanic rubble.

This dramatic part of the range was a rocky waste composed of red rock striated like a giant turtle shell and liberally adorned with ancient petroglyphs. All that grew here were sparse bunches of Mormon tea, prickly pear, and ocotillo. Such ragged life had a tough fight, competing as it did with so much rock.

Mostly, the area was a beguilingly beautiful, three-dimensional statue of a dinosaur's mouth that seemed to have been carved from one massive chunk of volcanic ash and basalt and set down here in the heart of the Arizona desert. The cobalt blue of the sky arching over the awful formations gave it a mind-jarring depth.

"Don't see him," Hawk grunted, continuing to stare through the glass, sweeping the single sphere of magnified vision up and down the uneven floor of the canyon beyond and below him.

"We saw him turn into that canyon, lover. He's gotta be there, looking for his mine. If he really is the Dutchman, like you

159

think he is."

"He is," Hawk growled, stung by her having called him "lover" again. Every time she used the moniker, it was like razor-edged claws raking the back of his neck.

He collapsed the spyglass and then began moving carefully down the steep, stone-carpeted slope toward where Saradee sat her palomino, holding the rope reins of Hawk's appropriated Apache mustang. His Apache carbine hung down Hawk's back by its leather lanyard, and his Apache bandanna ruffled in the hot breeze, the dry edge of which burned his eyes and made him forever thirsty. He was fortunate it was the monsoon season, and water was plentiful in the natural tanks among the rocks.

He paused now beside one such tank—little more than a shallow, egg-shaped dimple eroded out of the mosaic-like stone slope, in the shade of a square basalt boulder. He cupped the tepid water to his mouth, sucking it up and feeling the freshness roll down his throat. When he'd slaked his thirst, he removed his bandanna, soaked it, wrung it out only a little, and wrapped it around his head once more.

The wet cloth was instantly refreshing, cooling.

Hawk's thoughts were on the bearded stranger. Hawk figured the man, the "Dutchman"—who else could he be?—was heading for his secret mine, taking a roundabout route due to the comings and goings of the small bands of Apaches that roamed this stony wilderness, protecting their Thunder God from interlopers.

If so, the Dutchman might very well lead Hawk to Pima Miller and Jodi Zimmerman.

As long as the girl had actually been heading for the mine herself, of course. It was entirely likely she'd only been spewing hot air about knowing where the mine was located. Hawk didn't doubt she was more than a little soft in her thinker box. She might have only imagined she'd discovered the Dutchman's famously secret mine.

But following the so-called Dutchman had been Hawk's only hope of catching up to Miller, for it was impossible to track anyone through such rocks as those that comprised the Superstitions. Of course, Hawk could have let the man go in hopes of catching up to him later, in less forbidding territory.

But it was more than likely that Miller would head for Mexico after this, and Hawk might never get the chance to finally give him the bullet he was due. The bullet that he'd inadvertently given to the man's woman, Nan-tee, leaving their infant son an orphan.

Killing Miller wouldn't make up for Hawk's deadly mistake, of course. But it would make him sit a little easier, if such a thing were possible.

No, he wouldn't let Miller go. He'd try everything he could to run him down as fast as he possibly could. He didn't have anywhere special to be. If he died here, hunting Miller, so be it.

Men had died for worse causes than killing a killer like Miller. One who'd left his own boy behind . . .

Hawk continued down the slope. He tossed the spyglass up to Saradee. She tossed his rope rein down to him, and he had to leap, Apache-like, onto the rope saddle, which sported no stirrups. He reined the horse around—it was a fiery mount, and he had to keep it on a short leash lest it throw him—and rode along the bottom of the canyon they'd been following all morning.

The canyon slanted upward and doglegged to the right. The horses' hooves clacked on the canyon floor's solid stone slab. The hot breeze wheezed among the towering peaks and ratcheted the branches of a near ocotillo.

Hawk turned the mustang around a mushroom-shaped scarp into the mouth of the canyon that he and Saradee had seen the Dutchman turn into about an hour ago. This was a narrow,

161

winding cavity that appeared to climb gradually toward little but the blue sky far beyond.

They rode for an hour, the sun hammering down on them, and then suddenly Hawk's horse stopped and tossed its head and rippled its withers.

"Hold on," Hawk said, tightening his hold on the horse's rope rein, squeezing his knees against the mustang's sides. Getting pitched here onto solid rock could mean death or at least a broken bone or two.

In the distance, a gun popped. Saradee's palomino jerked, sidestepped. There was another pop and then another until it became obvious that several guns were being triggered farther up the trail, which appeared to grow steeper not far ahead. The gunfire continued—sporadic but angry, spanging shots—and then Hawk could hear men yelling, as well.

The sounds were growing louder.

From up trail, the trouble was moving toward him and Saradee.

Both Hawk and the girl leaped down from their horses, tied the reins to some tough, brown shrubs growing between boulders, and ran up the trail. They stopped at the brow of the next steep rise. From here Hawk could see the canyon they'd been following twist around to the right and climb more steeply before disappearing in chunks of red basalt capping a razorback ridge.

Hawk swung the Apache carbine around to his front, and poked his finger through the trigger guard, his heart beating faster. He dropped to one knee, ran a hand across his mouth, and stared up to where the canyon trail climbed and disappeared in the crags.

He was thinking that the Dutchman had run into an Apache patrol.

"Hawk!"

He turned to his right. Saradee was standing and pointing toward where several dark, willowy figures clad in calico headbands were scrambling down from the giant, jutting rocks protruding straight up from the ridge. The Apaches were running down toward Hawk and Saradee.

Just then, one of the Apaches dropped to a knee, raised a carbine to his shoulder, and showed a flash of teeth in his brick-red face as he snapped off a shot, his rifle barking hollowly, the slug screeching off a boulder slightly upslope from Hawk and his blonde companion.

Hawk snapped up his own carbine and returned fire once, twice, three times, the rifle screeching and lurching in his hands.

"Free the horses!" he shouted, rising and snatching his mustang's reins from the shrub he'd tied them to. At the same time, Saradee did the same. They couldn't risk their horses being killed out here in this natural sarcophagus. Better to run them down later.

Neither mount needed encouragement. As the Apaches continued firing their repeaters while they ran down the slope, both mounts gave shrill whinnies and then scrambled around wildly and galloped back down the slick, rocky slope, their hooves slipping so that several times they both nearly fell.

Hawk ran up the slope toward the Apaches. He'd known from being in Apache country before, and encountering Apaches from several different bands, that there was no running from the warriors. They were like wildcats. You had to bring the battle to them, and you cut loose with as much ferocity as they did. It was your only chance.

Hawk just hoped that he and Saradee weren't so badly outnumbered that their efforts would be in vein.

Suddenly, Hawk wasn't so sorry to have Saradee at his side. She had no trouble, even facing Apaches, to bolt forward whooping and hollering, every few steps stopping, raising her own carbine, and triggering .44 rounds toward the little, savage men bolting toward her.

Hawk felt a grim smile shape itself on his lips as he ran around the left side of a cabin-sized boulder, hearing Saradee screeching and firing on the boulder's opposite side. The girl was too damned much like himself.

Gonna be a shame to kill her . . .

He paused in his own sprint toward the ridge to snap off another round. He watched one of the Apaches fold like a pocketknife and turn a forward somersault off the boulder he'd just fired from.

Hawk glanced to his right as Saradee triggered her own carbine. An Apache about thirty yards upslope from her gave a screech, dropped and rolled. He piled up about ten feet in front of the blonde, who gained her feet, strode purposefully toward the howling brave bleeding from the bullet wound in his bare chest, and calmly blew the top of his head off.

She glanced at Hawk, winked, and cast her gaze upslope as she ejected the spent shell casing and seated a fresh one in the chamber. Hawk moved forward, aiming his own carbine straight out from his right hip, sliding it from side to side. Two more figures ran leaping down from the ridge straight above him, and then he saw two more leaping down from above and left.

At the same time, the shooting on the other side of the ridge was growing louder, as though the separate shoot-out was moving toward him.

Rifles crackled above Hawk. He dropped behind a boulder as the bullets plunked into the rocks around him. He snaked his rifle over the top of the rock, aimed at a lean brave running low between rocks, making his gradual way toward Hawk's position.

Hawk fired, watched his bullet kick up rock dust upslope from the brave continuing to work down toward him. At the same time, he spied movement in the upper-left periphery of his vision.

Hawk ejected the spent shell casing and looked toward where the canyon trail disappeared among the boulders capping the ridge, above and to his left. A man and two horses were running down from the ridge along the canyon trail. The man was running fast but stopping now and then to trigger lead back in the direction from which he was fleeing.

Crouched behind his covering rock, the rogue lawman began sliding fresh cartridges from the loops on his leather lanyard through the loading gate on his carbine. Two loud blasts sounded from upslope, not far away. The slugs hammered the opposite side of his covering boulder, blowing rock shards up and over his head.

He edged a peek over the rock to see the raisin-like face of a middle-aged Apache aiming an old Spencer repeater at him from the notch between two abutting boulders, twenty yards upslope from him. Hawk ducked as the rifle lapped flames toward him. The bullet screeched through the air where his head had been and puffed dust in the trail at the canyon bottom.

A rare apprehension raked the rogue lawman. During his peek over the top of the rock he was crouched behind, he'd seen more than merely the old Apache bearing down on him. He'd seen at least three more braves dropping down from the rocks capping the ridge. They seemed to be angling toward him and Saradee from the left, as if they were breaking off from the separate fight over that way.

His blonde partner must have gotten the same idea.

"Hey, Hawk!" Saradee called. She was belly down behind a large scarp to Hawk's right, sort of angled toward him, her carbine in her hands. He could see her bright, white smile through her delighted grin beneath the brim of her hat. "I think we might be about to powwow with old Geronimo—what do you think of that, lover?"

She laughed and fired her carbine.

CHAPTER 20
POWWOWING WITH GERONIMO

Another rifle blast caused Hawk's covering rock to quiver. Shards flew.

Gritting his teeth, Hawk lifted his head and rifle above the rock, planted a bead on the raisin-like forehead of the middle-aged Apache bearing down on him, and fired.

The Apache's head jerked back and then the man's arms and rifle came up as he flopped back and down and out of sight. He hadn't hit the ground before Hawk was up and running, triggering his carbine from his hip as he wove between boulders. One, two, three Apaches hit the dust and then one retaliating slug tore across the rogue lawman's left shoulder. The peripheral pain was an icy burn.

He shot the Apache who'd caused the burn but another appeared between two cabin-sized slabs of rock and sailed a slug over Hawk's left shoulder. He tried to return fire but his Winchester's hammer pinged on an empty chamber.

He ran another step then dove behind a wagon-sized boulder and immediately started reloading his carbine. Something moved to his hard left. He dropped the half-loaded Winchester, slid the Schofield from his cross-draw holster and raised the pistol as he clicked the hammer back.

Hawk stayed the pressure on the Schofield's trigger. He blinked. Pima Miller was hunkered down behind a boulder only a few yards up the slope from Hawk's position. The outlaw was hastily reloading Hawk's Henry, casting quick, sharp, shrewd glances toward the rogue lawman.

Hawk's heart thudded.

Rage welled in him. It was about to explode like a barrel of coal oil, when something moved on the boulder above Miller. Instinctively, Hawk shot the Apache bearing down on Miller. The warrior gave a shrieking cry. His own momentum drove him on over the boulder, dropping his rifle and clamping his hand across the bullet hole below his breastbone just before he turned a somersault and hit the rocky ground beside the outlaw Hawk was hunting.

Miller glanced at the dead Apache, and grinned. "Thanks, Hawk! 'Preciate that!"

Then he twisted around, aiming Hawk's Henry repeater, and fired somewhere upslope beyond Hawk's position. Hawk clicked the Schofield's hammer back but before he could aim again at his adversary, he saw another Apache running along the slope beyond the outlaw.

The brave was bearing down on Miller who just then saw him and triggered an errant round.

Hawk's Schofield barked twice. The Apache jerked as he ran, dropped to his knees, his bow and arrow clattering beside him, blood welling from the two holes in his chest, and collapsed facedown. He rolled on down the slope to pile up against a boulder thirty yards away from Miller.

Miller smiled. Hawk's heart continued to thud against his ribs as he tightened his grip on the Schofield, boring a hole through Miller with his eyes.

"Behind you!" the outlaw cried.

Hawk twisted around and triggered his Schofield. His bullet sailed wide of the Apache storming toward him, but two shots sounded from downslope. The Apache grunted and bounded upslope and then rolled back down past Hawk.

Hawk looked over the writhing Apache at Saradee. She was

crouching behind a rock thirty yards away and on his right.

The Apache was trying to gain his feet while sliding a bowie knife from behind his deerskin sash. Hawk shot the brave through his right temple and then looked over the dead Indian toward Saradee, who, looking beyond Hawk, said, "I see you found one of your friends, lover!"

Hawk was only vaguely aware of clouds having moved over the sun as he turned back to Pima Miller, who was on his knees now and aiming Hawk's Henry repeater over the top of his rock. Miller was looking at Hawk over his right shoulder, grinning that faintly jeering grin of his.

"We're in this together, Hawk! You an' me now! Even your purty friend, if you trust her." The killer lifted his chin toward the ridge. "I left three saddlebags filled with gold over yonder. Couldn't get 'em off the mesa. Leastways, not with them redskins houndin' my heels. The girl's dead. Died hard!"

The Indians were still shooting but more sporadically. Saradee was returning fire with her carbine. Miller squeezed off a shot and then looked at Hawk again as he ejected the spent cartridge. It clattered onto the rocks and rolled as he slid another one into the Henry's breech.

"Hawk, for chrissakes—get your head down!" Saradee admonished him.

The rogue lawman ignored her. He was staring grimly at Miller, not bothering to keep his head down any longer. He had killing on his mind. There was nothing else.

Only killing Pima Miller. That was why he was here.

Hawk rose stiffly from behind his cover. He did not look up-slope. He was staring at Miller, who suddenly looked fearful. He laughed to try to cover it, but then his eyes grew dark, afraid.

"Hawk, fer chrissakes!" he shouted, glancing nervously up-slope from where suddenly no more rifles barked, as though Hawk suddenly rising from behind his rock had befuddled the

Indians to silence. "It's us against them, now, Hawk. We gotta put the past behind us. I left thousands of dollars in gold up yonder. Next mountain to the north! *Hundreds of thousands of dollars!*"

Behind Hawk, Saradee laughed. Hawk only vaguely heard her. He was on his feet now and he was moving toward Miller. He could feel the Apaches' eyes on him. He could feel their rifles trained on him.

He didn't care. Linda and Jubal were beckoning.

This was as good a day as any to join them. No one here deserved to live, anyway. Not Miller. Not Saradee.

Not himself.

He was tired.

He just kept seeing that poor Indian woman he'd killed with a bullet meant for Miller. He kept seeing that little brown baby that Miller had left behind. He kept seeing in the far, misty background Linda and Jubal waving and smiling and beckoning him home.

A chill wind rose. Hawk heard it howling among the crags. The red rocks around him had turned gray as death.

"Hawk!" Miller cried. "You stop right there, goddamnit, or I'll shoot ya with your own gun!"

Hawk wasn't aware that he'd moved so swiftly until he saw his right, moccasin-clad foot lift. Then the Henry was rising up and over the boulder Miller was crouched behind. It turned in the air and then dropped out of sight. Hawk heard it clatter onto the rocks.

Behind Hawk, Saradee was laughing hysterically.

"Miller, do you really think Gideon Hawk gives a shit about *money*?" she cried.

Silence except for the moaning wind now hovered over the slope. That and Saradee's bizarre laughter that Hawk could barely hear.

Miller stared up at the rogue lawman standing over him, staring down at him. Miller's lower jaw hung. His narrow eyes were dark, terrified.

"Why, you're plum crazy," he rasped.

And then suddenly Miller was dragging his pistol out of its holster but before he could get it even half raised, Hawk smashed the butt of his carbine against the dead center of the man's forehead. The blow snapped Miller's head back against the rock with a crunching thud.

It stunned the killer, who sat staring dumbly at Hawk's belly.

"That there was for the woman," Hawk grunted.

He rammed the butt of the carbine against Miller's head again.

Miller grunted.

Hawk said, "That there's for the boy."

Again, he rammed the gun against the outlaw's bloody forehead.

"That was for the sawbones in Spotted Horse."

He raised the rifle once more, gritting his teeth and narrowing his eyes.

"This one's for me."

And then he drove the butt against the killer's head one more time, harder than before. A resounding, crunching blow.

Miller's head bounced off the boulder. It jerked forward. The boulder behind him was red, speckled white with brain matter. Miller's shoulders followed his head over his knees, and then the killer rolled downslope three times before coming to rest on his back, his arms and legs akimbo.

His bashed-in forehead faced the sky. His lips were stretched back from his teeth in silent agony. His close-set, sightless eyes stared at nothing.

A horse nickered.

Hawk lifted his gaze from Miller. His grulla stood a ways

downslope, beyond Miller. The girl's Morgan was there, as well, idly cropping the sparse brush growing around the base of a rock.

Hawk's grulla stared at its rider, head down, nose working. It twitched its ears and whickered with quiet urgency.

Hawk smiled.

Thunder rumbled.

He turned toward the upslope. Ten or so Indians had formed a semicircle around him, about twenty yards away. They crouched cautiously over their cocked rifles, all of which were aimed at Hawk's chest and belly.

"Sorry, Hawk," Saradee said behind him. She was no longer laughing. "I done capped my last shell. I'm fresh out. I reckon this is it, you crazy bastard."

Hawk looked at the braves. Most were young and clad in green, red, or gray calico headbands. They wore breechclouts and moccasins. Some wore deerskin leggings, the tops turned down.

They stared at Hawk quietly, mouths open, disbelief in their chocolate eyes. Their long, blue-black hair blew in the chill wind.

Cold raindrops began spitting down from the gray sky that was tearing on the highest crags.

Not all of the Chiricahuas facing Hawk were young. One was older, maybe late fifties, early sixties. Short and stocky, bandy-legged, streaks of silver in his long hair, he stood atop a boulder upslope from the others. His face was the nut-brown of old, worn leather, the skin drawn taught over high, knobby cheek-bones. He wore a calico shirt and high-topped moccasins, a red sash around his lean waist.

A medicine pouch and a talisman of porcupine quills hung from his neck. His silver-black eyes were set deep in craggy sockets. He held a Spencer repeater down low by his side, the rifle's rear stock trimmed with brass rivets.

The wind swirled, carrying the older Chiricahua's distinct scent down toward Hawk. He smelled like the old, wild things of the desert.

The older Apache stared at Hawk. Hawk stared back at him. They stood silently regarding each other for nearly a minute.

And then Hawk turned his face a little to one side, quirked his lip corners with the respect due a formidable fellow warrior. And then he dropped his own carbine and held his arms out from his sides, palms raised slightly.

Opening himself to a life-ending hail of lead.

He waited.

The old warrior chief continued staring obliquely down at the rogue lawman.

Thunder crackled quietly at first—a long, ripping tear that grew louder and louder. When it finished echoing around the crags, the old man shouted something skyward, as though to his own Apache god.

And then all the young warriors turned and scrambled back up the slope. When they were out of sight, the old warrior dropped down off his boulder, glanced once more at Hawk, and then ambled in his lurching, crouching, bandy-legged gait up the slope. He held his carbine down low at his side, the lanyard swinging free.

The rocks at the top of the ridge seemed to swallow him up.

Thunder pealed.

Hawk lowered his arms. Rain lashed down at him. Still, he continued staring at where the old warrior had disappeared.

"Sorry, Hawk," Saradee said, coming up to stand beside him. They were both soaked, the rain hammering them.

Saradee patted the rogue lawman's chest. "Maybe some other time, lover. Come on," she said. "I'll buy ya a drink . . . somewhere warm. I know a place in Phoenix."

She slogged off down the rain-washed, rocky slope, thunder clapping, lightning dancing around her.

And still Gideon Hawk stared up the slope toward the misty crags. He squinted his eyes against the rain. He was looking for Linda and Jubal. He wanted to see them there, beckoning.

But they were gone.

Hawk dropped to his knees, sobbing.

The wind and rain lashed him.

Thunder was a giant war drum exploding in his head.

He didn't see the old Dutchman, Jacob Walzer, smiling down from his relatively sheltered hiding place among the crags not far from where Geronimo and his Chiricahuas had disappeared.

★ ★ ★ ★ ★

BLOOD AND LUST IN
OLD MEXICO

★ ★ ★ ★ ★

CHAPTER 1
RAINY NIGHT IN SONORA

The Rio Concho Kid sagged back in his rickety chair and listened to the soft desert rain drum on the cantina's tin roof while a lone coyote howled mournfully in the Forgotten Mountains to the south.

The Kid was pleasantly drunk on *bacanora,* a favorite drink of the border country. He smiled sweetly as he reflected on happier times, hopeful times when he and his reputation were still young and, if not innocent, at least naive.

Mercifully, just when his thoughts began to sour, touching as they did on the smiling visage of a fresh young Apache girl named Elina, who was so long dead that he could just barely remember the texture of her hair but no longer recall the timbre of her voice, hooves hammered the muddy trail outside the remote cantina's batwing doors.

For an instant, a single owl's cry, like a fleeting call of caution, drowned that of the coyote.

Over the doors, out in the dark, rainy night, a large shadow moved. The smell of wet horse and wet leather, as well as the faint fragrance of cherry blossoms, wafted in on the chill damp air.

Leather squawked and a horse chomped its bridle bit.

Boots thumped on the narrow wooden stoop, and then a shadow appeared and became a young, red-haired woman as she pushed through the batwings and stopped, letting the louver doors clatter back into place behind her. Hunted brown eyes quickly scanned the long, dark, earthen-floored cantina, finding its only customer, the Kid, lounging against the wall opposite the bar consisting of cottonwood planks laid across beer kegs.

The barman, Paco Alejandro Dominguez, was passed out in his chair behind the clay *bacanora* bowl, snoring softly, his thick gray hair tumbling down over his wizened, sun-blackened face. His leathery, hawk nose poked through the hair, nostrils expanding and contracting as he snored.

The girl glanced behind her, nervous as a doe that had just dropped a fawn, and then strode forward to the Kid's table.

She was a well-set-up girl, twenty at the oldest, her thick, wavy, rust-red hair falling down over her shoulders and onto her plaid wool shirt that she wore open to the top of her cleavage. Between her breasts, a small, silver crucifix winked in the salmon light of the mesquite fire crackling near the bar's far end and in front of which a kitten snoozed in a straw basket.

The girl wore black leather slacks held snug to her comely hips by a leather belt trimmed with hammered silver, five-pointed stars. Black boots with silver tips rose to her shapely calves. There were no spurs. This was a girl who could ride—she had the hips and the legs for it—but who had a soft spot for horses.

Her hair was damp, as was her shirt, which clung to her full bosom, and her eyes were just wild enough to make the Kid's trigger finger ache.

"Buy a girl a drink?" she said quickly in a thick Spanish accent.

The Kid looked her over one more time, from the tips of her boots up past her breasts pushing out from behind the damp wool shirt, to her eyes that flicked back and forth across him with a faint desperation. The Kid smiled, shook his head. His dark eyes looked away from the young girl, no more than a child.

She slammed her fist on the table. *"Bastardo!"*

"I ain't gonna contest it," the Kid said mildly and casually lifted his gourd cup to sip his *bacanora.*

She lifted her mouth corners, leaned forward against the table, giving him a better look down her shirt, and said in a smoky, sexy rasp: "I could make you a very happy *hombre* tonight, *amigo.*"

The Kid looked at her well-filled shirt. A few years ago, when he was as green as a willow sapling, such a sight would have grabbed him by the throat and not let go for several hours. "And a dead one. Oh, true, there's worse things than dyin', but I'm enjoyin' this evenin' here with the rain and my drink and the prospect of a long sleep in a deep mound of straw out in the stable with my mare, Antonia. Run along, *chiquita.* Spread your happiness to someone who needs it more than I do tonight."

The Kid reached into the breast pocket of his buckskin shirt for his tobacco makings, but stopped suddenly and pricked his ears. Hooves drummed in the distance, beneath the patter of the rain on the tin roof and the cracking and popping of the pinyon fire in the mud-brick hearth.

The girl wheeled toward the batwings with a gasp.

The hoof thuds grew quickly louder. The girl's horse whinnied. One of the newcomers' horses whinnied a response. Over the batwings, large shadows moved, and then boots thudded on the porch and a big man in a wagon-wheel sombrero pushed through the batwings.

Two men flanked him, turning their heads this way and that to see around him, into the cantina.

"No, Chacin," the girl said in a brittle voice, backing away from the door, brushing the tips of her fingers across the Kid's table. "I won't . . . I won't go with you. I'd rather *die!*"

All this had been in Spanish, but the Kid, who'd been born Johnny Navarro in the Chisos Mountains of southern Texas, near the Rio Grande, though he'd acquired his nickname while riding the long coulees along the Rio Concho, knew the rough and twisted border tongue as well as he knew English.

The big man, dressed in the flashy gear of the Mexican *vaquero,* complete with a billowy green silk neckerchief, moved heavily into the room, bunching his thick, mustache-mantled lips in fury. His chocolate eyes fired golden javelins of rage as water dripped from the brim of his black-felt wagon-wheel sombrero.

"*Chiquita,* my orders are to bring you back to the General! You're lucky you didn't kill him—at least not yet!"

Suddenly, moving with more agility than the Kid would have thought possible in a man so ungainly, he swiped one of his big paws at the girl and caught her shirt just as she'd turned to run. The shirt tore with a shrill ripping sound, buttons popping, exposing a good portion of her pale left breast behind her partially torn chamise.

She screamed, *"No!"*

The big man reached for the silver-plated Colt Navy conversion pistol holstered high on his right hip.

"Oh, now, dangit," the Kid said with an air of great despondency, rising heavily from his table and brushing his right hand across the Smith & Wesson Model 3 Schofield revolver holstered high and for the cross draw on his left, denim-clad hip, "that ain't no way to treat a lady, an' you *know* it!"

CHAPTER 2
THE RIO CONCHO KID RIDES

The big Mexican must not have heard the Kid's indictment, for he slid his long-barreled Colt from its holster and was thumbing the hammer back when the Kid's own revolver roared like close thunder, causing the earthen floor to jump and the ceiling to buffet.

"Ah, Mariett-ahhhh!" the barman cried, lurching straight up out of his chair, still half asleep.

Dust sifted from between the herringbone pattern of cottonwood and mesquite branches to the floor.

The big Mexican, Chacin, squealed pig-like and fell back against a table, clutching the hole in the dead center of his chest. The hole was pumping blood like a geysering spring. He got his boots beneath him, held himself upright though listing badly to his left, regarding the Kid with shock and fury blazing like lamps in his dark eyes.

The girl backed away from him, covering her mouth with both her gloved hands. Chacin squeezed his eyes closed and fell with a heavy thump to the earthen floor, and lay with one leg quivering as he finished dying.

"Dios!" exclaimed the barman, Paco Alejandro Dominguez, crossing himself as he looked over the bar to the big man on the floor.

The Kid clicked his Schofield's hammer back and aimed at the two men who'd entered with Chacin. They both stood in crouches, hands on their holstered weapons, staring at the Kid

181

apprehensively. One of them was slowly inching his walnut-gripped Remington up out of its black-leather holster thonged low on his right thigh. His hand was shaking.

He stared at the Kid's gun. Smoke slithered like a little gray worm from the round, dark maw.

Chacin's men looked at each other, wide-eyed. Then, keeping their hands on their holstered weapons but keeping the weapons in their holsters, they shuffled backward through the batwings to fade away in the dark, wet night.

"Kid!" said Dominguez, his rheumy eyes round with fear. He jutted a gnarled finger at the big, dead Mexican on the floor. In Spanish, he said, "That is Chacin Velasco, General Constantin San Gabriel's right-hand man!"

The Kid turned to the girl who was still staring down at the dead man, both hands closed over her mouth. She turned to him slowly, lowering her hands. She said in a voice the Kid could barely hear above the pattering rain, "*Muchas gracias, senor.* It is unfortunate that I cannot give you my life, which I owe you for saving, because I am afraid I have just cost you yours."

Boots thumped on the porch. The Kid turned toward the front of the cantina once again, just as Chacin's two men, apparently realizing that they themselves were dead men unless they killed the man who'd killed Chacin, came bursting through the batwings like Brahma bulls through a loading chute.

Their gloved hands were filled with iron.

The Kid's Schofield thundered twice, sending both men bounding back through the doors, triggering their pistols into the cantina floor, and into the cool, wet night. They dropped with heavy smacking thuds, causing the horses to whinny and nicker and pull against their reins.

The Kid turned to the girl who stood smiling at him. The smile irritated him nearly as much as his having to kill three men just now when he was merely wanting to drink himself drunk and then to stagger out to Dominguez's stable and to sleep long and hard, old Antonia's somnolent breaths lulling him into peaceful dreams.

"What the hell is this about, *senorita?*"

She still had that nettling smile on her face. Her eyes were dreamy. "It's about love," she said. "What else is there?"

The Kid scratched the back of his head with his gun barrel. He was beginning to think she was soft in her thinker box. "Huh?"

"Love is a powerful thing. There will be more men where these men came from," she said, sobering and glancing at Chacin who lay still now in death. "I apologize, but it is true. If you help me to safety, you will be well rewarded."

Her eyes were smoky, insinuating, vaguely desperate, and she thrust her shoulders back slightly, impulsively, like a girl who knew exactly how desirable she was and used it to her best advantage.

The Kid looked at Dominguez. The old barkeep arched a brow at him.

"Get your horse," the Kid told the girl, breaking the "top-break" Schofield open to reload. "I'll fetch mine from the barn and meet you on the trail."

When he'd replaced the revolver's spent cartridges, he dropped it into its holster, snapped the keeper thong over the hammer, and walked toward the cantina's back door, casting incredulous glances at the beautiful girl behind him. He went out into the misty darkness laced with the smell of pinyon smoke and wet sage. He went into the adobe stable flanking the cantina—it was little more than an ancient, brush-roofed ruin—and found old Antonia snoring softly in her stable by a pile of aromatic hay.

A moody sorrel with gray spots sprayed across her hindquarters and a white star between her copper eyes, Antonia blew and stomped, cranky about being saddled so late, and in this weather, to boot! And the Kid said, "Know just how you feel, girl."

When he'd stuffed his old-model Winchester down into his elk hide saddleboot trimmed with Chiricahua beads, he mounted up and rode out, Antonia's hooves clomping dully on the wet ground. The girl sat her horse, a rangy Appaloosa, near some rocks and brush along the trail. The Kid saw her outline against the stars that were trying to break through the thin clouds that rolled across the sky like ink-stained tufts of gauze.

"Come on." He said it quietly, but the moody night was so strangely silent that it sounded like a yell. "I know a place."

CHAPTER 3
LA PISTOLA SAYS IT BEST

A long, keening wail rose on the night's damp wind, ensconcing all of *Hacienda del la General Constantin San Gabriel* in wretched torment and poignant misery.

Around the *hacienda*'s walled grounds, the peons prayed in their tiny, thatch-roofed hovels while babies cried, dogs howled, goats brayed, and pinyon logs snapped in fieldstone hearths, the gray smoke ribboning like halfhearted prayers up sooty chimneys.

Inside the sprawling, cavern-like, tile-roofed adobe casa, the General himself lay moaning in blood-soaked sheets. He groaned as he chomped down on a swatch of leather cut from a boot as his gray-bearded, one-eyed attendant, Juan Mendoza, stitched the nasty knife wound in his side.

Kneeling in a dark corner near a crackling stove, *Padre* Vicente, cloaked in ragged shadows, muttered over his prayer beads while a fat black cat washed its face on a window ledge beside him.

"That bitch! That bitch!" the General moaned. "I demand her beautiful, conniving head on a platter!"

The priest's muttering grew louder as he clutched his silver crucifix in both hands before him, occasionally pressing his lips to it.

"*Si, si,*" said Juan Mendoza, pinching up the skin around the ragged, bloody wound. "Chacin will bring her kicking and screaming, General. She will get her comeuppance for what she did to you. Imagine such an insult . . . on your wedding night, no less!"

Mendoza squinted his lone eye, poked the fire-blackened point of his needle through the pinched skin, and drew the catgut taut.

The General threw his bearded head back on his pillow and bellowed at the herringbone rafters.

"The worst of it is," he cried, "I *loved* that red-haired bitch!"

When Mendoza had finished stitching the wound and was dabbing at it with arnica, hoof thuds rose beyond the window. Horses splashed through puddles and blew and shook their bridle bits.

"Chacin!" the General hissed, lifting his head from the pillow and staring out the arched window. His eyes glowed with emotion as he stared into the night. He rose still higher and yelled in his weak, pain-pinched voice, "Chacin—report to me! Did you bring her?"

Outside, there was only the clomping and snorting of the horses beyond the wall of the General's wet garden.

"Chacin!"

General San Gabriel flung his covers away and dropped his pale feet to the cold flagstone floor.

"General!" admonished Juan Mendoza, placing a hand on the General's shoulder. "You must rest!"

The General brushed the man's hand away and heaved himself up off the bed, gritting his teeth against the searing pain in his side, where that bitch stuck the knife in just when he'd disrobed her fine body and was going to reward her with his own . . .

He stood, his broad torso bare, and grabbed his fleece-lined, red velvet robe off a chair back. The General was a tall, regal man with an impeccably trimmed mustache and goatee, hawk nose, and close-set, flinty eyes—the hard, shrewd eyes of a veteran of the bloody Mexican-American War and many, even bloodier battles against the hated Apache and Yaqui Indios.

For all of his sixty-two years, the General's coal-black hair and beard owned not a single strand of gray. His body was straight and, in spite of a slight paunch, as hard and sinewy-strong as that of an old warhorse.

With Mendoza and *Padre* Vicente hovering nervously around him, voicing their objections, the General drew the robe around his lean hips, and stepped into a pair of wool-lined doeskin sandals. He grabbed a Navy Colt conversion .36 off a low table beside his favorite, brocaded chair, quickly checked the loads, and dropped the brass-framed piece into a deep pocket of his robe.

He walked, cursing under his breath, through an arched door that gave access to his garden that was impeccably cultivated by the peons who'd come with the land he'd been granted by the government in Mexico—thirty-thousand acres of prime grazing land as payment for his near-lifelong service in the Mexican army.

His slippers clacked and scuffed against the flags as, holding one hand to the freshly stitched wound, he shuffled across the dripping garden and through an opening in the six-foot-high adobe wall into the soggy, muddy yard bordered by the *hacienda*'s several barns, the bunkhouse, and many pole corrals.

Lights from the peasants' shacks shone down the southern hill in the wooly darkness. A fine mist continued to fall, though several stars winked dully through the clouds.

Several riders sat their horses in front of the bunkhouse on the far side of the broad dirt yard from the General—part of the posse he'd sent after his bride. The riders were speaking in conspiratorial tones to four other *vaqueros* who stood smoking on the bunkhouse's brush-roofed gallery, the bunkhouse door open behind them and showing the flickering orange light of a fire.

Breeze-brushed, rain-beaded lanterns hanging beneath the gallery roof tilted shadows to and fro.

"Chacin!" the General bellowed, mindless of a pecan branch dribbling cold raindrops on his head and down his back. Mendoza and *Padre* Vicente stood in the opening in the wall behind him, cowering against the rain and hissing their disapproval of their *patrõn*'s impetuousness.

The three riders whipped their sombrero-mantled heads toward the General. They glanced at each other dubiously and then, with a reluctant air, galloped over and stopped their horses in the hock-high mud before the *patrõn*. Chacin Velasco was not among them.

Frowning, the General looked around. "Where is Chacin? Where is the girl? Where is my *wife*?"

"General, Lieutenant Velasco is dead!" intoned the *vaquero* known as Rubio something-or-other, his eyes concealed by the broad brim of his flat-crowned straw sombrero. "Him and two others were gunned down by a man as fast as God's angry fist from heaven!"

As if to punctuate the man's testimony, his horse whinnied and tried to buck, but the rider kept the wild-eyed barb on a tight rein.

General San Gabriel glowered at the man, his pain-addled brain slow to comprehend the information. Lieutenant Chacin Velasco, his most loyal officer . . . *dead*? It couldn't be. Chacin was not only proficient and quick with a gun, but he'd been the fiercest fighter the General had ever known. And he'd known a few!

Chacin had killed more Apaches than even the General himself!

"Nonsense," the General said though the shocked, apprehensive stares of the men before him tempered his resolve. "You must be mistaken. Who could kill Chacin? Surely not that little bitch who stabbed me when my defenses were down!"

Rubio and the man sitting the horse next to him both turned to the third rider, who said, "The Rio Concho Kid!"

"Who?"

The third rider repeated himself. And then in a few hastily spewed sentences, he filled his boss in on the rest of what had happened at Dominguez's cantina barely two hours ago. He and his two partners had ridden up to the cantina, where they were to rendezvous with Chacin, only to find Chacin and the two other *vaqueros* dead as tombstones.

Paco Alejandro Dominguez had informed them about who had done the killing only as an admonishment to let the man go. To go after such a man they'd need an army!

General San Gabriel stared up at the riders before him, silently fuming. "And you three listened to that old reprobate and did *nothing* but turn tail and *run*?"

"*Jefe*, you may not have heard of the Rio Concho Kid." The stocky man sitting in the middle of the small group shook his head slowly, darkly. "He is very deadly. He was just back from the War Between the States when he killed thirteen soldiers— *American soldiers!*—and desecrated their bodies in the most horrible way imaginable. Very deadly, boss. The Rio Concho Kid. It is said that wherever he rides a demon follows in the form of a ghost-faced owl. This winged demon looks after the Kid."

"An *owl?*"

"*Si, si!* The Apache bird of grace and deliverance. You see, the Kid avenged the murders of his Apache brothers and sisters—he is half Apache himself though he more resembles his Anglo father—and, once they were avenged, the spirits of the dead sent the owl to follow and protect him until the Kid, too, enters the world of the spirits."

"The Rio Concho Kid," said the General, eyes sharp with fury. "Owls! Spirits! *Apaches!* Let me tell you what I think of you three, riding off and leaving Chacin's body to molder in that fetid cantina . . . *unavenged!*"

"No, General!" Rubio shouted as the old warrior pulled the Colt Navy out of his robe pocket and raised it, clicking the hammer back.

Rubio raised both his hands in front of his face a half second before the General's roaring Colt blew a hole through Rubio's right hand and into his right cheek, just beneath his eye.

Pow! Pow!

The other two riders flew off the backs of their horses to hit the ground with wet thuds. All three horses wheeled, whinnying shrilly, and ran off across the yard, buck-kicking wildly.

The General walked over to the stocky *vaquero* who was still writhing and groaning. "But why waste words when *la pistola* says it best?"

He aimed the smoking Colt down at a slant and triggered a finishing round into the *vaquero*'s broad forehead.

Behind the General, Mendoza stood hang-jawed in shock.

Padre Vicente sobbed, clutching his crucifix to his breast and staring toward the stars as though praying that God had not witnessed this atrocity.

Presently, hooves thudded.

The General turned his attention from the dead men sprawled before him toward another rider, this one with his face bizarrely masked in white, riding into the yard from the north.

190

CHAPTER 4
SATAN RIDES TO US THIS EVENING, AMIGOS!

The Rio Concho Kid brought his mare to a halt beside a jutting escarpment near the brow of a night-capped ridge. Leaning forward in his saddle, the Kid looked up at the top of the hill where an old Spanish mission church hulked, pale in the rain-scoured starlight.

An orange light flashed in the church's bell tower, over the black square of the broad open doorway. The Kid jerked his head back as the bullet hammered the front of the escarpment, inches from his face, the ricochet's shriek nearly drowning the rifle's flat report.

Behind the Kid, the girl gasped.

The Kid raised his own rifle and sent three rounds screeching toward the bell tower and the shadow crouching inside. The rifle in the bell tower flashed again, but this time the orange flame lapped toward the ground.

As the Kid pulled his rifle down while pumping a fresh round into the chamber, he watched as the shadow in the bell tower slumped. The bushwhacker screamed a Spanish epithet, and then he fell forward out of the bell tower, his black silhouette turning a somersault against the cream tan of the adobe church.

There was a resounding thud and a splash as he struck a mud puddle. The lookout's rifle clattered to the muddy ground beside him.

Harsh voices rose from inside the church as did the metallic rasps of five or six rifles being cocked.

The Kid leaned forward in his saddle once more, clamping his rifle under one arm, raising both hands to his mouth, and shouting in Spanish, "Flee, you dogs. The Rio Concho Kid's come calling. He aims to take up residence here this evening, and he's not in the mood for company!"

A man's girlish shriek echoed inside the church. Boots clomped. Spurs rang.

A man shouted, *"Satanas cabalgo con nosotros esta noche, amigos!"*

A shrill Spanish curse.

More boot clomping and spur ringing. A few minutes later, while the Kid waited back behind the escarpment with the girl, hoof thuds rose from behind the church. They dwindled away to silence.

"All right," the Kid said, touching spurs to old Antonia's flanks and riding out from behind the scarp and onto the ridge.

The man he'd shot lay sprawled a few feet from the front of the block-like adobe church squaring its shoulders against the starry sky from which the storm clouds had disappeared. The damp air was cool and fresh, smelling like wild rose and cactus blossoms and brimstone.

"You sure know how to clear out a place." The girl stopped her horse suddenly. The Kid halted his own mount, turned toward her.

It was hard to see her face in the darkness, but he thought she was appraising him dubiously. Her long, red hair fluttered in a vagrant breeze.

"The Rio Concho Kid . . . ," she whispered.

Just then something gray flickered off to her left. She gasped as she turned her head and saw a ghost-faced owl wing past her. Its eyes glowed like umber coals in the darkness. The small, dove-gray bird gave its raucous, unsettling cry, which echoed harshly off the front of the church, before lighting on the front ledge of the bell tower and lifting a wing to preen.

The girl shuddered as she stared up at the sinister creature. "They say you're protected by Apache devils," the girl muttered. Her voice was thin, rife with caution.

"Guided, more like," the Kid said. "Not even an owl can protect me from some of the trouble I manage to court."

He swung down from his saddle and began leading Antonia to the front door. "Come on, if you've a mind. I told you I knew a place to shelter for the night, and this is it. If you don't like it . . . or the company . . . you're free to drift."

The Kid led Antonia into the church, pleased to see that the desperadoes had left a crackling fire near the front of the church, where an altar had once stood though it had long-since crumbled to jutting shards. What looked like a rabbit was spitted over the low flames.

The Kid had nearly finished unsaddling Antonia before slow clomps sounded, and he turned to see the girl leading her impressive Appaloosa through the large open doorway.

CHAPTER 5
TOMASINA DE LA CRUZ

The Kid walked back into the church after a thorough scout of the ridge, after both horses had been unsaddled and he'd made the girl comfortable by the fire. The blaze's warmth was welcome on such a damp and chilly evening.

She sat beside the fire, knees raised, a blanket over her shoulders. She was leaning forward and clutching the toes of her low-heeled, silver-tipped black boots. On the soles of each a red turtle had been stitched in red.

Her eyes were chocolate brown sprayed with flecks the same color as her hair, which, threaded with faint crimson highlights, hung straight down across her shoulders.

The Kid stopped before her, his rifle on his shoulder, and thumbed his brown Stetson back off his forehead. She looked up at him coyly, bouncing back and forth nervously on her rump while clutching her boot toes—an alluringly girlish gesture, thought the Kid.

But then everything about her—the smoothness of her skin, the fullness of her lips, the depth of her gaze, the sunset red of her hair—was strangely, almost uncomfortably alluring. Even her brandy-like smell, which he'd noticed on the trail, was intoxicating.

She glanced at a tin plate on which lay the lightly charred rabbit that the desperadoes had been roasting over the fire. Only a quarter of the carcass was missing. A cup of black coffee sat next to it, smoking.

"I left most of it for you, *senor*," she said softly.

The Kid leaned his rifle against the wall and sat down near his saddle. He doffed his hat and gloves, scrubbed his hands through his close-cropped, coal-black hair, brushed a buckskin-clad sleeve across his broad, weathered forehead, and then set the plate on his knee.

He tore the rabbit in two, and glanced at the girl, who watched him steadily, expectantly, as though waiting for him to break out in song.

"The Rio Concho Kid," she said, making him uncomfortable again with her close, dubious scrutiny. "I did not know when I walked into *Senor* Dominguez's cantina that I would find such a man as you there."

"Just my luck." The Kid pushed a chunk of the rabbit into his mouth.

"I should have known that only the Rio Concho Kid could have killed Chacin Velasco so swiftly, without flinching."

She seemed to wait for the Kid's response, which did not come.

"How many men have you . . . ?" She let her voice trail off, her eyes brightening with trepidation, realizing that she might have crossed a dangerous boundary. "If you don't mind me asking, *senor.*"

"Enough that I can clear a church of the devil's hounds right fast," the Kid said, taking another bite of the rabbit. "You gonna tell me who you are and who you're runnin' from and why, or you intend on keepin' it under your hat?"

He continued to eat, and when the girl said nothing, he glanced at her. She was staring up into the darkness beyond the fire's umber, cinder-stitched glow. "The owl?" she said.

"Ah, don't mind him," said the Kid. "He comes, he goes. Tumbleweed, that one. Sorta like me an' ole Antonia. But, unlike me, he's somehow managed to keep a price off his head.

Now, if you don't mind explainin' why I'm not still pleasantly drunk and half asleep at Dominguez's place, and who I should be watchin' out for . . ."

"I am Tomasina De La Cruz," she said in her quiet, mysterious voice that was as captivating as the rest of her. "And I am on the run, as you say, from General Constantin San Gabriel."

The Kid choked on a bite of rabbit, and scowled across at her. "How in the hell—if you'll pardon my privy talk, *senorita*—did you manage to lock horns with *that* fork-tailed Apache-killer?"

Tomasina De La Cruz jerked a look at him, her eyes feisty. "I did not want to lock horns with him! I did not want to lock anything with him!" A chinking appeared in her armor as her voice trembled, and a shiny veil dropped down over her eyes. "It was my father who did. He wanted me to marry that dirty old man!"

"Why?"

She turned away from the Kid once more and raised her knees higher, wrapping her arms around them, as though for protection against some unseen beast in the darkness. "It was the arrangement. You see, my father owns a *hacienda* on the other side of a mountain pass from the General, who came to the country of the Rio San Gezo only a few years ago. Having been in the military most of his life, he never married."

"And then he met you." The Kid knew how the General must have felt. The girl had a definite pull. The Kid felt it himself. A pull like only one other he'd ever felt.

"*Si*, he met me when my father invited him to *La Colina de Rosa*, on the opposite side of the Forgotten Mountains from the General's *hacienda*. He told me later he fell in love with me the first time he laid eyes on me." Tomasina shivered with revulsion.

"I take it the feeling wasn't shared." The Kid had been rolling a quirley with chopped Mexican tobacco and brown wheat paper. Now he reached for a brand in the fire, touched it to the quirley, sucked the peppery smoke deep into his lungs, and blew it out through his nostrils.

"No," she said, shaking her head slowly. "No, no . . ."

"And the General is not a man to take no for an answer."

"*Si.*"

She nodded gravely and then turned to the Kid again. "*La Colina de Rosa* has fallen on hard times. Our side of the mountains is in a drought. For the past three years, all the clouds pass over us and continue on over the mountains to drop their snow and rain on the General's *hacienda*. His creeks run deep with water, his grass grows stirrup-high. His cattle are fat and happy!"

Tomasina spat this last out like a bone as she kept her angry, wet gaze on the Kid. "My father and mother thought it best I marry the General, who could better provide for me. No one cared that I loved another!"

This last she fairly screamed. The scream rocketed around inside the church for too long, and the Kid winced and cast his gaze toward the open doorway, worried someone might have heard.

"*Senorita,* I know you're upset, but—"

She cut him off with "The marriage was arranged despite my protestations, *senor.*"

"Despite the fact you were in love with another."

"*Si*—Ernesto Alabando." She whispered the name, stretching her mouth to show all her small, pretty white teeth in an adoring smile. Slowly, her jaws drew taut, and she pressed her lips together until they formed a knife slash across the bottom half of her face.

Again, she turned her blazing eyes on the Kid.

"I tried to run away to Ernesto. The General, however, is a

197

jealous man, and a suspicious one, as well. He had ordered a man, a gun-toting leper—a bounty hunter—to keep a watchful on *La Colina de Rosa* . . . and me. When the leper foiled my attempt at escape, the General demanded we be married straightaway. After the ceremony at *La Colina,* he took me to his *rancho.* That night, after a grand but quiet meal—just the two of us and his servants—he ushered me off to his sleeping quarters, and disrobed me."

Tomasina De La Cruz clutched herself and shuddered as though deeply chilled.

"The thought of lying with this wheezing, warty, lusty old dog who had made me so unhappy, so lonely for Ernesto, *my one true love*—he so incensed me, you see, that before I knew what I was doing, I had grabbed one of the General's own fancy stilettos and stuck it in his guts!"

She cried for some time into her hands, her shoulders jerking, burnished copper hair falling down over her raised knees to hide her face.

"Pardon me, *senorita,*" the Kid said after what he thought was a discreet length of silence. "But . . . did you say *the Leper?*"

CHAPTER 6
A PLEA AND AN OFFER

Tomasina De La Cruz lifted her head, sniffed, brush tears from her cheeks, and nodded. *"Si. El Leproso."* She turned to him. "You know this man—this hideous creature?"

The Kid tossed his quirley stub into the fire. "Yeah. I know him."

The image of the man's misshapen face cloaked by a flour sack with the eyes and mouth cut out, caused icy fingers of dread to walk up and down his spine.

The girl crawled over to the Kid, knelt beside him, and placed both her hands on his right forearm. Her eyes were large as saucers, rife with beseeching. "Then you know what an awful man he is. A beast."

"A beast, all right," the Kid said, nodding, looking down at the girl's slender hands on his arm. "And damn handy with that shotgun of his." It was a sawed-off, double-barreled coach gun that the Leper, a Mexican bounty hunter, kept loaded with rock salt, because most of the higher-paying bounties were for men brought in with their ghosts intact.

The salt would make a mess of a man, but, if delivered to the right areas, it rarely killed, although its victims often wished they were dead.

"Por favor, senor," the girl said, squeezing his arm. "Will you help me? It is most likely that the General will send *El Leproso* for me, as he did once before."

"Help you do what, *senorita*? Help you *get where*?"

199

"To San Gezo. A two-day ride, only."

"What's in San Gezo?"

"Ernesto," she whispered, stretching her lips back away from her small, white teeth again. "My life's one true love. He will take me away to somewhere the General and *El Leproso* will never find us!"

The Kid looked down at her hands again. They burned into him, evoked a passion he'd rarely felt in his twenty-eight years. He lifted his gaze to her eyes. They were like a deer's eyes, wide with earnest pleading and boundless love, gazing up at him from beneath her brows.

Her rich, red lips were parted. Behind her shirt, her breasts rose and fell slowly, heavily.

Ernesto was one lucky boy!

The Kid tore his arm from her grip, and turned away, repelled by his own passion evoked by this girl's love for her beau. Of course the General had tumbled for this girl. What man wouldn't?

Lucky Ernesto!

The Kid stared at the church wall left of the fire. It danced and pulsated with reflected firelight. But it was the Kid's own shameful lust he saw there in that crenellated, flame-lit wall.

This girl was a succubus. She had him in her snare.

But she loved another.

He jerked with a start when he felt her arms wrap around him from behind. He watched one arm snake across the other one, over his belly. She pressed her body against his back. It was warm, supple, yielding. He could feel her breasts mash into him.

They, too, were warm, compliant.

Frowning, he turned, placed his hands on her naked shoulders. Her head came up with the rich mass of copper hair. Her eyes bored into his. He lowered his own gaze, and a hot shaft of desire was plunged into his loins.

She'd taken off her shirt. She sat before him with her lovely, pale breasts bared to him, the pink nipples like tender rosebuds.

"I told you back in the cantina, Kid," she said softly, in that gut-wrenchingly sexy voice of hers, the tip of her pink tongue flicking at her lips as she spoke, "that if you helped me I would make you a very happy man. Well, maybe not happy. I know what happened to you, Kid. Everyone has heard about . . . your family . . . your woman . . . the soldiers. All the death, all the killing. The bounty on your head back north of the border. But at least let me reward you for your efforts tonight, as promised."

As he stared at her, rapt, she smiled gently and placed her hands on his. She lifted his hands, cupped them to her breasts.

She whispered very softly, "I have never lain with another. Not even Ernesto. Not yet. I guess that was partly my appeal for the General."

The Kid's tongue lay heavy in his mouth. "And . . . you would . . . lay . . . ?"

She smiled that surreal smile of hers. "You are a good man. Ernesto wouldn't mind. I will by lying with him soon."

Her soft, smooth skin fairly burned in the Kid's palms. The pink nipples raked him gently. He'd just started to roll his thumbs across the tender buds when the owl's ear-rattling shriek rose, echoing like large stones rattling around in a barrel plunging down a steep, rocky hill.

The Kid looked past the girl toward a rear door, and shouted, "Tomasina, *down!*"

He shoved the bare-breasted girl away to his right. At the same time there was a bright flash and a thunderous roar.

As the Kid reached for his holstered Schofield .44, he grimaced against the tooth-gnashing sting of the rock salt tearing into him.

CHAPTER 7
EL LEPROSO

The Kid groaned as he used his right hand to raise the Schofield. He looked toward the rear door to see the shadowy figure in high black boots, long gray duster, gray mask, and a low-crowned, black sombrero trimmed with silver stitching take one long step toward him, shifting the sawed-off shotgun in his hands slightly.

The Kid sucked back the pain of the salt wounds in his chest, shoulder, and neck, and cut loose with the Schofield, which leaped and roared in his hand. The bounty hunter known as the Leper jerked back slightly. The shotgun issued another blast of deafening thunder, flames jutting from the second barrel.

One of the Kid's slugs had hit its mark, however, and most of the rock salt hurled from the Leper's second barrel sprayed the fire, scattering ashes and half-burned branches. The Leper got his boots under him and dashed behind a large stone pillar on his right, about ten feet from the door.

The Kid's slugs chewed into the pillar, pluming rock dust and shards. When the Schofield's hammer clicked on an empty chamber, the Kid holstered it, grabbed his rifle from where he'd leaned it against the wall, and quickly jacked a fresh round into the breech.

He ran toward the half-naked girl lying on the floor near the fire and saw the Leper edge his shotgun out around one side of the pillar. The Kid fired the Winchester, jacked and fired two more times as he dove onto the girl, keeping her down and

202

shielding her tender skin from a possible rock-salt blast.

The Kid lifted his head in time to see the Leper run out from behind the pillar toward the open door—a black-and-gray blur, the silver on the man's black sombrero flashing like starlight.

A jeering laugh rose like a scream.

The Kid's Winchester belched three more times, spitting orange flames and hot lead toward the bounty hunter. The Leper was too quick, however. The Kid's shots merely hammered the church walls around the door as the killer bounded out into the darkness from which he'd come, laughing.

"Stay here!" the Kid told the girl, and, as the horses pitched and whinnied shrilly near the front of the church, he ran for the back door, punching cartridges through his Winchester's loading gate.

He bounded out the back door and stopped ten feet out from the church, aiming his Winchester from his right hip and whipping his gaze around, expecting a gun flash or the flicking of the Leper's jostling shadow.

Nothing.

Then a laugh sounded in the distance directly out from the church. The Kid wheeled to face it, saw the pale shapes of tombstones stretching away in the starry darkness, with here and there the large shadow of a shrine or an ancient crypt.

Out among those hunched figures, a gun flashed. A pistol popped. The bullet screeched past the Kid's left ear and spanged shrilly off the rear wall of the church behind him.

The Kid ran ahead and left and dove behind a near tombstone as the pistol flashed twice more, one slug tearing up gravel just inches behind the Kid's left boot. The other barked into the face of the stone behind which the Kid crouched.

The Kid shifted his rifle to his left hand—he'd become accustomed to shooting well with either—and edged his left eye and his Winchester around the gravestone's left side. He couldn't be sure in the darkness, but he thought a pale figure moved among the stones beyond him, about forty yards straight out from the church's back door.

Ka-chooo! Ka-chooo! Ka-choo—Ka-chooo!

The Winchester's reports echoed loudly off the church and caused the horses inside to whinny again shrilly.

The Leper's infuriating, mocking laugh rose again, this time from the Kid's right and maybe a little farther out from where the bounty hunter's gun had flashed.

"Kid, it's been a while!" he yelled in Spanish. "This works out well for me, *amigo.* I can bag two heads on one ride—yours and the girl's! *Amigo,* the General wants her *bad!*"

"Over my dead body!"

"That is very much my intention, my friend."

"He must want her alive," the Kid yelled, staring around the right side of his covering gravestone now, desperately trying to pick the bounty hunter out of the darkness. "Thus the rock salt!"

Despite the burning, bleeding wounds in his chest and shoulder, the Kid knew he'd been lucky so far. Usually, *El Leproso* didn't make such careless missteps as that which he'd made inside the church. The man's judgment had no doubt been clouded by Tomasina's heartrending beauty.

The Kid had no idea who the bounty hunter was behind that mask—if man he was and not a demon, as was surmised by the superstitious peons of northern Sonora. The Kid only knew that the bounty hunter known as *El Leproso* was as cold-blooded a killer as you'd likely ever find this side of the Sierra Madre.

And the man had been on the Kid's trail ever since the Kid had wreaked holy vengeance on the American cavalry soldiers who'd killed his Chiricahua Apache family and the Apache girl he'd intended to marry, and a two-thousand dollar bounty had been put on his head by President Grant himself—the very man the Kid had fought so nobly for in the Great Rebellion.

El Leproso called from the darkness: "The General wants his beloved very much alive, Kid! You see, he wants to give her to his men for a few magical nights in their bunkhouse and then watch them shoot her down like a hydrophobic dog in front of his garden wall!"

The Kid aimed at the place from which the man's voice had come. The Winchester roared four times quickly, the slugs squealing through the darkness, screaming off rocks and ancient shrines.

The Kid hunkered down behind the marker, listening, waiting.

Silence closed over him, louder than before. His heartbeat quickened hopefully. Had one of his slugs taken down the bounty hunter?

As if in response to his silent query, a laugh rose—shrill and far away but as mocking as before.

"We'll meet again, soon, Kid!" called the Leper. "Please tell the girl she is most beautiful, even more lovely disrobed. But she must die just the same!"

Howling laughter.

Presently, hooves thudded. They dwindled quickly as *El Leproso* rode off in the night, and silence like a dark ocean tide washed in behind him.

A shadow flickered over the Kid's head. He jerked with a start, started to raise the Winchester. But it was only the ghost-faced owl lighting on a tombstone a few feet away—a small, gray apparition in the darkness, about the size of a dove.

The owl turned its pale face to him. Its small eyes glowed as though from a fire within.

"You might've warned me a little earlier in there," the Kid grouched, canting his head toward the church.

The owl gave a sharp cry and flew away.

"Same to you," the Kid said.

CHAPTER 8
TAINTED WATER

Pancho Montoya stood on the brush-roofed gallery fronting his remote stage relay station, near the door he'd propped open with a rock to let some of the stove heat out. He'd finished serving menudo and tortillas to the small batch of passengers who'd just pulled in on the stage, and now the stocky, apron-clad station manager was about to enjoy a cigar.

To that end, Pancho started to scratch a lucifer to life on the clay *ojo* hanging from the rafters to his right, but stopped when something caught his eye. He scowled off across the desert directly east of the station.

The wicked desert wind had been blowing all day, kicking up sand and grit and tossing tumbleweeds this way and that. So it was difficult for Pancho Montoya to see who was approaching the station, the horse and its rider slowly taking shape amid the jostling veils of windblown sand.

Odd for a man to be riding in from that direction—across the desert as the hawk flies, where there were no trails except a few ancient Indio trails but mostly only *banditos,* renegade Yaqui, and rattlesnakes. Why not take the relatively well-maintained stage road that swept into the station from the north and continued on beyond it to the southwest?

But, then, earlier that day, two others had come from that same direction . . .

Holding his stove match in one hand in front of his chest, his cigar in the other hand, Montoya scowled into the barren, wind-whipped desert at the oncoming rider. Gradually, the station manager was able to see that the horse was a fine, coal-black Arabian. Its rider was a tall man in a gray duster that flapped in the ceaseless wind. He wore a thick lanyard across his chest, and the barrel of a rifle or shotgun jutted up from behind his right shoulder. He batted tall black boots against the horses' sides as he held the sleek mount at a steady lope. Moving as one, they swam up out of the storm like a murky mirage.

The stranger was a pale man wearing a bullet-crowned black sombrero, which was thonged tightly beneath the rider's chin to keep it from blowing off his head in this maddening wind.

No, thought Montoya. Not a pale-faced man.

A man wearing a mask. Because of the wind, of course.

But then another thought occurred to Montoya as horse and rider continued to ride through the buffeting veils of blowing sand. As he continued to stare, riveted, at the gray-masked rider who was now within seventy yards and closing quickly, a dark apprehension nibbled at the edges of Montoya's consciousness.

The station manager crossed himself with the unlit cigar.

"*Mierda*," he whispered. "*Santos, por favor perdõname.*" Saints, please spare me.

Montoya heard the horse's dull thuds as it entered the yard, its tall, masked rider checking it down to a trot. The stranger passed the stagecoach sitting before the station house, tongue drooping, awaiting the storm's end and a fresh team. He reined to a halt before Montoya, who winced at the knot of pulsating nerves at the back of his neck, hard as an oak knot.

"*Senor* Montoya," said *El Leproso* as he swung down from his silver-horned Spanish saddle complete with a garish, three-point breastplate, each of the points being a hammered silver Spanish medallion. The Leper wrapped his reins over the hitch rack and looked up at Montoya, his dark eyes hard to read through the dusty flour-sack mask. "We meet again."

The eyes were red-rimmed. One sat slightly lower than the other, and, as Montoya had noted before, the left one tended to wander slightly. The Leper's lips were also red. Thick and red and oddly, irregularly shaped. And they smiled, showing the grimy, yellow teeth behind them.

The knot at the back of Montoya's neck grew tauter, but he suppressed a shudder of revulsion and turned his wince into a smile. "*El Leproso*, welcome!"

The Leper slipped his horse's fancy silver bit from its teeth, so it could draw water from the stock trough fronting the hitch rack, and then came up the gallery steps. He was a tall, lean man, and Montoya had to tilt his head back to look up at him.

The bounty hunter still wore that wet, red smile as he said, "Don't shit an old shitter, Pancho. Just tell me how long it's been since that half-breed and that redheaded girl passed through here."

Montoya's knees turned to putty. He stammered.

The Leper stared at him, canted his head one way and then the other, waiting. Montoya looked at the two pistols holstered on the bounty hunter's hips, behind the duster, and the shotgun jutting up from behind his right shoulder.

He'd heard it was loaded with rock salt.

"You're gonna tell me now, or you're gonna tell me later," the Leper said softly, the burlap mask buffeting against his nose as he breathed, his flat, walleyed stare as menacing a thing as Montoya had ever seen. "But you're gonna tell me."

"Two hours."

"Headed where?"

"I thought I heard the girl mention San Gezo."

The bounty hunter frowned behind his mask. Then he nodded and his thick, misshapen lips shaped another grin. "I see," he said wistfully.

He turned to the clay *ojo* hanging from the rafters, beside

Montoya. As he plucked the gourd dipper from the water pot and scooped up some water, he glanced at the station manager once more. "I don't care that you're not all that happy to see me, Pancho. I'm so damn happy to see you again, after all these months, *mi amigo,* that it makes up for the tenderness you so sorely lack with regards to my pretty ol' self."

Montoya wasn't sure what the bounty hunter had just said, and he didn't think it mattered. So much of what the killer said was mere nonsense that probably came from a man riding alone so much for most of his life. The station manager had heard that the man he knew only as *El Leproso* had contracted his hideous disease long ago, when he was very young.

For some reason, possibly because of some demon's curse on humanity, it hadn't yet killed him.

What Montoya was most concerned about now, however, was the precious water that the man had dippered up from the *ojo* and was holding about six inches from his disfigured face with its red lips rimed with dust.

El Leproso stared at Montoya as though reading the disgust in his mind. The bounty hunter swung the dipper out slightly, water sloshing onto the gallery's scarred wooden floor at his boots, and said, "Drink?"

Montoya smiled tensely and shook his head.

"You don't mind if I take a little, do you?"

Montoya looked down, the smile painted on his face, and shook his head though his guts writhed like snakes until he thought he would gag.

"Gracias, amigo."

The Leper drank loudly, slurping the water up through the hole in his mask, sounding like a dog. When he was through with one dipperful of the water, he scooped up some more and continued to drink loudly until he'd had his fill.

Then he dropped the dipper back down in the pot with a

splash, and wiped his mouth with his dirty duster sleeve. He hitched his double cartridge belts and two black holsters on his hips. Each ornately tooled sheath contained a silver-chased, pearl-gripped Navy Colt .44. He adjusted his sombrero's chin thong as he dropped down the gallery steps and plucked his reins from the hitch rail.

When he'd swung up into the saddle, he pinched his dusty hat brim to the station manager.

"Till next time, Montoya . . . when I can stay longer and enjoy more of your delicious water."

He swung the sleek black Arabian around and rode away.

Hoof thuds died beneath the sighing wind.

Montoya turned his head slowly to the *ojo,* and grimaced.

CHAPTER 9
SHADOWS IN THE WIND

Atop a wind-battered ridge, the Rio Concho Kid stared through his brass-chased spyglass.

A ragged shadow moved out on the darkling plain.

Thunder rumbled. The Kid glanced at the sky. A vast, arrow-shaped cloud mass nearly as dark as night but with its belly laced with thin wisps of cottony white was edging toward him from the southwest, the same direction the wind was from. Again, thunder rumbled, causing the gravelly ground to vibrate. From the same direction, a vast shadow was sweeping across the land.

The Kid directed the spyglass once more to the northeast.

The gray shadow remained, flickering between curtains of windblown sand. The Kid lowered the spyglass, felt his jaws tighten.

That's right, El Leproso. You keep comin'. I'd like nothin' better than to scour your ugly visage from my back trail once and for all!

How many years now, off and on, had the Leper been after him? Four? It felt like ten. He'd seen the man only a few times, mostly up north of the border.

The Kid glanced at the girl sitting a ways down the ridge behind him, the lower half of her face covered with a checked bandanna against the blowing dust. Her hair blew out behind her shoulders.

The air had cooled, and she wore a fringed elk-skin jacket, which, she said when she'd unwrapped it from her bedroll and donned it earlier, had belonged to her lover, Ernesto Alabando, a wandering *vaquero* who had ridden for a time for her father, before there were no longer any cattle to tend at *La Colina de Rosa.*

She yelled from behind her neckerchief and above the wind, "San Gezo is just over the next pass!"

"Still a half day's ride." The Kid shook his head. "We'll never make it before it rains and turns these arroyos to rivers!"

He looked down the ridge past Tomasina and their ground-reined horses to the abandoned goat herder's shack in the crease between this ridge and the next. "We'll spend the night here, finish our journey in the morning." He offered a wan smile. "Don't worry, *senorita,* you'll be with your beau again soon."

She smiled with her eyes, crawled up to him, and rested her hand against his cheek. She held his gaze for a time, and again he felt the heat of the girl penetrating every cell in his body. At the same time, a dark cloud swept through him, for he knew that all the pent-up passion inside her was reserved for Ernesto Alabando.

She would do anything, even lie with another, compromise her purity, to see her lover again.

She lowered her hand from the Kid's face.

"He's out there, isn't he?" she asked, letting her gaze flick toward the eastern plain. *"El Leproso."*

"Yes."

"Will we be safe here?"

"As safe here as anywhere."

Thunder boomed violently, and the rain began to fall at a slant—heavy raindrops the size of silver dollars.

She smiled again, confidently. "You have a plan, don't you?"

He grinned devilishly. "Of course, I do, Tomasina." He

climbed to his feet and took her hand. "Come on. Let's get inside before we have to swim for it!"

Hours later, when the rain had dwindled to a steady cadence on the stone shack's leaky brush roof, the Kid turned from where he'd been cleaning his guns at the stout wooden table.

He looked at Tomasina where she lay on the cot near the scorched stone fireplace. A fire danced and popped and smoked against the raindrops tumbling into it through the chimney. It cast a gentle glow upon the girl's right cheek and shone in the highlights in her hair.

She was even more beautiful in repose than she was awake. Asleep, she looked like a child. A sweet and tender, copper-haired, rose-lipped virginal child, eyelids pale as a dove's wings.

And then it wasn't Tomasina whom he was gazing at but his own life's one true love, the beautiful Apache princess Elina, whom he'd met when he'd returned to Arizona Territory after the war.

After rising to the rank of first lieutenant and witnessing so much killing, Johnny Navarro had yearned for the healing that he thought he could find only with his mother's people, the Chiricahua Apache, though his mother herself had died several years before from pneumonia. His father, Wayne Navarro, had been a rancher from the Great Bend country of Texas, and he'd disowned the Kid when the Kid had joined the Union army to fight against the Confederacy.

"Elina," the Kid whispered, reaching out to close his hand over the sleeping girl's shoulder. "Elina . . ."

She'd been killed by a drunken cavalry patrol—her and the rest of her small band, the People of the Ghost-faced Owl, when they'd been camped just north of the border in New Mexico Territory, in their traditional hunting grounds. The patrol had assumed they were the Apaches who'd been harassing the freight road between Lordsburg and Las Cruces, and they'd slipped into the canyon one night, set up their Gatling gun, and killed Elina and her entire band, while they'd slept in their wickiups.

The Kid had gone to Las Cruces with two braves for supplies. When they'd returned and the Kid saw the results of the massacre, he went as mad as a bruin fighting his way through a wildfire.

When the heavy clouds of insanity had parted, he'd stalked and killed every soldier in the patrol, some with the Gatling gun they'd used on the people who'd adopted him. He'd hacked out their eyes and cut out their hearts with his bowie knife, so that in the next world they would have no eyes to see with, no hearts to pump their blood with.

He'd left the killers' hearts and eyes for the coyotes and bobcats to fight over.

The ghosts of the killers would linger forever in the nether world, blind and hollow as scarecrows, wailing their eternal regrets for what they'd done to Johnny Navarro's people and Elina, his life's one true love . . .

And for two years following, he'd killed every soldier and lawman who came after him. Now it was mostly bounty hunters dogging his trail. He'd culled the herd until he was down now to the most dangerous stalkers—men like *El Leproso* . . .

His hand must have tightened on the girl's shoulder. She groaned, opened her eyes, turned to him. Her gaze shifted to something behind him. Her lower jaw sagged, and then the owl gave its raucous scream.

Chapter 10
Trickery by Starlight

The Rio Concho Kid swung around, his gun in his hand, clicking the Schofield's hammer back. The owl sitting on the ledge of the window behind him merely blinked its little eyes that reflected the crimson flames of the fire dancing in the hearth.

The Kid lifted the revolver's barrel, depressing the hammer.

"Does he follow you everywhere?" the girl asked.

"Pretty much."

The Kid rose and walked over to the table where his freshly cleaned and loaded Winchester lay.

Tomasina flung her blanket back and sat up, dropping her long legs over the edge of the cot. She was staring at the strange gray owl staring back at her from the window ledge.

"He's saying something . . . with his eyes. What?"

"He's telling me I need to keep my head clear. A real pain in the old caboose sometimes."

The Kid donned his hat and walked to the door.

"Is he out there?" Tomasina asked, her voice quavering slightly.

"That's what I'm gonna find out." He placed his hand on the leather-and-steel latch. "You stay here, keep your head down."

"Kid?"

He looked at her. She leaned forward, arms on her knees. "What was her name?"

He hesitated, turned to the door, felt a knot grow in his

throat. "Elina," he said, and then opened the door and went out.

He took a moment to draw a deep breath, to suppress the clinging, gnawing grief and sorrow, the frustration of knowing that his life should have turned out so much differently from all this killing, all this lone wandering and running. He and Elina should be together. They should have a child, maybe another on the way.

They should have a small *rancho* along the Rio Concho, so many good years ahead . . .

He looked carefully around the old goat herder's shack, finding no boot prints but his own and the girl's in the clay mud. After he investigated the old lean-to stable and found both horses calm and undisturbed, he walked up the east ridge and hunkered down at the top.

About two hundred yards out on the dark eastern plain, a pinprick of yellow light danced in the velvety darkness. The Kid removed his spyglass from the pocket of his doeskin jacket, and, lying on his belly, propped on his elbows, he stared through the glass, adjusting the focus.

That he was staring at *El Leproso*'s camp and small cook fire there was little doubt. The man himself sat under a lean-to canopy, which he'd likely hastily erected for shelter against the storm. From this distance, even through the spyglass the Kid couldn't see much, but he made out a long shadow stretched out beside the flickering fire, leaning back against what appeared to be a saddle.

The shadow was capped with a black sombrero. Beneath the sombrero was the gray splotch of the bounty hunter's mask. As the Kid studied the camp, he watched the slender shadow of *El Leproso* rise, throw a stick on the flames and then pour a cup of coffee before sitting back down against his saddle and leisurely crossing his legs.

The Kid stared through the glass. His heartbeat quickened.

El Leproso . . .

The old hunter took his time. He had patience. The Kid would give him that.

"What do you say we finish this, my old friend?" the Kid said under his breath, feeling his pulse throb in his temples. "Right now. Tonight."

He collapsed the telescope and returned it to his pocket. Rising, he picked up his Winchester, backed down the ridge a few yards and then turned and made his way along the slope toward the north.

He walked slowly and quietly, as he'd learned on his boyhood hunts with his Apache cousins along the Rio Bravo and the Rio Concho, which had given the Kid his nickname after he'd killed two US marshals along that tributary of the Rio Grande two years ago, when the lawmen had tried to arrest him and, failing that, tried to shoot him.

When he'd walked about six hundred feet north, he turned and headed east.

The Leper's fire flickered ahead and on his right though the Kid often lost sight of it, for he kept his head low, wending his way through pockets of wet brush and boulders, a flooded arroyo gurgling on his left.

He paused for a breather between two large boulders. The owl's winged shadow fluttered over him, whistling softly through the chill, damp air, and lighted on a mesquite. The owl stared at its charge with its superior air, its umber eyes pulsating softly.

Annoyed, the Kid whispered, "Don't you have some pocket mice to hunt?"

The owl continued to stare at him obliquely.

The Kid sighed and continued walking, angling now almost directly toward the fire flickering ahead about fifty yards away but growing gradually larger as the Kid closed on it.

When he was forty yards from the fire, he hunkered down behind a boulder, and crouched there, still as stone, all his senses attuned. He did not look at the fire, for the light would compromise his night vision. He peered into the darkness around it, watching for movement, listening for sounds.

There was only the faint sighing of the wet earth and dripping plants, the yodeling of a distant coyote and the slight rasping of a burrowing creature somewhere off to the Kid's left— probably a kangaroo rat rebuilding its nest after the storm.

Very faintly he could hear the snapping of the Leper's fire. His keen nose did not tell him where the Leper's horse was tied, and that caused a fingernail of caution to rake the small of his back.

Usually, on a night as still as this, he could smell a horse from fifty yards away.

He could smell the fire and the coffee and beans that had been cooked over it, but not the horse.

The Kid squeezed the neck of his Winchester. He'd already levered a cartridge into the chamber. Now, pressing his tongue against his lower lip, he very slowly and quietly raked the hammer back with his right, gloved thumb. He sat with his back to the boulder between him and the fire.

Now he doffed his hat and turned his head to peer with his right eye around the side of the boulder. He could see only the low column of flames dancing beneath the tarpaulin erected atop two mesquite poles. The bounty hunter was likely on the other side of it, as he'd been before.

This was not a fair fight between honorable combatants. This was kill or be killed. The Kid would shoot *El Leproso* through the fire without warning.

He leaned hard to his right and gritted his teeth as he snaked the rifle along the right side of the boulder and pressed his cheek to the stock. He steadied the weapon and stared down the barrel, half closing one eye and mentally slowing his heartbeat and leeching every scrap of nervousness from his hands.

Now he could see the area beneath the tarpaulin clearly.

He blinked. His heart thudded.

Beyond the fire lay vacant ground.

His heart thudded again as the Kid rose slowly to his feet, continuing to aim over the Winchester's cocked hammer and down the barrel . . . at nothing but sand and gravel.

The saddle that *El Leproso* had been reclining against was gone.

His coffeepot and all the rest of his gear were gone.

No wonder the Kid hadn't smelled the man's horse.

He'd pulled out.

In the night's hushed silence, a girl's distant scream vaulted toward the stars.

Somewhere behind the Kid, the owl added its own bitter wail to that of the girl's.

To Tomasina's . . .

The Kid lowered the Winchester and ran.

Chapter 11
San Gezo

The Kid reined Antonia to a halt atop a hill and stared down the other side into the village of San Gezo.

It was a small collection of peasant shacks and stock pens circling a big, brown church. The church and its customary cemetery were the centerpiece of the village's central plaza, where a stone fountain stood, surrounded by craggy poplars.

The pale hills that surrounded the village were stippled with green, for the recent rains had nourished the local foliage. But it was not the foliage the Kid was interested in.

Since the first wash of dawn, he'd been following the tracks of a single shod horse. They'd led him here to the outskirts of San Gezo. The Kid knew why *El Leproso* hadn't killed Tomasina when he'd outfoxed the Kid the night before, and circled around and nabbed her.

The General wanted her alive, to torture and kill her himself, or to watch his men kill her.

He likely wouldn't pay for a corpse.

But why had he brought her here and not directly to the General? Most likely, the Kid decided, he needed supplies and to rest his horse, for it was a three-day ride back to the General's *hacienda*. The night before, *El Leproso* hadn't taken the time to grab the girl's horse, so he'd need one of those, too, and the village was the best place around to find one.

But he wouldn't need the horse. Because the Kid had no intention of allowing the Leper to bring Tomasina back to the

General for killing.

Carefully sweeping the morning-quiet village with his gaze, the Kid slid his Winchester out of its saddle boot, cocked it one-handed, and rested the barrel across his saddlebow. He brushed his right hand across the walnut-gripped Schofield holstered for the cross draw on his left hip, then nudged Antonia with his heels.

He started down the hill and into the outskirts of the village, where the humble stone, adobe, or tin-roofed plankboard shacks and stock pens crowded close along the trail.

Chickens pecked around some of the shacks. A rooster crowed. Goats and pigs foraged. Somewhere on the other side of the village, in the pale hills to the southwest, a lone dog barked as though at something it had trapped under a gallery or in a privy.

The fresh morning breeze was touched with the aroma of breakfast fires and the winey fragrance of rose blossoms.

As the Kid continued toward the square, he saw a few people moving about their yards. A boy in peasant pajamas was hauling a wooden bucket of water from a flooded wash. When the boy saw the tall, grim stranger on the blaze-faced sorrel, his eyes widened under a mussed wing of short, black hair, and the boy hurried toward a tumbledown shack on the right side of the street.

He went inside and turned a frightened stare on the Kid as he closed the sagging plank door behind him.

The Kid slowed Antonia down more and, squeezing the neck of his Winchester, followed a slight bend in the street.

On the far side of the bend lay the plaza and the church ahead and on the right, a row of pale adobe shops and a wooden barn with adjoining blacksmith shop on the left. An old man in a straw sombrero sat on a bench outside one of the shops.

He was long-faced and reed thin. His skinny legs were

crossed, his feet bare. He was smoking a cigarette. As he watched the Kid without expression, he shook his head once and crossed himself.

At the same time, the Kid heard a gurgling, groaning sobbing. He swept the square with his gaze, the hair under his shirt collar prickling almost painfully.

Then he saw Tomasina.

She stood in front of the church's stout wooden doors, partly concealed by the morning's cool, blue shadows. She was not alone, for she was standing on the shoulders of an old, gray man in a brown clerical robe and rope-soled sandals. The old *padre* was groaning and sighing, shifting his weight from one foot to the other as he balanced the girl on his shoulders, his gnarled hands wrapped around her ankles.

Tomasina sobbed as she looked toward the Kid, whose heart turned a cold somersault in his chest when he saw the noose around the girl's neck. The rope trailed up from the noose to the bell tower where it was tied to the large, cast-iron bell's clapper.

The rope was nearly taut. If the *padre* dropped her, she'd hang. She'd suffocate if her neck didn't snap first.

The Kid swung his right boot over his saddle horn, dropped straight down to the ground and, holding the Winchester in one hand, took two lunging steps toward the *padre* and the girl.

"*Kid, no!*" she screamed.

The echo of her yell hadn't died before one dust plume rose mere inches in front of the Kid. The crack of a rifle flatted out over the village, echoing dully.

The Kid's boots lifted more dust as he skidded to a stop, slinging his arms out for balance and jerking his gaze to his left, the direction from which the lead had been slung.

The Leper was on one knee in front of the stable, aiming a sixteen-shot Henry rifle with a brass receiver against his shoulder. Gray smoke curled from the barrel.

The Leper's double-barreled shotgun poked up from behind his right shoulder.

The lips behind the mask were spread in a delighted grin as *El Leproso* ejected a spent shell and pumped a fresh one into the chamber.

Chapter 12
Boot Hill Shoot-Out

The Leper canted his masked head toward the girl and the *padre*. "A wretched way to die—hanging."

The old *padre* continued to grimace and groan, shifting his weight to balance the girl on his shoulders.

"Let me go, *Padre,*" Tomasina said. "I'm dead, anyway."

"Never, my child!" the old, gray-bearded man said, though the Kid could see that his knees were buckling and he was beginning to stoop forward beneath his burden. The girl probably didn't weigh much over a hundred pounds, but even that was too much weight for his ancient, spindly frame.

"Let me cut her down, damn you," the Kid snarled.

The Leper straightened slowly, lowering his Henry slightly but keeping it cocked and ready. "Over my dead body."

He sidestepped away from the stable, heading toward the fountain and the cottonwoods that stood between the stable and the church. The burlap mask buffeted against his contorted face as he breathed.

Rage seared through the Kid's veins like acid. All the years he'd been trying to stay ahead of this man only to confront him now, with the girl's life in the balance. Once the Leper was dead, both the Kid and the girl would be free . . . if the Kid could kill him fast enough, before the old *padre*'s back gave out.

The trouble was, the Kid was well aware that *El Leproso* was his most formidable foe. What else did the man have except his ability to maim, torture, and kill?

"That can be arranged!" The Kid took one running step forward and threw himself to the ground, clicking his Winchester's hammer back and firing.

The Leper laughed and stepped to his right as the Kid's bullet plunked into the cottonwood behind him. The Leper aimed his Henry from his right hip and fired three fast rounds, smoke and flames stabbing toward the Kid, who rolled to his left as each bullet blew up dust just inches to his right.

The Kid rolled onto his belly, jerked his Winchester up and fired his own three rounds quickly, watching in frustration as *El Leproso* dove behind the fountain. When the Kid's reports had stopped echoing, he could hear the bounty hunter laughing, taunting him.

"It is all right, *Padre*," Tomasina was saying in a gentle voice as she gazed sympathetically down at the old brown-robe, who was grunting and wheezing shrilly through gritted teeth as his shoulders continued to slump beneath the girl's weight. "Please . . . just let me go, *Padre*. Drop to your knees!"

"Never!"

The Kid glanced at the fountain. He couldn't see the Leper crouched behind it though he could hear the killer's hysterical laughter.

"Tomasina, look down!" the Kid shouted as he swung toward her, gaining a knee.

Pumping a fresh round into the Winchester's chamber, he slammed the stock against his shoulder and lined up his sites on the rope above the girl's head. He drew his index finger back against the Winchester's trigger.

At the same time that his own gun belched, he felt a searing burn in his upper left arm. The blast of the Leper's own rifle reached his ears as he watched his slug carve a dimple out of the church wall just a hair right of the taut rope above Tomasina's head.

The bullet burn across the Kid's arm punched him backward. He dropped his rifle and threw his right arm out to steady himself. At the same time, *El Leproso* stepped out to the right of the fountain and walked along it toward the Kid, aiming his rifle straight out from his right hip.

Smoke and flames lapped from the barrel.

The Kid sucked a sharp breath as the bullet carved a burning line across the nub of his right cheek and across his right ear before thumping into the street behind him.

El Leproso threw his head back and laughed. "Look at it this way, Kid, your running days are over. Now you can join that Apache whore you were so fond of. I heard the soldiers really had fun with her . . . really made her *howl like a whore* . . . before they cut her to ribbons with their Gatling gun!"

Fury a raging puma in the Kid's heart, he rolled sideways as *El Leproso* drilled another round at him. The Kid palmed his Schofield and leaped to his feet, firing once as the Leper threw himself behind a cottonwood. The Kid fired again, tearing bark from the tree, and then wheeled and sprinted toward the church.

Laughing wildly, *El Leproso* sent three rounds buzzing like enraged hornets around the Kid's head.

All three slugs slammed into the side of the adobe hovel beside the church a half second before the Kid bounded into the break between the *casa* and the church. He continued running, sprinting hard down the shady, trash-strewn gap. He dashed around the corner and pressed his back to the church's rear wall, breathing hard, gritting his teeth against his fury and the hot burn in his arm and across his cheek and ear.

He looked around.

To his right hunched the *casa* and a stable flanking it. Inside the *casa*, a baby was crying. To the Kid's left, beyond the church, lay open ground rolling off toward the pale, cactus-stippled hills. Straight out behind the church was a small cemetery adorned with shrines.

Quickly, the Kid tripped the catch and broke the Schofield open to expose the cylinder. He plucked out his spent cartridges, tossing them into the dirt at his boots, and replaced them with fresh from his shell belt. He snapped the gun closed, spun the cylinder, and pressed his back harder against the church's cool wall, pricking his ears to listen for *El Leproso*.

The man was coming.

But from which side of the church?

He got his answer a second later.

El Leproso stepped quickly around the corner to the Kid's left, aiming his Henry along the rear wall from his shoulder. The rifle's black maw appeared to open like a lion's jaws.

As the rifle thundered, the Kid lurched straight out away from the wall, dove over a tombstone, rolled off a shoulder and came up shooting.

Bam! Bam!

He glimpsed *El Leproso* jerking back behind the corner of the church as the Kid's bullets chewed adobe from the wall where the hunter had been standing a half second before.

The Kid heaved himself to his feet, ran back across the graveyard, and lofted himself into the air as the Leper's rifle barked twice more, one slug nudging the Kid's left heel as he careened over another stone and slammed into the ground behind it.

The Kid twisted around, squatted on his heels.

Stretching his Schofield over the gravestone, he saw *El Leproso* dashing toward him, crouching, holding his rifle low across his belly in both hands, the shotgun jutting from behind his right shoulder.

The Kid fired two shots. One slug kissed the nap of the man's gray duster sleeve; the second slug blew the Leper's sombrero down his back, where it hung by its thong.

Fleet as a puma, *El Leproso* dove to his left behind a shrine bright with fresh flowers and bordered by a rusted wrought-iron fence.

The crazy killer's hysterical laughter rose from behind the shrine, vaulting over the pale stones toward the lightening morning sky.

"I think you're too late, Kid!" the bounty hunter squealed. "I think I just heard that old fool's knees pop. Oh, well—there's an even bigger bounty on you!"

He edged his hatless, burlap-wrapped head around the side of the shrine.

The Kid held his breath though his heart was leaping wildly in his chest, and fired the Schofield.

His slug tore into the shrine's tall upright stone.

As *El Leproso* snaked his Henry around the side of the shrine, the Kid ducked behind his own covering gravestone. In the corner of his eye, the words carved into the stone caught his fleeting attention, and he knew a moment's vague befuddlement.

Ernesto Alabando.

Tomasina's one true love.

The Leper's slug loudly hammered the stone, cleaving it in two along a hair-thin fault line.

Both sides slumped away, leaving the Kid exposed.

He bounded off his knees, ran crouching to his right, wanting to save the last cartridge in his six-shooter because he'd never get a chance to reload. A thundering blast much louder than a rifle report rose from the direction of the shrine. The Kid knew immediately that what he'd heard was the Leper's double-barreled shotgun being brought into play.

The squash-sized fist of rock salt blew up a dogget of earth and nudged the Kid's left boot into the other one. The Kid left his feet. When he came down, his head glanced off another tombstone as he slammed onto his right shoulder and lay with his foot stinging now as badly as his cheek and his ear.

He felt as though a rail spike had been driven through his right temple. Warm blood trickled down that side of his face. He lay on his back, arms and legs akimbo, his vision flickering as the ground rolled like ocean swells around him.

In the back of his head a voice was screaming, *"Tomasina!"*

"I'm not gonna kill you, Kid!" the Leper shouted. The Kid heard his footsteps growing louder as the stalker walked toward him. "Gonna make you hurt *bad*. Have *fun* killin' you *slow*!"

The Leper laughed.

The Kid suppressed his misery, gathering himself.

Bunching his lips and hardening his jaws, he rolled onto his left shoulder and extended the cocked Schofield toward *El Leproso,* who just then stopped and grinned behind his mask as he aimed his double-barreled shotgun at the Kid's face.

At the same time, a raucous screech rose on the Kid's right—a sound like an entire flock of eagles in an ear-rending dustup over a dead rattlesnake.

The bounty hunter jerked slightly with a start and the rock salt fired from the roaring shotgun blew up rocks and dust a good foot ahead and left of the Kid's extended revolver.

The Kid triggered the Schofield, watched his slug drill a quarter-sized hole in the Leper's dusty mask, through the dead center of *El Leproso*'s forehead. The man's head jerked violently back. Then it straightened on his shoulders, wobbling slightly.

The Leper opened his gloved hands, and the smoking shotgun fell slack against his chest, dangling by its lanyard.

El Leproso stood staring at the Rio Concho Kid. Slowly, the smile left his thick, red lips behind the mask, which grew red quickly as the killer's blood ran down the inside of it. The

Leper's eyes rolled back into his head until only their whites were visible through the holes cut in the cloth.

El Leproso fell straight back atop a grave, kicking up tan dust painted gold by the morning sunlight. He lay there as though he'd been dropped from the sky.

The Kid glanced at the owl perched atop a tombstone about fifty feet away. Smugly, the bird was preening under a half-raised wing.

Tomasina . . .

The Kid climbed heavily to his feet, dropped his empty pistol, leaped the dead Leper's body, and sprinted along the side of the church toward the front. He dashed around the corner, and stopped, raking air in and out of his chest.

A cold stone dropped in his belly.

The *padre* was on his hands and knees, bawling, his tears dribbling into the dirt beneath him.

Tomasina hung by the rope around her neck, twisting slowly from side to side.

The Kid screamed her name, and, sliding his bowie knife from his belt sheath, sprinted over to her, leaped into the air. He swiped the knife across the rope once before gravity drove him to the ground.

"Tomasina!" he cried, desperately bounding off his heels once more, slashing at the rope above the girl's head until the last strand broke.

The Kid dropped the knife. The girl fell into his arms.

He collapsed to his knees, holding the girl's slack body across them. Her cheeks were pale, her eyes closed.

"Tomasina," the Kid cried, shaking her, feeling tears mingle with the blood on his cheek.

Her chest moved. Her lips fluttered. She drew a breath, and her eyes opened.

The Kid stared down at her, his lower jaw hanging in shock.

"I . . . I came here to join Ernesto . . . in the cemetery," she rasped out barely audibly. She stared up into the Kid's relieved eyes. "He is there, where *El Leproso* put him."

"Ah, Tomasina," the Kid said.

"I came to join him . . . because I thought life was only big enough for one love. For only *one true love.*"

She smiled, lifted her arms weakly, wrapped them around his neck. "But now I know that's not true, Kid."

"Me, too, Tomasina," the Kid said, laughing with exhilaration. "Me, too!"

The Rio Concho Kid lowered his head to Tomasina's, pressed his lips to her ripe mouth, and kissed her long and tenderly.

The Rio Concho Kid and Tomasina De La Cruz will return . . .

ABOUT THE AUTHOR

Peter Brandvold has penned over seventy fast-action westerns under his own name and his pen name, Frank Leslie. He is the author of the ever-popular .45-Caliber books featuring Cuno Massey as well as the Lou Prophet and Yakima Henry novels. Head honcho at "Mean Pete Publishing," publisher of harrowing western ebooks, he lives in Colorado. Visit his website at www.peterbrandvold.com. Follow his blog at: www.peterbrandvold.blogspot.com.

A
Child's
War

World War II Through the Eyes of Children

By

Kati David

Four Walls Eight Windows, New York

Expanded version of book originally published in Dutch as
Hinkelen Langs De Afgrond.
Published by Bzztôh, The Hague, Netherlands, 1987.

First English-language edition published by:
Four Walls Eight Windows
PO Box 548
Village Station
New York, N.Y. 10014

Library of Congress Cataloging-in-Publication Data:

David, Kati, 1935–
[Hinkelen langs de afgrond. English]
A child's war: World War II Through the Eyes of Children
by Kati David.
p. cm.
"Expanded version of book originally published in Dutch as
Hinkelen langs de afgrond"—T.p. verso.
ISBN: 0-941423-24-7 : $17.95
1. World War, 1939–1945—Children—Biography.
2. World War, 1939–1945—Personal narratives. I. Title.
D810.C4D3413 1989
940.53'161—dc19 88-34463 CIP

To the Unknown Child of past and present wars.

"Knowledge and reason only play a limited part in a child's life. Its interest quickly turns away from the real things in the outer world, especially when they are unpleasant, and reverts back to its own childish interests, to its toys, its games and to its fantasies. The danger in the outer world which it recognizes at one moment and to which it answers with its fear, is put aside at another moment."

—Anna Freud, *War and Children* (1943)

"What does not kill us, makes us stronger."

—Nietzsche

Contents

Acknowledgments

To those persons who shared their memories with me, and in particular the fifteen on whose true life experiences these stories are based. Without their confidence and their willingness to share their personal memories and most intimate feelings with me these stories could never have been written.

To Marian Turski, editor of *Byli wówczas dziećmi*, a collection of childhood memories of World War II in Polish, who gave me permission to adopt Pavel's story.

To all those who have gone out of their way to help me by finding people to interview, by giving me at all times the opportunity to discuss children's inner life, and by accompanying my writing with editorial advice. From the many I only mention a few:

Joke Landsman, Pamela and Jim Knight, Rebecca Rass, Nechama Tec, Edith Velmans, Hester Velmans, Myriam Wenger, my sister, Anki, my husband, Peter, and my children, Andrea and Paulo.

A
Child's
War

About *A Child's War*

It may sound strange, but when I think of my own childhood years during the war I always get a good feeling inside. Today, half a century later, I still remember how terrible the war was, and I realize that it is only by a miracle that we survived. But even then, the first thing that comes back to me when I think of those times is the comforting love of my mother.

When World War II started I was five, and when it ended I was ten. My family was Jewish and we lived in Amsterdam. As soon as the first rumors arrived that our lives were threatened, my mother's attitude toward her children changed. Instead of spending her days playing bridge and organizing mundane outings with her friends, she made my sister and myself the center of her life. And the egocentric little girl I was secretly enjoyed suddenly receiving so much more attention.

Gradually, outings like going to the movies, parks, and swimming pools became forbidden to Jews. But I didn't mind a bit: staying at home seemed just as much fun. The growing food shortage didn't bother me either; I loved to be in the kitchen while my mother prepared the most delicious dishes out of the scarce ingredients.

In the evenings my parents would sit together, trying to figure out how to avoid being deported. With the door ajar I could follow their discussions from my bed. Once, when I heard my father say that he was considering sending only us children into hiding because he did

not have enough savings to pay for all of us, I panicked. Being left behind and having to live with other people seemed to me the worst thing of all. I was much more afraid of that than of being sent to a camp with my parents. By that time I had heard many stories about concentration camps, that you could freeze from the cold and starve of hunger and that most people even died. But all that did not seem so terrible as long as we could stay together as a family.

At night, before falling asleep, I would try to imagine what our life would be like there. And the more often I thought about it the less frightening it seemed. I even became a little curious to see those barracks with long rows of bunks on top of each other. Sometimes I pictured myself playing outside with the other children, a thing which I hadn't been able to do for a long time. And then I also saw myself returning and telling everybody about life in the camp. The idea that I might not live to record it did not occur to me, because even though I knew that people were dying all over I was convinced that such a thing would never happen to me or to a member of my family.

By the second year of the war we were one of the few Jewish families in Amsterdam that had not yet been deported. We still lived in our apartment, but life became increasingly difficult. The police came to our house eighteen times to round us up. Every time my mother managed to convince them that we, the children, had a mysterious and contagious illness. She would bring out a fake doctor's certificate and go through lengthy explanations. When the police finally retreated, she would give them a piece of jewelry, an expensive coat, or an album of my father's stamp collection as a token of gratitude. In the meantime my sister and I had to keep quiet under the covers in our room,

[2]

which had been generously sprinkled with disinfectant. After the first few times it became a terrible ordeal to jump into our beds as soon as somebody rang the bell. But we kept doing it, of course, and were pleased to be able to do something to help save the family.

Once the usual excuses did not work and we were taken to the Gestapo. My mother, in her determination to fight the impossible, asked to see the commandant and made up some incredible stories. The commandant couldn't have believed any of them, but he was incapable of resisting her charm. And at three o'clock in the morning, we found ourselves in the street. The only who was not pleased was me, because once outside I realized that I had left my doll's cradle behind!

In the fall of 1943 the Hungarian government allowed those Jews abroad who possessed a Hungarian passport to return to their country of origin. And so we found ourselves on a transport of about two hundred people traveling to Budapest. Our family and friends there had difficulty believing what we had gone through, and one aunt kept complaining that life in Budapest wasn't what it had been before, because there were no silk stockings to be found. She had no way of knowing that three months later she would find herself in Auschwitz.

Soon, the Germans broke their alliance with the Hungarians and took over completely.

My father was deported right away and my mother, my sister, and I were locked up in so-called Jewish houses guarded by Hungarian Nazis. The cruelty of the Hungarian Nazis deeply shocked me. It seemed outrageous that human beings could despise their own countrymen so deeply. Back in Holland it had been relatively easy to accept that the Germans were treating us badly. After all, they were the enemy. Here in Budapest, where the Hungarians behaved worse than the

Germans, I felt trapped because I believed that there was nobody we could trust and no place where we could hide.

Things happened fast in Hungary and before long we were caught up in the battle of Budapest. The bombardments were heavy and uninterrupted, but I quickly got used to them and was not afraid. On the contrary, in a strange way I found them exciting, especially at night because then the bombs looked like fireworks. Once, when we were staying in a fifth-floor apartment, we were woken by a deafening noise. The house was cracking and swaying, and the next morning we found out that the second floor had been completely destroyed. To know that I had survived, when the house had collapsed, gave me a sense of victory and reaffirmed my feeling of invulnerability.

To me the houses that had been destroyed by the bombings looked like enchanted castles full of hidden treasures. Once I found a crystal vase in the rubble that had remained perfectly intact. It was to me a proof that miracles did exist. I loved those ruins because they were not like any other playground. They were real houses that the grown-ups had built for themselves and then destroyed. And now that they had done that the ruins belonged to the children.

Being a girl did not stop me from collecting cartridges and shrapnel. They gave you such an exciting feeling when you held them in the palm of your hand. Those very objects had been used for real; they had made a difference in the big game of the war. Once I found a button of a uniform and I was sure that it had been lost by a soldier in the heat of battle. I couldn't stop thinking of him and kept wondering if he was still alive. How I admired those men in uniform. I felt that way whether I wanted to or not. Until my late teens I

[4]

remember finding men in uniform always virile and handsome.

My favorite game, playing father and mother, had lost its attraction. Since the war had begun, my parents hadn't even raised their voices to me. Playing father and mother without being able to scold your children was no fun at all. Why should I scold them when they behaved so well? They were just as well behaved as I was. When my parents asked me to do a chore I would obey immediately. Not because I liked it—I hated it just as much as before—but because I had to show them that I wasn't that spoiled little girl anymore. Shrewd as I was, I supposed they would do their utmost to let me stay with them if they knew that I wouldn't be a bother, even if I was only a child of seven. So instead of playing father and mother I became a devoted nurse for the wounded soldiers. It was a noble task because they were not ordinary patients, they were real heroes who had risked their lives for their wives and children. By taking care of them and saving their lives with the bullets flying around my ears, I became a heroine.

During the war the norms had changed. What had been "bad" before was "good" now and vice versa. I remember thinking how nice it was to be allowed to do things that were usually forbidden. Calling people nasty names was a sin, but when I said that the Germans were mean monsters, my parents didn't object. They only warned me not to repeat such things in front of other people. That just made it more exciting because it meant that I was big enough to share their secrets. And how elated we were, my sister and I, when we followed the example of other people who were looting the shops that had been broken into by the Russian soldiers. We knew very well that we were doing something forbidden, but that only added to our joy. Unfortunately our booty was disappointing—there wasn't anything left in

the shops and we were very hungry. But all the same we were proud of the paper goods we had found, and we cherished them for a long time as a reminder of having been real looters.

I remember how my whole outlook changed when my father was deported. Convinced as I had been that nothing serious could happen to me or to anybody in my family, I suddenly sensed that my father might not be completely invulnerable after all. For the first time I was afraid, not of the Nazis nor of the bombings, but of the possibility that he might not return. I was only nine at that time, but I realized that without my father we would have lost the war whatever the outcome, because nothing could ever be as it was before.

During those dark days I became very dependent on my mother, and the fear of losing her as well constantly occupied my mind. One early morning the Nazis came to fetch her and a few other women to clean the nearby barracks. I was terribly anxious and was convinced that they used the cleaning up as an excuse to do something terrible to the women. When she hadn't returned in the evening I knew that I had been right. But late that night I was wakened by roars of laughter. My mother was there, telling the other roommates of her adventurous day. "And this German officer," I heard her say, "gave me a carpet beater and told me to beat an enormous rug. But I said that nobody had ever taught me how to do that and asked him to show me. And this idiot starts beating the rug like mad! And I stood there pulling faces behind his back and telling him how strong and how clever he was. . . ." When I heard her boasting like that, I became furious and indignant. My mother, the only adult person that I had left, was taking risks like that! Imagine what would have happened if another officer had seen her. They might very well have beaten her up and sent her to a

camp. I thought she had behaved scandalously for somebody who had to take care of two little children. She had behaved as if she were a child. If anybody had the right to behave like a child it was me! And even I would never do such a thing with the Germans. I was wiser than that, though I knew very well that it must have been fun and satisfying to do it. I was so angry that I resolved that this was going to be the first thing I would tell my father when . . . if . . . he came back. . . .

Actually I didn't even have to wait for my father's return, because I was constantly communicating with him in my mind. I kept reassuring him that I did my best to be brave and to be nice to mother even if she did foolish things. Naturally I trusted him, in his turn, to do the utmost to stay alive. And I also told him that I knew that this was very difficult for him because unfortunately it didn't depend on his own will alone. But even then, the least I could do was to promise him that he could count on my courage, because the worst thing would be if he came back and found that we hadn't made it to the end.

My secret conversations were my only way to be in touch with my father. In front of my mother and sister I didn't dare mention him. Who knew what they'd say— maybe they thought he'd never return, or even worse, maybe they knew something they didn't want to tell me. Instead of asking, I preferred to live with the benefit of the doubt.

As the siege went on, the Nazis realized that the Russians would win the battle sooner or later. Knowing that they in their turn would be the object of revenge, they put their last energies into murdering as many Jews as they could. During the night they emptied the houses near the Danube and took the people—men, women, elderly, and children—to the banks of the river. There they forced them to undress and walk for hours

[7]

in the freezing cold. At dawn they executed them and threw the corpses into the Danube. This was the winter of 1944–45, one of the coldest of our century.

In her despair my mother decided that we would be safer hiding in an apartment than staying in the shelter with the others. And so we waited for the siege to end in one of the half-destroyed deserted apartments. Looking back I still wonder how we managed to survive without food and water. But nonetheless some of my best memories go back to the dreadful days we spent there.

The only useful thing that the inhabitants had left behind was an eiderdown. My mother put it around her shoulders, and my sister and I cuddled up to her. And while we sat there together I forgot the cold and the hunger and just felt the sweet tenderness of my mother. I was so happy when she whispered in my ear how she loved me and when she tenderly stroked my hair. Never before and never after have I felt so close to her.

None of us remembers how long it took before the Soviets came to liberate us. It must have been five or six weeks. During those endless days and nights I kept myself busy, communicating with my father, cuddling up to my mother, and inventing tricks to keep reality at a safe distance. When I heard my mother and sister complain about being hungry, when I heard them say we would die if it went on much longer, I told myself that they were exaggerating. We hadn't eaten anything for many days, that was true, but here we were, still alive, which proved that you could keep going without any food. And anyway, I reminded myself over and over, I still had my "iron reserve." I had managed to save a lump of salt, a few packets of sugar, and even a piece of bread, which I carefully preserved in my muff. Knowing that I had food in reserve was like a guarantee that I wouldn't die from hunger. At the same time it also kept

me busy thinking of the moment that I would finally break into it and share it generously with my mother and sister.

I think that I was able to ignore my hunger by postponing it. And my trick worked perfectly, because even today I am not aware of having suffered real hunger. On a few occasions I did encroach on my "iron reserve." But I would only allow myself to do so if I knew that I could replace the eaten item by something else, preferably more nourishing. I must have connected emptying my muff with giving in, which meant the beginning of the end.

Another way of making myself feel better was to rub two stones, which I also kept in my muff, together. After some time they would start sparking and give a little light and warmth. And then there were the games of fantasy, when I would imagine myself a princess being taken by a handsome prince to his luxurious palace, where helpful servants were busy filling a tub with steaming hot water.

When I grew tired of cheating myself in my fantasy I would start bargaining with fate. I would spend hours and hours counting my buttons and then those of my mother and sister. The first one stood for yes, the second for no, and so on. If the last one said yes, the war was going to have a happy end. And somehow I always managed to count in such a way that the outcome reassured me.

My ritual games and secret prayers had worked: the miracle happened and my father returned. He had been in Bór, a labor camp in Yugoslavia. Only a few of his fellow prisoners survived; when the Germans knew they were going to lose, they started executing as many men as they could. It was sheer luck that the partisans came in time to liberate my father. When he finally arrived in Budapest, I had just turned ten. But even today I remem-

ber the moment I saw him again as the happiest of my life. I think that I must have sensed that fate had given our family a second chance.

We returned to Holland with one of the first Red Cross transports. And once we were back it seemed as if there had never been a war. There was no rubble in the streets, the electricity was working, and water came out of the taps. The schools had already started and the fact that I was Jewish did not seem to make any difference. I not only had the same rights but also the same obligations as the other children.

But my joy over all these novelties was shortlived because peace wasn't what I had imagined at all. I had imagined life after the war as a dream, that I would be free and able to do whatever I wanted. But now that peace was here at last, my parents suddenly started treating me like a little child. They came up with these stupid rules, like always answering with at least two words and letting older people help themselves first.

During the war, we children had always come first whenever my mother managed to lay her hands on some food. Now that there were delicacies to be had, they were passed around with quiet elegance. The guests were supposed to serve themselves first, and being the youngest, I had to wait until the end—till the very cookie I fancied was already taken! Though I was able to understand that this was the way things were supposed to be, I disliked formality profoundly and felt that after all my sufferings I didn't deserve to be treated like an ordinary child.

Life had become terribly boring. The routine of getting up every morning at the same time, going to school, returning home—day in day out, week in, week out—seemed totally senseless. The things we were taught had no practical value; they wouldn't be of any help if you had to protect yourself from danger. Instead

of trying to catch up in class, I sat and daydreamed about those times when we were hiding and running and trying to save our lives. And although I knew that it wasn't right, I couldn't help hoping that something dramatic would happen again. A bomb, a fire, even a disaster like a flood would do. It wasn't that I wanted anybody to get hurt or killed, but I wanted to be part of something that happened, something that mattered, something that was exciting. Just once would do, just so I could feel once more what it had been like.

It took me several years to discover that activities like learning, sports, and arts could also present a challenge. But gradually I adapted and found that I wasn't so different from the other children. The only difference maybe was that I felt more compassion for those who suffered. One of my classmates, who was always singled out because her father had been a collaborator, became my best friend. When my parents found out they were furious, and however much I pleaded that it was unjust to blame children for the mistakes of their parents, they would not hear of it. Though I did sympathize with their point of view, I wouldn't give in: at the age of twelve I had decided that I would have to live according to my own moral standards.

This, in broad outline, is how I experienced the war. When my book* appeared in Holland I got many reactions from people who had also been children during World War II. A Dutch friend of mine confessed that she remembers that last winter, when people were dropping dead on the street from starvation, as the happiest time of her childhood. Being the younger of two she had always felt that her parents preferred her elder sister, who was an excellent student and always well behaved.

*Een Klein Leven, Bzztôh, The Hague, 1984.

[11]

During that winter the schools stayed closed, and while her sister did her homework my friend spent her time wandering outside. At the end of the day when she returned she was never empty-handed. There was always a piece of wood for the stove, a pocketful of rotten apples, or some frozen potatoes that she had found or stolen somewhere. And instead of scolding her for dirtying her coat her parents would rejoice and praise her for her talents.

My friend's example made me wonder about the criteria we parents use. About the reasons why we love our children and how these differ in war and peacetime. But above all it proved to me that children have their own way of perceiving things. My friend was not Jewish and she had lived through the war under totally different circumstances. But still her nostalgia for that terrible winter of starvation reminded me of my own feelings during the worst times of all.

In my book I also wrote about my fascination with the bombings and the soldiers' uniforms. It wasn't easy to do so, but my need to be honest was stronger than my fear of being criticized for it. My honesty paid off; a great number of people who had also been children during the war went out of their way to tell me that they had felt exactly the same way. Once I knew that my fascination with the bombings was not unusual I wondered if we who were children during the war had something in common. And if this was so, was it also something universal? In other words: would children from different national, religious, social, and political backgrounds basically *all* have felt the same way?

The only way to find out was to ask them directly, which meant interviewing a wide cross section of people who had been between five and ten years old during World War II. It also implied that I would have to work with distorted and romanticized memories. As my in-

terest did not focus on historical facts, but principally on children's feelings, that didn't bother me. My own experience had taught me that the passing of time makes it easier to recognize one's truest feelings. It was only after forty years that some of my own feelings had lost their shamefulness and become endearing instead. Another advantage of interviewing adults would be that they could speak with hindsight about how the war had influenced them and what impact it had had on their lives.

For two and a half years—during most of which time I lived in Geneva—I searched for people who had been children in Europe during World War II. Altogether I interviewed over one hundred people from twenty-three different countries. It didn't make any difference to me if they were children of Jews, Resistance fighters, or Nazis. The only qualifications were their experience of the war and their age. The younger they had been, I found, the more their memories were loaded with emotion. Once they started recounting events that had occurred after their eleventh or twelfth year, they tended to rationalize more, and political considerations began making an appearance.

What amazed me most was their readiness to tell me, a total stranger, their most intimate childhood memories. The only thing I had told them about myself was that I too had been a child during the war and that my perception of the events was far different from what people expected it to be.

Most of the people I interviewed, and in particular those on whose true experiences the stories in this book are based, needed very little prompting. Their memories practically poured out of them without interruption. Once they had recounted their stories they seemed relieved, and later, when they had read the transcripts, they often expressed their gratitude; several of them

said that for the first time they felt able to put it behind them. Most of them had never before told the whole story of their life during the war to anyone. Not because they had felt inhibited, but because nobody had shown genuine interest. And they had not wanted to burden their partners or children with those painful events.

Those interviewed were middle-aged, mostly professionals, and hard-working people. They gave me the impression of being well-balanced and strongly family-oriented.

In analyzing these one hundred stories I found that all the children, even under the most different circumstances, had largely had the same reactions and that they showed a consistent pattern. While physical deprivations like cold and hunger left them relatively indifferent, their main fear had been of being separated from their parents. The majority had not been afraid of the bombings; most children had even been fascinated by them. A few people remembered being afraid during air raids, but they said that the adults had passed their own fear on to them. Even in these cases the memories of the bombings were positive because during those fearful moments they had received enhanced affection. Those children who had been separated from their parents suffererd infinitely more than the others. But even then, most of them had managed admirably well to cope with their problems as long as there was still something to fight and hope for.

One of the few questions I asked the ex-children was how they felt today about the fact that they had to go through the war at such an early age.

I have always felt that the war had made me a stronger person. To know that I faced horrible dangers and still survived has given me self-confidence and the certainty that I can overcome whatever happens in

everyday life. The war also gave me a true sense of appreciation. I see it as a privilege to be alive and can be happy with the most insignificant little things.

Of the hundred people, only three felt outright bitterness about having had to go through the war. All the others said that even though it was terrible, something positive had come out of it. Having to witness so many horrors and to confront so many problems made them aware of their inner strength. They also felt that the war gave them different values. Instead of taking everything for granted, like those who do not know what suffering is all about, they learned to be grateful for everything. This seemed to be a general attitude, independent of whether they had suffered a lot or a little. Actually those who had had the most difficult time seemed the most philosophical, as if they had been able to convert all the misery and sadness into an intense appreciation of the things that were good and beautiful.

Only a small minority expressed hate toward the Germans. When asked about the enemy, most people said that they had learned that nobody is entirely good and nobody is entirely bad, that there is some good and some bad in everybody, including themselves. And usually we concluded by saying that it would be wrong to point a finger at the enemy, without recognizing the potential danger in all of us.

—New York, 1989

FIORELLA

ITALY

"Mamma, why do I never get a banana anymore?"

"Because there is a war on, my little Fiorella."

The war had been going on for more than two months now. They kept on talking about the Fascists and the Communists, about Hitler and about Mussolini.

But not a word about bananas. That's why I asked:

"What do bananas have to do with the war?" Mamma smiled, and said, "That's much too complicated. You're too young to understand," and she gave me a kiss. With her it was always like that. She could never give me a decent answer. She'd give me a kiss instead. She hoped that then I'd leave her in peace. But it made me very angry. And also that she laughed at me. She thought that I was too little to understand what war was all about. But it wasn't true. I wasn't a baby anymore, I was almost seven.

Thank goodness Papa was so different. With him I could talk about anything I wanted to. And I didn't have to worry about making a fool of myself. He always took me seriously and treated me like an adult. Papa never read fairy tales to me, just stories from the *Divina*

[17]

Commedia by Dante. When I asked him what war really was, he said, "War is when people fight each other."

But they didn't fight just for fun. They had to have a reason. So I asked, "What do they do it for?"

"For freedom. Some people have certain ideas about freedom. And others have different ideas about freedom."

But I still didn't understand. "What is freedom?"

"Freedom is what every human being needs to lead a happy life. But the freedom of one person should not hurt the freedom of the other."

He explained things so beautifully. I hadn't understood it all, but I did know what he meant: as long as you didn't hurt anybody, you could do whatever you wanted. That was the freedom for which Papa and his friends were fighting. I said: "Papa, I want to help you. I want to fight with you."

From then on he always let me stay in the room when his friends came. Then he would take me on his lap and say: "Don't tell anybody what has been said here. Nor who you've seen here. But I want you to listen and to remember what you've heard."

Mamma was never at those meetings. Afterward, when they had left, she'd ask me who had been there and what they did. But I said, "I've promised Papa not to tell anyone." Then she'd get angry and shout at him: "You're teaching your daughter to lie!"

Papa wouldn't answer. He knew that she didn't like him being in the Resistance. The war was bad enough without that kind of game, as she called it. She thought he was taking too many risks. Papa understood that she was against it. Papa always understood everything.

We had to leave Milan when Papa's boss found out that he was in the Resistance. In Genoa he found a job right away, but a month later somebody told on him and he had to go underground. Papa's best friend was

the director of the hospital, and he said; "I'll give you a room and we'll pretend you're sick. You come and go whenever you want."

Mamma and I lived on the fifth floor, and when there was an air raid we had to run down all those stairs as quickly as we could. The street would be full of people running here and there. They ran as fast as they could to the underground shelter. But when they got there, they'd stop short and hang around the entrance. They all waited until the very last moment to go down because the shelter was too small and terribly stuffy.

Once, as we got to our places, there was a terrible noise outside. A bomb must have exploded nearby. The people threw themselves at the entrance, but it was too small for all of them at once. They fought like crazy to get inside. They yelled and hit and kicked as hard as they could. I was thrown to the ground, and all I could see were arms and legs and faces with bulging eyes and wide-open mouths. They stepped on me, and I felt somebody's heel cut into my shoulder. It hurt terribly, but I didn't want to scream. I didn't want to be like these people. What kind of people were they? They came to save their lives and ended up trampling each other to death!

An old lady who had been crushed underfoot died. When Mamma heard that she decided that from now on we would spend the nights in a tunnel near our house. At least that way we wouldn't have to rush down all those stairs. Some nights we ran to the shelter eighteen times!

I loved being in the tunnel. There were whole families living there. They'd sit around eating and drinking, and afterward they'd start singing. And all the children played together. Whenever they asked me to join in I always said yes. It was fun being with kids who were so different. I knew that Mamma didn't really like my

playing with them, just because they were so different. But she didn't say anything because she knew there was nothing she could do about it.

At night, when I was lying on my mat, I watched the trams ride through the tunnel. I watched the people too. There were people walking up and down all night long. If you listened long enough you could hear how they all lifted and put down their legs at the same time. And then, when you closed your eyes, you felt the ground move up and down, like waves. I loved it, to be rocked asleep like that.

But we had to leave Genoa. We couldn't buy a thing with our ration books and didn'thave enough money for the black market. In the country there would be more food, and there wouldn't be any bombs. But so what? I wasn't scared, and I didn't mind being hungry. In the country I'd see Papa even less. At least in Genoa I could go and visit him in the hospital. Being with Papa always made me feel better. Then I'd know all this misery had a reason. Because after the war, when the Fascists had lost, everything would be different.

Sometimes Papa told me about the things he did in the Resistance. One day, he had to deliver a gun someplace and they came up with a clever trick. His friend put Papa's leg in a plaster cast with the gun inside! Who would question somebody's broken leg? Poor Papa, for three and a half hours he walked like that! I loved those stories, they made me feel proud. And also relieved, because of the happy ending.

We found a big room in the village street above the pastry shop. Or what had once been the pastry shop. All that was in the shop window now were empty bonbon boxes and dusty porcelain statuettes. Behind that hung a curtain, and that's where the baker's family lived. There were two little girls and a boy my age.

The boy, Giorgio, helped us carry the suitcases upstairs. When he put them down, he stayed where he was and took out a red handkerchief. He started to blow his nose as if he had a terrible cold, but I knew that he was just pretending. When he finished he wiped his face all over and said, "Your father didn't come?"

"He had to stay in Genoa. In the hospital."

"Is he very sick?"

"Yes, kind of . . ."

"How long's he been sick?"

"A year and a half. But sometimes they let him go out."

"My father isn't around much either."

"Where is he?"

"In the mountains."

"With the partisans?"

How stupid to blurt it out! But when I saw him playing with the red handkerchief it made me think of the partisans. And then, when he said that his father was in the mountains, I was nearly sure that he was on our side. Giorgio bent over and whispered, "Want to help us?"

"Oh yes, please!"

And then he said loudly, so that Mamma could also hear it, "If you feel like it, I could come and pick you up tomorrow afternoon. Then you can meet the rest of us."

Giorgio and his friends were helping the partisans. Just before you got to the village there was a big hill, and from there you had a good view over the road. It was the lookout. The children stayed on the hill all day, and if they saw something suspicious they were supposed to run down screaming and yelling as hard as they could. Then the men in the village could quickly hide.

Once, when playing on the hill, we saw military

trucks below us on the road. We hadn't seen them coming! Quickly we ran down the hill, shouting loudly. My foot got caught and I fell down, head over heels. There was a silence. . . . What had happened to the others? Then there was a crack and next to me I heard a thump. . . . I felt spatters on my face. I wiped myself and saw my hands. They were full of blood and strange white flecks. Giorgio! He was lying on the ground, right next to me, his head all in pieces . . . with stuff coming out. . . . I couldn't stand the sight of it. Home! Home! Mamma, Mamma, Mamma, Mamma!

Mamma immediately undressed me and put me in the tub. Only a minute later they were banging on the door. She shouted, "Who is there?"

"Open up! Open up! Open!"

"Coming, coming. . . . Just a second."

She got me out of the tub and carried me over to the bed. Two men in uniform entered the room.

"We are looking for partisans. We know they are here."

"There's only my daughter here, and she is sick in bed."

They looked in all the corners, in the closet, and under the bed. I was afraid that they would find my dirty clothes. But Mamma had managed to bundle them up, out of sight.

In the evening Giorgio's mother came. She wanted to know everything; what we had been doing that day and what he had said. I realized that those things had suddenly become important. Giorgio had been the same as ever, but for her it made a difference because it had been the last time. So I tried to tell her everything as well as I could. I kept asking myself if she wanted to know the other thing as well: how in the end he had been lying there covered all over with gore. But luckily she didn't want to hear about that.

[22]

A few weeks later Papa came to visit. He had heard about the accident and was proud of me for having helped the partisans. It hadn't surprised him of his own Fiorella. When he said that, my stomach turned over from fear that he might ask me all kinds of questions. I couldn't talk about Giorgio, even with Papa. I dreamt about it every night, and in the daytime I kept seeing Giorgio, the way he'd been lying there. However hard I rubbed my eyes, that smashed head with blood and white gobs wouldn't go away. But Papa had come about something different.

He said, "I want to take you somewhere, Fiorella."

We walked a long way until we came to a forest. He said we were safe there, then looked for an open space between the trees and put a gun in my hand. It was terribly heavy, and I nearly dropped it. But Papa said, "I want you to learn how to use it." He showed me how to load it and how to pull the trigger. It was very difficult, and I was very clumsy, but he said there was no hurry—that I should just keep practicing until I could do it. When I got a little better, he said, "Now we'll bury it. You have to remember this place and when you need it you can come and get it."

We got a message: we should go to Dr. Arrigoni's right away. Papa told us that Dr. Arrigoni was also against the Fascists and that we could trust him. When we rang the bell he took us immediately into his office and told Mamma, "Your husband has been arrested. Somebody in the hospital betrayed him. He was probably taken to the municipal prison." Mamma stood there, not saying a thing. She just looked straight ahead of her, staring outside. As if there was something to see out there in the fields. Dr. Arrigoni took a roll of lire out of his pocket and stuffed it into her handbag. How old her bag looked, all flabby and the color worn off. The

[23]

clasp that used to shine so brightly was dull and gray. Strange that it only struck me now. Did this mean we were poor? It was the first time I wondered about that.

Mamma lowered her head and began to cry softly. She said, "Thank you, doctor. Thank you. You are a good man. . . ." and left the room without looking up. When she was at the door Dr. Arrigoni laid his hand on her shoulder and said, "You have to let me know if there is something you need. Don't forget that you can always count on me."

On our way home I thought: Dr. Arrigoni sent for us because he had a message. He had to inform us of something we didn't know yet. But that wasn't so! I knew it before he had said it. I had known it all the time. Back when we were still in Milan. But I'd never wanted to think about it. I just didn't want to know it. That's why it had still happened so unexpectedly.

At the entrance to the prison there was a woman sitting behind a little window. She was screwing the top off a thermos. When she saw us she just went ahead and began filling her cup. I was sorry we had arrived at this very moment, but it was too late now to go away. The woman cocked her head to find out what we wanted.

Mamma said, "Good morning. Uh, excuse me. Please . . . I just wanted to know if my husband is here. His name is Guipponi, Ernesto Guipponi."

How politely she spoke. She did her very best. It hurt me to hear her talk like that. She never did that. The woman behind the window put a piece of bread in her mouth and said, "That traitor? I don't even know if he's still alive!"

Mamma took a step backward in fright. She had wanted to ask so many questions, but now she knew that it made no sense. There was so much hatred in that voice that there was nothing left to hope for.

[24]

I had never heard anybody speak in a tone like that. I didn't know that people could hate that way. Mamma had always said that the world was full of bad people, but I had never wanted to believe her. I couldn't imagine that somebody could be totally bad, through and through. But she'd been right. Now I had to admit it. But that wasn't all. There was something else, something that was even worse. The woman was Italian. She was not German, so she wasn't even our real enemy. The first person I really hated was an Italian. And that was the worst, because you shouldn't hate somebody from your own country. But she was a Fascist, which meant that she was with Hitler and Mussolini, against us. That's why I had to hate her. But it would have been a lot easier if she had been German.

There was a wooden bench nearby, and we walked over to it. We didn't want to leave yet; we wanted to wait. What we were waiting for we didn't know. But who could tell?—someone else might take that woman's place. Somebody who would give us some information. Maybe she was very tired; she might have been sitting there all night.

I heard something. Was it my imagination? Were those screams? No, they couldn't be! But they kept coming back. Mamma just sat there, all hunched up. I didn't dare to ask, but I still wanted to know: "Do you think that they . . . Papa?"

"Yes . . ." she sobbed and started to cry. I put my arm around her shoulder, and we sat like that. But I didn't believe that it was Papa. Nor anybody else either, because although there were other prisoners in there too, these were not human voices. Nobody could scream that loudly. They must have used instruments that imitate sounds, just to frighten us.

Suddenly it was quiet. It was nearly five o'clock. If we wanted to catch the last train we had to leave. But

then it started again, even louder than before. Though it was hardly possible. Or had we already forgotten? We couldn't leave now. We *had* to stay.

A bell rang. It sounded like a siren. A man with a big bunch of keys walked toward us. He opened the door and said, "It's eight o'clock. You can't stay here any longer."

Everybody was excited and was talking about the liberation. The war couldn't last much longer. The Fascists had lost, and we had won. That was nice, but I couldn't be happy. I didn't feel anything special.

One evening we heard a car stop. It was a taxi and somebody got out. Papa! Papa! He was back! It couldn't be! But it was! Suddenly the war was over for me and I could be as excited about the liberation as everyone else.

Papa wanted to lie down because he felt a little tired. I went to sit next to him and touched his hand. But he pulled it back as if he'd had an electric shock. I asked him if I had hurt him and he replied: "Yes, but it's not your fault." He lifted his head and said: "Fiorella, I hardly recognize you. You've gotten so tall. You're getting to be a real young lady. And *what* a young lady. I didn't know that I had such a beautiful daughter."

"Papa, Papa, you are back. I am so happy!"

He had fallen asleep and I could look at him now, silently. How he had changed! So old and skinny and *ugly*. When that word came into my mind I was ashamed of myself. It wasn't his fault, was it? And after all, what did it matter? Even if he were the *ugliest* man in the world, he would still be my father and I would love him just as much! I saw the hand that I had tried to touch before. His fingers were twisted and swollen and there were black spots where his nails should have been.

[26]

He made a strange noise during his sleep. It was like a kind of coughing and a little fluid was coming out of his mouth. First just a little bit, but then more and more, and suddenly there was a squirt of blood. I heard Mamma cry beside me and I pulled a little closer. But I couldn't comfort her.

Dr. Arrigoni said that it would be wiser to take him to the hospital. They might still be able to do something for him there. But after one week he had a terrible bleeding and the next day another one. Papa died on April 26, the day of the liberation. My papa had been the best and the sweetest one of all. In ten years, he had taught me everything I knew.

Today Fiorella says:

"The moment I saw that little boy with his brains all over the place stays engraved in my mind. It is like an open wound, and whenever I have a problem I refer to it. In my dreams I relive the scene and see myself running home covered with blood. But telling my story has worked like a catharsis. Afterwards I had nightmares again, but somehow I was always able to get out of them, and the people I had seen dead were alive again. I saw them alive and they were happy. Then they returned to oblivion, but good oblivion, without black thoughts.

"By having me sit in on his secret meetings, my father awoke in me a sense of responsibility. It worked as a seed that grew inside me. Maybe it was a sad childhood for that reason. Because being so young I was already quite old. But when I think of the child I was back then, I have no regrets. I don't mind having lost the innocence of childhood."

Fiorella is a translator and lives in Milan, Italy.

ROBIN

ENGLAND

Ripping good news on the BBC! England has declared
war on the Jerries. Finally! They should have done that
as soon as Hitler swallowed up Czechoslovakia. But no,
those chaps in Whitehall couldn't make up their minds.
Mr. Chamberlain had to wait until Hitler had invaded
Poland. Perhaps it's just as well that Hitler did that. At
least it made Mr. Chamberlain decide at last.

We know all there is to know about the Jerries. Dad
was in the trenches right through World War I. Those
three medals he has weren't for nothing. Nobody knows
as well as Dad what dirty scum those Jerries are.

There's a photograph of Dad in his Coldstream
Guards uniform on our mantelpiece. I often look at it
and wonder if I'll look as smashing in my uniform as he
does in his. Will I be just as handsome as he is? In the
photo he's twenty-one, and I'm only seven now, so it's
hard to tell.

I hope there will be another war when I grow up.
Because I don't see the point of being in the army
without being in a real fight. And as a pilot they
wouldn't let me drop any bombs if it was peacetime. I
want to join the RAF. I'm not the only one, of course,

and I hope they'll have enough bombers to go around. All the boys in my form want to become pilots. Except Jeremy, of course. He's going to be a teacher. But he doesn't count. He isn't a boy, he's just a sissy.

When I ask Dad how many Jerries he shot he won't say. Of course it doesn't really matter—it isn't important at all. Peter is so proud that his father killed sixteen. He never stops boasting about it. If only I could say: "*My* Dad killed seventeen" (or, even better: nineteen), he'd have to keep his big mouth shut.

Our bomb shelter is at the top of Mum's rock garden. We'll never hear the end of it! She keeps saying that it took her twelve years to get it looking nice. Women have no idea what war is all about and the sorts of sacrifices you have to make. The girls I know are like that too. I hope they're not *all* like that, or I'm never going to get married.

The shelter is like a room, only with very thick walls and no windows. After the war we could use it as a workshop. Or even as a garage, if we have a car. You can climb on top and from there you can see the sea and the walls of the shipyard where my Uncle Jack works. He told me that Barrow-In-Furness is where they make the very best submarines.

Thank goodness we don't have Mr. Johnson as often as before. What a rotter! It's incredible how that chap can get all worked up about little things while his country is at war! Ridiculous. And he's always out to get me. The other day he said: "Robin! How much is seven times eight?"

Now I know my tables, all of them. Back to front and inside out. Seven is the only one I have a little trouble with. Eight's no problem. But you see, I wasn't sure if eight times seven was exactly the same as seven times eight. And then I wasn't completely sure if it was

[30]

sixty-five or fifty-six. So I said, "I think I know, sir. But I'm not quite sure. . . ."

"Robin, this isn't the first time that I'm testing you on the seven times table."

"Yes, sir. And I do know it, it's just that it's rather difficult. Once you get to the middle—"

"Which of you chaps can tell me what seven times eight is?"

"The same as eight times seven," I heard the sissy say.

"And how much is that, Jeremy?"

"Fifty-six, sir."

Fifty-six! I knew it! Why hadn't I said it? Why did I always have to mix it up with sixty-five? Well . . . who cares. . . . Mr. Johnson can get stuffed.

These days we have more important things to learn than the seven times table. Like first aid. With that you'd better not make any mistakes. If you give somebody too loose a bandage he could bleed to death. And if you make it too tight he could lose his arm, because you'd cut off the blood. Miss Lockwood explained it all to us. If I know the reason I have to do something, I don't have any trouble remembering. We practiced with real bandages, and one time Miss Lockwood let me bandage her arm. She told me I'd done rather a good job. She should know. She's a real nurse with a uniform and all. I'm glad there are women like that, too.

After school they're teaching us how to put out fire bombs. We each get our own pump and our own bucket. There's a huge mountain of sandbags in the playground. When the gym teacher leaves we always stay to play war. The team that captures the sandbags wins. The only one who never joins in is Jeremy. He hates his gas mask, too. It is rather a nuisance having it dangling around your neck all the time. But who'd make a fuss about that! Anyway, Mum always puts a pack of sweets

[31]

inside, in case of emergency. She gets mad when I've eaten it. But I know that she'll just put another pack in again. Because she'd never risk not putting one in, of course.

Sometimes, in my bed, I can hear the buzzing of the German bombers. It's very soft and it comes in waves. It sounds as if they're growling: "We are very close, but from down there you can't see us." Those dirty cowards only dare come here after dark. But then at last, all at once you hear *pom, pom, pom, pom, pom, pom . . .*—very fast—and then you know that our antiaircraft guns are going off. And then you hear the sirens howling and you have to run to the bomb shelter.

I wish Joyce would start to cry, because then I could say: "Don't be a baby! Why would they want to bomb *our* house? It's only the shipyard they're after." But Joyce isn't crying. She is quite brave, actually. That's not so hard when you're sitting on your mother's lap.

Dad usually goes to the kitchen to make some tea. But tonight he's staying in here with us. The bombing has never been this bad. Even if there's no tea tonight, will there be a biscuit anyway? The biscuits are stored in here. That's why I like the air raids. But I won't ask. I'll wait. Joyce will start whining for one soon enough.

But Joyce doesn't seem to be too interested in biscuits tonight. She's just listening to the noise of the bombs and watching the flame of the paraffin lamp, which is flickering and keeps wanting to go out because of the shaking.

At last something happens! Dad lights two matches. He holds them above the tobacco in his pipe and his whole face starts to move. Then he inhales deeply, chews quietly on his pipe, and says: "Looks like we'll be here for a while. So why don't I go make us a pot of tea anyway." And before Mum can open her mouth he's

gone. He makes a dash for it—with the bombs falling all around! What a hero, my Dad is. He isn't afraid of anything. I won't be, either, when I'm big.

On the last day of school we got our cards. They're splendid, with your photo on the left with a stamp across part of it, and to the right is written things like your name, your age, place of birth, religion, and the color of your hair. We had to sign underneath, and then Mr. Johnson gave us each a transparent case with a cord through it. He told us it was to carry the cards around our neck. That's typical of Mr. Johnson, inventing such a thing. We aren't babies, are we? *He* doesn't wear *his* papers around his neck, does he?

All the parents came to the station to say good-bye. Some mothers were crying, but my Mum didn't, luckily. I was glad when the train finally started moving. More and more children started yammering. I couldn't stand it. Especially not now, with everything so exciting. I'd never been on such a long journey, and I was awfully curious to find out where I would end up. A castle, I hoped, with a drawbridge and a moat around it. I'd often had dreams about it. And why not? This could be my lucky day. They had plenty of castles where we were going.

If only I didn't have such a bellyache. I don't even know if it's real pain, it just feels like a big, heavy rock in there. And then suddenly a stitch in my side. Oh—I can't stand it! Everything starts to spin and I don't even know where I am. And then once I open my eyes again I feel even worse. Because I see that I'm still lying here in this cold attic.

Last night I stared into the flame of the candle for a very long time. I kept thinking about Mum and Dad. I even prayed. I don't usually. Not because I don't want

to (Mum told me to say my prayers every night), but I just forget. I asked Our Father to send the Luftwaffe over here to bomb this house. But Our Father didn't hear me because nothing happened. Nothing ever happens here. It's so far away and dull that nobody is interested. Not even Our Father.

I have to call her Auntie Jane but I don't feel like it. When she brings me my food she asks me how I'm feeling. But I'm not feeling any better and I still can't eat a thing. When I ate three spoonfuls of soup it just came right out again. And not only that little bit of soup, but a lot more. I don't understand how that can happen, if you haven't eaten for days. I really must be very sick. If it goes on much longer they'll have to send me home. Because they don't even have a doctor here. They've never even heard of doctors here.

Of course it had to be Jeremy who got the castle. He gets driven to school in a Rolls Royce every day, like a little lord. Lucky fellow! And we have to *walk* three and a half miles each way! But the worst is, *he* isn't even enjoying it. The only thing he can tell us is that the rooms are big and cold and that the Duke and the Duchess are never there. When I asked him how many gun slits there were, he said he hadn't counted and he couldn't care less. He just wants to go home. Well, what can you expect from such a Mummy's boy?

After school we have to help sweep out the stable and take care of the little lambs. They're a lot of work. They're the stupidest animals there are. But such sweet things! And I'm very good with them, they listen to me. The other day, a mother sheep died. And they let me feed the little one with a bottle. And now it's my job to feed him until he's big enough to do it by himself.

Auntie Jane is a wonderful cook. Every morning we have bacon and eggs. The eggs are still warm when you go and collect them from underneath the hens.

At night we listen to the radio. The war is going splendidly. We are bombing all the German cities: Bonn, Frankfurt, Hamburg, even Berlin! More than a million Jerries dead already. And a good thing too, those dirty Jerries. It's about time someone taught Hitler a lesson.

There are some strange goings-on here. Every morning at six o'clock a military truck stops in front of the house and five men get out. They stay here all day and are picked up again in the evening. They're prisoners of war. That means they're soldiers who lost and were taken prisoner. And they just let those fellows walk around here, if you please! No guards! Auntie Jane and Uncle Jack had better watch out! Those chaps do work quite hard, that's true. And they don't get paid either, but still . . . they're the enemy, aren't they? They would have killed us if they could have, wouldn't they? And we could have and we didn't! We took them prisoner and brought them all the way back to England. And now that they're here we act as if they aren't even our enemies, but just ordinary workmen.

Auntie Jane lets them eat with us. She says that makes it easier for her. The first day I was really rather nervous, even though I'm pretty brave. I made sure to sit at the other end of the table. What if one of them asked me something? Then I'd have to answer and look him in the eyes.

But I've gotten used to them by now and they're very quiet. When they do talk it's to each other, and I can't understand them anyway. There are three Germans and two Italians.

One time I was walking near the barn. They're allowed to rest there after supper. One of the Germans was cutting a piece of wood with a knife. He did it so fast and so neatly that I couldn't help watching. Of

course he noticed and winked at me to come closer. It wouldn't be right to run on now. It was too late. When I came closer I saw that he'd carved a little dog. He stretched out his hand and said: "For you. Take it."

It was a frightfully good dog. How do you do that, make a dog out of just a piece of wood? But of course I couldn't take it, so I said, "No. No."

"You not like it?"

"Yes, I do. That's not it . . ."

How could I tell him what I was thinking? So I just turned and started to walk away. But he called after me, "I make different thing for you! Tell me what."

"I don't know."

I looked at him as I said it. It was the first time. It was different from what I'd thought. His eyes were very ordinary, they weren't frightening at all. In fact they didn't even look unfriendly. He asked: "A bird? A cat? An Indian?"

I love Indians. Winnetou's my favorite. Before I knew it, I'd said, "Yes!"

"Good," he said. "But you must help. I need big piece of wood."

In the woodpile I found the top of an old butter-churn. He started on it right away. How fast his hand moved! I loved looking at it.

"You learn also?" he asked, and he took my hand so fast that I didn't even have time to think about it. But it wasn't scary at all, his hand was big but felt very light. When he started carving again it seemed as if I were the one doing it. It was smashing to see the mouth come out, slowly. Then he said, without stopping, "You get paint. And horse's hair. Beautiful Indian!"

At school everyone is jealous of my mask. And they all want to know who gave it to me. It's none of their business! They'd really let me have it if they heard I got

if from a prisoner of war. And a German one, too. And that he made it specially for me.

It's not that I'm ashamed of it. Not at all. But they wouldn't understand. They only see the Germans as wicked scum. They don't see that they're just people, too. Ordinary people, just like us.

Barrow-In-Furness looks totally different from before. Everything has been flattened and all you can see are ruins. Shrapnel and fragments of shells everywhere. I got a beautiful collection in a few days.

Down the street two houses have been destroyed. They look just like two old forts, and after school we go there with a whole gang and play. We hide behind the walls that are still standing and pelt each other with stones. All you have to do is pick them up. There are heaps, all over.

I also have some live cartridges that I bought from two chaps who broke into the RAF armory. One of them even picked a real Sten gun. At first I wouldn't believe him, but he showed it to me. He kept it locked inside his desk at school. Taking it home would be too risky.

One day when I got home I saw the *Daily Express* lying open on the table. Normally, we weren't allowed to touch it until Dad had read it. Had *Mum* all of a sudden gotten interested in politics?

Closer up I saw some names in big letters: Auschwitz, Mauthausen, Bergen-Belsen. Never heard of them. And, lower, lots of photographs. Strange photographs. Loads of dead people piled in a ditch. And living skulls looking at you with huge eyes. What was this? I didn't understand! And what about those spooky figures standing behind the barbed wire? And those bald people in striped clothes? There were also photographs of big steel doors. The captions said they were the ovens where

[37]

they'd been burning—people. Fancy! Burning people in ovens? What a load of nonsense! Who'd dream up something like that? It must be a joke. But a very bad joke. They only did it to sell newspapers. Now that the war is over, the papers are going to go out of business. My own Dad says so.

But I keep having to look at those photos, over and over again. They are so strange, so different. Maybe that's why I find them so interesting. Once Dad was done with the paper I asked him if I could cut them out. Now I have saved them and look at them every time I want to have this weird feeling again.

Today Robin says:

"The war remains perhaps the most memorable period of my life. I feel it has been a real foundation, a reference point. Without the war I would see my life as rather dull. But when I look back now, I come to this great plateau—crowded with marvelous events—which is this experience of the war. I wouldn't have missed it. Highly positive.

"My encounter with the prisoners of war was an interesting experience, too. To discover that people I feared and hated—that I had been taught to fear and hate—were just like us, and not at all the gruesome, terrifying enemies one heard talk about. I suppose this was one of my first lessons in understanding other people, in not accepting first impressions as complete and final and irrevocable."

Robin is a journalist. He has two children and lives with his wife in Geneva, Switzerland.

MARICA

RUMANIA

"How stupid of me," Mrs. Shapiro cries. "I nearly forgot to give the child some sweets." She turns around and hurries back into the room. Mr. Shapiro stays with us in the hall. But he and Tata* don't speak anymore. The maid brings us our coats and Tata takes them from her. Now here comes Mrs. Shapiro, she's almost running. She holds out a big box of chocolates for me and says, "Just help yourself, dear . . . I don't even know your name." "My name is Marica," I say, and I take a bonbon. Not the biggest one—on purpose—and a kind of which there are many. "Another one for the road," she says. And when she sees I'm not moving, she takes a few chocolates out of the box and stuffs them into my pocket.

"Perhaps you'd like one too?" She asks suddenly, looking at Tata. Tata answers: "No, thank you, Mrs. Shapiro." Mrs. Shapiro says, "Too bad, they are very good." Tata nods at her and at Mr. Shapiro and says, "Come darling, we have to go."

*"Father" in Rumanian.

Out on the street I ask Tata, "What should I do with those chocolates?"

"Just eat them."

"But they are bad people."

"That's the way the world is. Don't let it bother you."

"Tata?"

"Yes, my sweetheart."

"Are we going home now? Or do we still need to see other people?"

"We're going home, my angel. I've been everywhere."

Tata never told me why he was going to see all those people. But he didn't have to, I was there and could see for myself. He asked them if they could lend him some money because all of his money was in the business. And the Germans had taken away his business because he was a Jew.

But everywhere the answer was *no*. And not because those people didn't have enough money. They actually had a lot of money. When we were at Mr. Weinberger's, he went to the wall and started turning a knob until suddenly a tiny little door opened up. And when that little door was open, I saw a hole, and in it there were blocks of gold! I could hardly believe my eyes. Later, when I asked if what I'd seen was real, Tata said it was. Mr. Weinberger is very rich, but I still wouldn't want him to be my father. He is much too old and has a crooked nose with big holes and dirty hairs sticking out.

There is a suitcase on the bed and Tata and Mama are putting all kinds of things in it. When I ask what they are doing, Tata says, "Why don't you pack your toys in the meantime? You can take whatever you can carry by yourself."

I go to the room and take my toys out of the closet

[42]

and the drawers. Most of the time, when Tata and Mama tell me to do something, I ask, "Why?" but this time I don't ask. Because I know it won't help anyway. They are so busy right now that they don't have time to explain things.

But it's okay for me to be by myself for a while. I am four years old already, and not at all a baby anymore. You know what? I'll show them that I can pack my toys easily all by myself.

I do have a lot of toys. And I'll have to carry them all by myself. But I can't leave them behind, just like that, can I? So—how shall I do it?

I guess there are lots of things I never play with. Those will just have to stay here for now. I'll just take along the toys I love best.

Like my darling rocking horse. But he is much too big to carry! And my little stove? I just got all the new pans. . . . And my doll's pram?

I know! I have an idea! I'll stuff all my toys into the doll's pram. Then I won't have to carry them.

Tata calls, "Marica, are you done?" "Yes, Tata," I say proudly. "Everything is in the pram." "Come on! Hurry up!" he says. "We have to be in the ghetto before four o'clock."

In the ghetto they put us in a room with at least thirty other people—strangers, and we don't know any of them. Some are very old. And there are little children who keep crying all the time.

"Tata?"

"What is it, Marica?"

"When can we go home?"

"I don't think we'll go home very soon."

"But we can't stay here, can we?"

"Anything is possible, my darling. The Germans can do whatever they want with us. They could leave us here. But they could also come and get us."

[43]

"I hope that they will come and get us soon."

"Don't say that, sweetheart. If they come and get us, it will be to take us to a camp."

It is nearly dark and we still have the Dnjestr to cross. And I am so tired from all that standing. We have been standing here all day, waiting for the boat.

"Marica! Here comes the boat!" says Mama.

"I don't believe it."

"Yes, yes it is! Let me lift you up. Then you can have a look."

I see a boat alongside of the shore. Could that be it? It is so small. . . . The boat I had imagined was not like that at all: that one was like the white one I once saw in a magazine.

People are already climbing on board. But the boat is almost full already. There is much too little room for all of us. And the soldiers keep shouting all the time: *"Raum machen! Schnell! Schnell!"** More and more people are crowding on. We are just about the very last to climb on board. And we are standing at the very edge.

I am so afraid that we're going to drown. But I won't cry. I press my Nyú-Nyú against me. He is so wonderfully soft, and yet so sturdy, too. Lucky for me that I have him with me. "If I fall in the water, you'll save me—won't you?" I whisper in his ear. I repeat it over and over, very fast, over and over again, so that nobody can hear me.

The people are screaming. They cry: "We're sinking!" And then suddenly a stern voice shouts: "Don't panic! If we all stay calm, nothing's going to happen." Tata says, "Grab my belt and hold on tight."

Something plops into the water. I look up and Tata says, "Don't worry, my darling. It was only my coat."

*"Make room! Hurry! Hurry!"

[44]

Dr. Weiss has promised to come and have a look at Tata. He happens to be here in Mogilev* too. Tata has had typhoid for so long, and he just isn't getting any better.

Where is Dr. Weiss? Why isn't he here yet? I know he has to work very hard. But can't he come and take a look at Tata, just for a moment? If he waits too long he may not be able to help him anymore.

Tata is asleep all the time. At least that's what I think he's doing because he never says anything. Except last night. Last night he suddenly started talking very loudly. Mama said it was because of the fever. What he was saying was all mixed up—you couldn't understand a thing. The only word that kept coming back was *"Palestine."* In the ghetto he had met a man who said that you could go to Palestine if you had family there. And Tata has a sister there, Aunt Leila.

Here's Dr. Weiss! But . . . he looks so thin . . . and he hasn't shaved. . . . He used to be such a good-looking doctor. But what do I care? As long as he makes Tata better.

The doctor leans over Tata. With his thumbs he pulls Tata's eyelids up and then pushes them back again. Then he lifts Tata's arm, feels his wrist, and folds his arm over his chest.

He looks at Tata and thinks for a long time. Then he stretches his back and sighs a deep sigh. "I'm afraid that it's already happened," he says to Mama.

I'm not allowed to be there when they come and get Tata. That's why I am standing here, outside. But I am so big now that I can look inside, through the window. I see two men putting him down on a big plank. And

*Camp in the Ukraine.

[45]

then I can just see his hair as they carry him out. There's hardly any left because it all fell out from typhus.

Dear Tata . . . Now you're gone. . . . Will I ever see you again? Can that be true? You really won't come back again? I can't imagine it. Somewhere, I'm sure, we will meet again. I don't know where. But somewhere, there must be such a place. There must be.

Tata must have caught cold standing in line for water. Every morning in the cold, without his warm coat. If only he could have kept his coat he would never have gotten sick. And if I hadn't taken along my Nyú-Nyú there would have been enough space. And he wouldn't have had to let his coat fall into the water.

Grandma is in the same barracks as Aunt Judith, Aunt Nina, Uncle Otto, and Bruno. I think they have a lot more to eat than us. I don't know how they get it. Maybe from that friend of Aunt Judith's. She met somebody here who works in the kitchen. But when I go there I never get anything. Once, Aunt Nina gave me a potato, but she said, "Just this once. I can't give you something every time."

The other day, I saw Grandma chewing on something. But when I asked her what it was, she said, "Nothing. I'm only doing that because my teeth are bothering me." When I came home I said to Mama, "Why doesn't she just say that she doesn't want to give me anything?"

Mama has gotten a whole loaf of bread. Great! For once we have something too. But we have to watch out that they don't steal it. When there was nobody in the barracks Mama sewed half of it inside the mattress. And the rest we carry in our pockets.

The bread came from a German who lives near the camp. Mama gave her the dress that Tata had bought

[46]

her in Paris that time. The only thing she still has left to exchange is her silk nightgown trimmed with lace.

All that time we didn't have a thing. And now that we have the bread, suddenly we also have some money— sent to us by Uncle Dan in Bucharest. Uncle Dan and Aunt Anna are still living there in their beautiful villa. They're really lucky, because in Bucharest there is hardly any war.

Mama has given me some money. I walk to the fence to buy something. The peasants there have so many good things to eat: sauerkraut, pickles, and sometimes poppyseed cakes. . . . The cake is the most expensive, but that's what I really want.

Yum . . . It tastes so good. . . . It reminds me of before the war. . . .

Mama comes into the barracks. When she sees me sitting on my wooden bed she asks, "Is it good?" "Great," I say. "It tastes like before . . ." "Well-done," she says, and she asks me for the change.

I look for the change, but I can't find it anywhere. Where is it? It can't have disappeared just like that! I look everywhere, but it's gone.

Mama starts to scream. She yells mean things like, "Rotten child," and, "I can never trust you!"

How mean! I didn't do it on purpose, did I? The pastry is still in my mouth, but suddenly it isn't good anymore. I tell her, "Now it tastes like shit."

Uncle Otto has been sent to a camp in Poland. The camps there are not like here. There you have to work very hard. And if you can't work anymore they kill you.

They say that from now on there will be a transport to Poland every week. And suddenly everybody is very scared here in Mogilev.

[47]

A few days ago Mama said, "Marica, I have a surprise for you."

"What?" I asked.

"You can go to Palestine with the Red Cross."

"And what about you?"

"I can't go. It's only for children."

"How is that possible? Only for children?"

"Yes, for orphans. The Germans are making an exception for them."

"But I'm not an orphan! I have a mother! I have you."

She isn't going to make me go with those filthy children, is she? Those children behind the barbed wire over there. Their heads are shorn and they walk around in those ugly uniforms. Whenever I see them I always think, *How lucky I am that I'm not one of them!*

"Of course you're not an orphan, sweetheart. But what difference does that make? As long as you arrive safely in Palestine. Then Aunt Leila and Uncle Daniel can take care of you."

"And you . . . When are you coming?"

"As soon as possible."

"And if they send you on? Just like Uncle Otto?"

"Well, then . . ."

"Don't send me away! I'd sooner go with you to Poland!"

"Come on! Don't say such silly things." She shouted and started to cry.

But I didn't say silly things. I really meant it.

I want to stay with her, but she won't listen to me. And she even says that it is for my own good. But that isn't true. If that were so, Aunt Nina would send Bruno to Palestine too. But Bruno can stay here, with his own mother.

For two days she has been busy with my coat,

sewing the names and the addresses of all our family members into the lining. In case I need them. Ha! That's what she thinks! She also thinks that I am going—first to Bucharest, from there to Constanza, and from there to Palestine. Ha! At the gate I'll say, "I'm not an orphan. I have a mother. Look, she is standing right there!"

But I didn't say anything at the gate. I thought, *I'd better go. She doesn't want me to stay with her anyway.*

We've now been traveling for two days. The cattle car is so full that we can't sit down. Luckily I have a place near the wall. And there is a little crack between two boards through which I can look outside. As long as I can do that I don't have to look at the children. It is bad enough that I have to smell their stench and hear their cries.

It looks like the train is now slowing down. It is creaking and squeaking. Are we going to stop at last? Yes. Now we really are standing still.

Nothing is happening. We are just standing and standing. Now I hear footsteps and somebody unbolts the door. At last!

"Get out!" they shout. "You have ten minutes to eat and to pee."

When I'm finished I go back quickly because I want my old place back again. But I am not the first one in there. Another girl is there already. She is much older, she must be at least sixteen. She is holding a little baby in her lap, and she says, "Look at this—isn't he a darling? I found him lying in the ditch. I couldn't leave him there, could I?"

The other children climb into the car and the attendants shout, "Hurry! Hurry! We're leaving!" But just as they are closing the door the baby starts to cry.

The door opens again. An attendant asks, "Is there a baby in here?" Nobody says anything. It is dead quiet.

The only thing you can hear is the little noises the baby is making. Now she calls to the other attendants and climbs into the car. "Come here, you, with that baby," she says. The girl steps forward. She hugs the baby to her chest and looks at the attendant.

"Give me that child! You know very well that isn't allowed."

"No, I won't give him to you!" the girl shouts.

"Hurry up! That's an order."

The girl begins to cry. She begs, "Please . . . Can I keep him? I'll share my rations with him. He won't be any trouble to you."

"You still don't understand, do you, you stupid girl?" she yells and hits the girl so hard that she falls down. But the baby isn't even crying. He isn't hurt because the girl had wrapped herself around him before she fell. Now the other attendants join in. They grab the girl and drag her out of the car.

When the train drives off I can see her through my crack, walking away. And I watch her for a long time. She cradles the baby in her arms and her head is bent forward. She must have been doing that because she is singing him a song.

Suddenly I so much longed to be that little baby. He is very poor and has nothing at all. And yet he is so very, very lucky. Because he has that girl, who loves him so much.

The throbbing in my ear and the cut in my foot aren't even that bad. At least I don't have to be embarrassed about that. But that diarrhea . . . Whatever I eat, it comes out right away. I can't help it. I really can't keep it in.

Mrs. Niculescu is so nice. She says that I really shouldn't worry. My stomach is all upset. And she says that that is normal after two years in the camp.

She put my bed in front of the window, and I can look outside all day long. Sometimes the sun shines right into the room. Then everything suddenly changes color. And then everything seems beautiful again. Just like back then, way back then, when we were still in Csernovic. I have already been here in Birlad at Mr. and Mrs. Niculescu's three months. When the train arrived here they brought us to a shelter for the night. But when I saw those mattresses on the floor I started to cry because I did not want to stay with those horrible children any longer. The man who worked in that shelter came over to comfort me. That was Mr. Niculescu, and he said that if I liked I could sleep at his place that night. But when I woke up the next morning I had such an earache that they called the doctor. And he said that I was too sick to travel like that.

But tomorrow, I'm finally leaving to go to Uncle Dan and Aunt Anna. I've got a ride with a driver who has to take two German officers to Bucharest. In a real limousine! They musn't know that I am Jewish, of course, but who's going to tell them? Not me!

I don't like it all here at Uncle Dan and Aunt Anna's. And that son of theirs, that Axel, I can't stand him at all! He is spoiled like a little prince. He doesn't even go to school, his teachers come to the house. One for the languages, one for doing sums, and one for the piano. And on top of that a priest comes because they've had themselves baptized and now they are Catholic.

Aunt Anna has three rooms, all for herself alone: one for sleeping, one for doing her makeup, and one for her clothes. And then she even has a whole bathroom all to herself! I once counted her shoes—only the white ones—and she had twenty-four pairs of those! When I saw that, I had to think of Mama, who had exchanged all her things, up to her very last pair of shoes.

[51]

Aunt Anna did not come to the station. She was in bed with a migraine again. In the beginning I thought that that was a terrible disease. But the maid told me that that's what the rich call a headache.

In my compartment there is a couple who are also going to Palestine. I've told them that I traveled by train from Mogilev to Birlad and from there by limousine to Bucharest. They said, "You're quite brave, for a girl of seven." They kind of like me, I think. That's lucky, because we've still got a long way to go. And it's good if you have somebody to talk to on the way.

In Constanza the people of the Red Cross are waiting for us on the platform. They ask me my name and say that I have to go with the other children onto the boat. But I don't want to. I don't want to go on the boat with those orphans. Why do they keep sticking me with the orphans? I'm not an orphan!

Everybody else is already on board but I won't budge from my seat. A nurse walks up to me and says: "Come on, little girl. You don't have to be scared." "I'm not scared!" I shout. "I don't want to go on the boat with those children." She is very patient and explains to me that for children without parents there is no other possibility. But when I insist that I still don't want to, she gets up to get some help.

Here come two strong men . . . What shall I do now? I start to bawl loudly. And then suddenly I hear the lady from the train say, "The little girl can sleep with us in our cabin."

I have been living for two years now on the kibbutz. I feel really at home here with Aunt Leila and Uncle Daniel.

But I still keep having to think of those poor chil-

[52]

dren. On the second night at sea, the boat with the orphans was torpedoed. And all the children drowned.

The boat I should have been on was sunk. And the boat I didn't belong on arrived safely in Palestine. Everybody thinks I'm such a clever girl because I was so smart. But I couldn't have known, could I? It was just bad luck for them. And it was just good luck for me.

I was lucky only because I was disobedient. If I had been a good girl I would also have been unlucky. And then I would have been dead. Just like the other children.

Today Marica says:

"Being sent away with those orphans was the most traumatic thing for me personally. My mother explained it all, that it was to save me and that it would be better where I was going. But even if I understood I couldn't help feeling rejected. And since then, things have never really worked out between my mother and me.

"I see the war as a negative experience only. I was only four when I learned the ugly side of human nature. There was no kindness and cooperation among the members of my family. What I saw was antagonism and grabbing and who gets what and more.

"I somehow decided that I wasn't a good person when I saw that girl giving up her life for the little baby she had found. I couldn't analyze it at that time, but I knew there were two choices: you stay alive or become a saint. And since I could not make that kind of a noble choice, I felt that I was bad. And later, when I heard that the boat on which I was supposed to be was torpedoed and that all the other children had drowned, this feeling got reinforced."

Camp Mogilev was liberated six months after Marica left. She and her mother emigrated to the United States, and Marica lives with her husband and son in New York.

PAVEL

Czechoslovakia

"Hello Mama," I said as I opened the gate. But she was bent so low over the tub that she didn't even look up. She just said, "Your dinner is on, Pavel. I'm coming in a minute."

I went to the stove and lifted the lid off the pan. Bean soup again. How silly of me to hope for something else. It was an ordinary weekday, after all.

Mama came in. She dried her arms and rolled down her sleeves. "I know what you are thinking," she said. "Just a little more patience, my boy. On Sunday I'll make poppyseed noodles for you and then you can eat until your belly bursts."

She filled my plate and put it before me on the table. The smell slapped me in the face. . . . Eat it quickly, that was the best thing to do. And think about something else. I shut my eyes tight and told myself that I had a plate with poppyseed noodles in front of me.

Somebody knocked at the door. It was the mailman, with a letter. Mama opened it hastily. I recognized the handwriting right away and knew that it was from

Tata.* Tata had been in the hospital for three long months, all the way in Bratislava. He had had an accident at work. Mama told me that a block of stone had fallen on him, but I didn't really believe it. Stone blocks don't simply fall on experienced men who work in the quarry. I knew that from Tata himself.

Once Mama took me along with her to the hospital. Tata was sitting up in bed with lots of pillows behind his back. Both of his legs were in plaster. And the color of his face was not brownish like before but all white.

"Hello, Pavel," he said and stuck out his hand. It felt moist and sticky on the inside.

"Come here," he said, and I knew that he wanted me to sit on the edge of his bed. My hand was still in his. He was holding it, but without any strength. I suddenly thought of those big strong hands I had always admired. There were two other men in the ward. But it was very quiet. The only thing I could hear was Mama crying softly on a chair behind me.

"How are you doing, Tata?" I asked.

"Very well, my boy. Especially now that I see you. You have grown again. . . . You will certainly be very tall, later."

Talking had made him tired. Under his chest hair I could see his ribs go up and down. For a second I thought that I even saw his heart beating.

"How nice that you came," he said. He let my hand go and sunk back into the pillows.

It was time to go. I stood up to say good-bye. As I bent forward he kissed my forehead. I thought that he had tears in his eyes, but I didn't dare look to see if it was really so.

*"Father" in Czech.

When Mama had read the letter she went to the stove to stoke the fire. Then she took the letter from the table and threw it into the flames. The only thing that I managed to read before that were the words at the bottom of the page. They were underlined twice and said, "Nobody should read this letter."

"What does Tata write?" I asked.

"That I should come and see him on Sunday."

"And about himself? How he is doing?"

"He writes that they have come and taken away Dr. Jezdinsky. You know, the doctor who took such good care of him."

"How come? Why?"

"Because he's Jewish."

She took a candle from the drawer and put it on the little table next to the statuette of the Virgin.

"What are you doing?" I asked.

"That one is for Dr. Jezdinsky. I'll light it tonight."

It was time to go to school. When I was standing at the door she said: "Here are three cents to get some yeast at Müller's on your way back. You won't forget?"

"No, Mama!"

That I surely wouldn't. If I had to get yeast, she must have some flour. And if she had flour, she was going to bake. I already saw her taking the fresh bread out of the oven. I knew the lovely smell that would spread through the house.

It was busy in the shop. Mr. Müller was serving Mrs. Vítek, Stěpán's mother. Stěpán was in my class. We used to be friends, but lately he wouldn't even look at me. He came to my place once and said that I didn't have a single toy that was worth owning.

The whole class was a little jealous of Stěpán because he was the only one who had real leather shoes. We all walked on clogs with canvas on the top. Once,

[57]

when I asked Mama how Štěpán's father had managed to become so rich all of a sudden, she got mad and said: "It's all goods stolen from the Jews."

Mrs. Vítek was ready. She had ordered her groceries. And Mr. Müller promised that the errand boy would get it to her soon. As she walked to the door, he rushed past her in order to open it for her.

Once back behind the counter, he told the other customers what decent and kind people the Víteks were. He knew Mr. Vítek well from the weekly political meetings.

When my turn finally came, Mr. Müller didn't even bother to open his mouth. He just nodded his head for me to say what I wanted. I put my three cents on the speckled rubber mat and said, "A package of yeast, please."

He tossed it onto the counter right under my nose. When I stretched out my hand to take it, he hissed, "Just tell your mother she'd better come to the store soon."

"Yes, Mr. Müller, I'll tell her."

When I came home Mama asked, "Well? Did Mr. Müller say something?"

"Only if you would come to the store."

Without answering she went over to the shelf with the clock and took down the booklet that was lying next to it. It had a faded blue jacket, and long ago it had had "Müller's groceries" written on it in gold letters. She sighed and sat down at the table with it. I knew exactly what was going to happen next. First she would start leafing through the booklet. Then she would sit and stare into space for a long time, her head resting on her hands. And finally she'd start crying.

The best thing was not to be around. That's why I said, "I'll just go to the square, to see if the other boys are there."

The boys were trading stamps. I heard Zdenko say: "Not that one!" To which Stěpán answered, "But it's such a beautiful one." Zdenko shouted impatiently, "How many times do I have to tell you that I only want Czech stamps. Real Czech stamps, without Hitler on them!"

"I'm going to tell my father on you!" Stěpán shouted angrily. He was so furious that he got all red. The other boys laughed at him and shouted: "Mad Stěpán! Mad Stěpán! That's what you get when you walk around in Jews' clothes!" Stěpán became angrier still. He gathered up his stamps and screamed: "You just wait! I'm going to tell my father everything!" "Then you can also tell him that *we* don't walk around in Jews' clothes and that my mother is praying for the Jews!" I shouted after him.

When I came home Mama said, "Pavel, when I finish ironing, you have to help me carry the clean laundry to Mrs. Čemková." I always went with her when there was too much laundry to carry alone. But I also had a date with Janěk. After dark we were going to go and secretly eat cherries in old Kováček's orchard. So I said, "Okay, Mama. But on the way back I have to stop by at Janěk's."

"That late?"

"He wasn't in school today. And I promised the teacher to bring him his homework."

She mumbled something that I couldn't understand. But then she said, "As long as you see to it that you are back before dark."

Janěk was already waiting for me outside. Kováček didn't live far from Janěk's house, only about ten houses further on. But we'd never seen his house because his yard was surrounded by a very high hedge. That made us curious. We didn't talk on the way. Janěk must have

been thinking about the cherries, as I was. I already saw myself sitting on a branch, high up in the tree. With one hand I'd pick the cherries and with the other I'd put them in my mouth, one after another, until I was so full that I couldn't swallow another one. And then I'd stuff my pockets full of cherries as well. And when I came home I would give those to Mama. How happy she would be! And she'd forget her anger completely.

We arrived at the hedge. Janĕk asked, "Shall I go first?"

"All right," I said.

He clicked his tongue and said, "When you hear me do this three times, you come too."

When we were inside you could still see the trees. They were a shade darker than the sky, but you could hardly tell one from the other. I thought, *We'll never find the cherry tree. It's much too dark already.*

Janĕk nudged me. "There! That's it, I bet!" he said.

If that was really it, then it was very near us. We only had to cross a small piece of grass. Janĕk crept in front of me, glancing left and right as if danger lurked everywhere.

When we were almost there, I heard something. Janĕk took one step back.

"Did you hear *that?*" he asked, scared.

"Yes! What was it?"

"I don't know. . . . An animal, maybe."

"Let's go back," I whispered.

I was scared. Everything seemed so creepy in the dark there.

Then I bumped into something. It was not a stump or a shrub. It was something . . . that was moving . . . that was alive. . . . And now it even made a sound— *Ooww . . . ow . . . ow . . .*—like a complaint or a moan.

Janĕk whispered, "I touched it! It's human . . . it's a child. . . ."

Again we heard: "*Ooww . . . ooww . . .*"

"Pavel!" Janĕk hissed. "Give me your hand, here!"

I felt a leg and then an ankle and then a rope. . . .

"Is it tied up?" I asked with difficulty. My throat had suddenly become so dry that I could hardly speak.

"Yes! And the rope is tied to the tree!" Janĕk shouted, his voice shaking.

"What shall we do?" I asked.

"I don't know," Janĕk said. "But let's wait awhile. Maybe they'll come to fetch it soon."

We hid behind a bush. But nobody came. We had completely forgotten about the cherries. The only thing we could think about was trying to find out who could have left that child here.

We waited and waited. But nothing happened. Finally I said, "We have to go home. We can't stay here all night." Janĕk was about to answer when we heard footsteps. They belonged to somebody who had come out of the house. Then we recognized the voice of the old Kováček. He said, "Come here, you dirty Jew."

We heard him doing something, and then he walked away. Back to the house.

"He must have taken the child with him," I said.

But then it came again, that moaning sound: "*Ooww . . . ooww . . . ooww . . .*"

We crept to the tree and blindly groped all around. Suddenly I held a leg in my hand. The rope was still tied around it. The old man had just shortened it. The child was now lying next to the tree.

"How could he! We must go to the police!" I cried— much too loud.

Janĕk covered my mouth with his hand and whispered, "We have to be careful, Pavel. It is a Jewish child. . . ."

"But he is tied up. That's not allowed."

"I know that. But we still can't go to the police."

"Why not?"

"Because it's dangerous."

"How come?"

"When they find out that it's a Jewish child, they'll come and get him."

"But we have to do something! We can't leave him here just like that, can we?"

"Let's come back tomorrow. Now it's too late anyway."

"All right then."

"Pavel . . . Will you promise me something?"

"What?"

"That this will be our secret. Just between the two of us."

The next day I was in the schoolyard before Janĕk. "What happened to you?" I asked when he finally arrived. He was walking like an old, broken man. "My father beat me up," he sighed. "And I couldn't sleep all night. Not because of that, but because of the child."

Then I had been luckier. I got a box on the ear and was sent straight to bed. But I also slept badly because I kept feeling that *"Ooww . . . ooww . . . ooww . . ."* coming in waves through my whole body.

"Do you still want to go back, then?" I asked.

"Of course. We have to know if the child is still there."

The bell rang. Janĕk and I were not in the same class. He was nine and I was eight.

Quickly I asked, "What do we do then?"

"This afternoon I have to take the goat out, anyway. I'll stop by at your place."

The teacher said that we would have a visitor. Lieutenant Veselý, the leader of the Hlinkaguard*,

*Organization of Slovak Fascists.

wanted to talk to us. When he entered we all stood up. He looked at the class, cleared his throat, and said: "We have received complaints about this class. A few pupils have said insulting things about members of the Hlinkaguard. Such incidents are inadmissible and will be punished severely."

He paced up and down before the class. It was dead quiet; nobody dared to move. Suddenly he stopped and clicked his heels. He took a piece of paper from his pocket, looked at it, and asked, "Is there a certain Pavel here in this class?"

My heart beat in my throat and I said, "Yes, that's me."

"Oh, so I see." He looked at me from top to toe. Then he pulled a face and said, "So that's you. And, Pavel . . . Do you also have a family name? For instance your father's?"

"My father's name is Novák. Jan Novák."

"And where is Jan Novák? In the army?"

"My father is in the hospital. He had an accident."

"An accident! What a pity!"

He said it in a tone as if it were actually quite funny. There was giggling behind me.

"So, while your father is in the hospital, your mother is praying for the Jews. Did I understand that correctly?" The children thought it was funny. Drops of sweat trickled down my back.

"My mother prays for the people who suffer. And for those who are unhappy. And so for the Jews also."

He snorted and said: "Just tell your mother to go easy on her knees. Otherwise they may be worn out by the time she needs them for herself. So worn out that there'll be nothing left of them. Just like there'll be nothing left of the Jews, very soon."

Now the class burst out laughing. When there was silence again, he said in an almost friendly tone, "Pavel!

Why don't you join the Hlinkaguard? You'll get a beautiful uniform."

"But you have to pay for it yourself. My mother doesn't have the money."

"Then you'll have to wait until you earn some money yourself."

"The money I earn won't go into buying a uniform."

He got mad, shook his fist, and shouted: "You good-for-nothing! You'll never amount to anything! Soon you'll be walking around with a star, just like the Jews!"

He clicked his heels, said, "Heil Hitler," and stomped out of the classroom.

On the way home Zdenko caught up with me. "Don't take it too hard," he said. "That Vesely is the biggest bastard of all. My father said it himself."

"Really?"

"That crook knocked old Mr. Schwartz's teeth right out of his mouth."

"How come?"

"Because he didn't get up to say, 'Heil Hitler.' "

"But the old man is paralyzed. He can't get up."

"That's just it. That's why he's such a rat."

I started awake. Somebody was tapping at the window. I had fallen asleep with my head on my exercise book.

It was Janěk. "Wait!" I called. "Let me help you with the goat." I went outside and we tied her up to a big nail.

We pretended to be doing our homework. But instead we were making plans for the evening. We were going to go to Kováček's garden before dark because we wanted to be able to see the child. At least, if he was still there. Mama stuck her head around the door and said: "Pavel, I'm just taking the laundry over to Mrs. Mednanska."

She had just walked out when we heard her scream. It sounded like a disaster.

We jumped up and ran outside. The clean wash was lying scattered all over the ground and the goat was drinking from the bucket. "Take that bucket away from him," she screamed. "There is chlorine in it!" Janĕk flew to his goat and pulled its head out of the bucket. And Mama went on moaning, her hands in the air, "Mother Maria! Good Heavens! Have Mercy!"

I stood there as if paralyzed. Everything that had happened these last few days came back to me. Only bad things were happening. . . . I ran up to Mama and shouted: "Forgive me! I thought we had tied the goat up so well!" I clung to her and burst into tears. Mama didn't say anything anymore, and after a while she began stroking my hair. When we had stood there for quite a long time, she said, "Just take the goat back. And better not say anything. Either it will die, or it will live."

On the way I said to Janĕk, to make him feel better: "Well . . . At least it's just a goat."

"I know . . . but I love my goat," he said, and then I saw that he too had been crying.

"Do you still want to go see the child?" I asked.

"Of course. We can't just abandon him."

Because it was still light out, we found the child immediately. It was a boy of about three. He was asleep. But we couldn't see his face because it was covered with his hand.

"What a stink," Janĕk said as he bent over him. I also smelled it, and then I saw that his legs were covered with dirty brown stains. He had done it in his pants. . . . Not once, but many times.

"Sssh . . ." hissed Janĕk. "Somebody's coming." He

grabbed my arm and didn't let go until we were sitting behind a bush.

It was Kováček's wife. She had a bowl in her hand and called, "Poldi! Poldi!" When she was at the child's side, she slapped the bowl down on the ground and shouted, "Dinner! Dinner! I have potatoes for you!"

The child woke up. When he saw the bowl he got up on all fours and threw himself onto it. His head inside the bowl, he started to eat and gobbled everything up down to the very last crumb. Like a famished dog. . . .

"Now drink!" she said when the bowl was empty, and she held a mug to his mouth. Poldi lifted his head and started to drink. He took such big gulps that we could hear the chug-chugging in our hiding place. The woman went back into the house.

I felt like saying something to Janěk. But I didn't know what. I couldn't speak. What I had seen was so horrible that I didn't have words for it.

Janěk was also silent. We just sat there, staring into space behind that bush. But suddenly, as if he came to his senses and remembered what we were there for, he said: "Let's go see him."

Poldi lay on his back. His eyes were open. They were big blue eyes, but they weren't seeing anything. He had a sweet little face, but it was covered with dirt and scabs. I said, "Poldi! Here we are again."

"We came back, Poldi. We are your friends," Janěk said.

Poldi looked at us. At last. And then, again he did it: "*Ooww . . . ooww . . . ooww . . .*" I took out my handkerchief and started to wipe his face.

"You like that, don't you," I said.

"*Ooww . . . ooww . . . ooww . . . ooww . . .*" again. Now tears were rolling down his cheeks.

"Poldi," Janěk said. "When we come back tomor-

row, we'll bring you something nice to eat. Will you wait for us?"

"*Ooww . . . ooww . . . ooww . . .*" we heard again. But now it sounded different. As if he had understood us.

"We have to go!" I shouted. Somebody had rung the bell at the house. Janĕk had also heard it. He said in a rush, "Bye, Poldi! Be brave." And we ran to the hedge. Before I climbed over I glanced back. I thought I saw Poldi lift his hand just for a second.

I ran home as fast as I could. I only stopped once I got to the door. The whole world started whirling around me. I was so tired I just sank down on the steps. "What's the matter, Pavel? What are you doing here?" I heard Mama ask. She didn't say anything about my being so late. For a moment I thought she knew where I had been, and I decided to tell her everything. But then I remembered my pact with Janĕk. And I also realized that she couldn't do anything for Poldi either. It would only make her miserable. So I just said, "I think I'll go to bed right now."

"You don't want to eat anything?"

"Thanks, Mama. I had a plate of poppyseed noodles at Janĕk's."

"That's good. Sleep well, my boy. And don't worry about the laundry. It's hanging on the line to dry again."

From my bed I could hear her washing and undressing herself. They were familiar noises, and I was glad to be safe at home. When she started her evening prayer I got out of bed and knelt down next to her. She looked at me and I asked, "Mama, would you help me pray tonight for somebody?"

"Of course, Pavel. Who do you want us to pray for, then?"

"For Tata . . . and for a little Jewish boy who is very unhappy. . . ."

The next morning Mama said that I had slept very restlessly. I kept calling out, "Poldi! Poldi!" in my sleep.

Janĕk was not in school. When I stopped by on the way home his mother told me that he was sick. And she also said that she had found the goat dead that morning.

Janĕk woke up when I came in. His cheeks were bright red. I sat down, but after quite a while he still hadn't said a word. Maybe he didn't like it that I had come. So I said, "I should go. . . ." But then he whispered, "No, not now. Just wait a little longer."

There was a knock at the door and Janĕk's mother went to open it. When she'd left the room he pulled a bottle out from under the blankets. There were stewed pears in it. "Take it," he whispered. "My godmother gave it to me. I want you to take it to Poldi."

The bottle felt warm. As if it also had a fever. I quickly hid it under my coat. Then he said, "You can go now. And don't forget to take a spoon with you."

That evening, when I stood outside the hedge, I suddenly got a bad feeling inside. As if my heart was trapped in an iron vise. *Don't be a baby*, I kept telling myself. *You're only afraid because now you're alone.*

Poldi was lying on his back. One arm was stretched out and he held a bunch of grass. He had eaten some of it, but afterwards he had thrown up. His mouth was all covered with green.

"Poldi!" I cried, "You shouldn't eat grass! Look here, see what I brought you. . . ."

But he wouldn't listen. He didn't even move his head. He only stared at me with those big blue eyes. And then suddenly I felt that iron vise squeezing my

heart again. "Poldi . . . Poldi . . .," I begged. "Look here, look at these beautiful pears. . . ."

But nothing happened. Everything was just as quiet. The only thing that moved was a green fly walking over Poldi's chin.

I started to shake him. But he seemed made out of stone. "Please, come on now, Poldi, please!" I yelled.

The vise squeezed harder and harder. My whole chest ached. I dropped the bottle and ran toward the house. Old Kováček sat outside, on a bench. When he looked up I bawled, "Poldi! Poldi! He is *dead!*"

Today Pavel says:

"Despite the passage of time, I've never stopped seeing that little Poldi, that little Jewish boy who wanted to live, to live without fear, without being tied to a tree by the leg, without dying with a mouth full of bitter grass.

"What can I say about people like the Kováčeks, who promised Poldi's unfortunate parents that they would hide Poldi and save him from the gas chambers? Only that human cruelty is always waiting for an opportunity—it is waiting for that opportunity even now."

Pavel still lives in Nitra, the Slovak town where these events took place. He is married and works as a dental technician.

INGE

GERMANY

It's half past ten already and the sirens haven't gone off yet. Aren't they going to bomb us tonight? Or maybe they won't come till after midnight? I really can't stay awake that long. I've already fallen asleep once, or maybe even twice. It's awful to be woken up by those sirens when I'm fast asleep. Then I'm so tired I just can't get dressed. My arms and legs feel like they weigh a hundred pounds. And then, when I'm dressed, I have to rush, in the dark, quick-quick, down all those stairs.

But in our cellar it's always very nice. In the beginning I didn't know what was going to happen. Because before, when Vati* and Mutti** would talk about the neighbors, they would say things like "They're not our sort," or "We should keep the children away from them."

Mutti now seems to have forgotten all that. She chats with the neighbors as if she's always liked them a lot and as if she'd never said all that. I just hope that she doesn't mind my playing with the children next

*"Father" in German.
**"Mother" in German.

[71]

door all the time now. If Vati were here I could ask him. Or he'd say something about it himself. Because he's always so sure about everything.

I haven't seen Vati for months and months—a year at least—more than a year. When the telephone was still working he used to call often. He'd say, "Tonight we are going to the opera," or ". . . . to the concert," or ". . . to the theater." He has such a wonderful life there in Berlin. Mutti says that he goes all over the place with the Führer. That is his job.

Sometimes he sends presents. Once a green satin evening dress for Mutti with a matching fur stole dyed exactly the same color green. But where is she going to wear it? She never goes out. He's not planning to let her come to Berlin, is he? I hope not. On the little card that was with it, he'd written "Your Adolf . . ." How strange. That is his middle name, but he had never used it before.

For Christmas he sent me a porcelain ballerina. She has a pink tutu and makes a beautiful pirouette on her tiptoes. But unfortunately she is standing on top of a swastika. Such a delicate little doll on a big black swastika. They just don't seem to go together. How come Vati didn't see that? Wasn't that clear? But of course I didn't say anything about it, not even to Mutti.

Before, I thought that psalms were meant to be sung in the church only. But now I know that people go to church in order to learn them for when they really need them. The louder the noise of the bombs outside, the more beautifully we sing in the cellar. The other day, when the house next to ours was hit, the noise was terrifying. All that creaking and crashing coming from next door made me ache all over. The whole cellar was shaking and we all held our breath. But then suddenly— as if it had been planned—our voices melted together

and a beautiful sound rose out of us as if it were coming out of one throat.

Mutti says it's been only three months since the bombing started. But that's not possible, they have been bombing us for years! Or at least one year. How else could she have changed so much in three months? She looks so stern now she's pulled back her beautiful hair. And her face is so pale. But of course I can't say that to her.

Mutti is terribly scared. She says that the bombs will fall on our house sooner or later. And then we'll be hurt, or maybe even killed. When she is so frightened I always snuggle up close to her. That helps, because then the shaking stops immediately. Often we sit like that for hours, clutching each other. Sometimes she starts kissing me and stroking my hair. And then she often says, "My little Inge, you are my very dearest girl. . . ." I never knew that she could be so sweet, so tender and so soft. How wonderful to have a mother who can cuddle with me like that. When I'm sitting so close to her I feel that she can protect me from anything. It's funny really that I never knew I had such a sweet mother. I'm not supposed to say it, not even think it, but I like the bombings. Because then I can cuddle up close to Mutti.

Poor Mutti. Being afraid of the bombs is one thing. But her biggest worry is that they will come for Karl and take him away. He just turned thirteen, and if they find him he will be sent to the front immediately. They don't make any exceptions. Vati being so important in Berlin doesn't seem to make any difference. "On the contrary," Mutti says, and then she starts to cry.

That's why she decided that we too should leave. The Red Cross is organizing transports to the East and the people said there already is peace over there. I wonder what peace looks like; I don't remember the time before the war. The only thing I can imagine going

[73]

with peace is toy shops full of dolls and beautiful tiny clothes. And lovely cream cakes like éclairs.

Now that Mutti has made up her mind I don't mind leaving at all. The cellar is getting emptier and emptier. Most of the neighbors have already gone. Where have they gone? When they leave they don't say anything, they just look sad. According to Mutti, they don't know themselves. But they can't stay here, in the cellar. The whole city of Bonn is a heap of rubble. It is a miracle that our house is still standing. But the water mains have been destroyed, and there is nothing to eat anymore.

The peace in the East is not at all what we had expected. It has taken us a week to get here, but at long last we have arrived in Lansberg-an-der-Wachte. Mutti says that it is near the Polish border. The other morning we heard a strange rumbling from behind the hills. It got louder and louder and we thought it was cannons. In the evening the sky turned red. It was beautiful, but we couldn't enjoy it because we knew that danger was coming closer to us.

We were woken in the middle of the night last night. What was going on? Who were those people? Were they human? With those weird eyes? And those big, furry hats? They didn't speak. They only made loud sounds and chased us outside. Some people were so tired after the long trip that they couldn't get up and stayed lying down. Once they had got us to stand in a long line they went inside. And a few minutes later we heard shots.

Mutti is black and blue all over, and all scratched and cut too. I can't bear to look at it. We were walking along that muddy road through the fields when suddenly two of those soldiers came up to her. They grabbed her arms and dragged her away. When she told us not to stop and to go on, one of them gave her an

[74]

enormous blow. He threw her into the ditch and then we heard terrible screaming. I felt all sick, as if my body was being torn open.

Karl said we had to go on. But I couldn't, my legs were trembling. Then he lifted me and carried me on his back. The noise got weaker and weaker, it did not sound like screaming anymore. Or was it only because by then we were too far away to hear it?

Since that day Mutti looks like a little old woman. She always wears a kerchief around her head. Fortunately not a black one, that would be even worse.

As we walk along I always look down at the ground. You never know. The other day I found a potato. I nibbled at it, very slowly. It was delicious. I never knew that raw potatoes could taste so good. And I never would have thought that you could just eat weeds and grass. But unfortunately they don't really help against the hunger. For a little while you feel filled up, but then your stomach starts grumbling just as badly again. How wonderful it must be, just for once, not to have to think of your stomach—to forget that you have one.

The other day a cow was mooing in a barn. They sent Mutti to milk her. And when she returned with a full bucket the soldier turned it upside down. I thought that was really mean. What have we done that he is punishing us for?

Sometimes we sleep in empty houses. But most of the time outside, under the stars. The other day I found a horse blanket in a barn. But somebody took it off me while I was sleeping. When I think of my little bed at home I just can't imagine that I ever slept in there. What a life I had, like a spoiled little princess! When I sneezed Mutti would say, "Oh, oh, Inge, let's hope you're not getting a cold again!"

I remember Mutti always made me drink chicken soup when I was sick. Without that there was no way,

she said, for me to get better. Since we left home I haven't even sneezed once. That's just as well, because here we don't have any chicken soup.

I don't know which is worse, the hunger or my poor aching feet. I should have taken along those high shoes with the rubber soles. But when we left home it was summer and Mutti thought we were going to where there was peace. Since my sandals broke I have been wearing old rags tied around my feet. That is very hard to walk in, especially when it rains.

In the beginning I was very much afraid of the soldiers. But the Russians never harm children. Mutti says that I'm lucky that I'm only nine. That's why I always hang around, because you never know what you can get. The other day when they slaughtered a horse one of the soldiers threw the head at me. The thing was so heavy that it slipped out of my hands. But he even tied a rope around it for me and I could drag it to Mutti all by myself. How proud I was! Food for a week!

Mutti was very happy when she saw me arriving dragging that head. She thought I was a clever girl and said that I could take care of myself very well. But I didn't like it when she put it like that. Why is she so sure that I can get by all by myself? Does she think I don't need her anymore?

Once they made us stop for a few days. The women had to make new pants for the soldiers. For every pair of pants they sewed they got a slice of bread. When Mutti got hers she gave it to Karl.

Boys always come first. There's no getting around it, mothers love their sons more. It seems that it's always been that way. It's not just Mutti. All the German mothers are like that. It's normal, and I shouldn't blame her for it. That's why I wouldn't have minded a bit if she'd given me a smaller piece. A little less than half, like a third. Even, if necessary, a tiny little piece. But

she didn't give me anything. None at all. And that I minded—a lot. So much so that I just can't forget it. That I hardly can forgive her for it. Does it mean that she doesn't love me at all? Or did she do it because she thinks I can take care of myself? But doesn't she understand that I do my very best only because I want to help her? Because I know that she is having such a hard time?

I can understand why she is so worried about Karl. Just the other day two soldiers came and took him away. He didn't even dare to look back to wave good-bye. That afternoon I couldn't find Mutti. She had disappeared too. But late the following night they came back together. Mutti didn't say a word. She didn't have to; I knew very well that she'd gone to the lieutenant and that she had slept with him. I can understand that. She sacrificed herself for her child. She is a heroine. But I can't tell her that of course. You can't talk about that kind of thing. What a pity, because those are the things that really matter!

The first time it snows we are walking through a village. School is just out and the children start throwing snowballs. I bend down because I want to make one too. But then I see my feet covered by bloodstained rags. I get a shock. What is going to happen next? Next, next . . . I don't want to think about it. I never think about the next day. I am just happy when the evening comes. That is the best time. Then I think, *How nice that I'm still alive.* Suddenly nothing else matters anymore.

Every night, before falling asleep, I give myself a little present. I make up a little story. Not just an ordinary story, but something really special. Something that doesn't have anything to do with ordinary life. Usually it is about a young prince who is handsome and rich. His life is perfect, only he is a bit lonely. That's why he always has himself driven around in his golden

carriage. One day, when he happens to pass by, he sees me lying there and orders his coachman to stop. He steps out, comes nearer, and slides his strong arms under my back. In a moment he lifts me carefully, as if I am very fragile. And while I am still asleep he carries me to the carriage.

In the beginning, in Lansberg-an-der-Wachte, there were more than three hundred of us. Now, after eight months, we are hardly a hundred and fifty. Of course we all know each other a little. Once I asked Mr. Schmidt where he thought all the others had gone.

"Most of them are dead. They died from hunger or they were shot because they couldn't walk anymore. A few have also fled."

"How did they do that?"

"They simply ran off."

"Is that why there was shooting last night in the middle of the night?"

"Yes, those two were unlucky. It was a brother and a sister. I knew them quite well. They left a letter for their relatives with me. In case they didn't make it."

"And you, don't you want to run away?"

"I am much too old and too tired. And nobody is waiting for me anymore. My wife died when our house was bombed."

"Do you know where they are taking us?"

"I suppose to one camp or another. And there they'll let us slowly starve to death."

A few days later I heard somebody whispering in the middle of the night, "Not now, idiot. There is a full moon."

"Can't you hear the Russians snoring? They're dead drunk. They had three bottles of vodka."

I saw two figures move and thought, *I have to follow them*. The only other thing I remember is that we

walked endlessly. Until we saw a train that was standing still, and we climbed into it. I think I slept for a very long time, and when I woke up I was here in Berlin.

I've been here for three weeks now and my eczema is already a lot better. My feet still hurt a lot, especially my small toe. It is totally frostbitten and will probably have to be operated on. I only hope that they don't have to cut it off. But actually I'm not afraid of anything anymore. Nothing really bad can happen now that Mutti and Karl have also arrived in Berlin. The Red Cross told them where I was, and so they came looking for me here.

We have been back in Bonn a year, but we haven't heard anything yet from Vati. We don't even know if he is alive or dead. One evening, very late, somebody rings the bell. Could it be him? That's what we keep hoping, but it always turns out to be somebody else. That's why I don't even dare to think of his return.

Then we see a skinny man coming up the stairs. That can't be him—Vati is heavy and round. But it *is* him all right! Only there is nothing left of him! I can't believe it. My Vati has come back! It is a miracle! They had taken him to Russia and after one year they let him go.

That night I can't sleep. I am so happy and excited that I can only think of Vati. My prince didn't even come. Where is he? With him you never know. He is so sensitive and modest and prefers to stay in the background. But now I don't have time to think of him. I am much too busy making plans for our new life. At last we are together again!

Vati keeps on wearing his mess tin and mug on his belt and he doesn't want to eat out of anything else. He hardly ever says anything and most of the time he sits in the big chair, looking straight ahead. I tell him all

kinds of stories about the bombing and about our long march through Poland. But it is as if he doesn't hear me. When I ask him what he did all that time he says that we could never understand. Only his friends know what he's gone through. And then he goes to the bar again and stays there endlessly, talking to his friends.

Once, when Mutti went there to fetch him, he got very angry. When they came home and the front door was shut, he started to hit her. Karl and I couldn't stand it and tried to separate them.

Since that time Mutti never goes to fetch him again. But when he comes home drunk he beats her up all the same. And he is stronger than the three of us together. Poor Mutti! I try to comfort her. When she is sad she seems so delicate and small. Then I throw my arms around her and let her cry on my shoulder. And we sit like that for a long time. Just like before, in the cellar. And then I am her little Inge again and I love her just as much as back then.

Today Inge says:

"I am not bitter. I think that people who have gone through so much suffering are somehow richer and that happiness and sadness affects them in a much stronger way. Emotions that spring from love, nature, music, and literature touch us deeper than those who have never been hurt or wounded. I also think that people who have suffered a great deal want their lives to make sense to themselves and to others. In a way I am even grateful for all that was decided for me."

Inge's father became an alcoholic and died shortly after the war. Inge lives with her husband and son in Hamburg, where she works as a librarian.

Jules

BELGIUM

"Papa! Papa! I want to go with you. Down to the corner."

"No question, Jules. You just go upstairs. Then you can help Maman with the beds."

"I don't want to go upstairs. I want to go down to the corner."

"Don't whine, Jules. I have to leave. I'm late already."

Now I start to cry very loudly. As if I'm hurt. Then he always listens.

"Come on. . . . What's the matter?"

"I don't want to stay home. I want to go with you. To the corner."

The other day the ice cream man was standing at the street corner. And I was allowed to go there all by myself. With twenty centimes in my hand. To buy myself an ice cream.

"But what is there for you at the corner?"

"I want to go look . . ."

"At what?"

"At the soldiers. I want to look at the soldiers. In Leopold Street."

[83]

"Why?"

"They're so beautiful."

"No way—you're not going, Jules. And stop it!"

I start to cry again.

"Why do you want to go to the corner? The soldiers march right by our house. Why should you wait for them there?"

"Because!"

" 'Because' is no good reason!"

Leopold Street is very long. You can see the soldiers when they are still very small. And then they get bigger and bigger. And suddenly they are close by. And at the corner they have to make a turn. That is so beautiful! And it goes so fast! And you can only see it there. There at the corner.

He is angry now. I start stamping my foot.

"I want to go down to the corner!"

"If you want to see the soldiers you just look out of the window."

The front door is already open. He is going outside. Try the garden. . . . Quickly!

"I don't want to stay inside. I want to be outside. In the garden!"

"All right then. You can go in the front garden. But I warn you! Stay inside the gate!"

I've been standing here a very long time. But nobody has come by. The soldiers must all be in Leopold Street. Maman shouts from upstairs, "Jules! Jules!"

Just let her shout.

"Jules! Jules! Jules!"

"Yeees. . . ."

"What are you doing there?"

"I'm watching."

"It's much too cold. It's raining, even!"

She comes out of the house. She wants to take me inside.

"I want to stay here! I want to wait!"

"For what?"

"The soldiers."

"Maybe they're not coming by today."

"Yes. They are."

"How can you know that?"

"I know it. They will come. They come every day."

Papa . . . Maman . . . It is dark. It is night. They say, "Come, darling. . . . Don't get scared. You don't have to worry." They tuck the blanket in around me. The big woolen blanket. I'm completely inside it. My head too. But I can still look outside.

Papa is carrying me. He is going down the stairs. We are walking down the street! Like that! I don't have to walk. He carries me all the way. Until we get to the underground shelter.

I love it when they come in the night, the planes that throw the bombs. Sometimes I can hear the bombs even before we get to the shelter. Then I see lots of little lights. It's so beautiful! Just like fireworks! And all that noise! So very loud!

The other day Papa lost his slipper. But he didn't stop. He left it lying in the street. He just ran faster to the shelter. And held me tight against his chest.

But in the cellar it's not so much fun. There Papa gives me to Maman. And I sit on her lap. Papa goes upstairs. And he stands talking with the other men and looking at the bombs. He can see them all. He can see them fall. And he sees the lights. I wish I was finally grown-up!

I passed the butcher's house with Maman. But I didn't see the bed. When the bomb fell on his house, the butcher was sleeping. And he fell down in his bed! Two floors!

[85]

If a bomb falls on our house I'll do what that old woman did. When she heard the noise she crept under the table. And after that the firemen came. She had slept under the table for three nights!

I hope the bomb comes soon. Maman doesn't like me to say that. She says that bombs are dangerous. And that they can kill people. Yesterday seven people died. But we don't even know them. And they live all the way in the Emma Street. That can't happen here.

This soldier here has something wrong with his foot. He can't stand up straight very well. He's wobbling a bit. Papa says that he can't fix it. If he touches it again the foot could break off. And then the soldier couldn't stand up at all anymore.

This soldier is naughty! He won't stand up straight! That's why he has to go to jail. To punish him. But then I won't have enough soldiers. Then I have only two short lines of four. If he isn't in jail, I have three lines. And that's much better. But he keeps wobbling! And that spoils everything!

Maman says that she can't buy me any more soldiers. There is a war on and they don't have any soldiers left. But I think she is telling lies. It isn't possible! Soldiers belong to wars, don't they? Like guns. And airplanes. And cannons. Maman is only saying that to tease me. Because it's my birthday soon. I'll be four.

Papa has counted them. There are twenty-seven of them. The soldiers that march by every day. The one that walks alone on the side is the boss. That is the chief. Papa says that he is a lieutenant. He walks so beautifully straight. All of them walk straight. But he walks even straighter. They march so beautifully in step: *tip, tap, tip, tap, tip, tap* . . . They march so well in time. They fling their legs up. All at the same time.

Completely straight. It is so nice to look at. And then, when they lower their legs, I suddenly see a tunnel. Could I slip through there very fast? I don't think so. It *should* be possible. But there wouldn't be enough time.

Papa also used to be a soldier, when he was young. He still has his cap. It is lying in the bottom of the wardrobe. The other day, when I heard the soldiers, I quickly went to fetch his cap. I put it on and went and stood outside on the front step. And when they passed by I held up my hand against it. And the lieutenant saw it. He looked at me and I saw his head moving! I shouted, "Maman, Maman! He saluted me! The lieutenant saluted me!"

But Maman was not happy at all. She doesn't like the soldiers. She never wants to come see them when they march.

I put Papa's cap back in the wardrobe. But I can't find it anymore. It's gone. Maman says she doesn't know where it is.

Where is he? What's become of him? Where is Jacques? He must be hiding behind that bush! But I can't call out to him. Otherwise they could hear us. And then they would come and look for us. If they find us here . . .

Here I am, all by myself. I didn't even want to come. Jacques wanted to go in. He's always got to see everything. He didn't even know what was here, before. He only knows because of me.

When I passed this way with Papa I asked him, "Papa, why is there always a soldier standing there? At the big gate?"

"He is standing guard."

"What does he have to guard?"

"The Gestapo."

"But isn't this the house of the Baroness?"

[87]

"Yes. Before. But not anymore. Now it belongs to the Germans."

"Papa? What do they do at the Gestapo?"

"That's a secret. They're a kind of police."

"Are they strict?"

"Yes. Very strict."

"Do they do bad things?"

"Yes. Sometimes they do very bad things."

"What kind of bad things?"

"That's not for little children. You don't have to know that."

"But I want to know! What *are* they doing?"

"They interrogate people."

"Which people?"

"People they suspect."

"What is 'suspect'?"

"When they think that people are against them."

"Do they suspect us? The Belgians?"

"Yes. Some Belgians."

"Papa! What is 'interrogate'?"

"That is when they ask things."

"And why is that bad?"

"When the people don't want to answer, they get a beating."

"Really? Grown-ups? And do they beat hard?"

"Yes. Very hard."

"So that they scream?"

"I suppose so. I don't know! Please stop it—stop asking all those questions!"

When I told Jacques, he wanted to go inside. He said that you might be able to hear the screaming in the garden. And then he found a hole in the hedge and sneaked inside. I couldn't let him go alone, could I? But I knew Jacques would be careful. He is much older than me. He is seven years old already.

When I came home Maman spanked me. Very hard.

[88]

But I didn't scream. I didn't say a word. She doesn't know where I've been.

Maman is sewing a big flag. Black, yellow, and red. The Belgian colors. Papa is not going to the office today, because it's a holiday. It's peace. The war is over.

Leopold Street is full of people. The Germans are leaving. The people say that they are happy that the Germans are going. And that they hate the Germans.

The Germans are marching, with the lieutenant at their side. But they don't have guns now. They march in step: *tip, tap, tip, tap* . . . Just the same as always. Very straight, without looking to the side. Neatly and exactly, in step.

The people are looking at the soldiers. They're not shouting nasty things. They could if they wanted to. They could even hit them. But they don't do anything. They're very quiet, all of a sudden. Are they still a little bit afraid? Or do they just like to see them march?

Here they are! The Americans! All the people are waving flags. They shout: "Welcome Yankees!" and they are very happy. The soldiers are driving open cars— "Jeeps," says Papa—and they're throwing little packages around. "Chewing gum," says Papa. It tastes good, but you're only supposed to chew it. You musn't eat it. The soldiers are waving their arms. They talk to the people and laugh. One is sitting and the other is standing. They've hung their jackets around their shoulders, and rolled back the sleeves of their shirts. And their caps! They're nice caps, but they're on completely crooked!

Are these men soldiers? Real soldiers? I'm sure they can't march. Certainly not as beautifully as the Germans.

[89]

Maman gets me out the door every morning at a quarter past eight. And school starts at half past eight. When I come home she always wants to know what we did at school. And then she wants to see my exercise book and my homework pad. And then she says, "When your homework is done you can go outside."

Before, when the war was on, everything was more fun. Then she never had the time to bother me. She was always busy with the stove. And she spent all afternoon in the kitchen. And in the evening, after dinner, I was allowed to play outside. Then she'd listen to the radio with Papa.

Now that I'm bigger I'm allowed to do much less. And nothing exciting really happens. There aren't any bombs falling, there isn't even ever an air raid alarm anymore. And you can't find anything good anymore, no shrapnel or cartridges. Not even empty cartridges. There is nothing left from the war.

Before I go to sleep I always think back for a moment to the war. To the time when the soldiers were in Hasselt, and marched past our house every day.

Today Jules says:

"I think of those years of the war as the happiest of my childhood. My family has never been as close as then, and the years that followed now seem drab. To me the war seemed like a big game, where some win and others lose. Until the age of thirteen I played violent games with my friends. We had great respect for militaristic values like discipline, force, and power. But when I was drafted I refused the military service and today I am a pacifist. I believe that playing war games and playing with arms are things that you have to do as a child. These things should be reserved for children and forbidden to adults. War is too serious a game to be left to adults. Only children are capable of avoiding excesses."

Jules is a family therapist and lives in Québec.

YURI

SOVIET UNION

Back then, back then, when we were in the country, at
the dacha . . . When we ate fish every day . . . Fried fish
with boiled potatoes . . . Hot potatoes with big clouds of
steam coming out . . .

When I take a deep breath I can smell those potatoes. And I can see that fish with the hard brown crust
and the soft white underneath. . . . Oh, that can't be
true. . . . I just can't stand to think about it. . . .

That deliciousness, that wonderful taste . . . was
that me? Or was it another Yuri who was eating that?

Mama says that we were still at the dacha this past
summer. So—it's not even that long ago. That's when
the war began. I didn't know a thing then. . . .

I remember the day the war broke out. Grandpa
had taken me with him to the post office. He had to talk
to Uncle Ivan in Moscow. In Gorodetz, you have to go to
the post office to make a phone call. But when we got
there, a lot of people were standing there. They were
waiting for the twelve o'clock news because Mr. Molotov
was going to say something. I didn't understand what
he was saying, but in Grandpa's face I saw that it was

something bad. When I asked Grandpa what was happening, he said, "The Germans have attacked us. And now it is war."

"Who are the Germans, Grandpa?"

"The Germans are our enemy."

"And are they strong?"

"Yes, Yuri, very strong. But not stronger than us."

"So then we're going to win!"

"Yes, we always win."

"But then war is not so bad, is it?"

"Yes, it is, Yuri. War is always bad. But a little boy of five cannot understand those things yet."

I didn't like it at all that Grandpa said that. But now I know that war is very different from what you think, and that it is always bad.

At first I went every day with Sasha to the Psovsyway to look at the military trucks. The trucks rode in long lines to the border and they were packed with soldiers. I never knew there were so many trucks and so many soldiers in the world. Also, I had imagined the soldiers to be very different. I had imagined them laughing and singing. But they were very quiet. And when we waved at them they didn't even wave back. It was as if they were asleep with their eyes wide open.

After only four days, the trucks were coming back. In the beginning only a few, but then more and more. The same trucks, and the same soldiers. But their heads and their arms and legs were now bandaged. Not even with real bandages, but with dirty rags soaked in blood. And they weren't sitting upright, as before. They were sort of slumped over each other—as if they were lumps of bloody meat.

How long have I been lying here in bed, with all my clothes on? At times I think, *It's been years*. But a

moment later it seems like just a few days. Maybe that's because there is hardly any difference between night and day.

At first, we would go to the cellar when there was an air raid alarm. But one day Papa said, "From now on, we will stay upstairs. All that running up and down is only making us weak." But that wasn't the worst thing. He also said, "The children are to stay in bed. All day. There will be no getting up or walking about. There will be no exceptions."

Grandma has come to live with us. Papa does not want her to stay in her own house. Her house is at the edge of our town, near the German lines. They are shooting all the time over there.

Mama is still unhappy that we stayed in Leningrad. We tried to get out just before the Germans shut us in completely. We went every day to the train station and we even slept there a few nights. But there weren't enough trains, and the people were pushing so hard that we could not get on.

I feel so strange. . . . "Mama, Mama!"

"What is it, Yuri? Why do you keep kicking the blanket off?" Mama is next to me and she pulls the blanket back over me.

"Don't, don't! I don't want a blanket!"

"But, Yuri, you will catch cold!"

"No, Mama, I'm terribly hot!"

I don't want a blanket, but she doesn't understand. Can't she understand then that it keeps slithering around, and that it's going to roll itself up, with me inside!

Mama says, "Come on, darling. . . . Take a sip of water and try to get some sleep."

I have slept a little and now I'm crying. But that doesn't matter, I don't mind that at all. Because when I

cry my face becomes all wet and I have to keep sniffing. After I've done that many times my mouth is full of snot and slime. And I like that because it tastes salty.

What are we going to eat tonight? We have already eaten our bread. Every day we get one piece of bread— one hundred grams each, exactly. The same amount for adults and for children. And that is our food for the whole day.

We are lucky because Grandma has a garden, and she goes there often. She has to walk very far through the deep snow. And it's very dangerous because the Germans shoot at anything that moves.

The other day, she came back with a bag of potatoes. They were frozen, but that didn't matter. They tasted so good. But the next time, she had nothing. Everything in the garden had been stolen. She was so angry she cried. She shouted, "If I ever get my hands on those thieves, I'll scratch their eyes out!"

Mama didn't cook anything today. Let's hope there is still a little soup left over from yesterday. I really hope so, because otherwise . . . otherwise, we'll just have to go to sleep again without anything to eat.

I think there is some potato soup left. I'm almost certain of it. There *must* be just a little left. The pan wasn't empty yesterday, it wasn't even nearly empty. That soup couldn't have just disappeared, could it have?

Later, when Papa dishes it out, I'll ask him to scoop some up from the bottom for me. Yesterday I got a portion from the top. And that tasted so watery, because on top the soup is always thinner.

The ceiling has beautiful curly patterns. If you stare at them for a long time they start to move. And then all of a sudden they seem to come alive. Sometimes they get very thin and long and they all start dancing with

each other. Then I tell them to get short again but they don't take any notice of me.

Often they become even longer, and then suddenly they start attacking each other. Just like poisonous snakes. Then I shout, "Stop it! Stop it!" But they go on fighting. That's why I try not to look at the ceiling. I prefer to think about the time that Papa came home with a bag full of sugar. He had been given it at work, just like that—because families with children come first.

Oh, how delicious that was. . . . We got a teaspoon of sugar on our slice of bread. Every day, for at least two weeks.

How easy it all still was back then. I didn't mind at all having to wait all day for that slice of bread with sugar. Because that gave me something good to think about. What else could be better than thinking about a slice of bread with sugar?

But even then Papa was very strict. Our bread had to be cut in tiny little pieces. And they had to be eaten very slowly. We had to chew each piece a long time. But I didn't mind because that way it takes much longer to eat it. Only sometimes . . . sometimes, just once, I'd like to open my mouth very wide and just take a huge bite. One time, when Papa wasn't looking, I ate my soup very fast. But then I got cramps. The same cramps as when, before the war, I had an upset stomach. Luckily the cramps soon passed, but after that I felt terribly blown up. My stomach felt just like a balloon. And then—oh, how hungry I got all of a sudden.

Dmitri from next door is dead. It was just a few days ago that Papa got so mad at him. He walked in, without knocking. "Look here, here it is . . .," he said and pointed to a cookbook he was carrying. Papa shouted: "Stop it, Dmitri! Do stop reading all those

[97]

recipes. It will drive you mad!" But Dmitri pretended not to hear and walked to the table. He opened the book and said in a very strange voice, "Stir the butter into the eggs until the mixture starts foaming. . . ." Mama said, "Okay, Dmitri. We've heard it now. And please go back to your room." Then he began to cry and wailed, "But *look*, Olga! *Believe* me! There! There! There's the foam! I can smell it . . . I can taste it, really I can."

Papa walked up to Dmitri, put his hand on his shoulder, and pushed him out of the room.

And now they are talking about Dmitri. They don't know what they are going to do with him. Papa says that he still has the strength to drag Dmitri down the stairs and leave him in the street with the other bodies. But first he thinks we can keep him up here for at least ten days. It's so cold that it is freezing in here. And all that time we'll be able to use his food card. That will sure be nice.

In the closet, behind an old trunk, Mama found a bottle of cognac. It had been there for years, and nobody had remembered it.

I don't know what cognac is, but they are so cheerful. Tonight they have been drinking it in tiny glasses. First they poured the cognac into a thimble, and then into their glass. But when they finished that, Papa said at least twice more, "Let's have another round. Today we are celebrating."

Sasha and I also had some. A few drops in a glass of water. It didn't taste of anything. But after that I suddenly felt nice and warm.

Is it because of the cognac that they are suddenly talking so much? Papa says people are eating rats. *Brrr* . . . That must be horrible. But Mama says, "It's still better than dying from hunger." Who knows, maybe rats don't taste that bad. And Mama could make some-

thing delicious out of them, I'm sure. So you wouldn't even know that you were eating a rat. As long as you didn't think about that long, thin tail. . . .

We are lucky that Mama can make anything taste wonderful. Today we ate Papa's leather belt. First she soaked it for a very long time in water, and then she cut it into tiny little pieces. It was just like minced meat. That is—if I still remember well how minced meat tastes.

I've got my head buried under the pillow. But I can still hear everything. Papa is angry at Grandma again. He yells, "Mother! How many times do I have to tell you that you shouldn't drink so much water. You know very well that it's dangerous!"

"Oh, leave me alone—it fills me up. It helps the hunger. . . ."

"It doesn't do a thing! It makes you blow up like a balloon!"

"All right, all right . . . It does make me blow up. But it still helps. . . ."

"That's what comes from all that trekking to your garden—that's why you're so hungry."

Now Grandma starts to cry. I hate that. She says, "Please, Vladimir. Just leave me alone. I don't have to be around much longer. As long as you and the children can make it through . . ."

Papa is not so angry anymore. Whew! He gets up and takes out the bottle of cognac.

"If you're so thirsty, Mother, then take a sip of this."

"All right then, Vladimir. Let's drink together."

They empty their glasses in one gulp and Grandma says, "To tomorrow. . . ."

"And to all the other days," says Papa.

"But first to tomorrow. Because tomorrow, I'm going back to my garden."

Papa takes two books out of the bookcase. I know them, they are his favorite books. They are thick and are bound in leather. He says to Mama, "These I had saved for last. I had hoped to be able to keep them. . . ."

I am so impatient. I can hardly wait. When he goes to the black market he always comes home with such wonderful things. Once he had a piece of chocolate! Real chocolate . . . Mmmm . . . I'll never forget how that tasted. Every night before I go to sleep I think about it. Just for a moment. Because if you think about it too long, you start tasting it. And then you feel how it gets soft on your tongue. And how it starts melting. . . . But that's what I don't want to happen. Because it's so awful when you realize all of a sudden that you *don't* have anything in your mouth.

Papa's got a parcel. What could it be? Another piece of chocolate? No, that isn't it. He says, "There's hardly anything left on the black market. The only thing I could get was oatmeal." And then I hear him whispering to Mama, "Can you believe it, Olga . . . For a moment I thought that I could buy some meat. But Kouznetsov tapped me on the shoulder to warn me that it was human flesh."

This is our second winter in Levinka. We came here because we thought that there would be enough to eat in a small village like this. But that isn't true at all. I feel hungry more here than at home in Leningrad. There I lay in bed all day and I didn't know if I was asleep or awake. I'd stopped thinking about my stomach and I just felt as if I was floating.

The other day I suddenly had to cry. I missed Papa so much. He is still in Leningrad. But when I told Mama

I wished I'd stayed with him, she got mad and yelled, "Yuri! How can you say such a stupid thing?! We were nearly *dead!*"

"But there at least my belly left me alone. Here it's grumbling all the time."

"That's because there is still something in it. In Leningrad it was so empty that you didn't feel anything anymore."

"How come? Why does your stomach start to growl when you eat?"

"Because then it wakes up and starts asking for more."

"And when does it stop asking?"

"When you give it enough to eat."

So then, for the time being, my tummy won't leave me alone. Because all that we have left are blackened potatoes. The dandelions and the sorrel and the stinging nettles won't come back until spring.

Oh, I am so fed up with that growling in my stomach!

Last winter we still had the little goat. But in the end she too was hungry all the time, and she didn't give a drop of milk anymore.

If only the snow was gone, I could at least start searching for parsnips and turnips again. I know that there are all sorts of things under the ground. Oh, that parsnip I found last year! I stuffed myself. If I had taken it home Mama could have cooked it. Then it would have tasted even better. But then I would have had to share with the others.

Boris wasn't in school today and the teacher said that he would never come back. He had eaten grains of corn that had been lying under the snow. Poor Boris. . . . How could he have known that that made them poisonous?

Boris was always so terribly hungry. I remember

the day a group of us walked down the road a way. He pointed to the horizon and said, "Do you see, there, that dark line?" We saw a very thin line far away, so we said, "Yes!"

"Fine," he said. "Then you also see the forest. Because there, at *that* line the great forest begins, where everything grows . . . where you can find mushrooms, blackberries, raspberries, and strawberries."

"Hurrah!" we shouted, and we started to run in that direction. Only the forest did not come any closer, and after a while we were so tired we couldn't go on. We slumped down on the ground and asked Boris to tell us about the things that grew in the forest. He said, "The strawberries there are so big . . ." And he held his thumb and index finger at least two inches from each other.

"Oh!" we cried. And he said, "They taste so sweet . . . as sweet as honey. And if you bite into them they are just as soft as a breadroll."

We all sighed. I asked Boris, "When did you eat them?" But then he answered: "I haven't ever eaten any. My aunt told me about them."

When I came home I asked Grandpa if he would take me to that big forest sometime. But he said: "You silly boy. We are in the middle of the steppe. There are no forests here."

I have counted the potatoes, and now I'm sure that the grown-ups are eating in secret at night. That isn't fair. I would never have expected that of Grandpa and Grandma and Mama. Tonight, when they do it again, I'll go up to them and tell them it's not fair. Then they'll be ashamed, and of course they'll give me a little bit too. But they always wait so long before they begin. And it is very hard not to fall asleep first.

We are back in Leningrad. The war is over, but still I'm often hungry. Oh, how I would like to stuff myself so full that there wouldn't be room for a single bite! Maybe one day that could happen with regular food. But sugar—never. I could never, ever, have enough of sugar!

What I like best, the very best in the whole world, is chocolate. One day I got an American chocolate bar. It was first packed in silver foil and then once more in shiny paper.

I sometimes wonder how much chocolate they have in America. Could there be enough for everybody? And could there be children who eat chocolate every day? Surely not. That isn't possible.

Some time ago a group of German prisoners of war worked near our school. They had to dig holes and lay pipes underground. One day Alex was walking home with me. When we came to the prisoners he asked, "Whatever are you doing, Yuri? Why are you making such a big circle around them?" I pulled him along and said, "Watch out! Stay away from them!" Didn't Alex know what dangerous monsters the Germans were? But he pulled my arm and said, "Come on! Don't make a fool of yourself!" I was shaking all over and cried, "Careful! They'll grab us!" But Alex gave me a push and said, "Coward! Just look for yourself."

I looked and felt a shock. Not the shock I had expected. What I saw were not dangerous monsters but men who looked like skeletons. How hungry they were! Just as hungry as I had been. Suddenly I realized that Germans were also human. And from that moment on I couldn't hate them anymore.

But this morning we didn't see them. When we asked the teacher why, he said they had been sent to Siberia.

And now our class is being punished. We have to write an essay six pages long in which we have to explain why we hate the Germans and why those who give them food are betraying the Soviet Union.

I know exactly what I would like to write. But I can't, because then they would throw me out of school. What I would like to write is that I'm not sorry at all. That I am glad that for all those weeks I gave my school breakfast to the prisoners. And that I am happy that the other children did the same. I would also like to write that I had made some real friends. Some of them spoke a little Russian, and they told us about their wives and children back home. Germany is a very different sort of country, but still their stories reminded me of myself. And of our life before the war.

And once I'd written all that, I'd write about my friend Heinrich. He was only eighteen, but he made such beautiful things with his hands. He gave me a bow and arrow and I know that I'll never ever part from it.

Today Yuri says:

"I still feel that hunger is the most inhuman of human conditions. When your physical part is maimed, your spiritual part is dying too. It is very connected. When I see the Ethiopian children on TV, I understand them very well. They are passive. Passivity is the most exact word to explain my state of being at that time. Absence of any interest in anything except food. When there was food on the horizon, you just became a little bit more active.

"I get very upset when my daughter, who was born in America, starts to eat something and immediately throws it in the garbage. I understand that I am foolish, that it is another age, another world, another planet. . . . But nevertheless, I hate to see food not eaten.

"Suffering makes a genetically good person better and a genetically bad person worse. Personally, I am convinced that suffering from hunger, sickness, and the gulag have made me a better person in all aspects."

Yuri is a journalist. He has lived with his family in New York since 1976.

Yuri's story refers to the starvation winter of the siege of Leningrad (1941–42), during which half the population (two million adults and 200,000 children) starved to death.

CLAIRE

FRANCE

The needle was terribly thick and long, but I didn't even cry when the doctor gave me the shot. They put me down on a white table and Maman and Grandmère held me there. When the needle was in my bottom the doctor said, "Now we count slowly up to five." But he pulled it out when we got to four. In one hand he held the needle and with the other one he pinched my cheek. He looked at Maman and said, "Now our little Claire won't get typhoid."

Véronique didn't get a shot. She's still too little. She's only two. You'll see, she's sure to get typhoid, she always catches everything. And then Maman will have to sit by her bed all the time and I'll have to do all kinds of things for her. I'm never sick and now I'm not going to get typhoid either. But they say it's a terrible illness. Maybe you have it all your life. So then it's better this way after all.

When we came out of the Boulevard St. Martin we saw that the Place de la République was crowded with people.

"Maman, what are all those people doing there?"

"They're watching."

"What?"

"The Germans."

Maman and Grandmère had also stopped. There were so many people that you couldn't move. But nobody said a thing. It was quiet. You could see on the people's faces that they didn't like it at all.

"Maman? Is that them, there?"

"Shh . . . Yes. Quiet!"

How wonderful those men on motorcycles looked. They were sitting straight up and had beautiful suits. And those black boots . . . how they shone. They were happy because they were laughing and waving at the people. But the people only watched them, without doing a thing.

"Maman! Maman! Look over there! What are those things?"

"Shhh . . . Claire!"

"But what are they?"

"Tanks," she whispered.

"What?"

*"*Shhh!"

One of them was getting closer. How big it was, and what a noise it made! I felt the ground shake under my feet. There was a soldier up on top! I saw his head and his shoulders. And his fair hair. He laughed and waved at us. But look, there was the next one already! And the soldier on top was just as handsome. In a moment he would have passed by without seeing me standing there.

I would have loved to wave, just for a second. But I couldn't because nobody else was waving. But I wanted to . . . I had to . . . it was something I had to do! There must be something I was allowed! Why wasn't I ever allowed to do anything? Hey—he had nearly passed us already. . . . I could only see him from the side now. . . . The only thing I could still do was to stick my tongue out.

I felt Maman's hand against my mouth. She said: "If they catch you doing that they'll put us in prison!" Poor Maman, she's so dumb. She thinks that the grown-ups will be punished when the children do naughty things.

Maman is so different these days. She never laughs at my jokes anymore. And Madame Hirschfeld, I can't stand her at all. She comes over every day and never stops complaining. When I ask Maman why Madame Hirschfeld keeps on coming to our house all the time she gets angry. She says that we have to be nice to her because her husband has been taken to a camp.

When Papa was drafted, Maman was so worried that she cried all day long. She was afraid that he'd never come back. And when I said that everything would be all right, she wouldn't even listen.

One day I told her, just for fun, "You'll see, on Sunday Papa will return. . . ." And on Sunday morning, very early, somebody rang the bell. By that time, I'd completely forgotten that I'd said that. But it *was* Papa! He had run away and walked all the way back to Paris. I was so proud of myself and told Maman, "You see, I was right. But you never want to believe me."

Grandmère's bed is in the dining room now. Before, she used to sleep in the guest room. Now I'm not even allowed to go in there anymore. As if I didn't know about the big machine that prints those papers. Papa and Maman think that I don't see things. And that I can't keep secrets. I'm six years old now, but they still treat me like a baby.

Lucie and Pascale aren't allowed to come and play at our house anymore. Luckily it's summer and we can play outside all day. If only the war would be over before the winter.

Papa woke me up this morning.

"What is it? Where's Maman?"

"Maman and Grandmère left early this morning."

"Where to?"

"To the Midi. Paris is too dangerous for them."

"What about me?"

"For you it's not as dangerous. Nor for Véronique. Nor for me either."

"But why did they have to go?"

"You know that Maman is Jewish."

"Yes. But I'm a little bit Jewish too. Why couldn't I go with her?"

"Later, maybe. . . . First we have to see if they manage to get down to the South safely."

"And who's going to stay with me?"

"You'll be going to Courseulles-Sur-Mer. I found a nice children's retreat there."

"But I don't want to go there!"

"Come on, Claire. Don't whine. Lucky for you, you won't be on your own. Do you remember Marie-Ange?"

"That horrible girl . . . with red hair?"

"She's not horrible at all. She's very nice—you'll see. And she'll take care of you like a big sister."

How mean of Maman to leave like that, without saying a thing. But if she had told me I wouldn't have let her go. Of course, that's why she left without saying good-bye.

If only Papa was Jewish too, then at least we'd all be the same. And then we could all of us have traveled together to the South. But maybe it is difficult for five people to travel together. Who knows, maybe there'd have been no place to sit and we'd have had to stand all the way. Or we wouldn't have had anything to eat. But I think I wouldn't even have minded that. Not as long as all of us could have stayed together.

Oh, I hate them! I hate them all! The children and the Monsieurs and the Madames. They have a big garden here with swings and a big slide. But I couldn't care less. Lucie and Pascale and I used to play all day without swings or a slide.

And then that Marie-Ange . . . What a name for a nasty girl like that! When Papa comes for me I'll tell him everything. And then I'm sure he'll say, "Claire, you were right. I'd never have thought it of her." And then he'll surely tell her father. They know each other very well because he is also a typesetter.

I keep thinking all the time how to explain it to Papa. What it's like to be woken up by the bombs. It must be hard to imagine if you've never experienced it. I always find it hard to talk about things that are horrible. When I hear myself talking, I keep thinking, it wasn't *that bad*. But it was *that bad*, that's just it. Only I don't know how to say it.

So I woke up and it was pitch dark. I went over to Marie-Ange and I said, "I'm so scared . . . can I get into your bed?" And what do you think she did? She shoved me and said, "Get lost!" At first I thought she'd be sorry and say, "Oh, all right then, get in, Claire. . . . I was only joking." So I just crept under her bed. But she didn't say a thing and I kept waiting and waiting. It was so cold without a blanket and the floor was terribly hard. But the worst of all was that I didn't have anybody.

When I woke up I was all wet down there. I'd peed in my pants. But I'm not going to tell Papa that part. It will be bad enough when I tell him that it was terribly cold under the bed.

We're staying with Aunt Thérèse, me and Véronique. Aunt Thérèse is Papa's sister, but that doesn't

make her love me. I help her dry the dishes and I never leave my toys around. But she's never happy.

She never uses Maman's name, she just calls her "that Jewess." The way she says it, it sounds like something very bad. Something that I should be ashamed of.

There isn't even enough room at Aunt Thérèse's. That's why I have to sleep at the woman's next door. She's old and very ugly. But that isn't the worst. The worst is that she has a hump. A big hump on her back.

I can't stop thinking about that hump. And that rhyme keeps coming into my head. We always sang: "Crick-crack! If you touch the hump, it'll jump on your back!" It keeps buzzing through my head and it wakes me up at night. The first thing I do is to check if there is a hump on my back.

Aunt Thérèse won't let me go to school. She's afraid that people will ask questions. The only one I have here is Véronique. But she's far too little, she doesn't understand a thing. When I tell her how awful it is to sleep next to a hunchback it only makes her laugh. And she doesn't understand why I miss Maman so much, either. I think she likes it here at Aunt Thérèse's, because she's her little pet.

I just don't understand. If you don't like the Jews, then you should like the Germans, shouldn't you? Because the Germans hate the Jews. But Aunt Thérèse doesn't like the Germans either. Aunt Thérèse doesn't like anybody. Not even Papa. When she talks about him, she always says, "That stupid Communist. . . ."

The other day, Aunt Thérèse took us to the Bois de Vincennes. She had ironed our Sunday dresses and I had pink bows in my braids. There was a German soldier there who asked if he could come and sit next to us on the bench. He started talking to us and took me on his lap. And he said a lot of nice things about me being cute and smart. He showed us pictures of his wife

and children. After Aunt Thérèse had seen them, he asked, "Don't you think that our little girls look a little bit alike?" Aunt Thérèse didn't answer, but he didn't seem to notice. He said, "It's so nice for me to be with children—I'd love to play with them again. If you don't mind we could meet again some other day. I am free every afternoon from three o'clock on. . . ."

When we left he kissed us both. And he also gave each of us a bar of chocolate and a box of candies. I didn't want to go home yet and kept waving at him for a long time. But once we were home Aunt Thérèse said with a mean voice, "Hand over that stuff." And she threw everything into the stove. What a waste! I can't stop thinking about my chocolate bar and my box of candies. A German had given them to us—but did that mean that we couldn't eat them?

It's Thursday. Will Monsieur Philippe come again today? He nearly always comes on Thursdays. I can't wait for Monsieur Philippe to come. He always brings a letter from Maman and money for Aunt Thérèse. Maman writes such lovely letters. She always writes that she misses me. And that she hopes we'll soon be together again.

The bell rings. It must be Monsieur Philippe! *No!* What a surprise! It is Papa! But he's so pale and skinny.

"Papa! Papa! What happened to you?"

Aunt Thérèse is shocked too. I can hear it in her voice. "Where have you been? My God!" she cries out.

"In prison. They kept me in for nine weeks. But they couldn't prove anything."

"Papa! Papa! I'm so happy!"

He says: "Claire, I have some news for you. Monsieur Philippe is picking you up tomorrow. And he's taking you to Lyons."

"What about Maman?"

"Maman and Grandmère are there already. And I'll be there in a few days if everything goes well."

"And Véronique?"

"Véronique will stay with Aunt Thérèse for the time being."

Monsieur Philippe is very rich. He has a lovely car. A big Citroën. They're sitting in the front, he and his wife (I think she is his wife). She's so pretty and so nice. I have the backseat all to myself. When I'm tired I can lie down on it, she said. What an idea! There's much too much to look at. Through the back window I see the trees along the road. The leaves are touching each other overhead and it's as if we were driving through a long green tunnel. There are not many cars on the road and we are in the most beautiful one of all. The trees must be thinking, *Here they come, the king and the queen with their little princess.*

I wish the trip would last forever. I'm having such a good time with Monsieur Philippe and his wife. We even ate in a restaurant, at a table with a white tablecloth. When you're with Monsieur Philippe you completely forget that there's a war on.

I'm with Maman again, at last! I am so happy. But Maman is very nervous. She smokes at least a hundred cigarettes a day. When Papa leaves for Grenoble you cannot even talk to her. She's so afraid that something is going to happen to him. I know that he has to go to Grenoble because of the newspaper. But if it's really so dangerous and if Maman hates it that much, why does he keep doing it?

I'm going to school again and now I'm already in fourth grade. Next week Maréchal Pétain* is coming to

*Head of the collaborationist Vichy government.

[114]

Lyons and somebody in our class is to present him with flowers. I wonder who the teacher is going to pick. Not Odile again, I hope? She already did it the other day, when the mayor's wife was here. Anyway, she isn't even pretty. It's only because she has those blond ringlets, like Shirley Temple.

If the teacher had any taste she'd pick me. I don't have ringlets but I do have blond hair, much blonder than Odile's. And the rest of me's much nicer. I don't say that aloud of course, but that's the way it is.

And I think it's fun to curtsy. It's not hard at all: You have to nod your head, bend your knees, and then hand over the flowers. I'm pretty good at it now. That's because I've been practicing, in front of the mirror.

When the Maréchal sees me, he's going to like me a lot. And once I've given him the flowers, he'll say, "Thank you, my child." And then maybe he'll ask, "What's your name?" I'll look him straight in the eye and say, "Claire, Monsieur le Maréchal." I can just picture it. Also the way he'll touch my hair very lightly when he's already turned away to talk to somebody else.

Maman got a terrible shock when I told her I was going to present the flowers to the Maréchal. She kept on saying, "Imagine, our Claire is going to offer flowers to Pétain! I don't believe it!" But she did go with Papa to the cinema to see the news. When they came home they said, "It was another girl! Thank God!" They were so relieved that they didn't even remember that I'd been telling stories. That was a pity, because I'd made up such a good excuse. I was going to say the teacher had chosen another girl at the last moment when she saw that my shoes were brown. That way maybe they'd buy me a pair of white shoes.

Papa shakes me awake. He whispers, "Shhh . . . it's a roundup . . ." He carries me to the big bed and I cuddle up to Maman. I feel her whole body shaking.

[115]

They're outside, carrying flashlights, and some-times a beam of light comes in. The shutters are closed so they can't see us (I hope). We hear them come up the stairs and bang on the door. They shout: *"Aufmachen!"* but we don't move. We just stay in the bed, the three of us. I'm terribly afraid and I pray Grandmère doesn't open her door. She's all by herself in the apartment upstairs, poor thing.

It's getting lighter outside already and they are still going up and down the staircase. Papa sneaks to the window and looks through a crack in the shutters. He comes back and whispers, "There's a group of people out there. I can't see them. The only one I recognize is old Lodsky."

I'd fallen asleep. Mmm . . . how cozy it feels to lie so close to Maman. But she tells me to get up. Papa and Maman want me to go to school, just as if nothing had happened. After school I'm not allowed to go home but have to wait for someone I don't know to come and pick me up.

It's so quiet here, in the corridor. I don't dare go down. What if one of them is still down there? Papa and Maman said that nobody is going to harm a little girl. It's easy for them to say that.

I'd like to go upstairs. Just to see if Grandmère is still there. How can I go to school without knowing? But when I ring the bell she doesn't open the door. That's what she and Papa and Maman had decided among themselves.

I love it here, in Aiguebelette. The cows give us milk every day and the chickens lay eggs in their nests. We eat meat very often and on Sundays we have real crème caramel.

Madame Périssot says that the war is on here, too. But it's really hard to believe. We play all day long.

There's another girl too, her name is Jeanette. We often go and pick dandelions and feed them to the rabbits. When it rains we play in the barn. We have our own theater there, which we made ourselves with boards that were just lying around. And we also write our own plays: Jeanette let her husband go to the front. And now she's afraid he'll get killed because the enemy is much stronger. I'm the colonel on the enemy's side. When Jeanette comes to see me, I stand up straight. She's on her knees and looks up at me.

"Oh, mon Colonel . . . I'm so sorry . . ."

"About what?"

"That I let my husband go, Colonel."

"That you let your husband go where?"

"To the front, to fight."

"To fight whom?"

"I hardly dare tell, Colonel."

Now I'm losing my patience and I stamp my foot. "Confess! And be quick about it!"

Jeanette bursts out crying. "Oh, Colonel . . . You're the only one who can help me."

"Why should I help *you?* Stupid woman!"

"Because you are *good*. And the others are *bad*."

"How do you know that?"

"I know. And I can see it. You are much *stronger* and much *smarter* . . . That's why you're also *better*."

Now I take a deep breath and say: "You've been very silly. And now you're sorry. That's why I'll forgive you. You'll get your husband back."

Sometimes Jeanette wanted to be the colonel. But she played it very badly. So I told her that we should trade parts again.

Monsieur and Madame Périssot listen to the radio all the time. They say that the war is nearly over, it's only a question of a few more days. Madame Périssot is

very happy and says, "Just a little patience, girls, and then you can go home at last." And I'd hoped to stay here until at least the end of the summer.

Today Claire says:

"Once I had told my story I realized what an egoistic and spoiled little girl I had been. My parents were an extraordinary couple who went out of their way to save their children. With my mother being Jewish and my father working in the Resistance, printing an underground paper (the Communist paper L'Humanité) they had to take terrible risks. But instead of acknowledging the stress under which they lived, I did silly things to attract their attention.

"As a child you get used to the war. It kind of becomes normal. That is what is so terrible—or interesting—about children. They experience abnormal things and normalize them. In other words, what I lived was my childhood, not the war."

Claire has three grown sons and works as a children's dentist. She lives with her husband in Lyons, France.

ARJÉ

HOLLAND

"Arjé! Arjé!"

It's Mother. She's calling me. But I don't feel like answering.

"Arjé! Where are you?"

There she is again. As if I didn't know that Aunt Lea and Uncle Daan have arrived. It's Sunday morning and they always come for a cup of coffee.

I shout, "Just a moment! Let me finish reading *Brownie Bear!*"

Don't worry, I'm not going to stay all morning in my room. But I'm sure Father will be telling Uncle Daan the news right now. And I prefer not to be there for that.

Last night Father came to tuck me in. He never does that. Then he said, "I have to tell you something, Arjé. First something good and then something bad."

"What? Tell me, please!"

"Tomorrow afternoon we are going to the dunes. You and I."

He was silent for a moment. I saw him swallow. Now I really wanted to know. "And the bad news?"

"I have to turn it in on Monday morning—the motorcycle."

[121]

The bastards! For four years Father saved his money to buy himself a motorbike. He'd made a few trips with his friends. Once they went all the way to the Ardennes. And when the weather was nice he would take me to the dunes.

There is a knock at the door. It's Aunt Lea.

"Hello, my boy. I'm bringing you a piece of ginger-cake. You're so right to stay here and read *Brownie Bear*. We're only talking about sad things anyway."

Suddenly I have to cry. I don't know why. Not even because of the motorbike. But because of everything. And mostly because of the nice things. I love Aunt Lea so much. She lives nearby. Just like Grandma and Grandpa and Aunt Hester and Uncle David and Frits and Saartje. They all live here. I am never bored. When Mother is too busy in the shop I can always drop in on somebody.

"What's the matter with you, Arjé?"

"I don't know, Aunt Lea."

"Just tell me. Don't be shy."

"But it's nothing. I don't even know why I'm crying. It's just that I love you so much, you and Uncle Daan. And Father and Mother and Grandma and Grandpa and all the others. . . ."

"Is that why you're crying? Just because of that?"

"Yes!"

She gives me lots of kisses and I say to her, "Please don't leave. Don't leave, Aunt Lea. Stay with me forever."

She strokes my cheeks and my hair. She has such tender, soft hands. I don't dare to look at her because I am afraid she might also be crying. And then I'll start all over again.

"Aunt Lea?"

"Yes, sweetheart. What's the matter?"

"Can I ask you something?"

[122]

"Of course, my darling."

"Will you promise me that you'll never turn on the gas?"

"*What* do you mean by *that?*"

"I know that many people have done that."

"That's true. But don't worry, Arjé. We would never ever do a thing like that, Uncle Daan and I."

"You won't, will you? There—you promised!"

"Yes, my sweetheart. We don't think that's a very smart thing to do. You can't give up just like that. We feel the same way about those things as your father."

"And Uncle David and Aunt Hester?"

"Orthodox people think a little differently. They feel that you should always obey. But nobody in our family would do anything as stupid as turning on the gas."

Aunt Lea is right. Religious Jews are more obedient. The other day I saw that Grandpa's star is sewn onto his coat very neatly. Mine is only attached with a couple of loose stitches at the very tips. So if there is a sudden roundup I can rip it off like that.

Grandpa is sexton of the big synagogue. I go there every Saturday to help him. Father and Mother only go there on Yom Kippur. But Mother still cooks kosher because otherwise the family could never come and eat here.

Father doesn't like all that business about being kosher. Sometimes he's so fed up with it that he takes me with him to the Zeedijk. And there we have a great time eating smoked eel.

Father used to be a member of the Communist Party, so he's hated the Germans for a long time already. The first day of the war he said to me, "Arjé, remember one thing: the Germans can't be trusted. Just take care that they don't catch you."

One day last week, as I was leaving school at twelve,

I had to think of that again. The Germans had just held a big roundup and had taken the people to the Jonas Daniel Meijer Square. The people weren't allowed to stand up, but were made to crawl on their knees over the ground. It was such a terrible sight that I thought, *Father, you were right. I'll see to it that they never catch me.*

I've been sitting in front of the window with my roller skates on for hours. But now it is three-twenty-five. Another thirty-five minutes and I can go out on the street. Then I'll skate to the Alexander Boer Street. After school a bunch of kids always gather there and nobody ever asks any questions.

I've been at the Boersma's for two months now. They own a boarding house in the van Baerle Street and they have become my "Aunt" and "Uncle." My name now is Jantje van den Berg and I'm living here because my house in Rotterdam was bombed.

The other day a boy stopped me on the street. He wore a band with a swastika on his arm. He said, "We're having a party at the Concert Building. You're invited." I didn't have time to think and didn't know what to say in a hurry, so I just said, "I think I might be able to come." But of course I didn't want to at all. What would I be doing at a party with NSB*-ers? On the other hand, why not? After all, nobody knows who I am. And luckily it doesn't show that I'm Jewish. When I'm doing an errand for Mrs. Boersma they always want to know if everybody in our family has such lovely blond curls.

So I just went to that party. There were lots and lots of people. It was swarming with Nazi youth members. And they had the most wonderful things. Oranges, cookies, and real chocolate!

*Dutch Nazis.

[124]

At the exit you had to give your name and address. It took me by surprise, but I had no trouble quickly making up a false name and address.

Father and Mother are now in the van Baerle Street too. First they were in Arnhem, but it got too dangerous there. The other guests think that they are just ordinary boarders of the house. And I can't say "Father" and "Mother" to them because I live downstairs with the Boersmas. Of course, I go and see them often in their room. But I never stay very long because it's terribly stuffy in there. I don't know how they can stand to stay in that little room all day.

I can see in Mother's eyes that she cries very often. She says that she's applied for a new hiding place for Flipje. In Arnhem he happened to be in the same street as they were, one door down across the street. And Mother could watch him from behind the curtains, without his knowing it. Flipje was having a hard time. He was filthy and skinny. And she often saw him crying in the street.

What a shame that Flipje is only five. If only he were eight, like me, I'm sure he too could have come to the Boersmas.

We're all sitting together in the big room. Father, Mother, Mr. and Mrs. Boersma, and the other guests. Everybody is just sitting here, staring. Nobody says anything. It is dead quiet.

What's going to happen now? Are they coming for us? What are we waiting for?

The man they left behind says that they'll be coming back soon. He is sitting there so calmly, with his hat on. He doesn't even wear a uniform, just an ordinary raincoat. I bet he has a pistol in his inside pocket. Otherwise they wouldn't have left him alone with more than fifteen people.

[125]

Oh, it's taking so long! I can't stand waiting. And now I also have to go to pee, too. But I don't dare ask. It's getting worse. I can hardly keep it in. . . .

Why shouldn't I ask if I can quickly go to the toilet? He could always say no. But when I ask him, fortunately he says yes.

The corridor is empty and as I pass the stairs I look out into the street. Is there somebody standing out there as well? There must be. But what if there isn't. Why don't I just have a look and see . . .

The street is empty! I must try it. . . . It's now or never. Because if they take me away I'm lost. I'm sure of it. It's nearly dark already. Just before the curfew. Oh, and now I remember: Jansen, Johannes Vermeer Street 29. That's the nearest emergency address!

What a pity I couldn't stay there, at the emergency address. The very next day they took me here to stay with these people, in the Jordaan.* They are very strange people. When they talk to their children it's always something like "Shut up," or "Get lost," or "You idiot!" And that's when they're just talking. You should hear them when they're fighting. . . .

One time, they were going out. When she was standing in the door, she said, "I've put the string beans on. When the water boils, just put them in the bed." I didn't understand at all and asked, "Why in bed?" She snarled, "Oh, His Highness thinks we're scum, does he? But he'll just have to get used to it. Not everybody can afford an expensive cooking-box."**

I had no idea what boiling was. But when the lid had been making a noise for some time, I thought that must be it. And I put the pan in the bed.

*Old working-class neighborhood in Amsterdam.
**A box filled with hay that was used to save energy when cooking.

They'd hardly been back a minute when she said to him, "Go and get the string beans." And suddenly I hear him holler, "That bastard! Everything's burnt! The bed and the beans!"

He dragged me to the kitchen table and began to hit me with the carpet beater. He beat me and beat me. . . . And I screamed as hard as I could. But he didn't stop and just went on. For a very, very long time. So long, that in the end I didn't feel anything anymore.

The next day it hurt so much that I couldn't move. I was all stiff and black and blue all over. From head to toe, over my whole body. And all over you could see the round marks of the carpet beater.

And now here I am. All by myself in the attic. It must have been at least five weeks already. I don't even know if it was measles or diphtheria. But when I got the red spots and the fever, she said, "Go to the attic. If you stay downstairs you'll only give it to the girls."

Every morning a plate of porridge is put outside the door. And that's my food for the whole day. In the beginning I slept nearly all day, that made the time pass much faster.

Not too many walk through the Laurierdwars Street. Much less than a hundred a day. Yesterday there were eighty-seven and today, seventy-five. Tomorrow I'm going to count the bicycles and the cars as well.

It's in the evenings that I'm most bored. Then there isn't anybody outside. And you can't look inside anywhere either. Before, I liked to look inside because it was such a cozy sight. But now all the windows are blacked out.

When the family left for Maarn, and me with them, I thought, *It can't be worse than in the Laurierdwars Street.* But, what do you know! Here I don't even have a bed. I sleep in a chicken coop on a straw mattress.

And if I come home at night without any milk or cheese—watch out! Yesterday I biked all day without getting a thing anywhere. I was starving because I hadn't eaten anything all day except for that thin slice of bread at breakfast.

There was a bowl of pears on the table, but they didn't tell me to help myself. Before going to my shed I quickly snatched one. You should have seen the reaction! He unbuckled his belt, pulled down my pants, and put me across his knee. And then he started hitting away. Just because of that one measly pear! While the whole bowl was full! That was so mean that I've really had it with them.

Why should I stay with these people any longer? I'll run away. I won't live in hiding. I might just as well take care of myself. That's what I've been doing here, after all. All day, every day, pedaling into the wind. There isn't one farm between Wijk-bij-Duurstede and Bunnik where I haven't begged for food.

I wish I could see their faces when I don't come home tonight. They'll be furious that I took their bicycle! That'll show them.

Know what I'll do? I'll just ride over to that castle in Woudenberg. There they always give me food. I don't even have to ask for it. When they see me standing at the gate they already shout from the kitchen, *"Komm hier, Bursch! Du hast sicher Hunger."** The other day I got there around noon and the cook was sitting at the table with his mates. They said, *"Wir haben Bratwurst mit Kartoffeln,"*** and they gave me a plate piled high. It tasted wonderful. I hadn't eaten so well since home.

---

*"Come here, boy! You must surely be hungry."
**"We have fried sausages with potatoes."

It's nearly six o'clock. It's getting dark so early these days. I haven't found a place to sleep yet, and I'm so tired of that gnawing feeling in my stomach.

There are days that nothing works. Then I have to give myself courage. I tell myself over and over again: *Keep going, Arjé,* don't give up—you can't give up. I say Arjé, although my name is now Jantje van den Berg. But it only works if I talk to Arjé. Because isn't it Arjé who has to keep going, after all?

A little while ago I asked a farmer's wife who was milking a cow in the barn if I could sleep in the hay. Without looking up she snarled, "Get lost! Or I'll set the dog on you!"

But fortunately they're not all like that. Earlier this week I had a lucky break at another house. When I asked if I could sleep in their yard, they said, "That's fine. And you can also join us for dinner. Because we're celebrating a birthday."

There were also some other people. I thought that they might be in hiding, but of course you can't ask about a thing like that. I would so much have liked to know, because the woman reminded me terribly of Aunt Hester. She kept staring at me and when I looked back she got very shy. Then she smiled a little bit and I knew that in her thoughts she was far, far away.

Maybe it was because of that that I dreamed about Aunt Hester that night. I had no school because it was Wednesday afternoon and she'd bought us cakes. She asked: "Arjé, shall I sing you something?" and sat down at the piano. And she sang in a very lovely voice: "*Wien, Wien, nur Du allein . . .*"

What nonsense! Aunt Hester didn't even own a piano, and I remember that she can't sing. But the next day I kept thinking about that dream and I saw myself sitting in Aunt Hester's living room. And just that, the

thought of it, was very nice. I knew very well that it was only a dream. But it was such a wonderful dream. Because just for a little, everything felt like before.

It is such an elegant house. And I think, *I'm going to ring the bell here.* But maybe it is too elegant. "Rich people are misers," Mother always said. But I still want to try it. A lady opens the door and says, "Hello, my boy . . ."

"Good afternoon, Madam. Please excuse me for ringing your bell just like that. I am Jantje van den Berg. I'm from Zeist. Our house was bombed and I have to get to Zwolle. My uncle lives there."

Why I say Zeist, I don't know. I don't even know if they have bombed that place. But it is true that I want to get to Zwolle. Not because I have an uncle there but because it is on the other side of the IJssel. And everybody says they have more to eat over there.

The lady says, "Well, why don't you come in, Jantje. Do you want a cup of tea? Or do you prefer a glass of lemonade?"

"Lemonade, please. If you have it. . . ."

When we are in the living room, she says, "Now, tell me exactly what happened."

"Well, our house was bombed. And then my parents and my little sister went to Zaandam. That's where my Grandma lives. And they sent me to Zwolle, to Father's brother."

"Don't worry, Jantje. We will help you."

"How kind of you. Thank you very much, Madam."

"Jantje, may I ask you if you have a religion?"

In the entrance I had seen a cross hanging on the wall. So I say, "I am a Catholic. But we don't do much about it."

"That doesn't matter. I just wanted to know because I wanted to discuss it with the priest."

[130]

"Thank you. That's very kind of you."

"Will you come upstairs with me? I'll show you where you'll be sleeping. Of course you haven't got any things with you."

"No, I haven't, Madam."

She opens a wardrobe and takes out some underwear and a pair of pants and a sweater. Then she says, "Here are some clean clothes. Would you like to wash yourself too?"

"Yes, please Madam."

When I come out of the bathroom she is sitting there waiting for me. She gives me a pair of shoes and says, "Try these, see if they fit you."

They are almost brand-new, with real rubber soles. I put them on and say, "They feel good on."

"You can keep them. And I also have a winter coat for you. That little coat you're wearing is much too thin."

"Thank you very much, Madam. . . . But I don't know I can accept all this."

She presses a finger to her mouth and I understand that I should say no more. Later, when the husband comes home, I hear that they had a little boy of ten. And he died just a few months ago.

Oh, I have such a good time here! What a pity I can't stay a little longer. This morning after breakfast, she says, "Jantje, it's all arranged. The priest has taken care of everything. Tomorrow you leave for Zwolle. The only thing left for me to do is to go to Zeist and see if I can find any of your papers there."

As soon as she is out of the house I take my bicycle and leave.

It's the coldest winter in a hundred years. That's what the people who stand in line to buy food from the farmers say. They also say that there is nothing to eat

in Amsterdam anymore. And that people are dropping dead in the streets from hunger.

I must, I absolutely *must* get to the other side of the IJssel. Once I'm there I'll go on north. The further north you get, the more there is to eat.

But when I finally get to the IJssel I don't know how to get to the other side. There are German soldiers standing at the entrance to the bridge. You can also cross the river in a small boat, but you need money for that. And of course I don't have any. So finally, after wondering for a long time what to do, I decide to take the risk.

I cross the bridge on foot, my bicycle along. Just like that, without looking to the right or the left. My heart is beating in my throat and my ears are buzzing. And it works, nobody stops me or asks me any questions! But when I finally arrive at Zwolle, just at the first houses, my bicycle snaps in two. And this time it can't be repaired anymore. So here I am in Zwolle with a broken bicycle and an air raid alert too. How am I going to find a roof over my head before the curfew?

A man who has taken shelter in the same doorway asks, "Are you from Zwolle?"

"No, from Rotterdam. I'm on my way north."

"Don't think that there's any food left there either."

"They can't have less than in the West."

"You're not going on tonight, are you?"

"No. Tomorrow morning."

"And where are you going to sleep?"

"I don't know yet."

"You can come with me, once the alert is over. I'll take you to Red Sien. On the Island."

"Is there an island here?"

"No, that's where the whores live in Zwolle. But don't worry about that."

He takes me to the old town, into a little shop that is still open. It is filled with German soldiers buying cigars and cigarettes. A tall red-haired woman is standing behind the counter. When she sees us, she says, "You can go straight upstairs."

She has a little room up there with a built-in kitchen, and we wait there until she finally closes the shop. When she comes upstairs she asks the man, "Is the boy looking for shelter?"

"You've guessed right again."

"There's always room in the attic. And this one can stay as long as he wants to."

That was in March, and Zwolle was liberated on the fourteenth of April. Everybody is elated and is celebrating. But all I can do is cry. I keep having to think of Father, Mother, Grandpa, Grandma, and all the others. I ask myself, *What am I doing here? I'm all alone . . .*

Red Sien tries to make me feel better. The war is finally over and we can start all over again. But when she says that, I just have to cry even more. Because what does it all matter, without my parents?

We've written to the Red Cross in Amsterdam. It's been four months. But we still haven't heard anything. Red Sien tells me that that doesn't mean a thing because the mail is still all mixed up. She means well, but nobody has to tell me anything. I know that I won't see Father and Mother again, ever. That evening in Amsterdam, when I walked out of the house in the van Baerle Street, I already knew that.

Today Arjé says:

"Looking back it seems incredible I was able to face those dangers. But I think that the solidity and warmth of my family background before the war gave me the strength to do it.

"I am glad I did not let the Germans drag me away. Children sense danger sooner than adults, and I have always felt that by running away I saved my life.

"Something that has stayed with me since the war is a certain distrust of other people. But in spite of everything, I am an optimist and still believe in the good side of human nature.

"I have to admit that the war also had its positive side, because it taught me to live more wisely. The people around me always make an incredible fuss when something bad happens. I agree that bad things are a nuisance. But I know there are things that are much worse. To me nothing really bad can happen anymore. Probably because the worst has already happened."

Arjé's entire family was exterminated. Only Flipje, his younger brother, survived. Arjé is a photographer and lives with his wife and three children in Amsterdam, Holland.

HILJA

ESTONIA

They could come for us any day, the Russians. Ema*
has heard we're on the list for deportation. She's thinking all the time about what she should pack to take
with us. As many warm clothes as possible of course,
because it's very cold in Siberia. You're not allowed to
take any precious things, but she's sewn her engagement ring and her gold chain into the hem of her coat
all the same. She says jewels can sometimes save your
life.

To me it doesn't seem that bad at all to go to the
camp. They say it's very different there. So different
that you can't even imagine it if you haven't seen it for
yourself. I've heard that you only get food once a day
and you have to stand in line for hours. And for the
journey there they also have trains that are very different. Not coaches with compartments and benches, but
wooden boxcars like the ones they normally use for
animal transport. I've never been in one of those and
can't imagine what it looks like inside. I wonder if there
are any toilets in there. Certainly not. But then how do

*"Mother" in Estonian.

[135]

you go when you have to? It's a very long trip to Siberia. They say it takes at least a week. So they must have thought of something. I'd just like to know what.

The only thing that I'm afraid of is that they won't let me take Muki. I wouldn't like it at all in the camp without him because then I wouldn't have anybody to play with. No, without Muki I just couldn't do it. I've had him for so long. He's been my pet for five years. And when it's cold at night he always gets into bed with me.

Suppose I have to leave Muki behind. Who'll take care of him? And protect him? The war is just as dangerous for animals. People never think about that. They think only about themselves.

Ema and Isa* were afraid that they would take me to the camp too. That's why I'm now at Grandma and Grandpa's. To get out of town I had to dress up. I was wearing a skirt of Ema's that reached all the way down to the ground. And she gave me her black shawl to wrap around my head and shoulders. I really looked like a little old woman. Ema took me to the market and left me with the people who sell the potatoes. They're from the same village as Grandma and Grandpa and we have known them a very long time. When the market was over they took me along on the cart.

Grandma and Grandpa are very nice, but I'm so bored. There are no children to play with and nothing ever happens. The only thing I can do is read. But Grandpa's books are all so dull. There's just one that has a lot of pictures. It's a history book, about the time of Napoleon. But the pictures are all more or less the same—just men in uniforms covered in decorations and medals. And on their shoulders they have silly stiff

*"Father" in Estonian.

things that keep reminding me of the brushes at the end of broomsticks. But the men seem to like them a lot. They look terribly proud and I think they must all be very important in politics. Probably that's how I got those brushes and brooms confused with politics.

One day I was playing under the table. Grandpa didn't know. He had a visitor and they were talking. And suddenly I heard them talking about our brooms. Not just talking, but really arguing about them! At Grandma's they had two brooms. One for the inside and one for the outside. The one for the inside they used to sweep the rooms, and the one for the outside to sweep the steps and the hallway. The inside broom was old and worn out but it still swept pretty well. The outside one was new, but you could hardly use it because the stick was loose and wobbly. Grandpa had tried to fix it several times already, but it only helped for a little while.

Suddenly, Grandpa noticed that I was under the table. He said, "What are you doing there, Hilja? You want to discuss politics?"

I was a little scared of Grandpa, so I just smiled. But the guest said, "Maybe she does have an opinion. Go ahead, tell us what you think."

He was so serious. As if he really meant it. He had asked me to tell what I thought about our brooms. And if a grown-up asks you a question you have to answer.

"Our inside politics are old and worn out," I said, "but they still work all right. Our outside politics are new. But you can't use them because they keep wobbling all the time."

"What an intelligent child!" the guest shouted. "She's right! I fully agree with her!"

To which Grandpa said, "Leave the room, Hilja. You know you're not supposed to be around when I'm discussing with my guests."

[137]

I wondered why Grandpa sounded so angry. How could I have known the difference between broomsticks and politics? And what did it matter? I had been right, hadn't I? Grandpa couldn't possibly mind that the visitor had agreed with me and not with him? Somebody as old as him couldn't be so childish.

I am back in Tallinn with Ema. The Russians have deported Isa. They wanted to take Ema as well, but when she told them that she had a little girl they left her behind. What a relief! What would I have done otherwise?

Isa had to go in one of those cattle cars, and Ema went with him to the station. She told me all about it. But I'd rather have seen him off myself. Going to a camp is something very important. You aren't sure if you'll see each other ever again. Who knows, maybe it was the last time . . . I didn't even want to think about it. Still . . . I would so like to have given him one last kiss. Now I haven't even said good-bye.

But Ema said it is better this way. Because these things are much too sad for little children. As if I didn't know that. Of course it is very sad. But this way it is even sadder.

I didn't mind so much being hungry because then I can play the wedding game. Ema told me once what they'd eaten at her wedding. What a spread! To begin with, smoked salmon with toast and butter. After that bouillon with a very thin slice of lemon. And as a main course, schnitzels with peas and rice. And after that there was still the wedding cake! Three layers on top of each other, beautifully decorated.

When I was hungry I would line all those things up in a row, one neatly next to the other. I wouldn't start eating right away. First I'd look at them, taking my

time, trying to decide which I should begin with. (The cake didn't count. That was separate and came much later.) The hardest choice was always between the salmon and the schnitzel. Actually I liked the salmon a little better than the schnitzel; that's why it was better to save it for after the schnitzel. But the salmon was the starter, so you were supposed to eat it first.

That's why I ended up taking turns. And whether it was the schnitzel first or the salmon, it made no difference: the moment I took that first bite . . . Oh, what a joy! My mouth was suddenly full of water and the taste flowed all over my tongue. I waited to swallow for as long as possible, because then I'd lose the taste. And I'd only swallow once I'd decided to take another bite. It was all my imagination of course, I knew that very well. But whenever I'd eaten like that I wasn't hungry anymore and my stomach felt completely full.

And then there was still the cake. What a treat! Now I didn't eat because I was hungry, but only because it was so good. But to cut such a cake is not as simple as it seems. Actually it's very complicated because there arc so many possibilities. You can just go ahead and cut a slice from anywhere: from the top, the middle, or the bottom layer. But in a way that would be a pity because then it wouldn't look whole anymore. Maybe it was a better idea to lift the three layers off each other. Then you still had three different complete cakes. And then, if you wanted to have a piece, you only had to cut into one of them. I never was completely sure what to do. And once I'd finally made the decision, I still wasn't sure if I had chosen the best way. Sometimes I'd get so mixed up that my heart would start pounding. And then it would take a very long time before I could fall asleep.

He keeps coming back into my head, that man. I keep seeing him before me all the time. It makes no

difference if I have my eyes closed or open. I try to chase him away: "Go, go, go away!" I keep telling him. But he's back again before I've finished saying it.

He's there since the day I played over at Helvi's and the air raid came. They kept dropping more and more bombs. It was much worse than usual and it wouldn't end. But I wanted to go home because Ema would be worried about me. When it was quiet for a few minutes, Helvi's mother said, "Hilja, if you want to go home, you should try it now. Please watch out and stay as close to the houses as possible."

As soon as I was outside it started again. It would have been better to stay at Helvi's. But it was too late, I didn't want to go back.

The Pärnustreet looked completely different. The houses were burning as if they were made of paper.* The tram tracks had sprung out of the pavement and were sticking high up into the air.

There was nobody else in the street, except for one man. I had seen him walking in front of me and now he started to run. I'll stay close behind him, I told myself. All of a sudden I heard an enormous bang. A bomb? I fell flat on my stomach and covered my head with my hands. After a while I stood up and looked for the man. But I couldn't see him. Only a little heap of stuff. But that was him. He was it. . . . There was hardly anything left of him. He had shrunk down to nearly nothing.

How could that be? It couldn't be, could it? Just moments ago he was an ordinary man and now he'd turned into this little heap. In just one second. . . . A little while ago he was still walking ahead of me. A little while ago he was still a human being. A human being who was breathing. And now he couldn't do anything

*In Tallinn the Germans used phosphorus bombs and many of the houses were made of wood.

anymore. Nothing was left of him. Just that horrible little heap.

When I got home we rushed to the big bomb shelter in the park. The bombing got worse and worse. Everything was shaking, everything was trembling. But I didn't care. I could only see that man.

Later, when we went to look at our house, we saw that there was nothing left. Only one wall was still standing, the rest was rubble with smoke coming out. It was very strange because it didn't feel like my house. But the weirdest thing of all was that I thought I'd already seen that smoking rubble before. Somewhere completely different. In another world or another life. But that wasn't possible, of course. It could only happen in a dream. I must have dreamt about it.

Once, when I asked Ema if Isa was still alive, she said she didn't know. That's just as well. That means there's still hope. He's been away for two years now and we've never heard a thing. If Ema had received some news she'd certainly have told me. I'm sure about that. Nearly completely sure. That's why I don't want to keep asking her all the time. It would make her feel bad because it would keep reminding her of Isa. And she thinks about him so much already. I know, because I do the same thing.

Sometimes I wonder what would have happened if they had taken her too. Or if she disappeared, all of a sudden. During a war, anything can happen. If something terrible happened to her, that would become of me? How would I get on? I am too little to earn money. If they asked me my age I could of course lie and say I was twelve instead of nine. But even then they'd say, "We are very sorry, but you're still too young."

The only thing I could do to earn some money would be to help behind the counter of one of those

little shops at the movie theater. You can hardly call them real shops. They could easily let a child run them. They're just little stalls, with a few shelves to put things on. And the women they have standing in there are much too big. So big that you can't even see the sweets behind them on the shelves. Apart from that, I know much more about candy because I'm a child. I'd know exactly what the other children would like. And I'm also very good at adding and giving change and things, so I wouldn't have any trouble running the cash register.

In the mornings I could stay at home (since they only have picture shows in the afternoons and evenings) and take care of Muki. We'd only need one tiny little room. And I'd keep it very clean and tidy.

But whenever I've been thinking about my life on my own, I always feel bad about it afterwards. I feel ashamed because there's no reason to make that kind of plan. Ema is still with me, luckily, and she has promised never to leave me alone.

I feel so bad because everybody says that you have to love God. They say God is good and just. But that's not true at all. God is not good at all and He is not even just. That's why I can't love Him. It's a great shame. I really feel sorry about it. But I just can't help it. However hard I try, I cannot love Him.

The other day I heard a story. It was so terrible that I could hardly believe it. It was about Lodz, a town in Poland where there were many Jews. The Germans sent all those Jews to the camp. And as they were walking through the town with their suitcases, people started insulting them and beating them!

If God were good and just, He wouldn't allow that kind of thing to happen. He would do something to stop the deportations. But it seems as if He doesn't want to see those things.

Yesterday I spilled a little water on the piano. And five minutes later, when I tried to cut myself a piece of bread, the knife slipped and cut my finger. See, that kind of thing He doesn't miss. I think God wants to see only the small things.

We've been in Germany for three months now. Ema is working at the big aluminum plant here in Forchheim.

When we were back in Tallinn, I went looking for Muki every day in our old street. I kept on going there, but I never found him. One day I met the old lady who used to live above us on the second floor of our house. She told me she'd seen Muki. At least she thought it was him. She wasn't completely sure because he'd looked very skinny and was all covered in dirt.

So he was still alive, my darling Muki! I knew it! I'd always known! I knew he'd survive the bombs!

But when I called his name he wouldn't come. He was a little bit scared, naturally. I decided next time I'd bring him something good to eat. And then he'd come home with me. We didn't have much to eat but I was sure I'd find something. With me he'd never go hungry. He would soon feel at home again and start washing himself all day long. And then his fur would be beautifully shiny, like before.

I just couldn't understand where Muki could be. I'd gone there so often and I'd never seen him. Could the old lady have been wrong? When Ema told me we had to go to Germany, I cried and cried. I didn't want to leave Muki behind. But Ema was very nice. She hugged me and said Muki could come with us if I found him.

Finally, the day before we left, he came the very first time I called him. Muki! Muki! My darling! But how skinny he was. . . . And his fur was all dull and gray. . . . But who cared? He was still my own Muki.

[143]

I had a little pat of margarine with me and I let him lick it from my finger. Then he looked pleased, as if he hadn't eaten anything as good as that in a long, long time. And then he rubbed his head against my leg and I thought that I heard him purr, very softly. I stroked his back. But when I wanted to pick him up he sprang back. "Muki, Muki! Come here, come to Hilja," I cried. Then he came nearer, very slowly. He sniffed at my shoes and looked at me as if he recognized me. I bent down and picked him up, just like I'd always done. As I held him in my arms, I whispered in his ear: "Together again—at last!" But suddenly he slipped out of my hands. He ran away and disappeared into a crack between the stones. I waited until dark but he never came back.

Today Hilja says:

"The war has taught me that there are things you cannot control and have to take as they come. I know that every unpleasant situation will pass, one way or another. Therefore I am very rarely upset. Little things don't get me derailed. It has to be a major catastrophe to throw me out of focus. As long as I survive, it's all right. As an emotional experience, the war was positive for me, even though it had many negative aspects. It certainly made me a more balanced person and better able to cope with life.

"Another thing that has stayed with me is that I feel that nothing is totally good and nothing is totally bad. Nobody is totally bad and nobody is totally good. I'm not, neither are you. I must have sensed this from a very early age."

Hilja and her mother came to the United States in 1950, having lived for five years in a D.P. (Displaced Persons) camp in Germany. In 1957 the Red Cross informed them that her father had died in Siberia after one year of Soviet captivity. Hilja lives in New York, where she works as an ergotherapist.

FREDI

AUSTRIA

Another three nights of sleep and then it will be Sunday, and then we are going to the big arms show. All of us together: Vati, Mutti, Uncle Horst, Aunt Erika, and me. Liselore has to stay with Fräulein. She's only two and doesn't know anything about weapons.

I am already five years old and I know a lot about them. Not as much as Vati, of course, that would be impossible. Nobody knows as much as he does. Vati has even been to officers' school in Berlin. For nine months—and all that time he didn't come home. I didn't like that at all, but Mutti said that you have to make sacrifices for the Fatherland. When I asked her what "sacrifices" and "Fatherland" meant exactly, she explained it to me. It took very long, and I still don't understand it really. She also said something about security and protection. But I already knew that that was Vati's work. He was there to protect us. Us and all the other people in Austria and Germany.

When I grow up, I'll be able to play with the lead soldiers. Vati has a lot of them but they're behind a window on the shelf. They are very fragile, especially the old ones that belonged to Vati's grandpa. They are a

[147]

hundred years old at least, because he was a captain in the army of Emperor Franz Josef. But they are very beautiful, and on some of them there is still a bit of real gold left. You can tell exactly what rank each one is, if you know them well at least. Vati has taught me all of them.

Sunday I'll wear my sailor suit and my new cap with the gold buttons. It really looks like Vati's. I can just imagine us walking with our caps on. Vati in his uniform, of course, and his shining boots.

Mutti is very proud of Vati. She often sighs, "So young and already a major!" Uncle Horst is thirty-two, and he is still only a lieutenant. But Aunt Erika doesn't mind. At least she doesn't say anything about it.

The arms show was even bigger than I had thought. There were many, many machineguns, thousands of hand grenades, long, long cannons, and even a real tank! Vati took me inside and he let me look through a tiny little window. But I couldn't see a thing, just some black stripes. He told me not to worry, even grown-ups found it difficult to look through a slit.

"But *you* can, can't you, Vati?"

"Yes. But I had to learn how."

"And are you going to drive in a tank like this?"

"Not right now. Maybe later."

"Then I'll go with you!"

He laughed and said, "Come on, Fredi. You're much too little!"

"That's exactly why! There isn't enough room for big people!"

I felt Vati's hand on my shoulder and he said, "War is not a game, Fredi. You still have a lot to learn."

As if I don't know that the war isn't a game. It is because of the war that Vati is never home. And now he is going all the way to Greece.

"Vati?"

"Yes, my boy?"

"Can't you stay a little longer?"

"No whining, Fredi. You knew that today would be our last day together."

"Yes, I know."

"Fredi, what do you want to be when you grow up?"

"A soldier, of course. Just like you. You know that!"

"If that's what you really want, Fredi, then you have to be brave, very brave. Starting now. You mustn't cry when I leave. And when you're sad you can't show it. Not even to Mutti. It's very difficult, I know. But do you think you can do that?"

"Yes, Vati. I can, I really can."

"You promise that you'll do it?"

"I promise, Vati."

Some people have yellow stars on their coats. When I asked Mutti why, she said, "They have to." And when I asked her why they had to, she said, "It is compulsory." I don't know that "compulsory" is, but she said it in such a voice that I didn't dare ask anymore. Maybe she doesn't really know herself. Or she just doesn't want to tell me the real reason.

The other day I saw an old woman with a yellow star. She had a dark coat on and walked with her head bent. You could see that she didn't want to be noticed. When we came close to her she stepped aside, to the very edge of the sidewalk. She did it very clumsily and I was afraid that she'd fall.

Nobody told me, but I know for sure that those people do not like to wear their star. Maybe it is a kind of punishment. I wonder why they would want to punish such a shy old lady. She couldn't have done anything bad, could she? But what kind of punishment is that? If

you want to punish somebody, you should let him wear something ugly. Those yellow stars aren't ugly. They're quite nice. I don't think I'd mind so much if they made me wear a star like that.

My head still hurts a little because I fell. Mutti says I only got what I deserve. That's what happens when children try to race the elevator. And I had started off so well! The moment the elevator left our floor I started to run down the stairs. I was already on the mezzanine when it stopped on the second floor. But just then I bumped into two men carrying a big chest up the stairs. What happened after that I don't know, all I remember is a man's voice asking, "Do you see stars?" When I opened my eyes I was lying in his arms and I had to tell him which floor we lived on.

Mutti opened the door herself. The man clicked his heels and said, "Heil Hitler! Ma'am, here's your son. He fell down the stairs. But I don't think it's anything serious."

"Oh, my God! What happened? My darling, my little darling! I must call the doctor!"

"If you wish. But I could take a look at him—I am a doctor myself."

"Oh, that would be very kind of you, Captain."

". . . von Lenbach. Heil Hitler."

"I am Mrs. Goetsch. Anneliese Goetsch. Heil Hitler."

The captain drops in every day to see how I am doing. He says it's no trouble for him at all because he has a room at Mrs. Fischer's, on the second floor. Mutti is very grateful and gives him a cup of coffee. And then they talk about the war. They both agree that everything is going well. Hitler's army is so strong that nobody can beat it.

[150]

Yesterday the captain invited us to go to the mess hall with him. I could see that the other officers were jealous of him. They were all looking at Mutti and she was laughing happily. She looked very beautiful in her new coat. I didn't mind at all that the captain and Mutti were talking together. I could study the mess hall in peace. I had never seen so many splendid tables. And all those important officers. It was just like a party. They all looked terribly handsome in their black uniforms with those skulls on their collars. If you kept on looking at them those silvery skulls made you frightened. They weren't big or anything, they were actually quite small. But there was something about them. They made those uniforms look very different and much more beautiful.

Vati is back from Poland. He didn't like it there at all. There is no fighting going on, the soldiers just live in the town. Once when he was in the tram, a woman who had a baby in her belly accidentally got on the wrong car. In Warsaw the trams have separate cars for Germans. The ordinary people are not allowed to ride on them. A soldier pushed her off the tram while it was going. When Vati saw it happen, he immediately pulled the emergency brake and ordered a doctor to come and look at the woman and her baby. And after that he went right to the police station to report it. But the people there made fun of him, they said that it was normal and that things like that happened all the time.

Vati was happy when they sent him to the Eastern Front. We were allowed to see him get on the train, Liselore and I. But the station was very dark; there were no lights because of the bombings. Mutti was all pale and she cried hard when she had to say good-bye. And then, of course, Liselore started to whine as well. Only Vati and I were brave. When he kissed me he told me to take care of his women. That made me feel very proud.

[151]

I was shaking all over inside, but he couldn't have noticed that.

There was a telegram saying that Vati had been wounded. He had been taken to Silesia, and Mutti left immediately to see him. She wrote that he had lost his left leg when a grenade exploded nearby. But he was doing all right and she would stay in Silesia until they could come home together. I tried to imagine how Vati would look with only one leg. If he wore pants you wouldn't see it that much, it would look like he was limping. I hoped they would hurry up and give him an artificial leg. Maybe that's why they were still in Silesia. The telephone rang just as I was thinking about that. It was Mutti, and she said that Vati was dead. His wound got infected and he died within three days. I felt terrible, especially since I had been thinking all that time about an artificial leg.

Vati got a big funeral. But I couldn't be there because suddenly I got sick and had a fever. Afterwards they all came to our house, the family and the friends. They let me get out of bed and everybody was very nice. They pulled me onto their laps and weren't even afraid to catch my illness. Aunt Erika stroked my hair and said that I had grown again. When I said that I wanted to become as big as Vati she began to cry. Just like Mutti. I didn't like it at all that they cried like that in front of all those people.

Aunt Erika comes to see Mutti every day. I often hear them talk about Uncle Horst. Aunt Erika is terribly worried because she hasn't heard from him for nine weeks. Mrs. Rainer also visits us often. She is very sad. Mutti told me that her husband is in Russia. He has been taken prisoner.

I think very often of my dear Vati, and when Mutti goes to the cemetery I always go with her. Vati wasn't

just an ordinary person, he was a real hero. He didn't die for nothing, he died because he was fighting the enemy.

Mutti often stays in her room with the curtains drawn. She says that she's tired, but that's not true because I can hear her crying. Nobody comes to visit us anymore because of the bombing. Everybody else is in the cellar, but Mutti prefers to stay upstairs. She doesn't want to be with all those other people.

From the kitchen window I can see the planes coming, hundreds at a time. They look like dots in the sky. And then, suddenly, they start dropping their bombs. Many, many, you can't count them, at least thousands of millions. They make the sky all gray, as if it had started to rain.

There's not so much bombing now, and Mrs. Rainer came to see us. She asked Mutti to go with her to the Gestapo. Mutti knows the commandant and maybe he can do something for her husband. We can come too because Mutti is afraid to leave us alone at home.

The commandant is sitting behind a big table, and Mutti and Mrs. Rainer are sitting in beautiful leather armchairs. They have been talking for a long time, but I don't understand a word of it. Then suddenly the commandant gets up and says, "I am very sorry, Mrs. Rainer. At this stage I cannot do any more for you. I'm just doing whatever I can to save my own people right now." As he was talking he laid his hand on his back pocket, where his pistol is. It is quiet for a moment. Then I hear him sigh. I see him giving a tap to his pistol and then he says, "And then . . ."

When we're outside I ask Mutti, "Is the commandant going to shoot himself?"

"Yes, I think so."

[153]

"Why?"

"Because we have lost the war."

"But that doesn't mean you have to die."

"No. But he prefers that to giving himself up."

"Is he afraid of the enemy?"

"That isn't it, Fredi. You are too young to understand these things."

I keep remembering that commandant and can't forget the way he looked when he touched his pistol.

If he did it, he would become a hero. Then he would get a big funeral and his family would be as proud of him as we are of Vati. But I still feel sorry, because he wasn't that old. It's nice to have a father who is a hero. But it would be even nicer to have a father who is alive.

We were playing tag in the courtyard when suddenly a car drove in. An open car with four soldiers in uniform, with guns. Were they the enemy? What were they going to do? Would they start shooting at us, just like that?

The people shouted from the windows: "Yankee! Yankee! Welcome, Yankee!" When they heard that, the men started throwing shiny little packages at us. We ran up to them and they shouted, "Hello! Hello!" They were very cheerful and I wasn't afraid at all. I was only a little bit scared when I saw that one of them had a black face and black hands. When he noticed how I was looking at him he laughed, and then I saw that he had beautiful white teeth. But they only stayed a few minutes. Then the courtyard was empty again. We ran upstairs and Mutti said they were American soldiers and that those packages were chewing gum.

In the evening somebody rang the bell. It was an American soldier. He pointed at a package he was holding and said, "Rudi Hartmann." Vati had a cousin in America with that name, so the package must be from

him. Mutti suddenly got all shy and didn't know what to do. Liselore started shouting that she wanted to open the package and pulled the soldier inside. He said that he was a friend of Uncle Rudi's and that we should just call him Joe. I had already noticed that he was a captain, but he said, "Don't worry. Just call me Joe."

Oh, the things that came out of that package! Chocolate, egg powder, soap, toothpaste, cigarettes, and nylon stockings! Mutti loved those things, but she didn't know what to say to Joe. But I think he didn't even notice. He put me and Liselore on his lap and made us laugh by pulling funny faces. When he left he gave us a few more packages and chewing gum and promised to come back soon.

Mutti and Aunt Erika are going on a trip with Joe. He is driving them to Mauthausen* in his own jeep. Joe has heard a lot about Mauthausen and he wants to see it for himself. It's a shame I can't go along, but he says that it really isn't for children.

They'll be home late because it's a long way. That's why Mrs. Fischer is coming to look after us. I don't mind staying home one day without Mutti. She never goes out anymore, and once she's back she'll have lots to tell.

It's half past six. I hear Mutti! I run up to her but she doesn't even see me. When I ask her how it was she walks straight into her room. She drops onto the bed and starts to cry. Mrs. Fischer goes after her and shuts the door in my face. When she finally comes outside again, she says, "Just leave your Mutti alone."

"What happened?"

"Nothing happened. She's just crying."

*Concentration camp near Vienna.

"About Vati?"

"No. Not at all."

"Is it because of Joe?"

"No. That isn't it at all."

"But what is it then?"

"She didn't like the trip."

"What didn't she like about it?"

"Mauthausen. She thought it was horrible."

"Really?"

"Yes."

"Is that all?"

"Yes. That's all."

"Is it true? There really isn't anything else?"

"No. Believe me."

"So she's only crying because of that?"

"Only because of that. Are you satisfied now?"

"Yes. I am."

Aunt Erika has been living with us for two years now. The Russians took her apartment away. There are two other families here as well. All together we are eight grown-ups and seven children. It's very busy and there is always something going on. The other day, when I told Mutti that I was happy being with so many people, she didn't answer. She just patted my head and said that I was a good boy.

Today Fredi says:

"My greatest regret is that I could never discuss these things with my parents. Shortly after the war, my mother died in an accident. I'll never stop reading about the war, trying to understand my parents' attitude, but without wanting to whitewash it.

"I feel that my sister and I did not suffer too much during the war. My biggest grief was the death of my father. But I think that it affected me mostly because it devastated my mother totally. I hadn't really grasped it, my father having always been someone very distant. I only saw him three weeks a year and to me he was mainly a hero.

"The experience of the war has determined my life. It has made me more serious. I realized this when I came to work in an international environment. My American and English colleagues had totally different reactions than I did. What they had experienced as problems during their youth seemed ridiculous to me. I found that I had much more in common with my Russian colleagues, especially with a few friends whose fathers had been officers in the Red Army, maybe because they had lived in a political system that was not so different from that of the Third Reich."

Fredi is a physicist and works and lives in Geneva, Switzerland. He and his wife have three adult children.

HANKA

POLAND

My dear Tatus*, he's changed so much. Suddenly he looks so small and pitiful. He sits there and cries all the time. I don't want him to cry! *He* shouldn't cry. Everybody else can cry, but not him.

Mamusia** is also so different. She doesn't do a thing anymore. There are clothes all over the place and the kitchen is full of dirty pots and plates.

The only thing Tatus and Mamusia talk about is death and dying. They say that the Germans are going to kill all the Jews. And we are Jews. But we aren't going to die! I know that they're not going to kill us. I know that. But when I tell Tatus, "You will see, you will see, we will live," he starts to cry even harder.

They sit there all day, Tatus and Mamusia. They are waiting because they know that something terrible is going to happen.

The bell rings. Tatus and Mamusia are frightened.

Luckily it is not the Germans. It is Stanislaw, a friend of Tatus. He loves him very much because when

*"Father" in Polish.
**"Mother" in Polish.

he was in an accident Tatus saved his life. Stanislaw says, "I have good news," and he whispers something to Tatus and Mamusia. When he leaves, he says, "Tomorrow morning at ten o'clock."

It is ten o'clock and a man comes. A strange man. He bends down and says to me, "Come along with me." *What?* Do I have to go with *him?* I don't even know that man! And I don't want to know him! He is bad. Bad because he wants to take me away from Tatus and Mamusia.

"Just come with me," he says, and he picks me up.

"No, no! I don't want to!" I yell.

I beat his head with my fists. But it doesn't help, he doesn't let me loose.

"Come on! And quiet about it!"

Be quiet? And go along with some stranger? I'll show you! I'll kick you . . . I'll scratch you . . .

"What do you think you're doing," he hollers and grabs my arms.

"I'm not going! I won't go!" I yell.

My legs are free, I can kick him. And with my teeth I bite his ear.

"I'm sorry, Dr. Lipschitz," he says in the end, and he puts me down.

He has left, the stranger. But I know it won't help anyway. I'm sure somebody else will come and take me along.

I am squatting here in the corner next to the piano. Tatus and Mamusia are standing in front of the mantelpiece. They're just standing there and they don't say a thing.

Why do I have to go away? Why can't I stay with Tatus and Mamusia? Don't they love me, then? They do. They say it all the time. But they also say that I'm a nuisance. And too little. But that's just it! That's exactly why I want to stay with them.

Tatus and Mamusia are still not saying anything. And I'm just sitting here, in my corner. They don't say why I have to go away. And I don't dare to ask them.

I'm just sitting here, all by myself. Completely alone. There are two of them, they have each other.

And now look. It's happening again. They're coming to get me. . . .

How big and fat they are, these two women! They have scarves on their heads, just like peasants.

They come and pick me up. I start yelling. But they're holding me so tight! I can't move at all. There is no way I can hit or kick them. The only thing I can do is scream and yell.

Tatus and Mamusia are still not saying a thing. Do they think it's all right? They aren't doing anything to stop them. They just stand there in front of the mantelpiece. They just stand there and cry.

I am looking at the trees outside. That's what I do all day. For many days. Sometimes I see Tatus or Mamusia. Only for a moment. Just a glimpse of them. All I can see is a bit of a hand or a leg or a wisp of hair.

I know that they can't come to me and that's why they play hide-and-seek behind the trees.

This isn't even a house. It's a hut. One of the two women lives here with her husband and daughter. But she isn't nice at all, the little girl. She's fat and dumb and never wants to play with me. Whenever I say something to her she runs up to her mother and hides under her apron. She's a real crybaby and yet she is already five years old. We're the same age; she's two months older, even.

The man is nearly always gone. He watches the forest, that is his job. He has a uniform and boots and a gun.

[161]

When he comes home he always brings dead animals. The other day he asked me to help him with the rabbits. He was holding them and I had to pull the skin off. It was dreadful. Those poor darling rabbits. They looked so terrible. All naked, without their little coats. I felt sick but I didn't want him to notice. I want them to think that I am brave, these people.

The first day the woman said, "Your father and your mother are dead and you are never going to see them again." She also said that I wasn't allowed to talk about my family or to mention anyone's name. Not even my own.

So I'm not Hanka anymore. Maybe it's better this way. Because Hanka was such a sweet little girl. She wouldn't be able to stand it here. Hanka couldn't sit here all day without talking to anybody. The woman never says a thing, she doesn't even talk to her own little girl. The only time I hear her is in the morning when she opens the grate of the stove. Then she looks into the ashes and shouts, "Oh, it's going to be a terrible day!" and says that the house is going to burn down or that the Germans are going to come and find me.

Tomorrow I can go outside for the first time. Up till now I wasn't allowed to go further than the back porch. Disgusting! It isn't even a real toilet, it's a stinking hole with crawling worms and dirty flies around it.

Look . . . look here at the moss under the tree. It's like green velvet. I remember our piano stool, how I liked to stroke it. But real moss is even more beautiful than velvet. It's much thicker and much softer. And in the forest there's so much of it!

Mmm . . . How nice it is to lie here on the soft moss. When I look up I can see the clouds. How big they are and white! It looks as if they're floating. No, not on water, just through the sky. How far away are they?

[162]

Very far, or not that far at all? I'd love to sit on top of that big cloud there. Then I could walk around up there and look behind all those hills.

Mmmm . . . What is it I feel? I know—it's the wind. It's started to blow. And it's everywhere. It is stroking me, I feel it even on my cheeks.

Look! Up there! What's *that?* I've never seen anything like it! It's like a curtain. A glittering curtain. A curtain made of gold! Is it real or am I dreaming? No, I'm not dreaming. I now see what it is. It is the wind making a curtain when it blows those tiny flowers from the tree.

Oh, what a shame. . . . The curtain has gone. The petals of the flowers are all lying on the ground. They are yellow and white, but you can hardly see them anymore. You only see the green of the grass.

I love the smell of the forest this morning. The pine needles smell so good when it's been raining. They are all clean and crisp and they crunch under your feet when you walk on them.

"Good morning!" I say to the mushrooms when I see that they have raised their heads up for me.

They like it when I pick them. Otherwise, they wouldn't let go of the ground so easily. I can eat them all day long. Only those that are pink and brown, of course. I'd never touch the poisonous ones.

But I like strawberries even more. There are lots and lots of them now; down near the stream they are growing in long rows. I'll go there in a little while. But first I'll peel a few pine branches. Under the brown crust they are all white and shiny. When they're clean I thread the strawberries on them and then I walk through the forest, looking for a nice place to eat them.

Where shall I sit today? Maybe on that big flat stone near the river. I like it there when it's been raining all night. Because the water is very wild then and makes a

lot of noise. If you listen hard you hear voices—all kinds of voices mixed together. In the end they start calling you. I hear, *Hanka! Hanka!*

That's a pity, the sun is going down already. But I don't have to go back just yet. I can stay a little while longer.

On this side of the path the trees are very close to each other. Ordinary people can't even come here. But I can. I can go everywhere because I'm small and I know the way.

I love to play the tunnel game. Look, there's the opening! It's all dark inside and you have to run for a very long time. But at the end there's always a surprise: a beautiful flower or a special bird.

Oh, how long it is, this tunnel. I'd forgotten.

But there, now I'm getting to the end. I see a little spot of light and it grows bigger and bigger. I've got to keep running—just a little longer—and then I'll be out of the dark.

No flowers or birds this time . . . But oh, there is something much better! The whole field is filled with flowers—yellow, pink, white, and blue flowers. All those daisies . . . I've never seen that many. Know what I'm going to do? I'm going to make a daisy chain. But I can't. It's too late. I have to go home soon, and I can't wear it there. A beautiful daisy chain in such an ugly house. The flowers would die right away.

The light is still on. The man's brother is here, they are sitting at the table. He lives in Lesko, and when he comes he always gives news about the war.

"Hello my child," the man says and pats my head. How nice, he's never done that before.

The brother is leaving now and says to the man, "So you'll do it, as we agreed." The man doesn't answer. He pretends he hasn't heard. The brother gets mad and

shouts, "Do you want them to kill *you? You* and your *wife?* Remember what happened to the poor Drewnows I told you about!" "But what do I do," the man whispers, "if her parents do return, after all?" "Don't worry about that!" the brother shouts and slams the door behind him.

The man is sitting at the table again. His plate is full but he tells the woman that he doesn't want to eat.

Go! Go! I have to go! I can't stay here! Quick, quick, into my bed . . . under the covers . . .

"Take this out to the chickens." It is the woman's voice. She's talking to her daughter, because she's the one who always takes the scraps outside. So it must be evening, that's when they feed the chickens.

What happened? Where was I all that time? Did I sleep all day? There is the wall and the window. The same wall and the same window. So I am in the same room. I *am here* . . . I *am alive* . . . So, he didn't do it. . . . He didn't . . .

But who knows, maybe they are trying to fool me. Maybe he is waiting for me in the room . . .

I have to find out! I have to find out! Now!

The man is not in the room. When I ask the woman if he is out, she says: "Yes."

Quick! Quick! To my forest!

As if I'm flying, my feet are so light. . . . I have no breath left. But who cares! I'm there.

Hello, my darling tree. There you are. You are always there. You are always waiting for me.

I am so happy to be with you again. It's here that I feel safe. Because you are the biggest and the strongest. Just look how thick you are. When I stretch out my arms as far as they will go, I still can't get them around

you. You'd need three children to do that. But I don't want that! Because you are mine, all mine.

You are not only the biggest and the strongest, but also the richest. No other tree has as many branches as you. And you even have branches that are thicker than the trunks of other trees! If I didn't have you, my dear tree . . . It's with you that I want to stay. Always, all my life.

Now what do I hear? There they go again. The whole bird family. What a stir . . . they're so excited. They're making a terrible racket. Why are they doing that? Oh, I know already! They are warning each other about the thunderstorm. The big birds are telling the little ones to look for a hiding place.

The lightning . . . Look there! How beautiful. . . . Ah! That was a loud bang. So loud that it made everything shake.

I don't have to look for a hiding place. I am safe under my tree. Here I won't get wet and I can watch the sky.

I hope the thunderstorm lasts a long time. And that the noise will get louder and louder. And that it will come sooner and sooner after the lightning. So that the sky is lit up all the time.

If only the snow would go down a little. I remember, last year, how dark it was. And how terribly long it lasted. And then one morning, a little light came inside. And the next morning there was a little more light. And the day after that there was a crack between the snow and the top of the window.

At last I could look outside again! But I still had to wait for a very long time until I could return to my forest. Because my shoes had already worn out back then.

Luckily for me, someone else came to stay in the

hut this winter too. It was a woman and she was very nice. One day she said, "Your hair is terribly dirty and greasy. I'll wash it for you."

She got some snow and let it melt. And then she heated it, specially for me. In the beginning I didn't like it at all because it hurt a lot. It took her so long to get rid of those knots! And when, at last, she could get through it with the comb she still had to catch all those lice. But after that I felt wonderful, so fresh and clean.

She looked like my Aunt Mania, the woman. I was sure it was her. When I told her that, she answered, "No, sweetheart, my name is Poniatowka." Aunt Mania had a gold tooth on the side of her mouth. And the woman had a hole in exactly the same place. But when I said, "My Aunt Mania had a gold tooth there," she said, "Isn't that strange? But I'm really not your aunt. I am Poniatowka."

Once I woke up in the middle of the night. She was lying next to me and crying. I asked, "What's the matter? Why are you crying?" She said, "Don't worry about me, darling," and went on crying.

I still don't understand that. Why did she come over and cry so close to me if she wasn't my Aunt Mania after all?

It's the first day I've been outside. The sun is really warm now. Oh, look at those streaks of water at the side of the path. They're just like tiny little rivers! They were just born right now, those rivers. Before that they didn't exist. Before that they were snow. They make all kinds of trickling noises. How sweet, it's as if they're singing a song.

What's that, down there on the road? German soldiers? Quick! Quick! I have to hide! Luckily I'm near to the house and I can run to my hiding place.

I hear: *Hanka! Hanka!* Who's that? Nobody knows

my name. What can it be? I'm not moving out, I'm staying right here, safe.

Hanka! Hanka! I hear again, *It's me, your Mamusia!*

Tatus has been standing in line all day long. He was at the IRO* and they said we can't get a visa for Palestine here in Bucharest. We should have asked for it back in Budapest. But at that time the IRO did not have an office in Budapest.

We have been on the road for nearly a year, staying in lots of different places. We stay in one place until they tell us that they can't do anything for us and then we go on.

Aunt Cipi and Aunt Rochal and Uncle Mordechai are also going to Palestine. They have been in concentration camps and never stop talking about the horrible things they saw there. We're always with them and I can't stand those stories about the roll calls, the kapos, and the gas chambers anymore.

Tatus and Mamusia are just as nice as before. But they're very thin and pale because they spent all that time in a hole under Stanislaw's workshop, without any heat, and there wasn't even enough space to stretch their legs.

How lucky I was! I had such a lovely time in my forest. It was great, it was marvelous there. I wish I could hug my big tree once more again. . . .

*International Refugee Organization.

Today Hanka says:

"*After the war I lived in a fog, and until I got into therapy I couldn't deal with my feelings.*

"*What happened, in fact, was that I retreated from reality into the forest. The conditions were so extreme that I escaped into fantasy. I must have used a part of the mind that certain mystics can discipline themselves to enter. Today I wouldn't be able to let go of my senses like that. But as a child of four or five you have extraordinary powers to fool yourself.*

"*I think those were the most intense years of my life. It was an immediate, 'right now' existence, living day-to-day, alone with nature. I was so happy in that forest, I'd like to be able to recapture that. If I could be born a second time and able to record it better, I'd like to go through it again. I see it as a terrific loss, as if I have been thrown out of Paradise.*"

Hanka is a painter. She lives with her husband and two sons in New York.

ANDRÉ

SWITZERLAND

"Maman! Maman!"

"What's the matter, André? What *are* you doing?"

I'd stuck my head under her apron and pressed it against her belly. That always worked.

"Maman, you have to come. . . ."

"Where to?"

"To the garden."

"Come on, you don't need me for that. You can do that by yourself."

"But you have to come and look."

"At what?"

"At me on the swing. I can go very high. As high as Cécile."

With my back against the seat I pushed it up as high as I could, and when it fell I quickly jumped on it. When it came down I gave myself a push with my feet again. Suddenly I took off and flew up into the sky. All the way up! It went through my whole body, but it wasn't really scary. It was wonderful. Maman hadn't even seen me do it yet. She must have thought I'd never learn.

"I've only two more apples to do," she said, "then

I'll come and watch you—as soon as I've put the tart in the oven."

It would have been nicer if she'd come right away. Then we'd walk together right over to the other end of the garden, to the cherry tree with the swing. But she wanted me to go ahead without her. I could do that, too. Then she'd see on her way how beautifully I could fly.

It worked—again. This time it was even better. I hardly had to push myself off. I didn't even know how I did it. It went all by itself. I was already high, high up. But where *was* she? Wasn't she going to come right away? I always got a little scared if she left me alone for long. But why *should* I be afraid? It was going well, wasn't it? And it was fun. I knew how to have fun by myself. Just like Cécile.

Oh, no . . . Not now . . . Please . . . There they are again, the sirens. . . . That awful noise!

Here I am, on the swing, all by myself. I can't move my arms, either one. If I let go of the ropes I'll fall down. I've got to stop! Quick! Quick! Otherwise I'll still be here when they come. All alone by myself!

"André! André! What's the matter with you? You know when there is an air raid you must come in at once!"

She lifted me off the swing and took me inside.

"Come on—what are those tears for now?"

I couldn't tell her that, she wouldn't understand anyway. The other day I told her I'd seen the Germans close by, at night. And she hadn't believed me. She said it was nonsense because there were no Germans in Switzerland. There is no war here, she said. I didn't have to worry about that.

But that's all she said. Because she doesn't want me to be afraid. But I know it isn't true. Why would János be eating at our place, otherwise? Every Tuesday and

every Thursday? He ran away from the Germans. All the way from Hungary. They wanted to kill him because he was Jewish. He told me that himself.

I don't know exactly what "Jewish" is. But János doesn't seem to be anything special. He looks exactly the same way we do. He even looks a little bit like Eric, my big cousin. I can't see the difference. So maybe Eric's in just as much danger. And if *he* is, then we all are.

What about Papa having to stay in the army all the time? He only comes home on weekends. That's a sign too, isn't it? Sunday night, when he left, he said: "André, you're the man of the house. When I'm away, you're the boss." How could he say such a thing? Doesn't he know what Maman and Cécile are like? He knows very well that they'd never, ever listen to me.

But I don't want to think about that. I'm not that sure that something bad is going to happen. But I do know that the army isn't as safe as all that.

And if there's no war, why do we have those air raid warnings all the time? Maman says it's because the Allies are flying over. The English and the Americans. They're our friends and wouldn't do us any harm. But when I asked why we still had to stay inside, she said, "Just to make sure. In case they make a mistake."

"But can't they *see* where they are?"

"Yes, they can. But they're never really sure. From above everything looks very small. And we're very close to the border here. And on the other side it's war."

So I'd been right all along. There was a war after all. On the other side of the border. And we were close to the border. The Germans could come at any moment. Papa had said that himself. The other day I heard him say, "If they want to, the Germans can invade us overnight."

Since the day Papa said that I often see the Ger-

mans. When I'm in bed, with my pajamas on (so that I can't run away), they come out of the dark. I don't even dare cry for help. There are so many of them, they're so big and they're all over! With their evil faces, their filthy hair, and their sharp claws they look like the wolves in the stories.

Cécile says wolves aren't ugly at all. She's seen them herself, in the zoo in Basel. But she only says that because she doesn't want me to be scared. Because I'm still so little. I didn't want to go to Basel and stayed home with Maman. They let me because my throat was hurting a little anyway.

The station was packed. You'd think the whole world had come to Vevey. They'd decorated the platform with Swiss and French flags. They were even selling ice cream! Maman said she'd buy me one as soon as Jean arrived.

But when was that train going to get here? It was already ten minutes late. Maman said that wasn't very long for a train coming all the way from Lyons. They were very strict at the border because everybody wanted to get into Switzerland. The woman standing next to us said that people tried to hide themselves everywhere. They were even found hanging under the carriages, between the wheels. I didn't want to think of that. But I kept imagining what it would be like. It seemed terribly scary. Especially when the train was going . . . Just think! If you fell, the wheels would run over your hands and your legs. Or over your head. That was even worse, then you'd surely be dead.

The Germans only let children cross the border. And only if they were really starving. If they were, they were allowed to stay with a Swiss family for three months.

There he was. Oh . . . how skinny he was! His hair,

cut so short you could see his scalp. That wasn't the worst of it. The worst was that he smelled terrible. They all do. Maman said it was because of the powder for head lice. *Yechh!* And *that* had to come and stay in our house!

There was a label around his neck and Maman checked it one last time. It said "Jean Duclos." So it was really him.

Jean doesn't like our food. He doesn't dare to say it, but I can see it when he swallows. Once, when I asked him if he had to finish his porridge at home too, he said that they didn't have porridge in France. Then he bent his head and kept looking at the tablecloth. And after a while I saw tears running down his cheeks.

But Jean is naughty too. He plays with matches all the time. Secretly, of course. We found out when Cécile's doll caught fire. There's nothing left of her hair, just a few wisps! Now he has to stay in my room for three whole days and nights. When I ask him why he did it he won't answer. He just sits on the edge of his bed and stares straight ahead.

Maman is always angry at dinner time. It's all because Jean eats so little. She says he came to us to get big and strong. And if he doesn't eat he'll be just as skinny when he goes home. But now, Maman's asked Jean what he likes the best. And she's cooked it specially for him a few times.

Jean is finally eating normally and he's feeling more at home. You can tell because he takes my bicycle without asking. And he plays with the children next door as if they were *his* friends. I'm glad he's leaving soon. Then I'll have my room to myself again. It's such a mess now. There are far too many things in the closet and his books are always lying on my table.

I like to have houseguests. But not for too long. Jean is used to being here now and he just takes everything

for granted. He acts as if all my things were also his. He even does it with Maman. He lets her cuddle him as if he didn't have a mother of his own, at home. Maman has her hands full with Cécile and me.

It was a long trip to the nature preserve in the Jura. The whole class was hungry even before we arrived. When the teacher asked, "Who wants to eat?" we all shouted, "Me!" "Good, then let's eat," she said. "But first let's walk to that spot up there, between the trees."

We ran up to the place and got out our sandwiches. Then the teacher said, "Children! Do you see that stone wall over there?"

"Yes!"

"Well, that's the border."

I couldn't believe it. Were we so near to the border? It couldn't be true, she must be wrong. After all, those few stones there . . . That couldn't be a border, could it? Certainly not the border of a country that was at war. And occupied by the Germans. Wasn't that far too dangerous? If the Germans wanted to, they could step over that little wall, just like that.

"Look," the teacher said, "there is a German soldier over there. Let's go and see him." She got up and pulled me along. What was I to do? I couldn't tell her that I kept seeing Germans at night, could I? And that I had terrible dreams about them? Maybe I could have told her, but not with the others around. They were all following us and they weren't afraid at all. What should I do? I could quietly let go of her hand and stay behind. She wouldn't even notice. The other children were talking to her all the time. But we were getting closer and closer and she was still holding onto my hand. And then suddenly I heard her say something to the German. Oh God! What should I do? I looked back to where we'd come from, as if I'd seen something there. But the

children shouted, "Come on, André! What is it? Are you scared or something?"

I had to do something. My heart was thumping in my throat. I turned around and saw the German soldier. But he didn't notice and kept on talking to the teacher. That was lucky, I had a chance to get a quick look at him. I did it and he still didn't notice. I looked once more, not as quickly as before. And then I saw that he had normal eyes, nothing special! He had a human face, a nose and two eyes. He was wearing a uniform, just like Papa. Only the color was different. And all of a sudden I thought, *I'm not scared anymore!* The Germans aren't monsters, they're ordinary human beings, just like us.

One night the planes came very close. And it sounded as though they were dropping bombs. We went upstairs and looked out the window in the attic. We saw a lot of light over Renens. It was beautiful and I had to keep telling myself that it wasn't fireworks.

The next morning a whole lot of boys were standing around Pierre in the schoolyard. He said he'd been to Renens. He'd biked there right after the air raid, with his father. They had seen the firemen on ladders. Luckily there hadn't been any dead. A few people had been badly wounded. A woman who had jumped out the window had broken her leg. And a piece of a beam had hit a child on the head. Both had to be taken to the hospital by ambulance.

I was jealous of Pierre. He'd seen all those things after they'd just happened. If we went to look there later, it wouldn't be the same. They wouldn't let you get close to the houses. They might even have put barriers around them.

But I still wanted to go and take a look. You never know. I'd never seen something like that for real. And

who knew, maybe there'd still be something left to find. A fragment of a bomb, like the one Pierre got. I was so excited all day. After school we all went to Renens. What an adventure! Was this what war was like? I'd imagined something very different. I thought that it would be really scary. But now that I've seen a bombing I'm not afraid anymore. Not at all. I hope (but of course I won't tell anyone) that it will happen again soon. And this time I'll get there right away.

Today André says:

"I think that one is more afraid of war if one has never experienced it. For me the war has always stayed a menace that never became concrete. It made me more anxious because I could not confront it. So I do not know if you can confront it and still survive. In a sense I am more fragile than those who experienced the war and survived. I realize this when I compare myself to people who have lived through the war. They seem to have more self-confidence, even if they are weaker than I.

"The war can't be as terrible in real life as it is in our imagination, where the worst moments come one right after the other, like they do in films. We shouldn't forget that daily life goes on, families grow closer to each other, and stupid problems lose their importance.

"Until a few years ago I was an overanxious person. Then my best friend got a fatal illness and I nursed him until the end. Today I no longer live in fear of the disasters that life has in store for me. Confronting the worst has probably made me stronger."

André is a journalist. He lives and works in Lausanne.

BIRTHE

DENMARK

Far* always sends me to bed at seven o'clock, when I'm not at all sleepy. He tells me I can still read a little, but I don't feel like that at all. I prefer to look out the window, at the children playing outside. Jytte is always with them. She too is only five years old, but she's allowed to stay up till eight.

Jytte often goes on outings on the bicycle with her father. Far doesn't even have a children's seat on his. But that doesn't matter, I can sit on the bar in front. Only he's never gotten around to taking me along because he's always much too busy.

Far is always on the phone in the evening. I once asked Mor** if that was because of his job. But she said, "No. He is busy with other things." That's what I thought too, because his voice sounds so different. He is always getting angry and talks about those "dirty pigs" and says, "Just wait and see. We'll get them in the end." When I hear him talk like that I always have to shudder.

*"Father" in Danish.
**"Mother" in Danish.

And I pull the blanket up over my ears so that I don't have to listen.

Mor says that I'm much too curious. I can't help it, I keep having to think of that cupboard. The chocolates and Mor's cigarettes are in there. Far is the only one who has the key. Oh, how I'd like to look in that cupboard—just for a second. I'm sure I wouldn't care so much anymore once I knew what's in there.

I'll just go and take a peek! I'll do it now! Far is taking his nap anyway. He always does that after lunch. And his bunch of keys is lying next to him on the table. I've taken the keys. . . . He hasn't noticed anything. . . . I am tiptoeing to the cupboard now. . . . What if he suddenly wakes up? What do I do then?

He never wakes up all at once. First he stops snoring. And I can hear that from here, in the other room. I'll just have to listen very carefully. And if it gets quiet all of a sudden, I'll quickly put the keys back.

The lock opens easily. . . . I leave the door ajar a little bit. Then you can't hear it creak.

Oh . . . Look! What's that? What are those things doing here in the cupboard? And where have they come from? They don't belong to Far, do they?

My goodness! A soldier's cap! It looks like a real one. . . . The ones the Germans wear look exactly like this. And that band for around the arm . . . with that big swastika. And a stick that they use to hit people with. And also photos of men in uniform. What are those things doing *here?*

Oh . . . There's also a pistol. It couldn't be a real one, could it?

How heavy it is. I pick it up, just like that. Without thinking. Careful, Birthe! Hold it tight . . . it could slip out of your hand. How come my hands are so wet all of a sudden?

Since I looked in the cupboard I feel so mixed up inside. Everything is a big jumble in there.

I wish I'd never opened that cupboard. Then I wouldn't know what's in it. So I keep telling myself that I only *planned* to, but that in the end I didn't really do it. Sometimes I believe myself for a little while. But then suddenly I'm sure again that I did. So I just try not to think about it. But that doesn't always work. Especially not when it's dark and I'm lying in my bed.

If only I could tell somebody about it. But if I tell Mor she'll scold me, of course. And who knows, she might even tell Far.

I don't dare tell Jytte either. Because what would she think? She might even believe that Far is doing bad things. And that's not true at all. My Far doesn't do bad things. What he does is always good. Even if it's a secret.

Before, I always wanted to know all secrets. But now I know that secrets are not at all always nice.

Mrs. Christensen from downstairs is talking with Mor. Something terrible has happened. I can hear that.

This morning, when I came into the kitchen, Mor sat there crying. I knew right away that it was something to do with Far. She said that he'd gone to Copenhagen. But if that were true she wouldn't be so sad, because Far goes to Copenhagen often enough.

Poor Mor. . . . I'd love to help her. But I can't. The only thing I can do is to be a good girl. And not whine. That's why I stopped asking where Far is.

"I hear cars," says Mrs. Christensen, and she goes over to the window. Mrs. Christensen has had such a shock that her voice is hoarse as she says: "Two officers. They're coming in this direction. I'll just quickly go back downstairs."

I hear them coming up the stairs. That noise of their boots on the linoleum. They're nearly upstairs. In

[183]

a minute they'll be at the door. And then they'll click their heels . . .

Oh! I wish I wasn't here! That I could disappear. Or hide. But I can't even move. I'm all stiff and my legs feel like cotton wool.

How brave Mor is. When they ring the bell she goes to the door and opens it. One of the Germans says, "Hello, Mrs. Knudsen. *Heil Hitler!* Forgive us for disturbing you."

How polite he is. I'd never have thought it. Maybe they won't do us any harm. Who knows, maybe they are very kind. And maybe they've just come to tell us that Far will be coming home soon. Why not? Why didn't I think of that before?

"Can you tell me where my husband is?" Mor is asking.

"He is with us, at the Gestapo. But he'll be going to Kolding soon."

"And when can I see him?"

"Not right now. You'll have to have a little patience, Mrs. Knudsen."

He nods to the other officer. This one takes a step forward and puts Far's wallet, watch, and keys on the table. Then he says to Mor, "We just came to bring you your husband's personal possessions. And to ask if there is anything we can do for you."

Mor asks: "Can I send him a few things? His shaving gear and his toothbrush?"

"Don't worry about that, Mrs. Knudsen. He can get those from us. If we think he needs them."

"So all I can do is wait."

"I'm afraid so, Mrs. Knudsen."

It looks as if Mor is going to cry. But she stays brave. The German now says, "Oh, yes . . . I nearly forgot. Your husband asked me to tell you that your cigarettes are in the cupboard."

When they've left, Mor immediately calls Grandpa

[184]

and Grandma to tell them that Far is being sent to the prison at Kolding.

I wish I still was a tiny little baby, like Svend. He's been fast asleep all morning and hasn't noticed that anything's been going on.

Grandpa stops by every night to tuck us in. Sometimes, if he's in a good mood, he tells a little story. But when he found out that I had gone to the Aabenraa Road he got a little angry. He said that I'm much too curious, and since then he calls me a nosy little girl.

When I heard that there had been an attack in the Aabenraa Road I ran there immediately. I saw the soldiers and the horses just lying there in the middle of the road. The soldiers had at least been covered with blankets. But the horses . . . I still shiver to think of it. Those poor horses . . . I still see them before me, with their round bellies and their long thin legs. They were so sad, but also a little creepy. Those big bulging eyes seemed to be looking at me.

"Mor! Come here! Quick!"

She was already there and asked, "What's the matter with you, Birthe? You're all wet and your teeth are chattering."

"I had such a terrible dream! I dreamt that they were after me. Just like Erik . . ."

"Now where did you hear that story?"

"Jytte told me."

Suddenly I had to cry and I told her everything. That Jytte came to fetch me when she'd heard her mother talking on the phone. Her mother had been called by a friend who knew that Erik was dead. That friend had seen the Germans chasing him herself and she had also heard them firing as he climbed over a wall.

Jytte wanted me to go with her to the place where

[185]

it had happened. But I said no because I knew it wasn't allowed. "Come on," she said. "Nobody has to find out. It's not far from here and we'll soon be back."

When we got there there was nothing to see. We thought the story couldn't be true. But suddenly I saw a few red spots on the cobblestones. I realized it was blood. . . . Blood from Erik. . . . That had been his . . . Blood that had been inside him. . . . Not so long ago, maybe only an hour. . . .

And when I realized that just one hour ago Erik was still running, and climbing over a wall, and *alive*, I got so sick that I had to throw up.

"You see now, Birthe. That's what happens when you want to see everything."

"But I didn't want to at all! It was Jytte."

"It was very stupid of Jytte too. But you still went with her."

"I'll never, ever do it again, Mor! I promise!"

She gave me a kiss and said, "Now just go back to sleep."

Sleep? How could I go to sleep now? I was so scared. "Please . . . Don't leave me alone."

"What are you afraid of, my darling?"

"I'm so afraid for Far. That he—just like Erik . . ."

"Come on, Birthe. You shouldn't be thinking of things like that. Far is in Kolding. You know that, don't you?"

"But he's been there forever. And we never hear a thing."

"That's because they don't allow him to write. But they promised me that he'll be coming home."

"But *when?*"

"I don't know. I hope very son."

"You mean before Christmas?"

"I really hope so, sweetheart. But I can't promise."

At Christmas the family is always together. Either we go to Padborg or they come to Haderslev. This year Aunt Mette and Lars and Olaf are coming here. Without Uncle Jesper because he's still in Germany, in a camp.

I'm glad I saved all my pocket money. Now I can buy presents for everybody. This time I'm going to buy the nicest presents for Far and Uncle Jesper.

We still haven't had any news. Not from Far and not from Uncle Jesper either. But they will come for Christmas, I'm sure about that. The Germans are mean, but they can't be that mean. They'll let them go home, even if it's just for a few days. It will be terrible if they have to go back afterwards. But it will still be better than nothing at all. Then at least we'll have been together for a little while.

Aunt Mette and the boys have gone this morning back to Padborg. I had hidden Far's and Uncle Jesper's presents behind the couch, in case they showed up at the very last moment. But now I have to find another place for them.

They've called to say that Far is coming home. Oh, I'm so excited! I'm so happy. I've never been so happy in my life. At last I too have a Far again. Just like all the other children.

Mor says that we have to be very quiet in the beginning. We mustn't make any noise and walk on our tiptoes. But I don't mind that at all. I'll do anything for my darling Far.

The doorbell is ringing. That must be him. . . . Quick, quick, run to the door. . . . Oh, how far away it seems. How long it's taking to get there. . . .

When Mor opens the door I don't dare look right away. I hide behind her. And Svend keeps pulling at my skirt. He doesn't understand what is going on. He doesn't even remember Far anymore.

[187]

Far is standing with his arms around Mor. I hear her cry. But it's not from sadness. It's because she's so happy.

Now I finally dare to look . . . But is that Far? That skinny, gray man? Nobody told me that he's been sick! Far is sitting on the couch and Mor asks me to get the tea. I tiptoe to the kitchen and return with the big tray. Far says that he isn't thirsty right now. "A cookie?" I ask. "No, maybe later . . ."

And then suddenly, as we are having our tea, Far asks, "What is that rattling sound I keep hearing?" I don't know what he means, but Mor says, "Birthe, stop stirring your cup for a moment."

Svend is staying with Grandma and Grandpa because it was much too busy for Far. And I'm at Jytte's nearly all the time. Her mother doesn't mind, luckily. She says: "You have to be patient. It will pass. It's only been five weeks since he came home. . . ."

Sometimes I think that Far will never again be the way he was before. He doesn't do a thing all day. He just sits there in his chair and stares out the window.

The only time I really see Far is at the table when we're eating. And then he keeps hiding his hands. I've told myself a million times that I don't have to look at them. Two of his fingers don't have nails anymore. I know that they have pulled them out in jail. But he shouldn't find out that I know that.

But I would like to see them—just once. Then at least I'd know how they looked. And I'm sure that then it wouldn't be so difficult to pretend I don't notice.

I hate the Germans. Oh, how I hate them! When I think about them I just get the goose bumps. It's their fault that Far has changed so much and that we still haven't heard from Uncle Jesper.

On Liberation Day I stole three eggs from the cellar and took them to the big square. I smashed them right into the faces of those bitches whose heads had been shaved. At last they were getting what was coming to them! I didn't know what they had done exactly, but it was something to do with the Germans. So it had to be something very, very bad.

"Birthe, please. Try to control yourself," says Mor. I've laid my head in her lap but it doesn't stop. We're nearly in Padborg and I'm still howling. I sob, "I'm trying . . . I'm really doing my best . . . but I just can't . . ." "Come on, my little girl . . . I understand," says Mor. Mor understands. Of course she understands. Uncle Jesper was her own brother, after all.

When Aunt Mette called to tell us that the people of the Red Cross had found his body she also cried. They had recognized him because of his front teeth. They had a big gap between them. I remember that very well. I wish they hadn't recognized Uncle Jesper. At least then we could go on hoping. Then we could believe that he might still come back. But now it's certain, completely certain, that we'll never, ever, see him again.

It's all the fault of those rotten Germans. I'll never forgive them for killing Uncle Jesper. My big, strong Uncle Jesper! He loved Aunt Mette so much, he loved Olaf so much, he loved Lars so much. And me, as if I were his own daughter.

Today Birthe says:

"Although I know that there is now a new generation, I still feel a shiver when I think of the Germans. That's why I probably never wanted to think of those times. Before being asked about my memories, I did not even know that I remembered so much. When I read my story it was as if another part of me had opened up. My son asked me, 'Why didn't you ever tell me this?' He actually never knew that his grandfather had been in the Resistance. And now he is very proud of it.

"I think that the experience of the war has made me more human, and I do not mind having gone through it. But I realize that my mother was a very strong woman who did not make a big deal out of anything. Today I am just glad that I did not have to go through it with my own children."

Birthe lives with her husband and two sons in Connecticut.

ZSUZSA

HUNGARY

I was glad Fräulein was holding my hand when we came out of the church. Suddenly there was so much light that it hurt my eyes. It had been so dark in there. And now we were outside again. It had all gone so fast. The priest had said so much. I'd hardly understood any of it.

"Fräulein?"

"Yes, Zsuzsa."

"Am I a Catholic now?"

"Yes. Now you are Catholic."

"Is that what it is, to be baptized?"

"Yes, that's it."

"But don't they do it with water?"

"Yes, with Holy Water."

"Those few little drops. Was that Holy Water?"

"Yes, that's what it was."

"Fräulein?"

"Yes, Zsuzsa."

"If you are a Catholic, then aren't you a Christian too?"

"Yes, of course."

"So then when you're a Christian, then you're also a Catholic."

"No, that's not necessarily so."

"But why not?"

"That's much too complicated to explain. Why do you always have to know everything? Look, let me show you something. I have a surprise for you."

She gave me a little square box. It was tied with a red bow.

"Is that for me?"

"Yes, for you. From your darling mother. I was to give it to you after the ceremony."

It made me go hot all over. What could be inside that little box? I wanted to know so much. But what a pity, to have to ruin that beautiful bow.

"Oh! A little cross! On a chain! How lovely!"

"Let me see how it looks on you. It's beautiful! And the chain is just the right length."

"Is it real gold?"

"Yes. Just look at the box. It's from Bálint. At Bálint they only sell real jewelry."

"How sweet of Anyu* to surprise me! Couldn't we go by the workshop for a minute? I'd like to thank her."

"No, Zsuzsa. You know very well that you mustn't disturb her."

"Yes, Fräulein, I know that. . . ."

What a lovely little cross. I am going to wear it every day. All my life. And the chain is also so beautiful. Very thin, they go so well together. Anyu really knows how to pick these things out. She has such good taste. That's also why she is a dressmaker.

Why doesn't Anyu ever wear a little cross? She is a Catholic too, isn't she? I'm sure of it. So one person

*"Mother" in Hungarian.

[192]

wears a cross and the other doesn't. It's one's own choice. Grandma Gizi wears a cross and so do Aunt Teréz and Aunt Margit. They also go to church a lot. Grandma Gizi nearly every day, but Anyu never. Anyu and Apu* didn't even get married in the church. Otherwise I would have seen photographs of that. Everybody has photographs of that, even poor people. I once asked Fräulein why Anyu and Apu didn't have pictures of their wedding. And then I had to promise her that I would never, ever ask that question again.

I think that you can only wear a cross when you've been baptized, when you're a Catholic. That's what people decided, so you could tell who's Catholic and who isn't. But of course you also wear it because it's so pretty.

Aunt Ilonka also used to wear a gold chain like this. Not with a little cross but with a little star. One time I wanted to see how it would look on me, and she let me wear it for a little while. But I haven't seen her wear that little star for quite some time. I hope she hasn't lost it.

"Fräulein?"

"Yes, Zsuzsa. What's the matter?"

Anyu's workshop is in the Váci street; we passed very close to it on our way. Once, when Fräulein had gone to her uncle's funeral, Anyu came to fetch me from school herself. And afterwards she let me come back with her to the workshop. One of the seamstresses gave me a magnet that she used to pick up pins. You could pick up at least a thousand pins in one go with it. And you could make lots of nice things with that clump of pins. Another seamstress let me play with the bobbins of thread. First I put the nicest colors next to each other: red, blue, and yellow. And after that I sorted them into

*"Father" in Hungarian.

[193]

groups of each color and placed them next to each other in a row going from light to dark.

It is so nice and cozy in the workshop. Anyu is often busy with the clients, but I don't mind at all. I know that she is close by, in the salon. And when everybody has left I am allowed to sit for a moment on the elegant chairs in the salon. They are so beautiful! The wood is all gold and the cushions are made of pink silk.

Anyu is such a darling, she really wouldn't mind if we dropped in for a moment now, I thought. So I said: "Can't we . . . Just for a bit. . . ."

"Stop it, Zsuzsa! If you keep whining like that I'll have no more surprises for you!"

"What?" Another surprise?

"Yes. You're really being incredibly spoiled."

"What? Tell me, what?"

"You can have an ice cream on the terrace at Gerbaud's."

"Oh, how wonderful! I'd like mocha, please."

"See, how sweet your mother is! She even treats you to an ice cream. And at Gerbaud's, of all places. There aren't many girls of seven who can say they have eaten ice cream at Gerbaud's."

I knew very well that Anyu was spoiling me. It was already the third time she'd let me have an ice cream there. And the ice cream at Gerbaud's is so good. If you take mocha there's even a piece of chocolate on the top.

Tomorrow I'll tell Vera that I've been to Gerbaud's. Will she be jealous, I wonder? No, that isn't her way. But if she's never been there herself, she might not be too happy about it. Better not to say anything then. What a pity. It would be so nice to tell her about it. And it would be even nicer to eat an ice cream together on the terrace. At Gerbaud's there are so few children. At least I've never seen one there yet.

[194]

At Miss Tauber's it normally took a very long time before she opened the door. The room where she taught was at the very end of the corridor. And she also walked so slowly because there was something wrong with her leg.

When Fräulein rung the bell I thought, *Now I'm going to do it!* I'll rush down the stairs, into the street, and run to the Danube. To the spot where the stone steps go all the way down into the water. There I'll sit, take off my shoes, and dip my feet in the water!

But I waited just a little too long. Just as I was about to turn around I heard Miss Tauber switch on the light in the hall.

Fräulein took off my coat and stayed in the front room, reading a magazine. I always went ahead of Miss Tauber. That way it looked as if I was in a hurry to get to the piano. But that wasn't it at all. I only did it because then I didn't have to see how she dragged her foot.

When I was sitting on the piano bench Miss Tauber asked, "Did you practice well?"

Since she asked me that each time, I always had the same answer, "Yes, Miss Tauber. I did my best. But it was a little difficult."

And then she said, just as always, "All right then, let's hear what you have learned this week."

But just as I was about to begin, she suddenly said in a very different voice, "My dear child . . . I see that they've had you baptized. How smart of your parents."

She sighed deeply, and I quickly started to play. I'd just begun when the bell rang. Great! Now I could stop! And the lesson would be shorter, she couldn't keep me there longer than usual. I knew that at four another girl was coming.

How nice, Miss Tauber was staying away a long time. Suddenly Fräulein came into the room. Her voice

was all hoarse and she said, "They have come to fetch Miss Tauber. And we have to go with her."

There were three men in dark uniforms. They looked like policemen. They had bands with swastikas on their arms. They were very severe and said that they had very little time. We had to hurry and walk quickly to the car. When they noticed how Miss Tauber dragged her foot they were very mean. They laughed and said that they would soon teach her to walk faster. And she really was doing her very best!

When I saw her like that I was sorry that I'd always been such a nuisance to her. It wasn't her fault that I disliked playing the piano so much, was it?

At the police station Fräulein got very angry. She said it was a scandal. We had no business being there. And that I was only a little child. What did they want from us? We had to go home at once. Then they changed their tune and said very politely, "All right, we will take the child home. But you must stay a little longer."

The policeman rang the doorbell and Anyu opened the door. She gave me a big kiss and I saw right away that she'd been very worried. Apu was also home, and Aunt Bözsi and Aunt Ilonka were also there. I was so happy because I hadn't seen Apu for so long. When he came home in the evenings I was already in bed, and on Sundays they always went to visit friends.

But I soon found out that they weren't there for the fun of it. They were worried and wanted to know exactly what had happened. I tried to tell it as well as I could because I noticed that they thought it was very important. And when they'd asked me everything so often that I kept giving the same answers, they started talking among themselves. Very quietly, so that I couldn't hear.

I did so want to know why the police had taken Miss Tauber. But nobody told me anything. Was it a

secret that I didn't have the right to know? Or did they think that I already knew it?

The next day was washing day and then I could ask Juci, I thought. Fräulein and the maid laughed at Juci because she was so fat and stupid. But I loved her and I didn't mind at all that she was fat. She was very nice and I could discuss everything with her. And I didn't think she was stupid. Once, when I asked her if it was really true that there was a war on, she'd said, "Yes, it's been on for three years, already." And when I wanted to know why you could hardly notice there was a war on, she said: "Lucky for us, the Germans have left us alone so far."

I didn't exactly understand what she meant then, but at least now I knew for sure that there was a war on. Every time I asked Fräulein the same question, she'd start to laugh or she'd talk about something else completely.

Anyu was at the workshop, Fräulein was talking to her friend on the telephone, and the maid was making the beds. I sneaked to the scullery, where Juci stood before the washtub.

"Juci! I was at the police station yesterday!"

"Hey, what's that you're telling me now, my darling Zsuzsa? That's no place for little girls like you!"

"I was at my piano lesson and then they came to fetch us. The teacher, Fräulein, and me. But they let me go right away. And Fräulein came back last night at ten o'clock."

"And your teacher?"

"I don't know. I think she is still there. Anyu tried to call her. But there is no answer."

"What a crying shame! You hear so many things lately."

"Juci? Do you know why they came to get her?"

[197]

"Of course not, my darling. How would I know that? I don't know your teacher, do I?"

"Her name is Tauber. I thought maybe you also worked at her place."

"No. And the name doesn't mean anything to me. Is she Jewish?"

I didn't know what that was. But I had heard the word often. Always very softly and quickly whispered. As if it was something shameful. A kind of disease that you had to keep secret.

I said, "I don't know. How can you tell? Does it show?"

"Not really. . . . Well, maybe a little. . . . Most Jews have dark hair and big noses. They're good at learning and they're all rich."

When Juci said that I saw Miss Tauber before me. She had black frizzy hair and a crooked nose. And suddenly I remembered how she had sighed when she saw my little golden cross. I knew then for sure that she was Jewish.

The seamstresses now work here at home in the guest room and I'm allowed in there all the time. Aunt Bözsi and Aunt Ilonka are living in the Váci Street workshop and I go there every day with Fräulein. On our way there we buy food because they themselves never go out. Nobody is allowed to know that they live there now.

Once, when we were there, the caretaker rang the doorbell. Aunt Bözsi and Aunt Ilonka suddenly turned all white. Aunt Ilonka ran as fast as she could to the WC and Aunt Bözsi dove into the wardrobe, where Anyu's designs used to hang. Aunt Bözsi in the wardrobe! I'd never have thought it possible! She was much too round and much too fat! It was so funny to see those two fat

aunts playing hide and seek. But I couldn't even laugh. I had to sit still and be quiet.

Luckily the caretaker didn't notice anything. But Aunt Ilonka and Aunt Bözsi had a terrible fright. When we left they were still shaking.

Apu is going away. He has to go on a trip. I don't know where and I don't know how long he'll stay away either. He doesn't feel like going at all and I'm afraid that he isn't going to have a good time there.

He has to leave in six days' time. Anyu is working with the seamstresses to get his things ready. I have a bag full of patches and I have picked out the nicest ones. They look so nice together, so I'm going to make a little cushion out of them. It's a big job and I've already been working on it for three days. One of the seamstresses said that she wouldn't mind helping me. But I don't want that, I want to do it myself, otherwise it's not really mine. Apu has to take something that's all mine.

I don't know exactly what he is going to use my little cushion for over there. But you can do all sorts of things with it. It can keep you warm and is so nice and soft. Apu can only take very few things with him, just a rucksack. Luckily my little cushion will just fit.

I'm sure that Apu is going to miss me a lot when he's so far away. But then he'll suddenly remember that he has my little cushion. And then, when he touches it, he won't feel so lonely anymore.

We're allowed to take Apu to the train station. I am wearing my new coat for the first time. It is light blue and the collar and the buttons are made of navy velvet.

I am so happy that Apu can see me like this. In my new coat I don't look like such a little girl anymore but almost like a real young lady.

Apu is walking between Anyu and me. He hardly

says a thing and he looks very pale. But he is holding my hand firmly. I look at the other children who are walking next to their fathers. Some of them are crying and want to be carried.

We have to walk quite far because the train is terribly long. There are at least a hundred wagons and it's taking a long time for us to get to the one Apu has to go in.

I'm sure something is going to happen soon. At the last moment, when I'm saying good-bye to Apu.

There are German soldiers on the platform, some of them with big police dogs. They see me walking in my beautiful coat next to Apu. At Apu's wagon there will be a soldier too. And I'm sure that just as Apu is bending down to kiss me, he will say, "Sir, you don't have to leave. You have such a sweet little daughter. It would be a shame to leave her behind."

But it doesn't go that way at all. When Apu kisses me, nothing like that happens. He is pushed along with many other men into the carriage and can't even wave good-bye. And the German soldiers who have been looking on so quietly suddenly start shouting very loudly.

On the way home I feel terribly cold, and when I come home I have a high fever. Anyu puts me to bed at once and I must stay indoors for a whole week.

Fräulein says that it is a miracle that Anyu was able to leave the town. The heavy bombing started the day she left. The Russians are already very close and the Germans just don't want to leave. That's why we're living in the cellar now and have been for I don't know how long.

Every time the noise of the bombing gets louder, Fräulein starts to tremble. Then she goes all white and she gets so cold that I can hear her teeth chattering.

Fräulein is the only one I have left, the only one

who has stayed with me. I love her very much. I only wish she wouldn't be so afraid, I hate that. Sometimes I'm a little scared myself, but I can't tell her because I know that she herself is much more afraid. It wouldn't help anyway, because she is afraid of different things—like bombs. I don't really worry so much about them. Because you can see the bombs, you can hear them, and they are there for everyone. If they hit you it's just bad luck.

I am afraid of things that are much more scary. Of the real dangers—the ones you can't see. I am so afraid that something will happen to Anyu. She just left, just like that, all by herself, to look for Apu. And she doesn't even know where he is because we still haven't heard from him.

The best place to be is on my mattress under my quilt. And then I watch the shadows on the walls. It's like a strange puppet show with witches and fairies. Even though it's only the people around me, moving around in the candlelight.

But what I like most is to lie here with my eyes shut. Then the only things I see are big white clouds. And then a white horse and a white carriage come driving up over the clouds. A handsome young prince and a princess with long blond hair are sitting on the driver's box. When they come closer I see that they are not a prince and a princess at all, but my own Apu and my own Anyu. They drive on and on, they are flying high above me, way up in the air. I don't think they can see me, lying here in the cellar on my mattress. But then I feel myself lifted up very gently. And before I know it, I am sitting between them and together we fly above the white clouds in the blue sky.

What a bang! Everything is shaking! Everyone is screaming. There's no light. Somebody is shouting:

[201]

"Quick! Quick! The emergency exit!" I hear a few muffled bangs, and then I see lots of bright light shining
through a narrow crack. Everybody is relieved and people are beginning to push toward the exit. They are
pushing so hard that I can hardly stay on my feet. But
they're cheerful and keep saying, "How lucky we are! If
the emergency exit had been buried, we would all have
suffocated to death in here!"

Suddenly I hear somebody call, "Zsuzsa, Zsuzsa!
Where are you?"

The voice is coming from the outside and I shout
back as loud as I can, "Here! Down here, in the cellar!"

"Zsuzsa! Please . . . Answer me! It's me, your Aunt
Teréz!"

"Yes! I am right here! In the cellar!"

Thank goodness, she has heard me. She asks, "You
aren't hurt, are you?"

"No, not at all. I am all right!"

"What's keeping you? Why don't you come out?"

"There are a lot of people ahead of me."

"And what about Fräulein?"

"She is here too."

When I climb out we wait for Fräulein. Only she
doesn't come and everybody else is already out.

Aunt Teréz shouts, "Fräulein! Come on now! Hurry
up!"

"I'm coming!"

"What's the matter? You're not hurt, are you?"

"No, but I can't find it . . ."

"Can't find what?"

"The pan?"

"What pan?"

"The little pan with the food."

"Leave it! Who cares about that little pan?!"

"But there was still a bit of goulash left!"

[202]

"Come on, hurry up, will you! Forget the goulash! Everything could collapse any time now!"

"I've found it! I'm coming!"

The first thing we see coming out is the little pan. It is all covered with dust and the lid is only half on. That Fräulein . . . She's done nothing but tremble and shake. And now a bomb has fallen on our house, she only thinks about the leftovers in the pan.

When Grandma Gizi saw me she cried, "Come here, come here, my poor child! That mother of yours, she has abandoned you. And all because of that Jew. . . ."

Suddenly I understood everything. That Apu was Jewish. That was why they had deported him.

What a shame that Grandma Gizi did not like the Jews. I heard that clearly in her voice. But she said it so honestly. At least now I know why Anyu's family is so different from Apu's.

I have been here only a few days but already I feel completely at home. We often sit all together around the table, sorting lentils. And then we tell each other all kinds of stories. I didn't use to like lentils. But Grandma Gizi knows how to cook them in at least a hundred different ways. That's just as well, because there isn't anything else to eat anyway.

I am not such a baby anymore as when I was with Fräulein. The first day, Grandma Gizi gave me a little bowl with water and a towel and now I wash myself every day. I can also brush my own hair now, and I can nearly braid it all by myself too.

There is a mirror hanging on a nail in the wall. That's where Aunt Teréz and Aunt Margit stand when they put on their makeup. They don't mind if I watch them while they're doing it. It's such fun to watch, they do it so fast and so neatly. They look exactly like Anyu,

with their blue eyes and blond hair. Sometimes I also stand before the mirror to have a look at myself. What will I look like later? I won't be as beautiful as Anyu, that's for sure, because I don't have blond hair and blue eyes. With my curly brown hair and my green eyes I look much more like Apu, I suppose.

Uncle Laci says that the siege really cannot last much longer because the Russians are coming a little closer every day. In a few days, a week at most, we'll be liberated. Uncle Laci should know, because he sometimes goes outside. It's very dangerous, but he does it anyway.

I don't even remember how life was before the bombings. It's going to be strange not to live in a cellar anymore. And to see such a big difference between day and night.

Yesterday, when nobody was looking, I sneaked out of the cellar. I walked into the street, to the shop that had been bombed and where Uncle Laci had found two huge crystal vases. He had said that there were still lots of other things lying around. But when I arrived the shop was completely empty.

It started to snow. I didn't feel like going back at all. It was lovely in the street. I hadn't been outside for so long!

There was nobody around. But suddenly I saw a few people in the distance. They were smashing open a shop window that had been only a little damaged. I just wanted to take a look. And when I came nearer I saw that it was a toy shop!

If I took something now . . . was that stealing? Yes, of course it was. But weren't they all doing it? So then it must be all right after all. If a shop was destroyed by a bomb then you could take things.

I didn't know where to look first. There were two big, long boxes lying on the counter. I lifted the cover of

one of them and there was a doll with real hair and porcelain blue eyes! I quickly grabbed both boxes and ran home with them.

They're all mine, they belong to me. I rescued them myself from the bombs. In my little room at home I had twenty-seven dolls. They are all gone now. How lucky I was to find these! I already love them so much that I wouldn't exchange them for all the others.

What shall I call them? Such beautiful dolls have to have a very special name. Strange, suddenly I can't think of any. Am I such a bad doll's mother, then? I need two names and I can't think of one! Don't worry darlings—if I hold you both in my arms long enough, it will surely come to me.

Which one do I think is sweeter? Which one do I love more? It's difficult to say because they're exactly the same. They even have the same dress: light blue trimmed with white lace. The only difference is that one of them is a little bit damaged, she has a little spot on her left cheek.

Katika, the daughter of the caretaker, is always right behind me when I'm playing with my dolls. She keeps asking me where I found them and if there are any more. I know! I'll give her one of them! They are exactly the same anyway and I only need one. *Veronka!* That's a beautiful name! Suddenly I've found it. Without even thinking, it came to me, just like that. And I am very sure of it. That name, no other name, is the one that suits her. "Katika . . . Look . . . I'll give you this one."

She gets very shy and says: "Really, you mean it?"
"Yes. Here, take it."
"But I can't. I have no right, just like that . . ."

"Why not? They are both mine. I found them myself."

She takes the doll I give her and says:

"Hey, you're giving me the wrong one."

"What do you mean?"

"You gave me the one that is undamaged."

My sweet little Veronka. You are a bit wounded. But I'll make you all better and that spot on your face will soon heal. And if in the end there's still a scar, I won't mind at all. I'll love you just as much, maybe even more. The other doll is a tiny bit more beautiful . . . But I could never give you, my dear Veronka, away.

The Russians have come. It has been four weeks already. We are now living upstairs again and everybody is happy that we are finally free.

Nobody talks about Anyu. Grandma Gizi thinks that she is dead. Of course she doesn't say that, but I know what she thinks. The other day, when the door was ajar, I heard Aunt Teréz say, "I really can't keep her. . . . What am I to do with a child of ten?"

I ran into the garden and flung myself face down in the snow. I lay there like that for a very long time. In the end I got so cold that I stopped thinking completely. I may even have fallen asleep. Because I know that suddenly I remembered everything again. And I thought, *Please no, I don't want to get up anymore.* But then I realized I was all wet and so I got up anyway.

Anyu is back! My dear Anyu! I am so happy! I am so happy! I have never been so happy in all my life!

She came on foot, all the way from Sopron through the deep snow, with only one piece of bread to eat. And when she was finally home she saw that our building had been destroyed. She had a terrible shock because she was sure I was buried under the rubble! With her

last remaining strength she ran to Grandma Gizi's house and when she saw me here she collapsed.

When Anyu talks about her search for Apu she starts to cry. First she went to Aunt Magda, because Uncle Géza is a lieutenant and he was working in the concentration camp Sopron Köhida. But they weren't nice to her at all. They let her sleep on the couch but they kept it a secret. And they didn't want to help her either. Uncle Géza only said that Apu was not in his camp. And when she begged to ask about him at the other camps, he said that he couldn't do that. So then she went all by herself from one camp to the other but they never let her in. The only thing she could do was look at the prisoners behind the barbed wire. But they all looked alike because they were all bald and wore the same kind of clothes. Everywhere she went she'd shout Apu's name, but the prisoners were too far away to hear her.

I was at the station once when a transport arrived. The way they looked! Just like skeletons! They looked as if they don't even know where they were.

But when they passed close to us, my heart started to beat faster and faster. Suddenly I was sure that Apu was among them. He must be—surely he was one of these men, only we didn't recognize him!

But after a while the platform was empty. Everybody had left. Anyu said that he would have seen us even if we had not recognized him.

Whenever we go to the train station we carry a big sign that says, *"Stark Miklós, thirty-seven years old. Has anyone seen him?"* Once somebody stopped and said that he had slept in the same barracks as a man called Stark Miklós. But when they were freed Stark Miklós was so weak he stayed behind on his wooden bed. The

last thing he'd heard was that they had taken Stark Miklós to the hospital.

On our way home I asked Anyu: "Do you think that Apu is still alive?"

"I don't know, my sweetheart . . ."

"But he was still alive when they freed him! Once the war is over, you don't die, do you?"

"Most of the time, no. But sometimes, yes. Some people are so weak and exhausted that nothing can be done for them anymore."

"How horrible! But how could such a dreadful thing happen to him, of all people?"

"So many horrible things can happen. But we have to keep hoping."

We passed a cemetery and Anyu said that she felt like praying. I sat down to wait on a little bench while she prayed. When she'd finished she came and sat down next to me. It was very quiet and I didn't really know what to say to her. So I just said, "It's beautiful here." And then she said, "Yes, but life is not beautiful!" and she burst into tears. She cried so hard that her whole body shook. I so much wanted to comfort her but I knew that I couldn't. If only I could cry too, at least we'd be doing it together. But I couldn't cry, even though I wanted to very much, because I felt all dried up inside.

It's been two years since I've been in school here with the nuns. Anyu can't have me because she's working in the factory from early in the morning until late at night. If only Apu would come back, then everything would be back to normal!

Anyu says that it is not good to go on believing that he is still alive. Still, sometimes I'm all but certain that he is somewhere, that he still exists. He could still be too weak to travel, couldn't he? Or, who knows, maybe he's forgotten everything?

[208]

These days some people don't even remember their own name. I heard about a man who had forgotten that he had a wife and children. He was living in Germany and he had married again. But one day, as much as ten years later, he found the house key of his former home in his pocket. And suddenly he remembered everything!

One of the girls asked me why I never talk about my father. I couldn't tell her I believe that he is alive, somewhere. And the story about the hospital is none of her business. It's such a horrible thought that he could have died of exhaustion. Think of it—after the liberation, no less! Anyhow, that story might not be true at all. That's why I simply said, "My father died during the war." She looked at me as if she was about to ask more questions. So I said quickly, "He was a soldier."

That was not a complete lie, because when Apu was young he had been in the army.

Today Zsuzsa says:

"I still don't know the exact circumstances of my father's death. A few years ago I happened to meet somebody who was there when he died. When I asked him for details he said that he would tell me another time. But strangely enough I never asked him again. Maybe because I do not want to see the version with which I finally have come to terms revised.

"Looking back to those childhood years during the war, my biggest problem was that everything was kept secret. Nobody told me that my father was Jewish; I didn't even know what being Jewish meant. All I understood was that it was something shameful. When I found out that my father was Jewish I could not accept it. For many years I denied my Jewish origins and later I was ashamed of having denied it. It was only by marrying a Jew and having Jewish friends that I solved the problem.

"The war has left me with a certain distrust of human beings, especially when I suspect them of harboring racist feelings. Another thing that stayed with me is that I am not afraid of dying. Probably having been close to it so often makes death seem a very normal thing."

Zsuzsa lives in Geneva, Switzerland, with her husband. She has two married daughters. She works part-time as a laboratory technician.

Books from

FOUR WALLS EIGHT WINDOWS

Algren, Nelson.
Never Come Morning. pb: **$7.95**

Anderson, Sherwood.
The Triumph of the Egg. pb: **$8.95**

Boetie, Dugmore.
Familiarity Is the Kingdom of the Lost. pb: **$6.95**

Brodsky, Michael.
X in Paris. pb: **$9.95**

Brodsky, Michael.
Xman. cl: **$21.95,** pb: **$11.95**

Codrescu, Andrei, ed.
American Poetry Since 1970: Up Late. pb. **$14.95**

David, Kati.
A Child's War: World War II Through the Eyes of Children. cl: **$17.95**

Dubuffet, Jean.
Asphyxiating Culture and Other Writings. cl: **$17.95**

Howard-Howard, Margo (with Abbe Michaels).
I Was a White Slave in Harlem. pb: **$12.95**

Johnson, Phyllis, and Martin, David, eds.
Frontline Southern Africa: Destructive Engagement. cl: **$23.95** pb: **$14.95**

Null, Gary.
The Egg Project: Gary Null's Guide to Good Eating. cl: **$21.95,** pb: **$12.95**

Santos, Rosario, ed.
And We Sold the Rain: Contemporary Fiction from Central America.
cl: **$18.95,** pb: **$9.95**

Schultz, John.
No One Was Killed. pb: **$9.95**

Sokolov, Sasha.
A School for Fools. pb: **$9.95**

Wasserman, Harvey.
Harvey Wasserman's History of the United States. pb: **$6.95**

Weber, Brom, ed.
O My Land, My Friends: The Selected Letters of Hart Crane.
cl: **$21.95,** pb: **$12.95**

Zerden, Sheldon.
The Best of Health. cl:**$23.95,** pb **$12.95**

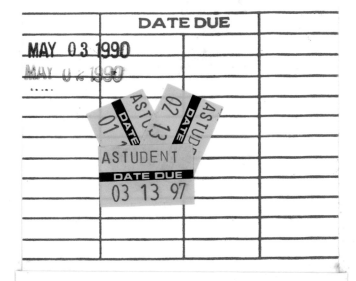

DATE DUE		
MAY 03 1990		
MAY 0 ∡ 1990		
.....		

ASTUDENT
DATE DUE
03 13 97

1-16